More praise for <u>Altered Carbon</u>

● ● ●

"Carbon-black noir with drive and wit, a tight plot, and a back-story that leaves the reader wanting a sequel like another fix."
—KEN MCLEOD

"*Altered Carbon* is a really impressive debut, an auspicious start to what will be an ongoing series. I look forward to seeing more from this talented author."
—SF Site

"A marvelous updating of Marlowe film noir . . . Morgan comes up with a twist on the soul-as-software idea that's both original and effective. . . . All the disturbing implications of the big SF idea are worked through to their conclusions, and there's some subtle musings on the true nature of identity hidden away beneath the enjoyable surface of the tale."
—*Starburst*

"First-rate . . . A mystery that could only derive from its particular SF setting, and one that validates this setting not by opening it up, but by enriching its texture and, like some Chandler and bit more Hammett, revealing ever-deepening layers of corruption and ever more sinister characters."
—*Locus*

"Exciting . . . Addictive . . . This is a ceaseless, permanently off-balance sprint through an all-too-grimly-familiar future where miraculous technologies are degraded through everyday use and abuse. There are occasional throwaway mentions of background details here that beg entire novels on their own; ubiquitous pieces of history dismissed in single lines that had my nose twitching, scenting something far bigger lurking, hidden under the surface. If Richard Morgan can use these to even come close to repeating the harsh triumph of *Altered Carbon* in his next novel then I would suggest we have another bona fide UK sf triumph on our hands. Go and get yourself a copy of *Altered Carbon* now, if only to forestall other people telling you how much you need to read this book." —*Infinity Plus*

Please turn the page for more reviews. . . .

ALTErED CArBON

...

RICHARD K. MORGAN

Ballantine Books
New York

A Del Rey® Book
Published by The Ballantine Publishing Group
Copyright © 2002 by Richard K. Morgan

All rights reserved under International and Pan-American Copyright Conventions. Published in the
United States by The Ballantine Publishing Group, a division of Random House, Inc., New York. Originally
published in Great Britain by Gollancz, an imprint of Orion Books, in 2002.

Del Rey is a registered trademark and the Del Rey colophon is a trademark of Random House, Inc.

www.delreydigital.com

Library of Congress Cataloging-in-Publication Data
Morgan, Richard K., 1965–
    Altered carbon / Richard K. Morgan.— 1st American ed.
        p.   cm.
    ISBN 0-345-45768-4
    1. Title.
    PS3613.O748 A78 2003
    813'.6—dc21

                                                                                    2002031165

Cover design by David Stevenson
Cover illustration based on a photograph © Lynn Saville/Photonica

Book design by Susan Turner

Manufactured in the United States of America

First American Edition: March 2003

10   9   8   7   6   5   4   3   2   1

This book is for my father and mother:

JOHN
*for his iron endurance and unflagging generosity of spirit
in the face of adversity*

and

MARGARET
*for the white hot rage that dwells in compassion
and a refusal to turn away*

ACKNOWLEDGMENTS

There is a vast distance between deciding to write a first novel and actually seeing it published, and the journey across this distance can be emotionally brutal. It comes with loneliness attached, but at the same time, requires a massive faith in what you're doing that is hard to sustain alone. I was able to complete this journey only thanks to a number of people along the way, who lent me their faith when my own was running very low. Since the technology imagined in *Altered Carbon* doesn't exist yet, I'd better get on and thank these traveling companions while I can, because without their support, I'm pretty certain *Altered Carbon* itself would not exist either.

In order of appearance, then: Thanks to Margaret and John Morgan for putting together the original organic material, to Caroline (Dit-Dah) Morgan for enthusiasm from before she could speak, to Gavin Burgess for friendship when often neither of us were in any condition to speak, to Alan Young for depths of unconditional commitment there isn't any *way* to speak, and to Virginia Cottinelli for giving me her twenties when I'd almost used mine up. Then, the light at the end of a very long tunnel, thanks to my agent, Carolyn Whitaker, for considering drafts of *Altered Carbon* not once but twice, and to Simon Spanton at Gollancz for being the man to finally make it happen.

May the road always rise to meet you!
May the wind be always at your back!

PrOLOGUE

Two hours before dawn I sat in the peeling kitchen and smoked one of Sarah's cigarettes, listening to the maelstrom and waiting. Millsport had long since put itself to bed, but out in the Reach currents were still snagging on the shoals, and the sound came ashore to prowl the empty streets. There was a fine mist drifting in from the whirlpool, falling on the city like sheets of muslin and fogging the kitchen windows.

Chemically alert, I inventoried the hardware on the scarred wooden table for the fiftieth time that night. Sarah's Heckler and Koch shard pistol glinted dully at me in the low light, the butt gaping open for its clip. It was an assassin's weapon, compact and utterly silent. The magazines lay next to it. She had wrapped insulating tape around each one to distinguish the ammunition: green for sleep, black for the spider-venom load. Most of the clips were black-wrapped. Sarah had used up a lot of green on the security guards at Gemini Biosys last night.

My own contributions were less subtle: the big silver Smith & Wesson, and the four remaining hallucinogen grenades. The thin crimson line around each canister seemed to sparkle slightly, as if it was about to detach itself from the metal casing and float up to join the curlicues of smoke ribboning off my cigarette. Shift and slide of altered significants, the side effect of the tetrameth I'd scored that afternoon down at the wharf. I don't usually smoke when I'm straight, but for some reason the tet always triggers the urge.

Against the distant roar of the maelstrom I heard it. The hurrying strop of rotor blades on the fabric of the night.

I stubbed out the cigarette, mildly unimpressed with myself, and went through to the bedroom. Sarah was sleeping, an assembly of low-frequency sine curves beneath the single sheet. A raven sweep of hair covered her face and one long-fingered hand trailed over the side of the bed. As I stood looking at her the night outside split. One of Harlan's World's orbital guardians test-firing into the Reach. Thunder from the concussed sky rolled in to rattle the windows. The woman in the bed stirred and swept the hair out of her eyes. The liquid crystal gaze found me and locked on.

"What're you looking at?" Voice husky with the residue of sleep.

I smiled a little.

"Don't give me that shit. Tell me what you're looking at."

"Just looking. It's time to go."

She lifted her head and picked up the sound of the helicopter. The sleep slid away from her face, and she sat up in bed.

"Where's the 'ware?"

It was a corps joke. I smiled the way you do when you see an old friend and pointed to the case in the corner of the room.

"Get my gun for me."

"Yes, *ma'am*. Black or green?"

"Black. I trust these scumbags about as far as a clingfilm condom."

In the kitchen, I loaded up the shard pistol, cast a glance at my own weapon, and left it lying there. Instead I scooped up one of the H grenades and took it back in my other hand. I paused in the doorway to the bedroom and weighed the two pieces of hardware in each palm as if I was trying to decide which was the heavier.

"A little something with your phallic substitute, ma'am?"

Sarah looked up from beneath the hanging sickle of black hair over her forehead. She was in the midst of pulling a pair of long woolen socks up over the sheen of her thighs.

"Yours is the one with the long barrel, Tak."

"Size isn't—"

We both heard it at the same time. A metallic double *clack* from the corridor outside. Our eyes met across the room, and for a quarter second I saw my own shock mirrored there. Then I was tossing the loaded shard gun to her. She put up one long-fingered hand and took it out of the air just as the whole of the bedroom wall caved in in thunder. The blast knocked me back into a corner and onto the floor.

They must have located us in the apartment with body-heat sensors, then mined the whole wall with limpets. Taking no chances this time. The commando who came through the ruined wall was stocky and insect-eyed in full gas attack rig, hefting a snub-barreled Kalashnikov in gloved hands.

Ears ringing, still on the floor, I flung the H grenade up at him. It was unfused, useless in any case against the gas mask, but he didn't have time to identify the device as it spun at him. He batted it off the breech of his Kalashnikov and stumbled back, eyes wide behind the glass panels of the mask.

"Fire in the hole."

Sarah was down on the floor beside the bed, arms wrapped around her head and sheltered from the blast. She heard the shout, and in the seconds the bluff had bought us she popped up again, shard gun outflung. Beyond the wall I could see figures huddled against the expected grenade blast. I heard the mosquito whine of monomolecular splinters across the room as she put three shots into the lead commando. They shredded invisibly through the attack suit and into the flesh beneath. He made a noise like someone straining to lift something heavy as the spider venom sank its claws into his nervous system. I grinned and started to get up.

Sarah was turning her aim on the figures beyond the wall when the second commando of the night appeared braced in the kitchen doorway and hosed her away with his assault rifle.

Still on my knees, I watched her die with chemical clarity. It all went so slowly it was like a video playback on frame advance. The commando kept his aim low, holding the Kalashnikov down against the hyper-rapid-fire recoil it was famous for. The bed went first, erupting into gouts of white goose down and ripped cloth, then Sarah, caught in the storm as she turned. I saw one leg turned to pulp below the knee, and then the body hits, bloody fistfuls of tissue torn out of her pale flanks as she fell through the curtain of fire.

I reeled to my feet as the assault rifle stammered to a halt. Sarah had rolled over on her face, as if to hide the damage the shells had done to her, but I saw it all through veils of red anyway. I came out of the corner without conscious thought, and the commando was too late to bring the Kalashnikov around. I slammed into him at waist height, blocked the gun, and knocked him back into the kitchen. The barrel of the rifle caught on the doorjamb, and he lost his grip. I heard the weapon clatter to the ground behind me as we hit the kitchen floor. With the speed and strength of the tetrameth, I scrambled astride him, batted aside one flailing arm, and seized his head in both hands. Then I smashed it against the tiles like a coconut.

Under the mask, his eyes went suddenly unfocused. I lifted the head again and smashed it down again, feeling the skull give soggily with the impact. I ground down against the crunch, lifted and smashed again. There was a roaring in my ears like the maelstrom, and somewhere I could hear my own voice screaming obscenities.

I was going for a fourth or fifth blow when something kicked me between the shoulder blades and splinters jumped magically out of the table leg in front of me. I felt the sting as two of them found homes in my face.

For some reason the rage puddled abruptly out of me. I let go of the commando's head almost gently and was lifting one puzzled hand to the pain of the splinters in my cheek when I realized I had been shot, and that the bullet must have torn all the way through my chest and into the table leg. I looked down, dumbfounded, and saw the dark red stain inking its way out over my shirt. No doubt about it. An exit hole big enough to take a golf ball.

With the realization came the pain. It felt as if someone had run a steel wool pipe cleaner briskly through my chest cavity. Almost thoughtfully, I reached up, found the hole, and plugged it with my two middle fingers. The fingertips scraped over the roughness of torn bone in the wound, and I felt something membranous throb against one of them. The bullet had missed my heart. I grunted and attempted to rise, but the grunt turned into a cough and I tasted blood on my tongue.

"Don't you move, motherfucker."

The yell came out of a young throat, badly distorted with shock. I hunched forward over my wound and looked back over my shoulder. Behind me in the doorway, a young man in a police uniform had both hands clasped around the pistol he had just shot me with. He was trembling visibly. I coughed again and turned back to the table.

The Smith & Wesson was on eye level, gleaming silver, still where I had left it less than two minutes ago. Perhaps it was that, the scant shavings of time that had been planed off since Sarah was alive and all was well, that drove me. Less than two minutes ago I could have picked up the gun; I'd even thought about it, so why not now? I gritted my teeth, pressed my fingers harder into the hole in my chest, and staggered upright. Blood spattered warmly against the back of my throat. I braced myself on the edge of the table with my free hand and looked back at the cop. I could feel my lips peeling back from the clenched teeth in something that was more a grin than a grimace.

"*Don't make me do it, Kovacs.*"

I got myself a step closer to the table and leaned against it with my thighs, breath whistling through my teeth and bubbling in my throat. The Smith & Wesson gleamed like fool's gold on the scarred wood. Out in the Reach power lashed down from an orbital and lit the kitchen in tones of blue. I could hear the maelstrom calling.

"*I said don't—*"

I closed my eyes and clawed the gun off the table.

PART ONE

ArrIVAL
(NEEDLECAST DOWNLOAD)

CHAPTEr ONE

Coming back from the dead can be rough.

In the Envoy Corps they teach you to let go before storage. Stick it in neutral and float. It's the first lesson and the trainers drill it into you from day one. Hard-eyed Virginia Vidaura, dancer's body poised inside the shapeless corps coveralls as she paced in front of us in the induction room. *Don't worry about anything,* she said, *and you'll be ready for it.* A decade later, I met her again in a holding pen at the New Kanagawa Justice Facility. She was going down for eighty to a century; excessively armed robbery and organic damage. The last thing she said to me when they walked her out of the cell was *don't worry, kid, they'll store it.* Then she bent her head to light a cigarette, drew the smoke hard into lungs she no longer gave a damn about, and set off down the corridor as if to a tedious briefing. From the narrow angle of vision afforded me by the cell gate, I watched the pride in that walk and I whispered the words to myself like a mantra.

Don't worry, they'll store it. It was a superbly double-edged piece of street wisdom. Bleak faith in the efficiency of the penal system, and a clue to the elusive state of mind required to steer you past the rocks of psychosis. Whatever you feel, whatever you're thinking, whatever you are when they store you, that's what you'll be when you come out. With states of high anxiety, that can be a problem. So you let go. Stick it in neutral. Disengage and float.

If you have time.

I came thrashing up out of the tank, one hand plastered across my chest searching for the wounds, the other clutching at a nonexistent weapon. The weight hit me like a hammer, and I collapsed back into the flotation gel. I flailed with my arms, caught one elbow painfully on the side of the tank, and gasped. Gobbets of gel poured into my mouth and down my throat. I snapped my mouth shut and got a hold on the hatch coaming, but the stuff was everywhere. In my eyes, burning my nose and throat, and slippery under my fingers. The weight was forcing my grip on the hatch loose, sitting on my chest like a high-g maneuver, pressing me down into the gel. My body heaved violently in the confines of the tank. Flotation gel? I was *drowning*.

Abruptly, there was a strong grip on my arm and I was hauled coughing into an upright position. At about the same time I was working out there were no wounds in my chest someone wiped a towel roughly across my face and I could see. I decided to save that pleasure for later and concentrated on getting the contents of the tank out of my nose and throat. For about half a minute I stayed sitting, head down, coughing up the gel and trying to work out why everything weighed so much.

"So much for training." It was a hard, male voice, the sort that habitually hangs around justice facilities. "What did they teach you in the Envoys anyway, Kovacs?"

That was when I had it. On Harlan's World, Kovacs is quite a common name. Everyone knows how to pronounce it. This guy didn't. He was speaking a stretched form of the Amanglic they use on the World, but even allowing for that, he was mangling the name badly, and the ending came out with a hard *k* instead of the Slavic *ch*.

And everything was too heavy.

The realization came through my fogged perceptions like a brick through frosted plate glass.

Offworld.

Somewhere along the line, they'd taken Takeshi Kovacs (D.H.), and they'd freighted him. And since Harlan's World was the only habitable biosphere in the Glimmer system, that meant a stellar-range needlecast to—

Where?

I looked up. Harsh neon tubes set in a concrete roof. I was sitting in the opened hatch of a dull metal cylinder, looking for all the world like an ancient aviator who'd forgotten to dress before climbing aboard his biplane. The cylinder was one of a row of about twenty backed up against the wall, opposite a heavy steel door, which was closed. The room was chilly and the walls unpainted. Give them their due, on Harlan's World at least the air resleeving rooms are decked out in pastel colors and the attendants are pretty. After all, you're supposed to have paid your debt to society. The least they can do is give you a sunny start to your new life.

Sunny wasn't in the vocabulary of the figure before me. About two meters tall, he looked as if he'd made his living wrestling swamp panthers before the present career opportunity presented itself. Musculature bulged on his chest and arms like body armor, and the head above it had hair cropped close to the skull, revealing a long scar like a lightning strike down to the left ear. He was dressed in a loose black garment with epaulettes and a diskette logo on the breast. His eyes matched the garment and watched me with hardened calm. Having helped me sit up, he had stepped back out of arm's reach, as per the manual. He'd been doing this a long time.

I pressed one nostril closed and snorted tank gel out of the other.

"Want to tell me where I am? Itemize my rights, something like that?"

"Kovacs, right now you don't have any rights."

I looked up and saw that a grim smile had stitched itself across his face. I shrugged and snorted the other nostril clean.

"Want to tell me where I am?"

He hesitated a moment, glanced up at the neon-barred roof as if to ascertain the information for himself before he passed it on, and then mirrored my shrug.

"Sure. Why not? You're in Bay City, pal. Bay City, Earth." The grimace of a smile came back. "Home of the Human Race. Please enjoy your stay on this most ancient of civilized worlds. Ta-dada-*dah*."

"Don't give up the day job," I told him soberly.

● ● ●

The doctor led me down a long white corridor whose floor bore the scuff marks of rubber-wheeled gurneys. She was moving at quite a pace, and I was hard-pressed to keep up, wrapped as I was in nothing but a plain gray towel and still dripping tank gel. Her manner was superficially bedside, but there was a harried undercurrent to it. She had a sheaf of curling hardcopy documentation under her arm and other places to be. I wondered how many sleevings she got through in a day.

"You should get as much rest as you can in the next day or so," she recited. "There may be minor aches and pains, but this is normal. Sleep will solve the problem. If you have any recurring comp—"

"I know. I've done this before."

I wasn't feeling much like human interaction. I'd just remembered Sarah.

We stopped at a side door with the word SHOWER stenciled on frosted glass. The doctor steered me inside and stood looking at me for a moment.

"I've used showers before, as well," I assured her.

She nodded. "When you're finished, there's an elevator at the end of the corridor. Discharge is on the next floor. The, ah, the police are waiting to talk to you."

The manual says you're supposed to avoid strong adrenal shocks to the newly sleeved, but then she'd probably read my file and didn't consider meeting the police much of an event in my lifestyle. I tried to feel the same.

"What do they want?"

"They didn't choose to share that with me." The words showed an edge of frustration that she shouldn't have been letting me see. "Perhaps your reputation precedes you."

"Perhaps it does." On an impulse, I flexed my new face into a smile. "Doctor, I've never been here before. To Earth, I mean. I've never dealt with your police before. Should I be worried?"

She looked at me, and I saw it welling up in her eyes, the mingled fear and wonder and contempt of the failed human reformer.

"With a man like you," she managed finally, "I would have thought they would be the worried ones."

"Yeah, right," I said quietly.

She hesitated, then gestured. "There is a mirror in the changing room," she said, and left. I glanced toward the room she had indicated, not sure I was ready for the mirror yet.

In the shower I whistled my disquiet away tunelessly and ran soap and hands over the new body. My sleeve was in his early forties, Protectorate standard, with a swimmer's build and what felt like some military custom-carved onto his nervous system. Neurachemical upgrade, most likely. I'd had it myself, once. There was a tightness in the lungs that suggested a nicotine habit and some gorgeous scarring on the forearm, but apart from that I couldn't find anything worth complaining about. The little twinges and snags catch up with you later on, and if you're wise, you just live with them. Every sleeve has a history. If that kind of thing bothers you, you line up over at Syntheta's or Fabrikon. I'd worn my fair share of synthetic sleeves; they use them for parole hearings quite often. Cheap, but it's too much like living alone in a drafty house, and they never seem to get the flavor circuits right. Everything you eat ends up tasting like curried sawdust.

In the changing cubicle I found a neatly folded summer suit on the bench and the mirror set in the wall. On top of the pile of clothes was a simple steel watch, and weighted beneath the watch was a plain white envelope with my name written neatly across it. I took a deep breath and went to face the mirror.

This is always the toughest part. Nearly two decades I've been doing this, and it still jars me to look into the glass and see a total stranger staring back. It's like pulling an image out of the depths of an autostereogram. For the first couple of moments all you can see is someone else looking at you through a window frame. Then, like a shift in focus, you feel yourself float rapidly up behind the mask and adhere to its inside with a shock that's almost tactile. It's as if someone's cut an umbilical cord, only instead of separating the two of you, it's the otherness that has been severed and now you're just looking at your reflection in a mirror.

I stood there and toweled myself dry, getting used to the face. It was basically Caucasian, which was a change for me, and the overwhelming impression I got was that if there was a line of least resistance in life, this face had never been along it. Even with the characteristic pallor of a long stay in the tank, the features in the mirror managed to look weather-beaten. There were lines everywhere. The thick, cropped hair was black shot through with gray. The eyes were a speculative shade of blue, and there was a faint, jagged scar under the left one. I raised my left forearm and looked at the story written there, wondering if the two were connected.

The envelope beneath the watch contained a single sheet of printed paper. Hardcopy. Handwritten signature. Very quaint.

Well, you're on Earth now. Most ancient of civilized worlds. I shrugged and scanned the letter, then got dressed and folded it away in the jacket of my new suit. With a final glance in the mirror, I strapped on the new watch and went out to meet the police.

It was four-fifteen, local time.

●●●

The doctor was waiting for me, seated behind a long curve of reception counter and filling out forms on a monitor. A thin, severe-looking man suited in black stood at her shoulder. There was no one else in the room.

I glanced around, then back at the suit.

"You the police?"

"Outside." He gestured at the door. "This isn't their jurisdiction. They need a special brief to get in here. We have our own security."

"And you are?"

He looked at me with the same mixture of emotions the doctor had hit me with downstairs. "Warden Sullivan, chief executive for Bay City Central, the facility you are now leaving."

"You don't sound delighted to be losing me."

Sullivan pinned me with a stare. "You're a recidivist, Kovacs. I never saw the case for wasting good flesh and blood on people like you."

I touched the letter in my breast pocket. "Lucky for me Mr. Bancroft disagrees with you. He's supposed to be sending a limousine for me. Is that outside, as well?"

"I haven't looked."

Somewhere on the counter, a protocol chime sounded. The doctor had finished her inputting. She tore the curling edge of the hardcopy free, initialed it in a couple of places, and passed it to Sullivan. The warden bent over the paper, scanning it with narrowed eyes before he scribbled his own signature and handed the copy to me.

"Takeshi Lev Kovacs," he said, mispronouncing with the same skill as his minion in the tank room. "By the powers vested in me by the U.N. Justice Accord, I discharge you on lease to Laurens J. Bancroft, for a period not to exceed six weeks, at the end of which time your parole status will be reconsidered. Please sign here."

I took the pen and wrote my name in someone else's handwriting next to the warden's finger. Sullivan separated the top and bottom copies and handed me the pink one. The doctor held up a second sheet, and Sullivan took it.

"This is a doctor's statement certifying that Takeshi Kovacs (D.H.) was received intact from the Harlan's World Justice Administration and subsequently sleeved in this body. Witnessed by myself, and closed-circuit monitor. A disk copy of the transmission details and tank data are enclosed. Please sign the declaration."

I glanced up and searched in vain for any sign of the cameras. Not worth fighting about. I scribbled my new signature a second time.

"This is a copy of the leasing agreement by which you are bound. Please read it carefully. Failure to comply with any of its articles may result in you being returned to storage immediately to complete the full term of your sentence, either here or at another facility of the administration's choice. Do you understand these terms and agree to be bound by them?"

I took the paperwork and scanned rapidly through it. It was standard stuff. A modified version of the parole agreement I'd signed half a dozen times before on Harlan's World. The language was a bit stiffer, but the content was the same. Bullshit by any other name. I signed it without a blink.

"Well then." Sullivan seemed to have lost a bit of his iron. "You're a lucky man, Kovacs. Don't waste the opportunity."

Don't they ever get tired of saying it?

I folded up my bits of paper without speaking and stuffed them into my pocket next to the letter. I was turning to leave when the doctor stood up and held out a small white card to me.

"Mr. Kovacs."

I paused.

"There shouldn't be any major problems with adjusting," she said. "This is a healthy body, and you are . . . used to this. If there *is* anything major, call this number."

I put out an arm and lifted the little rectangle of card with a machined precision that I hadn't noticed before. The neurachem was kicking in. My hand delivered the card to the same pocket as the rest of the paperwork and I was gone, crossing the reception and pushing open the door without a word. Ungracious maybe, but I didn't think anyone in that building had earned my gratitude yet.

You're a lucky man, Kovacs. Sure. A hundred and eighty light-years from home, wearing another man's body on a six-week rental agreement. Freighted in to do a job that the local police wouldn't touch with a riot prod. Fail and go back into storage. I felt so lucky I could have burst into song as I walked out the door.

CHAPTEr TWO

The hall outside was huge, and all but deserted. It looked like nothing so much as the Millsport rail terminal back home. Beneath a tilted roof of long transparent panels, the fused glass paving of the floor shone amber in the afternoon sun. A couple of children were playing with the automatic doors at the exit, and there was a solitary cleaning robot sniffing along in the shade at one wall. Nothing else moved. Marooned in the glow on benches of old wood, a scattering of humanity waited in silence for friends or family to ride in from their altered carbon exiles.

Download Central.

These people wouldn't recognize their loved ones in their new sleeves; recognition would be left to the homecomers, and for those who awaited them the anticipation of reunion would be tempered with a cool dread at what face and body they might have to learn to love. Or maybe they were a couple of generations down the line, waiting for relatives who were no more to them now than a vague childhood memory or a family legend. I knew one guy in the corps, Murakami, who was waiting on the release of a great-grandfather put away over a century back. Was going up to Newpest with a liter of whiskey and a pool cue for homecoming gifts. He'd been brought up on stories of his great-grandfather in the Kanagawa pool halls. The guy had been put away before Murakami was even born.

I spotted my reception committee as I went down the steps into the body of the hall. Three tall silhouettes were gathered around one of the benches, shifting restlessly in the slanting rays of sunlight and creating eddies in the dust motes that floated there. A fourth figure sat on the bench, arms folded and legs stretched out. All four of them were wearing reflective sunglasses that at a distance turned their faces into identical masks.

Already on course for the door, I made no attempt to detour in their direction, and this must have occurred to them only when I was halfway across the hall. Two of them drifted over to intercept me with the easy calm of big cats that have been fed recently. Bulky and tough-looking with neatly groomed crimson mohicans, they arrived in my path a couple of meters ahead, forcing me either to stop in turn or cut an abrupt circle around them. I stopped. Newly arrived and newly sleeved is the wrong state to be in if you plan to piss off the local militia. I tried on my second smile of the day.

"Something I can do for you?"

The older of the two waved a badge negligently in my direction, then put it away as if it might tarnish in the open air.

"Bay City police. The lieutenant wants to talk to you." The sentence sounded bitten off, as if he was resisting the urge to add some epithet to the end of it. I made an attempt to look as if I was seriously considering whether or not to go along with them, but they had me and they knew it. An hour out of the tank, you don't know enough about your new body to be getting into brawls with it. I shut down my images of Sarah's death and let myself be shepherded back to the seated cop.

The lieutenant was a woman in her thirties. Under the golden disks of her shades, she wore cheekbones from some Amerindian ancestor and a wide slash of a mouth that was currently set in a sardonic line. The sunglasses were jammed on a nose you could have opened cans on. Short, untidy hair framed the whole face and stuck up in spikes at the front. She had wrapped herself in an outsize combat jacket, but the long, black-encased legs that protruded from its lower edge were a clear hint of the lithe body within. She looked up at me with her arms folded on her chest for nearly a minute before anyone spoke.

"It's Kovacs, right?"

"Yes."

"Takeshi Kovacs?" Her pronunciation was perfect. "Out of Harlan's World? Millsport via the Kanagawa storage facility?"

"Tell you what, I'll just stop you when you get one wrong."

There was a long, mirror-lensed pause. The lieutenant unfolded fractionally and examined the blade of one hand.

"You got a license for that sense of humor, Kovacs?"

"Sorry. Left it at home."

"And what brings you to Earth?"

I gestured impatiently. "You know all this already, otherwise you wouldn't be here. Have you got something to say to me, or did you just bring these kids along for educational purposes?"

I felt a hand fasten on my upper arm and tensed. The lieutenant made a barely perceptible motion with her head, and the cop behind me let go again.

"Cool down, Kovacs. I'm just making conversation here. Yeah, I know Laurens Bancroft sprung you. Matter of fact, I'm here to offer you a lift up to the Bancroft residence." She sat forward suddenly and stood up. On her feet she was almost as tall as my new sleeve. "I'm Kristin Ortega, Organic Damage Division. Bancroft was my case."

"Was?"

She nodded. "Case is closed, Kovacs."

"Is that a warning?"

"No, it's just the facts. Open-and-shut suicide."

"Bancroft doesn't seem to think so. He claims he was murdered."

"Yeah, so I hear." Ortega shrugged. "Well, that's his prerogative. I guess it might be difficult for a man like that to believe he'd blow his own head clean off."

"A man like what?"

"Oh, come—" She stopped herself and gave me a small smile. "Sorry, I keep forgetting."

"Forgetting what?"

Another pause, but this time Kristin Ortega seemed to be off balance for the first time in our brief acquaintance. There was hesitancy blurring her tone when she spoke again. "You're not from here."

"So?"

"So anyone from here would know what kind of man Laurens Bancroft is. That's all."

Fascinated at why someone would lie so ineptly to a total stranger, I tried to put her back at her ease. "A rich man," I hazarded. "A powerful man."

She smiled thinly. "You'll see. Now do you want this lift or not?"

The letter in my pocket said a chauffeur would be outside the terminal to pick me up. Bancroft had made no mention of the police. I shrugged.

"I've never turned down a free ride yet."

"Good. Then shall we go?"

They flanked me to the door and stepped out ahead like bodyguards, heads tilted back and lensed eyes scanning. Ortega and I stepped through the gap together, and the warmth of the sunlight hit me in the face. I screwed up my new eyes against the glare and made out angular buildings behind real wire fences on the other side of a badly kept landing lot. Sterile, and off-white, quite possibly original premillennial structures. Between the oddly monochrome walls, I could see sections of a gray iron bridge that came vaulting in to land somewhere hidden from view. A similarly drab collection of sky and ground cruisers sat about in not particularly neat lines. The wind gusted abruptly, and I caught the faint odor of some flowering weed growing along the cracks in the landing lot. In the distance was the familiar hum of traffic, but everything else felt like a period-drama set piece.

". . . and I tell you there is only *one* judge! Do not believe the men of science when they tell you . . ."

The squawk of the poorly operated ampbox hit us as we went down the steps from the exit. I glanced across the landing area and saw a crowd assembled around a black-clad man on a packing crate. Holographic placards wove erratically in the air above the heads of the listeners. NO TO RESOLUTION 653!! ONLY GOD CAN RESURRECT!! D.H.F. = D.E.A.T.H. Cheers drowned out the speaker.

"What's this?"

"Catholics," Ortega said, lip curling. "Old-time religious sect."

"Yeah? Never heard of them."

"No. You wouldn't have. They don't believe you can digitize a human being without losing the soul."

"Not a widespread faith then."

"Just on Earth," she said sourly. "I think the Vatican—that's their central church—financed a couple of cryoships to Starfall and Latimer—"

"I've been to Latimer. I never ran into anything like this."

"The ships only left at the turn of the century, Kovacs. They won't get there for a couple more decades yet."

We skirted the gathering, and a young woman with her hair pulled severely back thrust a leaflet at me. The gesture was so abrupt that it tripped my sleeve's unsettled reflexes and I made a blocking motion before I got it under control. Hard-eyed, the woman stood with the leaflet out, and I took it with a placating smile.

"They have no right," the woman said.

"Oh, I agree . . ."

"Only the Lord our God can save your soul."

"I—" But by this time Kristin Ortega was steering me firmly away, one hand on my arm in a manner that suggested a lot of practice. I shook her off politely but equally firmly.

"Are we in some kind of hurry?"

"I think we both have better things to do, yes," she said, tight-lipped, looking back to where her colleagues were engaged in fending off leaflets of their own.

"I might have wanted to talk to her."

"Yeah? Looked to me like you wanted to throat-chop her."

"That's just the sleeve. I think it had some neurachem conditioning way back when, and she tripped it. You know, most people lie down for a few hours after downloading. I'm a little on edge."

I stared at the leaflet in my hands. CAN A MACHINE SAVE YOUR SOUL? it demanded of me rhetorically. The word *machine* had been printed in script designed to resemble an archaic computer display. *Soul* was in flowing stereographic letters that danced all over the page. I turned over for the answer. NO!!!!!

"So cryogenic suspension is okay, but digitized human freight isn't. Interesting." I looked back at the glowing placards, musing. "What's Resolution 653?"

"It's a test case going through the U.N. court," Ortega said shortly. "Bay City public prosecutor's office wants to subpoena a Catholic who's in storage. Pivotal witness. The Vatican say she's already dead and in the hands of God. They're calling it blasphemy."

"I see. So your loyalties are pretty undivided here."

She stopped and turned to face me.

"Kovacs, I hate these goddamn freaks. They've been grinding us down for the best part of two and a half thousand years. They've been responsible for more misery than any other organization in history. You know they won't even let their adherents practice *birth control*, for Christ's sake, and they've stood against every significant medical advance of the last five centuries. Practically the only thing you can say in their favor is that this D.H.F. thing has stopped them from spreading with the rest of humanity."

My lift turned out to be a battered but undeniably rakish-looking Lockheed-Mitoma transport decked out in what were presumably police colors. I'd flown Lock-Mits on Sharya, but they'd been a dull radar-reflective black all over. The red and white stripes on this one looked garish by comparison. A pilot in sunglasses to match the rest of Ortega's little gang sat motionless in the cockpit. The hatch into the belly of the cruiser was already hinged up. Ortega banged on the hatch coaming as we climbed aboard, and the turbines awoke with a whispery sound.

I helped one of the mohicans manhandle the hatch down, steadied myself against the lift of the cruiser, and found my way to a window seat. As we spiraled up, I craned my neck to keep the crowd below in sight. The transport straightened out about a hundred meters up and dropped its nose slightly. I sank back into the arms of the automold and found Ortega watching me.

"Still curious, huh?" she said.

"I feel like a tourist. Answer me a question?"

"If I can."

"Well, if these guys don't practice birth control, there's got to be an awful lot of them, right. And Earth isn't exactly a hive of activity these days, so . . . Why aren't they running things?"

Ortega and her men swapped a set of unpleasant smiles. "Storage," the mohican on my left said.

I slapped myself on the back of the neck, and then wondered if the gesture was in use here. It's the standard site for a cortical stack, after all, but then cultural quirks don't always work like that.

"Storage. Of course." I looked around at their faces. "There's no special exemption for them?"

"Nope." For some reason, this little exchange seemed to have made us all buddies. They were relaxing. The same mohican went on to elaborate. "Ten years or three months, it's all the same to them. A death sentence every time. They never come off stack. It's cute, huh?"

I nodded. "Very tidy. What happens to the bodies?"

The man opposite me made a throwaway gesture. "Sold off, broken down for transplants. Depends on the family."

I turned away and stared out of the window.

"Something the matter, Kovacs?"

I faced Ortega with a fresh smile gripping my face. It felt as if I was getting quite good at them.

"No, no. I was just thinking. It's like a different planet."

That cracked them up.

SUNTOUCH HOUSE

October 2

Takeshi-san,

When you receive this letter, you will doubtless be somewhat off balance. I offer my sincere apologies for this, but I have been assured that the training you underwent with the Envoy Corps should enable you to deal with the situation. Similarly, I assure you that I would not have subjected you to any of this, had my own situation not been desperate.

My name is Laurens Bancroft. Coming as you do from the colonies, this may not mean anything to you. Suffice it to say that I am a rich and powerful man here on Earth, and have made many enemies as a result. Six weeks ago I was murdered, an act that the police for reasons of their own have chosen to regard as suicide. Since the murderers ultimately failed I can only assume that they will try again, and in view of the police attitude, they may well succeed.

Clearly you will wonder what all this has to do with you and why you have been dragged 186 light-years out of storage to deal with such a local matter. I have been advised by my lawyers to retain a private investigator, but owing to my prominence in the global community, I am unable to trust anyone I could engage locally. I was given your name by Reileen Kawahara, for whom I understand you did some work on New Beijing eight years ago. The Envoy Corps was able to locate you in Kanagawa within two days of my requesting your whereabouts, though in view of your discharge and subsequent activities they were unable to offer any kind of operational guarantees or pledges. It is my understanding that you are your own man.

The terms under which you have been released are as follows:

You are contracted to work for me for a period of six weeks with an option for me to renew at the end of that time should further work be necessary. During this time, I shall be responsible for all reasonable expenses incurred by your investigation. In addition, I shall cover the cost of sleeve rental for this period. In the event that you conclude the investigation successfully, the remainder of your storage sentence at Kanagawa—117 years and 4 months—will be annulled and you will be refreighted to Harlan's World for immediate release in a sleeve of your own choosing. Alternatively, I undertake to pay off the balance of the mortgage on your current sleeve here on Earth and you may become a naturalized U.N. citizen. In either case the sum of one hundred thousand U.N. dollars, or equivalent, will be credited to you.

I believe these terms to be generous, but I should add that I am not a man to be trifled with. In the event that your investigation fails and I am killed, or that you attempt to in any way escape or evade the terms of your contract, the sleeve lease will be terminated immediately and you will be returned to storage to complete your sentence here on Earth. Any further legal penalties that you incur may be added to that sentence. Should you choose not to accept my contract from the outset, you will also be returned to storage immediately, though I cannot undertake to refreight you to Harlan's World in this case.

I am hopeful that you will see this arrangement as an opportunity and agree to work for me. In anticipation of this, I am sending a driver to collect you from the storage facility. His name is Curtis and he is one of my most trusted employees. He will be waiting for you in the release hall.

I look forward to meeting you at Suntouch House.

Yours sincerely,

Laurens J Bancroft

Laurens J. Bancroft

CHAPTEr THrEE

Suntouch House was aptly named. From Bay City we flew south down the coast for about half an hour before the change in engine pitch warned me that we were approaching our destination. By that time the light through the right-side windows was turning warm gold with the sun's decline toward the sea. I peered out as we started to descend and saw how the waves below were molten copper and the air above pure amber. It was like landing in a jar of honey.

The transport sideslipped and banked, giving me a view of the Bancroft estate. It edged in from the sea in neatly manicured tones of green and gravel around a sprawling tile-roofed mansion big enough to house a small army. The walls were white, the roofing coral, and the army, if it existed, was out of sight. Any security systems Bancroft had installed were very low key. As we came lower I made out the discreet haze of a power fence along one border of the grounds. Barely enough to distort the view from the house. Nice.

Less than a dozen meters up over one of the immaculate lawns, the pilot kicked in the landing brake with what seemed like unnecessary violence. The transport shuddered from end to end, and we came down hard amidst flying clods of turf.

I shot Ortega a reproachful look, which she ignored. She threw open the hatch and climbed out. After a moment I joined her on the damaged lawn. Prodding at the torn grass with the toe of one shoe, I shouted over the sound of the turbines. "What was that all about? You guys pissed off with Bancroft just because he doesn't buy his own suicide?"

"No." Ortega surveyed the house in front of us as if she was thinking of moving in. "No, that's not why we're pissed off with Mr. Bancroft."

"Care to tell me why?"

"You're the detective."

A young woman appeared from the side of the house, tennis racket in hand, and came across the lawn toward us. When she was about twenty meters away, she stopped, tucked the racket under her arm, and cupped her hands to her mouth.

"Are you Kovacs?"

She was beautiful in a sun, sea, and sand sort of way, and the sports shorts and leotard she was wearing displayed the fact to maximal effect. Golden hair brushed her shoulders as she moved, and the shout gave away a glimpse of milk-white teeth. She wore sweat bands at forehead and wrists, and from the dew on her brow they were not for show. There was finely toned muscle in her legs, and a substantial biceps stood out when she lifted her arms. Exuberant breasts strained the fabric of the leotard. I wondered if the body was hers.

"Yes," I called back. "Takeshi Kovacs. I was discharged this afternoon."

"You were supposed to be met at the storage facility." It was like an accusation. I spread my hands.

"Well. I was."

"Not by the *police*." She stalked forward, eyes mostly for Ortega. "You. I know you."

"Lieutenant Ortega," Ortega said, as if she was at a garden party. "Bay City, Organic Damage Division."

"Yes. I remember now." The tone was distinctly hostile. "I assume it was you who arranged for our chauffeur to be pulled down on some trumped-up emissions charge."

"No, that would be Traffic Control, ma'am," the detective said politely. "I have no jurisdiction in that division."

The woman in front of us sneered.

"Oh, I'm sure you haven't, Lieutenant. And I'm sure none of your friends work there either." The voice turned patronizing. "We'll have him released before the sun goes down, you know."

I glanced sideways to see Ortega's reaction, but there was none. The hawk profile remained impassive. Most of me was preoccupied with the other woman's sneer. It was an ugly expression, and one that belonged on an altogether older face.

Back up by the house there were two large men with automatic weapons slung over their shoulders. They had been standing under the eaves watching since we arrived, but now they ambled out of the shade and began to make their way in our direction. From the slight widening of the young woman's eyes I guessed that she had summoned them on an internal mike. Slick. On Harlan's World people are still a bit averse to sticking racks of hardware into themselves, but it looked as if Earth was going to be a different proposition.

"You are not welcome here, Lieutenant," the young woman said in a freezing voice.

"Just leaving, ma'am," Ortega said heavily. She clapped me unexpectedly on the shoulder and headed back to the transport at an easy pace. Halfway there she suddenly stopped and turned back.

"Here, Kovacs. Almost forgot. You'll need these."

She dug in her breast pocket and tossed me a small packet. I caught it reflexively and looked down. Cigarettes.

"Be seeing you."

She swung herself aboard the transport and slammed the hatch. Through the glass I saw her looking at me. The transport lifted on full repulse, pulverizing the ground beneath and ripping a furrow across the lawn as it swung west toward the ocean. We watched it out of sight.

"Charming," the woman beside me said, largely to herself.

"Mrs. Bancroft?"

She swung around. From the look on her face, I wasn't much more welcome here than Ortega had been. She had seen the lieutenant's gesture of camaraderie, and her lips twitched with disapproval.

"My husband sent a car for you, Mr. Kovacs. Why didn't you wait for it?"

I took out Bancroft's letter. "It says here the car would be waiting for me. It wasn't."

She tried to take the letter from me, and I lifted it out of her reach. She stood facing me, flushed, breasts rising and falling distractingly. When they stick a body in the tank, it goes on producing hormones pretty much the way it would if it was asleep. I became abruptly aware that I was swinging a hard-on like a filled fire hose.

"You should have waited."

Harlan's World, I remembered from somewhere, has gravity at about 0.8 of a G. I suddenly felt unreasonably heavy again. I pushed out a compressed breath.

"Mrs. Bancroft, if I'd waited, I'd still be there now. Can we go inside?"

Her eyes widened a little, and I suddenly saw in them how old she really was. Then she lowered her gaze and summoned composure. When she spoke again, her voice had softened.

"I'm sorry, Mr. Kovacs. I've forgotten my manners. The police, as you see, have not been sympathetic. It's been very upsetting, and we all still feel a little on edge. If you can imagine—"

"There's no need to explain."

"But I am very sorry. I'm not usually like this. None of us are." She gestured around as if to say that the two armed guards behind her would ordinarily have been bearing garlands of flowers. "Please accept my apologies."

"Of course."

"My husband's waiting for you in the seaward lounge. I'll take you to him immediately."

The inside of the house was light and airy. A maid met us at the veranda door and took Mrs. Bancroft's tennis racket for her without a word. We went down a marbled hallway hung with art that, to my untutored eye, looked old. Sketches of Gagarin and Armstrong, empathist renderings of Konrad Harlan and Angin Chandra. At the end of this gallery, set on a plinth, was something like a narrow tree made out of crumbling red stone. I paused in front of it, and Mrs. Bancroft had to backtrack from the left turn she was making.

"Do you like it?" she asked.

"Very much. This is from Mars, isn't it?"

Her face underwent a change that I caught out of the corner of my eye. She was reassessing. I turned for a closer look at her face.

"I'm impressed," she said.

"People often are. Sometimes I do handsprings, too."

She looked at me narrowly. "Do you really know what this is?"

"Frankly, no. I used to be interested in structural art. I recognize the stone from pictures, but . . ."

"It's a songspire." She reached past me and let her fingers trail down one of the upright branches. A faint sighing awoke from the thing and a perfume like cherries and mustard wafted into the air.

"Is it alive?"

"No one knows." There was a sudden enthusiasm in her tone that I liked her better for. "On Mars they grow to be a hundred meters tall, sometimes as wide as this house at the root. You can hear them singing for kilometers. The perfume carries, as well. From the erosion patterns, we think that most of them are at least ten thousand years old. This one might only have been around since the founding of the Roman Empire."

"Must have been expensive. To bring it back to Earth, I mean."

"Money wasn't an object, Mr. Kovacs." The mask was back in place. Time to move on.

We made double time down the left-hand corridor, perhaps to make up for our unscheduled stop. Mrs. Bancroft's breasts jiggled with her steps under the thin material of the leotard, and I took a morose interest in the art on the other side of the corridor. More empathist work, Angin Chandra with her slender hand resting on a thrusting phallus of a rocket. Not much help.

The seaward lounge was built, as its name suggested, on the end of the house's west wing. Mrs. Bancroft took me into it through an unobtrusive wooden door, and the sun hit us in the eyes as soon as we entered.

"Laurens. This is Mr. Kovacs."

I lifted a hand to shade my eyes and saw that the seaward lounge had an upper level with sliding glass doors that accessed a balcony. Leaning on the balcony was a man. He must have heard us come in, come to that he must have heard the police cruiser arrive and known what it signified, but still he stayed where he was, staring out to sea. Coming back from the dead sometimes makes you feel that way. Or maybe it was just arrogance. Mrs. Bancroft nodded me forward, and we went up a set of stairs made from the same wood as the door. For the first time I noticed that the walls of the room were shelved from top to bottom with books. The sun was laying an even coat of orange light along their spines.

As we came out onto the balcony, Bancroft turned to face us. There was a book in his hand, folded closed over his fingers.

"Mr. Kovacs." He transferred the book so that he could shake my hand. "It's a pleasure to meet you at last. How do you find the new sleeve?"

"It's fine. Comfortable."

"Yes, I didn't involve myself too much in the details, but I instructed my lawyers to find something . . . suitable." He glanced back, as if looking for Ortega's cruiser on the horizon. "I hope the police weren't too officious."

"Not so far."

Bancroft looked like a Man Who Read. There's a favorite experia star on Harlan's World called Alain Marriott, best known for his portrayal of a virile young Quellist philosopher who cuts a swath through the brutal tyranny of the early Settlement years. It's questionable how accurate this portrayal of the Quellists is, but it's a good flick. I've seen it twice. Bancroft looked a lot like an older version of Marriott in that role. He was slim and elegant with a full head of iron-gray hair, which he wore back in a ponytail, and hard black eyes. The book in his hand and the shelves around him were like an utterly natural extension of the powerhouse of a mind that looked out from those eyes.

Bancroft touched his wife on the shoulder with a dismissive casualness that in my present state made me want to weep.

"It was that woman, again," Mrs. Bancroft said. "The lieutenant."

Bancroft nodded. "Don't worry about it, Miriam. They're just sniffing around. I warned them I was going to do this, and they ignored me. Well, now Mr. Kovacs is here, and they're finally taking me seriously."

He turned to me. "The police have not been very helpful to me over this matter."

"Yeah. That's why I'm here, apparently."

We looked at each other while I tried to decide if I was angry with this man or not. He'd dragged me halfway across the settled universe, dumped me into a new body, and offered me a deal that was weighted so I couldn't refuse. Rich people do this. They have the power and they see no reason not to use it. Men and women are just merchandise, like everything else. Store them, freight them, decant them. Sign at the bottom, please.

On the other hand, no one at Suntouch House had mispronounced my name yet, and I didn't really have a choice. And then there was the money. A hundred thousand U.N. was about six or seven times what Sarah and I had expected to make on the Millsport wetware haul. U.N. dollars, the hardest currency there was, negotiable on any world in the Net.

That had to be worth keeping your temper for.

Bancroft gave his wife another casual touch, this time on her waist, pushing her away.

"Miriam, could you leave us alone for a while? I'm sure Mr. Kovacs has endless questions, and it's likely to be boring for you."

"Actually, I'm likely to have some questions for Mrs. Bancroft, as well."

She was already on her way back inside, and my comment stopped her in midstride. She cocked her head at an angle and looked from me to Bancroft and back. Beside me, her husband stirred. This wasn't what he wanted.

"Maybe I could speak to you later," I amended. "Separately."

"Yes, of course." Her eyes met mine, then danced aside. "I'll be in the chart room, Laurens. Send Mr. Kovacs along when you've finished."

We both watched her leave, and when the door closed behind her Bancroft gestured me to one of the lounge chairs on the balcony. Behind them, an antique astronomical telescope stood leveled at the horizon, gathering dust. Looking down at the boards under my feet, I saw they were worn with use. The impression of age settled over me like a cloak, and I lowered myself into my chair with a tiny frisson of unease.

"Please don't think of me as a chauvinist, Mr. Kovacs. After nearly two hundred and fifty years of marriage, my relationship with Miriam is more politeness than anything. It really would be better if you spoke to her alone."

"I understand." That was shaving the truth a bit, but it would do.

"Would you care for a drink? Something alcoholic?"

"No thank you. Just some fruit juice, if you have it." The shakiness associated with downloading was beginning to assert itself, and in addition there was an unwelcome scratchiness in my feet and fingers, which I assumed was nicotine dependency. Apart from the odd cigarette bummed from Sarah, I'd been nicotine-free for the last two sleeves, and I didn't want to have to break the habit all over again. Alcohol on top of everything would finish me.

Bancroft folded his hands in his lap. "Of course. I'll have some brought up. Now, where would you like to begin?"

"Maybe we should start with your expectations. I don't know what Reileen Kawahara told you, or what kind of profile the Envoy Corps has here on Earth, but don't expect miracles from me. I'm not a sorcerer."

"I'm aware of that. I have read the corps literature carefully. And all Reileen Kawahara told me was that you were reliable, if a trifle fastidious."

I remembered Kawahara's methods, and my reactions to them. Fastidious. Right.

I gave him the standard spiel anyway. It felt funny, pitching for a client who was already in. Felt funny to play down what I could do, as well. The criminal community isn't long on modesty, and what you do to get serious backing is inflate whatever reputation you may already have. This was more like being back in the corps. Long polished conference tables and Virginia Vidaura ticking off the capabilities of her team.

"Envoy training was developed for the U.N. colonial commando units. That doesn't mean . . ."

Doesn't mean every Envoy is a commando. No, not exactly, but then what is a soldier anyway? How much of special-forces training is engraved on the physical body and how much in the mind? And what happens when the two are separated?

Space, to use a cliché, is big. The closest of the Settled Worlds is fifty light-years out from Earth. The most far-flung are four times that distance, and some of the colony transports are still going. If some maniac starts rattling tactical nukes, or some other biosphere-threatening toys, what are you going to do? You can transmit the information, via hyperspatial needlecast, so close to instantaneously that scientists are still arguing about the terminology, but that, to quote Quellcrist Falconer, deploys no bloody divisions. Even if you launched a troop carrier the moment the shit hit the fan, the marines would be arriving just in time to quiz the grandchildren of whoever won.

That's no way to run a protectorate.

Okay, you can digitize and freight the minds of a crack combat team. It's been a long time since weight of numbers counted for much in a war, and most of the military victories of the last half millennium have been won by small, mobile guerrilla forces. You can even decant your crack D.H.F. soldiers directly into sleeves with combat conditioning, jacked-up nervous systems, and steroid-built bodies. Then what do you do?

They're in bodies they don't know, on a world they don't know, fighting for one bunch of total strangers against another bunch of total strangers over causes they've probably never even heard of and certainly don't understand. The climate is different, the language and culture are different, the wildlife and vegetation are different, the atmosphere is different, shit, even the *gravity* is different. They know nothing, and even if you download them with implanted local knowledge, it's a massive amount of information to assimilate at a time when they're likely to be fighting for their lives within hours of sleeving.

That's where you get the Envoy Corps.

Neurachem conditioning, cyborg interfaces, augmentation—all this stuff is *physical*. Most of it doesn't even touch the pure mind, and it's the pure mind that gets freighted. That's where the corps started. They took psychospiritual techniques that Oriental cultures on Earth had known about for millennia and distilled them into a training system so complete that on most worlds graduates of it were instantly forbidden by law to hold any political or military office.

Not soldiers, no. Not exactly.

"I work by absorption," I finished. "Whatever I come into contact with, I soak up, and I use that to get by."

Bancroft shifted in his seat. He wasn't used to being lectured. It was time to start.

"Who found your body?"

"My daughter, Naomi."

He broke off as someone opened the door in the room below. A moment later, the maid who had attended Miriam Bancroft earlier came up the steps to the balcony bearing a tray with a visibly chilled decanter and tall glasses. Bancroft was wired with internal tannoy like everyone else at Suntouch House, it seemed.

The maid set down her tray, poured in machinelike silence, and then withdrew on a short nod from Bancroft. He stared after her blankly for a while.

Back from the dead. It's no joke.

"Naomi," I prompted him gently.

He blinked. "Oh. Yes. She barged in here, wanting something. Probably the keys to one of the limos. I'm an indulgent father, I suppose, and Naomi is my youngest."

"How young?"

"Twenty-three."

"Do you have many children?"

"Yes, I do. Very many." Bancroft smiled faintly. "When you have leisure and wealth, bringing children into the world is a pure joy. I have twenty-seven sons and thirty-four daughters."

"Do they live with you?"

"Naomi does, most of the time. The others come and go. Most have families of their own now."

"How is Naomi?" I stepped my tone down a little. Finding your father without his head isn't the best way to start the day.

"She's in psychosurgery," Bancroft said shortly. "But she'll pull through. Do you need to talk to her?"

"Not at the moment." I got up from the chair and went to the balcony door. "You say she barged in here. This is where it happened?"

"Yes." Bancroft joined me at the door. "Someone got in here and took my head off with a particle blaster. You can see the blast mark on the wall down there. Over by the desk."

I went inside and down the stairs. The desk was a heavy mirrorwood item; they must have freighted the gene code from Harlan's World and cultured the tree here. That struck me as almost as extravagant as the songspire in the hall, and in slightly more questionable taste. On the World mirrorwood grows in forests on three continents, and practically every canal dive in Millsport has a bartop carved out of the stuff. I moved past it to inspect the stucco wall. The white surface was furrowed and seared black with the unmistakable signature of a beam weapon. I should know; I spent the better part of my youth making marks like that. The burn started at head height and followed a short arc downward.

Bancroft had remained on the balcony. I looked up at his silhouetted face. "This is the only sign of gunfire in the room?"

"Yes."

"Nothing else was damaged, broken, or disturbed in any way?"

"No. Nothing." It was clear that he wanted to say more, but he was keeping quiet until I'd finished.

"And the police found the weapon beside you?"

"Yes."

"Do you own a weapon that would do this?"

"Yes. It was mine. I keep it in a safe under the desk. Handprint coded. They found the safe open, nothing else removed. Do you want to see inside it?"

"Not at the moment, thank you." I knew from experience how difficult mirrorwood furniture is to shift. I turned up one corner of the woven rug under the desk. There was an almost invisible seam in the floor beneath. "Whose prints will open this?"

"Miriam's and my own."

There was a significant pause. Bancroft sighed, loud enough to carry across the room. "Go on, Kovacs. Say it. Everyone else has. Either I committed suicide or my wife murdered me. There's just no other reasonable explanation. I've been hearing it since they pulled me out of the tank at Alcatraz."

I looked elaborately around the room before I met his eyes.

"Well, you'll admit it makes for easier police work," I said. "It's nice and neat."

He snorted, but there was a laugh in it. I found myself beginning to like this man despite myself. I went back up, stepped out onto the balcony, and leaned on the rail. Outside, a black-clad figure prowled back and forth across the lawn below, weapon slung at port. In the distance the power fence shimmered. I stared in that direction for a while.

"It's asking a lot to believe that someone got in here, past all the security, broke into a safe only you and your wife had access to, and murdered you, without causing any disturbance. You're an intelligent man; you must have some reason for believing it."

"Oh, I do. Several."

"Reasons the police chose to ignore."

"Yes."

I turned to face him. "All right. Let's hear it."

"You're looking at it, Mr. Kovacs." He stood there in front of me. "I'm here. I'm back. You can't kill me just by wiping out my cortical stack."

"You've got remote storage. Obviously, or you wouldn't be here. How regular is the update?"

Bancroft smiled. "Every forty-eight hours." He tapped the back of his neck. "Direct needlecast from here into a shielded stack over at the PsychaSec installation at Alcatraz. I don't even have to think about it."

"And they keep your clones on ice there, as well."

"Yes. Multiple units."

Guaranteed immortality. I sat there thinking about that for a while, wondering how I'd like it. Wondering *if* I'd like it.

"Must be expensive," I said at last.

"Not really. I own PsychaSec."

"Oh."

"So you see, Kovacs, neither I nor my wife could have pulled that trigger. We both knew it wouldn't be enough to kill me. No matter how unlikely it seems, it *had* to be a stranger. Someone who didn't know about the remote."

I nodded. "All right, who else *did* know about it? Let's narrow the field."

"Apart from my family?" Bancroft shrugged. "My lawyer, Oumou Prescott. A couple of her legal aides. The D.H.F. director at PsychaSec. That's about it."

"Of course, suicide is rarely a rational act," I said.

"Yes, that's what the police said. They used it to explain all the other minor inconveniences in their theory, as well."

"Which were?"

This was what Bancroft had wanted to reveal earlier. It came out in a rush. "Which were that I should choose to walk the last two kilometers home, and let myself into the grounds on foot, then apparently readjust my internal clock before I killed myself."

I blinked. "I'm sorry?"

"The police found traces of a cruiser landing in a field two kilometers from the perimeter of Suntouch House, which conveniently enough is just outside the pickup range of the house security surveillance. Equally conveniently, there was apparently no satellite cover overhead at that precise time."

"Did they check taxi datastacks?"

Bancroft nodded. "For what it's worth, they did, yes. West Coast law does not require taxi companies to keep records of their fleets' whereabouts at any given time. Some of the more reputable firms do, of course, but there are others that don't. Some even make a selling point of it. Client confidentiality, that sort of thing." A momentary hunted look crossed Bancroft's face. "For some clients, in some cases, that would be a distinct advantage."

"Have you used these firms in the past?"

"On occasion, yes."

The logical next question hung in the air between us. I left it unasked, and waited. If Bancroft wasn't going to share his reasons for wanting confidential transport, I wasn't going to press him until I had a few other landmarks locked down.

Bancroft cleared his throat. "There is, in any case, some evidence to suggest that the vehicle in question might not have been a taxi. Field-effect distribution, the police say. A pattern more in keeping with a larger vehicle."

"That depends on how hard it landed."

"I know. In any case, my tracks lead from the landing site, and apparently the condition of my shoes, was in keeping with a two-kilometer trek across country. And then, finally, there was a call placed from this room shortly after three A.M. the night I was killed. A time check. There's no voice on the line, only the sound of someone breathing."

"And the police know this, too?"

"Of course they do."

"How did they explain it?"

Bancroft smiled thinly. "They didn't. They thought the solitary walk through the rain was very much in keeping with the act of suicide, and apparently they couldn't see any inconsistency in a man wanting to check his internal chronochip before he blows his own head off. As you say, suicide is not a rational act. They have case histories of this sort of thing. Apparently the world is full of incompetents who kill themselves and wake up in a new sleeve the next day. I've had it explained to me. They forget they're wearing a stack, or it doesn't seem important at the moment of the act. Our beloved medical welfare system brings them right back, suicide notes and requests notwithstanding. Curious abuse of rights, that. Is it the same system on Harlan's World?"

I shrugged. "More or less. If the request is legally witnessed, then they have to let them go. Otherwise, failure to revive is a storage offense."

"I suppose that's a wise precaution."

"Yes. It stops murderers passing their work off as suicide."

Bancroft leaned forward on the rail and locked gazes with me. "Mr. Kovacs, I am three hundred and fifty-seven years old. I have lived through a corporate war, the subsequent collapse of my industrial and trading interests, the real deaths of two of my children, at least three major economic crises, and I am still here. I am not the kind of man to take my own life, and *even if I were*, I would not have bungled it in this fashion. If it had been my intention to die, you would not be talking to me now. Is that clear?"

I looked back at him, back at those hard dark eyes. "Yes. Very clear."

"That's good." He unpinned his stare. "Shall we continue?"

"Yes. The police. They don't like you very much, do they?"

Bancroft smiled without much humor. "The police and I have a perspective problem."

"Perspective?"

"That's right." He moved along the balcony. "Come here, I'll show you what I mean."

I followed him along the rail, catching the telescope with my arm as I did and knocking the barrel upright. The download shakes were beginning to demand their dues. The telescope's positional motor whined crabbily and returned the instrument to its original shallow angle. Elevation and range focus ticked over on the ancient digital memory display. I paused to watch the thing realign itself. The finger marks on the keypad were smudged in years of dust.

Bancroft had either not noticed my ineptitude or was being polite about it.

"Yours?" I asked him, jerking a thumb at the instrument. He glanced at it absently.

"Once. It was an enthusiasm I had. Back when the stars were still something to stare at. You wouldn't remember how that felt." It was said without conscious pretension or arrogance, almost inconsequentially. His voice lost some of its focus, like a transmission fading out. "Last time I looked through that lens was nearly two centuries ago. A lot of the colony ships were still in flight then. We were still waiting to find out if they'd make it. Waiting for the needle beams to come back to us. Like lighthouse beacons."

He was losing me. I brought him back to reality. "Perspective?" I reminded him gently.

"Perspective." He nodded and swung an arm out over his property. "You see that tree. Just beyond the tennis courts."

I could hardly miss it. A gnarled old monster taller than the house, casting shade over an area the size of a tennis court in itself. I nodded.

"That tree is over seven hundred years old. When I bought this property, I hired a design engineer and he wanted to chop it down. He was planning to build the house further up the rise, and the tree was spoiling the sea view. I sacked him."

Bancroft turned to make sure his point was getting across.

"You see, Mr. Kovacs, that engineer was a man in his thirties, and to him the tree was just an inconvenience. It was in his way. The fact it had been part of the world for over twenty times the length of his own life didn't seem to bother him. He had no respect."

"So you're the tree."

"Just so," Bancroft said equably. "I am the tree. The police would like to chop me down, just like that engineer. I am inconvenient to them, and they have no respect."

I went back to my seat to chew this over. Kristin Ortega's attitude was beginning to make some sense at last. If Bancroft thought he was outside the normal requirements of good citizenship, he wasn't likely to make many friends in uniform. There would have been little point trying to explain to him that for Ortega there was another tree called the Law and that in her eyes he was banging a few profane nails into it himself. I'd seen this kind of thing from both sides, and there just isn't any solution except to do what my own ancestors had done. When you don't like the laws, you go somewhere they can't touch you.

And then you make up some of your own.

Bancroft stayed at the rail. Perhaps he was communing with the tree. I decided to shelve this line of inquiry for a while.

"What's the last thing you remember?"

"Tuesday, fourteenth August," he said promptly. "Going to bed at about midnight."

"That was the last remote update."

"Yes, the needlecast would have gone through about four in the morning, but obviously I was asleep by then."

"So almost a full forty-eight hours before your death."

"I'm afraid so."

Optimally bad. In forty-eight hours, almost anything can happen. Bancroft could have been to the moon and back in that time. I rubbed at the scar under my eye again, wondering absently how it had got there.

"And there's nothing before that time that could suggest to you why someone might want to kill you."

Bancroft was still leaning on the rail, looking out, but I saw how he smiled.

"Did I say something amusing?"

He had the grace to come back to his seat.

"No, Mr. Kovacs. There is nothing amusing about this situation. Someone out there wants me dead, and that's not a comfortable feeling. But you must understand that for a man in my position, enmity and even death threats are part and parcel of everyday existence. People envy me, people hate me. It is the price of success."

This was news to me. People hate me on a dozen different worlds, and I've never considered myself a successful man.

"Had any interesting ones recently? Death threats, I mean."

He shrugged. "Perhaps. I don't make a habit of screening them. Ms. Prescott handles that for me."

"You don't consider death threats worth your attention?"

"Mr. Kovacs, I am an entrepreneur. Opportunities arise, crises present themselves, and I deal with them. Life goes on. I hire managers to deal with that."

"Very convenient for you. But in view of the circumstances, I find it hard to believe neither you nor the police have consulted Ms. Prescott's files."

Bancroft waved a hand. "Of course, the police conducted their own cursory inquiry. Oumou Prescott told them exactly what she had already told me. That nothing out of the ordinary had been received in the last six months. I have enough faith in her not to need to check beyond that. You'll probably want to look at the files yourself, though."

The thought of scrolling through hundreds of meters of incoherent vitriol from the lost and losers of this antique world was quite sufficient to uncap my weariness again. A profound lack of interest in Bancroft's problems washed through me. I mastered it with an effort worthy of Virginia Vidaura's approval.

"Well, I'll certainly need to talk to Oumou Prescott, anyway."

"I'll make the appointment immediately." Bancroft's eyes took on the inward glaze of someone consulting internal hardware. "What time would suit you?"

I held up a hand. "Probably better if I do that myself. Just let her know I'll be in touch. And I'll need to see the resleeving facility at PsychaSec."

"Certainly. In fact, I'll get Prescott to take you there. She knows the director. Anything else?"

"A line of credit."

"Of course. My bank has already allocated a DNA-coded account to you. I understand they have the same system on Harlan's World."

I licked my thumb and held it up queryingly. Bancroft nodded.

"Just the same here. You *will* find there are areas of Bay City where cash is still the only negotiable currency. Hopefully you won't have to spend much time in those parts, but if you do, you can draw actual currency against your account at any bank outlet. Will you require a weapon?"

"Not at the moment, no." One of Virginia Vidaura's cardinal rules had always been *find out the nature of your task before you choose your tools*. That single sweep of charred stucco on Bancroft's wall looked too elegant for this to be a shoot-'em-up carnival.

"Well." Bancroft seemed almost perplexed by my response. He had been on the point of reaching into his shirt pocket, and now he completed the action awkwardly. He held out an inscribed card to me. "This is my gunmaker. I've told them to expect you."

I took the card and looked at it. The ornate script read LARKIN AND GREEN— ARMORERS SINCE 2203. Quaint. Below was a single string of numbers. I pocketed the card.

"This might be useful later on," I admitted. "But for the moment I want to make a soft landing. Sit back and wait for the dust to settle. I think you can appreciate the need for that."

"Yes, of course. Whatever you think best. I trust your judgment." Bancroft caught my gaze and held it. "You'll bear in mind the terms of our agreement, though. I am paying for a service. I don't react well to abuse of trust, Mr. Kovacs."

"No, I don't suppose you do," I said tiredly. I remembered the way Reileen Kawahara had dealt with two unfaithful minions. The animal sounds they had made came back to me in dreams for a long time afterwards. Reileen's argument, framed as she peeled an apple against the backdrop of those screams, was that since no one really dies anymore, punishment can come only through suffering. I felt my new face twitch, even now, with the memory.

"For what it's worth, the line the corps fed you about me is so much shit on a prick. My word's as good as it ever was."

I stood up.

"Can you recommend a place to stay back in the city? Somewhere quiet, midrange."

"Yes, there are places like that on Mission Street. I'll have someone ferry you back there. Curtis, if he's out of arrest by then." Bancroft climbed to his feet, as well. "I take it you intend to interview Miriam now. She really knows more about those last forty-eight hours than I do, so you'll want to speak to her quite closely."

I thought about those ancient eyes in that pneumatic teenager's body, and the idea of carrying on a conversation with Miriam Bancroft was suddenly repellent. At the same time a cold hand strummed taut chords in the pit of my stomach and the head of my penis swelled abruptly with blood. Classy.

"Oh, yes," I said unenthusiastically. "I'd like to do that."

CHAPTEr FOUr

"Y ou seem ill at ease, Mr. Kovacs. Are you?"
I looked over my shoulder at the maid who had shown me in, then back at Miriam Bancroft. Their bodies were about the same age.

"No," I said, more coarsely than I'd intended.

She curved her mouth briefly down at the corners and went back to rolling up the map she'd been studying when I arrived. Behind me the maid pulled the chart room door closed with a heavy click. Bancroft hadn't seen fit to accompany me into the presence of his wife. Perhaps one encounter a day was as much as they allowed themselves. Instead, the maid had appeared as if by magic as we came down from the balcony in the seaward lounge. Bancroft paid her about as much attention as he had last time.

When I left, he was standing by the mirrorwood desk, staring at the blast mark on the wall.

Mrs. Bancroft deftly tightened the roll on the map in her hands and began to slide it into a long protective tube.

"Well," she said, without looking up. "Ask me your questions, then."

"Where were you when it happened?"

"I was in bed." She looked up at me this time. "Please don't ask me to corroborate that. I was alone."

The chart room was long and airy under an arched roof that someone had tiled with illuminum. The map racks were waist high, each topped with a glassed-in display and set out in rows like exhibit cases in a museum. I moved out of the center aisle, putting one of the racks between Mrs. Bancroft and myself. It felt a little like taking cover.

"Mrs. Bancroft, you seem to be under some misapprehension here. I'm not the police. I'm interested in information, not guilt."

She slid the wrapped map away in its holder and leaned back against the rack with both hands behind her. She had left her fresh young sweat and tennis clothes in some elegant bathroom while I was talking to her husband. Now she was immaculately fastened up in black slacks and something born of a union between a dinner jacket and a bodice. Her sleeves were pushed casually up almost to the elbow, her wrists unadorned with jewelry.

"Do I sound guilty, Mr. Kovacs?" she asked me.

"You seem overanxious to assert your fidelity to a complete stranger."

She laughed. It was a pleasant, throaty sound, and her shoulders rose and fell as she let it out. A laugh I could get to like.

"How very indirect you are."

I looked down at the map displayed on the top of the rack in front of me. It was dated in the top left-hand corner, a year four centuries before I was born. The names marked on it were in a script I couldn't read.

"Where I come from, directness is not considered a great virtue, Mrs. Bancroft."

"No? Then what is?"

I shrugged. "Politeness. Control. Avoidance of embarrassment for all parties."

"Sounds boring. I think you're going to have a few shocks here, Mr. Kovacs."

"I didn't say I was a good citizen where I come from, Mrs. Bancroft."

"Oh." She pushed herself off the rack and moved toward me. "Yes, Laurens told me a little about you. It seems you're thought of as a dangerous man on Harlan's World."

I shrugged again.

"It's Russian."

"I'm sorry?"

"The script." She came around the rack and stood beside me, looking down at the map. "This is a Russian computer-generated chart of moon landing sites. Very rare. I got it at an auction. Do you like it?"

"It's very nice. What time did you go to sleep the night your husband was shot?"

She stared at me. "Early. I told you, I was alone." She forced the edge out of her voice, and her tone became almost light again. "Oh, and if that sounds like guilt, Mr. Kovacs, it's not. It's resignation. With a twist of bitterness."

"You feel bitter about your husband?"

She smiled. "I thought I said resigned."

"You said both."

"Are you saying you think I killed my husband?"

"I don't think anything yet. But it is a possibility."

"Is it?"

"You had access to the safe. You were inside the house defenses when it happened. And now it sounds as if you might have some emotional motives."

Still smiling, she said, "Building a case, are we, Mr. Kovacs?"

I looked back at her. "If the heart pumps. Yeah."

"The police had a similar theory for a while. They decided the heart didn't pump. I'd prefer it if you didn't smoke in here."

I looked down at my hands and found they had quite unconsciously taken out Kristin Ortega's cigarettes. I was in the middle of tapping one out of the pack. Nerves. Feeling oddly betrayed by my new sleeve, I put the pack away.

"I'm sorry."

"Don't be. It's a question of climate control. A lot of the maps in here are very sensitive to pollution. You couldn't know."

She somehow managed to make it sound as if only a complete moron wouldn't have realized. I could feel my grip on the interview sliding out of sight.

"What made the police—"

"Ask them." She turned her back and walked away from me as if making a decision. "How old are you, Mr. Kovacs?"

"Subjectively? Forty-one. The years on Harlan's World are a little longer than here, but there isn't much in it."

"And *ob*jectively?" she asked, mocking my tone.

"I've had about a century in the tank. You tend to lose track." That was a lie. I knew to the day how long each of my terms in storage had been. I'd worked it out one night, and now the number wouldn't go away. Every time I went down again, I added on.

"How alone you must be by now."

I sighed and turned to examine the nearest map rack. Each rolled chart was labeled at the end. The notation was archaeological. SYRTIS MINOR; 3RD EXCAVATION, EAST QUARTER. BRADBURY; ABORIGINAL RUINS. I started to tug one of the rolls free.

"Mrs. Bancroft, how I feel is not at issue here. Can you think of any reason why your husband might have tried to kill himself?"

She whirled on me almost before I had finished speaking, and her face was tight with anger.

"My husband did not kill himself," she said freezingly.

"You seem very sure of that." I looked up from the map and gave her a smile. "For someone who wasn't awake, I mean."

"Put that back," she cried, starting toward me. "You have no idea how valuable—"

She stopped, brought up short as I slid the map back into the rack. She swallowed and brought the flush in her cheeks under control.

"Are you trying to make me angry, Mr. Kovacs?"

"I'm just trying to get some attention."

We looked at each other for a pair of seconds. Mrs. Bancroft lowered her gaze.

"I've told you, I was asleep when it happened. What else can I tell you?"

"Where had your husband gone that night?"

She bit her lip. "I'm not sure. He went to Osaka that day, for a meeting."

"Osaka is where?"

She looked at me in surprise.

"I'm not from here," I said patiently.

"Osaka's in Japan. I thought—"

"Yeah, Harlan's World was settled by a Japanese *keiretsu* using East European labor. It was a long time ago, and I wasn't around."

"I'm sorry."

"Don't be. You probably don't know much about what your ancestors were doing three centuries ago either."

I stopped. Mrs. Bancroft was looking at me strangely. My own words hit me a moment later. Download dues. I was going to have to sleep soon, before I said or did something really stupid.

"I *am* over three centuries old, Mr. Kovacs." There was a small smile playing around her mouth as she said it. She'd taken back the advantage as smoothly as a bottleback diving. "Appearances are deceptive. This is my eleventh body."

The way she held herself said that I was supposed to take a look. I flickered my gaze across the Slavic-boned cheeks, down to the décolletage and then to the tilt of her hips, the half-shrouded lines of her thighs, all the time affecting a detachment that neither I nor my recently roused sleeve had any right to.

"It's very nice. A little young for my tastes, but as I said, I'm not from here. Can we get back to your husband, please? He'd been to Osaka during the day, but he came back. I assume he didn't go physically."

"No, of course not. He has a transit clone on ice there. He was due back about six that evening, but—"

"Yes?"

She shifted her posture slightly and opened a palm at me. I got the impression she was forcibly composing herself. "Well, he was late coming back. Laurens often stays out late after closing a deal."

"And no one has any idea where he went on this occasion? Curtis, for example?"

The strain on her face was still there, like weathered rocks under a thin mantle of snow. "He didn't send for Curtis. I assume he took a taxi from the sleeving station. I'm not his keeper, Mr. Kovacs."

"This meeting was crucial? The one in Osaka?"

"Oh . . . no, I don't think so. We've talked about it. Of course, he doesn't remember, but we've been over the contracts and it's something he'd had timetabled for a while. A marine development company called Pacificon, based in Japan. Leasing renewal, that kind of thing. It's usually all taken care of here in Bay City, but there was some call for an extraordinary assessors' meeting, and it's always best to handle that sort of thing close to the source."

I nodded sagely, having no idea what a marine development assessor was. Noting Mrs. Bancroft's strain seemed to be receding.

"Routine stuff, huh?"

"I would think so, yes." She gave me a weary smile. "Mr. Kovacs, I'm sure the police have transcripts of this kind of information."

"I'm sure they do, as well, Mrs. Bancroft. But there's no reason why they should share them with me. I have no jurisdiction here."

"You seemed friendly enough with them when you arrived." There was a sudden spike of malice in her voice. I looked steadily at her until she dropped her gaze. "Anyway, I'm sure Laurens can get you anything you need."

This was going nowhere fast. I backed up.

"Perhaps I'd better speak to him about that." I looked around the chart room. "All these maps. How long have you been collecting?"

Mrs. Bancroft must have sensed that the interview was drawing to a close, because the tension puddled out of her like oil from a cracked sump.

"Most of my life," she said. "While Laurens was staring at the stars, some of us kept our eyes on the ground."

For some reason I thought of the telescope abandoned on Bancroft's sundeck. I saw it stranded in angular silhouette against the evening sky, a mute testimony to times and obsessions past and a relic no one wanted. I remembered the way it had wheezed back into alignment after I jarred it, faithful to programming maybe centuries old, briefly awakened the way Miriam Bancroft had stroked the songspire awake in the hall.

Old.

With sudden and suffocating pressure, it was all around me, the reek of it pouring off the stones of Suntouch House like damp. Age. I even caught the waft of it from the impossibly young and beautiful woman in front of me, and my throat locked up with a tiny click. Something in me wanted to run, to get out and breathe fresh, new air, to be away from these creatures whose memories stretched back beyond every historical event I had been taught in school.

"Are you all right, Mr. Kovacs?"

Download dues.

I focused with an effort. "Yes, I'm fine." I cleared my throat and looked into her eyes.

"Well, I won't keep you any longer, Mrs. Bancroft. Thank you for your time."

She moved toward me. "Would you like—"

"No, it's quite all right. I'll see myself out."

The walk out of the chart room seemed to take forever, and my footsteps had developed a sudden echo inside my skull. With every step, and with every displayed map that I passed, I felt those ancient eyes on my spine, watching.

I badly needed a cigarette.

CHAPTEr FIVE

The sky was the texture of old silver and the lights were coming on across Bay City by the time Bancroft's chauffeur got me back to town. We spiraled in from the sea over an ancient suspension bridge the color of rust, and in amongst the heaped-up buildings of a peninsula hill at more than advisable speed. Curtis the chauffeur was still smarting from his summary detainment by the police. He'd been out of arrest only a couple of hours when Bancroft asked him to run me back, and he'd been sullen and uncommunicative on the journey. He was a muscular young man whose boyish good looks lent themselves well to brooding. My guess was that employees of Laurens Bancroft were unused to government minions interrupting their duties.

I didn't complain. My own mood wasn't far off matching the chauffeur's. Images of Sarah's death kept creeping into my mind. It had happened only last night. Subjectively.

We braked in the sky over a wide thoroughfare, sharply enough for someone above us to broadcast an outraged proximity squawk into the limousine's com-set. Curtis cut off the signal with a slap of one hand across the console, and his face tilted up to glower dangerously through the roof window. We settled down into the flow of ground traffic with a slight bump and immediately made a left into a narrower street. I started to take an interest in what was outside.

There's a sameness to streetlife. On every world I've ever been, the same underlying patterns play out, flaunt and vaunt, buy and sell, like some distilled essence of human behavior seeping out from under whatever clanking political machine has been dropped on it from above. Bay City, Earth, most ancient of civilized worlds, had won itself no exemptions. From the massive insubstantial holofronts along the antique buildings to the street traders with their catalog broadcast sets nestling on shoulders like clumsy mechanical hawks or outside tumors, everyone was selling something. Cars pulled in and out from the curbside, and supple bodies braced against them, leaning in to negotiate the way they've probably been doing as long as there've been cars to do it against. Shreds of steam and smoke drifted from food barrows. The limo was sound- and broadcast-proofed, but you could sense the noises through the glass, corner pitch sales chants and modulated music carrying consumer urge subsonics.

In the Envoy Corps, they reverse humanity. You see the sameness first, the underlying resonance that lets you get a handle on where you are, then you build up difference from the details.

The Harlan's World ethnic mix is primarily Slavic and Japanese, although you can get any variant tank-grown at a price. Here, every face was a different cast and color. I saw tall, angular-boned Africans, Mongols, pasty-skinned Nordics, and, once, a girl who looked like Virginia Vidaura, but I lost her in the crowd. They all slid by like natives on the banks of a river.

Clumsy.

The impression skipped and flickered across my thoughts like the girl in the crowd. I frowned and caught at it.

On Harlan's World, streetlife has a stripped-back elegance to it, an economy of motion and gesture that feels almost like choreography if you're not used to it. I grew up with it, so the effect doesn't register until it's not there anymore.

I wasn't seeing it here. The ebb and flow of human commerce beyond the limo's windows had a quality like choppy water in the space between boats. People pushed and shoved their way along, backing up abruptly to get around tighter knots in the crowd that they apparently hadn't noticed until it was too late to maneuver. Obvious tensions broke out, necks craned, muscled bodies drew themselves up. Twice I saw the makings of a fight take stumbling shape, only to be swept away on the chop. It was as if the whole place had been sprayed with some pheromonal irritant.

"Curtis." I glanced sideways at his impassive profile. "You want to cut the broadcast block for a minute?"

He looked across at me with a slight curl of the lip. "Sure."

I settled back in the seat and fixed my eyes on the street again. "I'm not a tourist, Curtis. This is what I do for a living."

The street sellers' catalogs came aboard like a swarm of delirium-induced hallucinations, slightly diffuse through lack of directed broadcast and blurring swiftly into each other as we glided along, but still an overload by any Harlanite standards. The pimps were the most obvious, a succession of oral and anal acts, digitally retouched to lend an airbrushed sheen to breasts and musculature. Each whore's name was murmured in throaty voiceover, along with a superimposed facial, coy little girls, dominatrixes, stubbled stallions, and a few from cultural stock that was completely alien to me. Weaving in between were the more subtle chemical lists and surreal scenarios of the drug and implant traders. I caught a couple of religious 'casts amidst it all, images of spiritual calm among mountains, but they were like drowning men in the sea of product.

The stumbling started to make sense.

"What does *from the Houses* mean?" I asked Curtis, trawling the phrase from the 'casts for the third time.

Curtis sneered. "The mark of quality. The Houses are a cartel—high-class, expensive whorehouses up and down the coast. Get you anything you want, they say. If a girl's from the Houses, she's been taught to do stuff most people only ever dream about." He nodded at the street. "Don't kid yourself, no one out there ever worked in the Houses."

"And Stiff?"

He shrugged. "Street name. Betathanatine. Kids use it for near-death experiences. Cheaper than suicide."

"I guess."

"You don't got 'thanatine on Harlan's World?"

"No." I'd used it offworld with the corps a couple of times, but there was a ban in fashion back home. "We got suicide, though. You want to put the screen back up?"

The soft brush of images cut out abruptly, leaving the inside of my head feeling stark, like an unfurnished room. I waited for the feeling to fade and, like most aftereffects, it did.

"This is Mission Street," Curtis said. "The next couple of blocks are all hotels. You want me to drop you here?"

"You recommend anywhere?"

"Depends what you want."

I gave him one of his own shrugs back. "Light. Space. Room service."

He squinted thoughtfully. "Try the Hendrix, if you like. They got a tower annex, and the whores they use are clean." The limousine picked up speed fractionally, and we made a couple of blocks in silence. I neglected to explain I hadn't meant that kind of room service. Let Curtis draw the conclusions he seemed to want to.

Unbidden, a freeze frame of Miriam Bancroft's sweat-dewed cleavage bounced through my mind.

The limo coasted to a halt outside a well-lit facade in a style I didn't recognize. I climbed out and stared up at a huge holocast black man, features screwed up presumably in ecstasy at the music he was wringing left-handed from a white guitar. The image had the slightly artificial edges of a remastered two-dimensional image, which made it old. Hoping this might indicate a tradition of service and not just decrepitude, I thanked Curtis, slammed the door, and watched the limousine cruise away. It began to climb almost immediately, and after a moment I lost the taillights in the streams of airborne traffic. I turned to the mirrored glass doors behind me, and they parted slightly jerkily to let me in.

If the lobby was anything to go by, the Hendrix was certainly going to satisfy the second of my requirements. Curtis could have parked three or four of Bancroft's limos side by side in it and still have had space to wheel a cleaning robot around them. I wasn't so sure about the first. The walls and ceiling bore an irregular spacing of illuminum tiles whose half-life was clearly almost up, and their feeble radiance had the sole effect of shoveling the gloom into the center of the room. The street I'd just come in off was the strongest source of light in the place.

The lobby was deserted, but there was a faint blue glow coming from a counter on the far wall. I picked my way toward it, past low armchairs and shin-hungry metal-edged tables, and found a recessed monitor screen swarming with the random snow of disconnection. In one corner, a command pulsed on and off in English, Spanish, and kanji characters.

SPEAK.

I looked around and back at the screen.

No one.

I cleared my throat.

The characters blurred and shifted. SELECT LANGUAGE.

"I'm looking for a room," I tried, in Japanese out of pure curiosity.

The screen jumped into life so dramatically that I took a step backwards. From whirling, multicolored fragments it rapidly assembled a tanned Asian face above a dark collar and tie. The face smiled and changed into a Caucasian female, aged fractionally, and I was facing a blonde thirty-year-old woman in a sober business suit. Having generated my interpersonal ideal, the hotel also decided that I couldn't speak Japanese after all.

"Good day, sir. Welcome to the Hotel Hendrix, established 2087 and still here today. How may we serve you?"

I repeated my request, following the move into Amanglic.

"Thank you, sir. We have a number of rooms, all fully cabled to the city's information and entertainment stack. Please indicate your preference for floor and size."

"I'd like a tower room, west facing. The biggest you've got."

The face recoiled into a corner inset, and a three-dimensional skeleton of the hotel's room structure etched itself into place. A selector pulsed efficiently through the rooms and stopped in one corner, then blew up and rotated the room in question. A column of fine-print data shuttered down on one side of the screen.

"The Watchtower suite, three rooms, dormitory thirteen point eight seven meters by—"

"That's fine, I'll take it."

The three-dimensional map disappeared like a conjuror's trick, and the woman leapt back to full screen.

"How many nights will you be with us, sir?"

"Indefinite."

"A deposit *is* required," the hotel said diffidently. "For stays of more than fourteen days the sum of six hundred dollars U.N. should be deposited now. In the event of departure before said fourteen days, a proportion of this deposit *will* be refunded."

"Fine."

"Thank you, sir." From the tone of voice, I began to suspect that paying customers were a novelty at the Hotel Hendrix. "How will you be paying?"

"DNA trace. First Colony Bank of California."

The payment details were scrolling out when I felt a cold circle of metal touch the base of my skull.

"That's exactly what you think it is," a calm voice said. "You do the wrong thing, and the cops are going to be picking bits of your cortical stack out of that wall for weeks. I'm talking about *real* death, friend. Now, lift your hands away from your body."

I complied, feeling an unaccustomed chill shoot up my spine to the point the gun muzzle was touching. It was a long time since I'd been threatened with real death.

"That's good," the same calm voice said. "Now, my associate here is going to pad you down. You let her do that, and no sudden moves."

"Please key your DNA signature onto the pad beside this screen." The hotel had accessed First Colony's database. I waited impassively while a slim black-clad woman in a ski mask stepped around and ran a purring gray scanner over me from head to foot. The gun at my neck never wavered. It was no longer cold. My flesh had warmed it to a more intimate temperature.

"He's clean." Another crisp, professional voice. "Basic neurachem, but it's inoperative. No hardware."

"Really? Traveling kind of light, aren't you, Kovacs?"

My heart dropped out of my chest and impacted soggily in my guts. I'd hoped this was just local crime.

"I don't know you," I said cautiously, turning my head a couple of millimeters. The gun jabbed and I stopped.

"That's right, you don't. Now, here's what's going to happen. We're going to walk outside—"

"Credit access will cease in thirty seconds," the hotel said patiently. "Please key in your DNA signature now."

"Mr. Kovacs won't be needing his reservation," the man behind me said, putting a hand on my shoulder. "Come on, Kovacs, we're going for a ride."

"I cannot assume host prerogatives without payment," the woman on the screen said.

Something in the tone of that phrase stopped me as I was turning, and on impulse I forced out a sudden, racking cough.

"What—"

Bending forward with the force of the cough, I raised a hand to my mouth and licked my thumb.

"The fuck are you playing at, Kovacs?"

I straightened again and snapped my hand out to the keypad beside the screen. Traces of fresh spittle smeared over the matte-black receiver. A split second later a calloused palm edge cracked into the left side of my skull, and I collapsed to my hands and knees on the floor. A boot lashed into my face, and I went the rest of the way down.

"Thank you, sir." I heard the voice of the hotel through a roaring in my head. "Your account is being processed."

I tried to get up and got a second boot in the ribs for the trouble. Blood dripped from my nose onto the carpet. The barrel of the gun ground into my neck.

"That wasn't smart, Kovacs." The voice was marginally less calm. "If you think the cops are going to trace us where you're going, then the stack must have fucked your brain. Now *get up!*"

He was pulling me to my feet when the thunder cut loose.

Why someone had seen fit to equip the Hendrix's security systems with twenty-millimeter automatic cannon was beyond me, but they did the job with devastating totality. Out of the corner of one eye I glimpsed the twin-mounted autoturret come snaking down from the ceiling just a moment before it channeled a three-second burst of fire through my primary assailant. Enough firepower to bring down a small aircraft. The noise was deafening.

The masked woman ran for the doors, and with the echoes of fire still hammering in my ears I saw the turret swivel to follow. She made about a dozen paces through the gloom before a prism of ruby laser light dappled across her back and a fresh fusillade exploded in the confines of the lobby. I clapped both hands over my ears, still on my knees, and the shells punched through her. She went over in a graceless tangle of limbs.

The firing stopped.

In the cordite-reeking quiet that followed, nothing moved. The autoturret had gone dormant, barrels slanting at a downward angle, smoke coiling from the breeches. I unclasped my hands from my ears and climbed to my feet, pressing gingerly on my nose and face to ascertain the extent of the damage done. The bleeding seemed to be slowing down, and though there were cuts in my mouth I couldn't find any loosened teeth. My ribs hurt where the second kick had hit me, but it didn't feel as if anything was broken. I glanced over at the nearest corpse, and wished I hadn't. Someone was going to have to get a mop.

To my left an elevator door opened with a faint chime.

"Your room is ready, sir," the hotel said.

CHAPTER SIX

Kristin Ortega was remarkably restrained.

She came through the hotel doors with a loping stride that bounced one heavily weighted jacket pocket against her thigh, came to a halt in the center of the lobby, and surveyed the carnage with her tongue thrust into one cheek.

"You do this sort of thing a lot, Kovacs?"

"I've been waiting awhile," I told her mildly. "I'm not in a great mood."

The hotel had placed a call to the Bay City police about the time the auto-turret had cut loose, but it was a good half hour before the first cruisers came spiraling down out of the sky traffic. I hadn't bothered to go to my room, since I knew they were going to drag me out of bed anyway, and once they arrived there was no question of me going anywhere until Ortega got there. A police medic gave me a cursory check, ascertained that I wasn't suffering from concussion, and left me with a retardant spray to stop the nosebleed, after which I sat in the lobby and let my new sleeve smoke some of the lieutenant's cigarettes. I was still sitting there an hour later when she arrived.

Ortega gestured. "Yeah, well. Busy city at night."

I offered her the pack. She looked at it as if I'd just posed a major philosophical question, then took it and shook out a cigarette. Ignoring the ignition patch on the side of the pack, she searched her pockets, produced a heavy lighter, and snapped it open. She seemed to be on autopilot, moving aside almost without noticing to let a forensics team bring in new equipment, then returning the lighter to a different pocket. Around us, the lobby seemed suddenly crowded with efficient people doing their jobs.

"So." She plumed smoke into the air above her head. "You know these guys?"

"Oh, give me a fucking break!"

"Meaning?"

"Meaning, I've been out of storage six hours, if that." I could hear my voice starting to rise. "Meaning, I've talked to precisely three people since the last time we met. Meaning, I've never been on Earth in my life. Meaning, *you know all this.* Now, are you going to ask me some intelligent questions, or am I going to bed?"

"All right, keep your skull on." Ortega looked suddenly tired. She sank into the lounger opposite mine. "You told my sergeant they were professionals."

"They were." I'd decided it was the one piece of information I might as well share with the police, since they'd probably find out anyway, as soon as they ran the make on the two corpses through their files.

"Did they call you by name?"

I furrowed my brow with great care. "By name?"

"Yeah." She made an impatient gesture. "Did they call you Kovacs?"

"I don't think so."

"Any other names?"

I raised an eyebrow. "Such as?"

The weariness that had clouded her face retreated abruptly, and she gave me a hard look. "Forget it. We'll run the hotel's memory, and see."

Oops.

"On Harlan's World you'd have to get a warrant for that." I made it come out lazily.

"We do here." Ortega knocked ash off her cigarette onto the carpet. "But it won't be a problem. Apparently this isn't the first time the Hendrix has been up on an organic damage charge. While ago, but the archives go back."

"So how come it wasn't decommissioned?"

"I said up on charges, not convicted. Court threw it out. Demonstrable self-defense. Course—" She nodded over at the dormant gun turret, where two members of the forensic team were running an emissions sweep. "—we're talking about covert electrocution that time. Nothing like this."

"Yeah, I was meaning to ask. Who fits that kind of hardware in a hotel anyway?"

"What do you think I am, a search construct?" Ortega had started watching me with a speculative hostility I didn't much like. Then, abruptly, she shrugged. "Archive précis I ran on the way over here says it got done a couple of centuries back, when the corporate wars turned nasty. Makes sense. With all that shit breaking loose, a lot of buildings were retooling to cope. Course, most of the companies went under shortly afterwards with the trading crash, so no one ever got around to passing a decommissioning bill. The Hendrix upgraded to artificial-intelligence status instead and bought itself out."

"Smart."

"Yeah, from what I hear the A.I.s were the only ones with any kind of real handle on what was happening to the market anyway. Quite a few of them made the break about then. Lot of the hotels on this strip are A.I." She grinned at me through the smoke. "That's why no one stays in them. Shame, really. I read somewhere they're hardwired to want customers the way people want sex. That's got to be frustrating, right?"

"Right."

One of the mohicans came and hovered over us. Ortega glanced up at him with a look that said she didn't want to be disturbed.

"We got a make on the DNA samples," the mohican said diffidently, and handed her a videofax slate. Ortega scanned it and started.

"Well, well. You were in exalted company for a while, Kovacs." She waved an arm in the direction of the male corpse. "Sleeve last registered to Dimitri

Kadmin, otherwise known as Dimi the Twin. Professional assassin out of Vladivostok."

"And the woman?"

Ortega and the mohican exchanged glances. "Ulan Bator registry?"

"Got it in one, chief."

"Got the motherfucker." Ortega bounced to her feet with renewed energy. "Let's get their stacks excised and over to Fell Street. I want Dimi downloaded into Holding before midnight." She looked back at me. "Kovacs, you may just have proved useful."

The mohican reached under his double-breasted suit and produced a heavy-bladed killing knife with the nonchalance of a man getting out cigarettes. Together, they went over to the corpse and knelt beside it. Interested uniformed officers drifted across to watch. There was the wet cracking sound of cartilage being cut open. After a moment, I got up and went to join the spectators. Nobody paid any attention to me.

It was not what you'd call refined biotech surgery. The mohican had chopped out a section of the corpse's spine to gain access to the base of the skull, and now he was digging around with the point of the knife, trying to locate the cortical stack. Kristin Ortega was holding the head steady in both hands.

"They bury them a lot deeper in than they used to," she was saying. "See if you can get the rest of the vertebrae out; that's where it'll be."

"I'm trying," the mohican grunted. "Some augmentation in here, I reckon. One of those antishock washers Noguchi was talking about last time he was over— Shit! Thought I had it there."

"No, look, you're working at the wrong angle. Let me try." Ortega took the knife and put one knee on the skull to steady it.

"Shit, I nearly had it, chief."

"Yeah, yeah, I'm not spending all night watching you poke around in there." She glanced up and saw me watching her, nodded a brief acknowledgment, and put the serrated point of the blade in place. Then with a sharp blow to the haft of the knife, she chopped something loose. She looked up at the mohican with a grin.

"Hear that?"

She reached down into the gore and pulled out the stack between finger and thumb. It didn't look like much, impact-resistant casing streaked with blood and barely the size of a cigarette butt, with the twisted filaments of the microjacks protruding stiffly from one end. I could see how the Catholics might not want to believe this was the receptacle of the human soul.

"Gotcha, Dimi." Ortega held up the stack to the light, then passed it and the knife to the mohican. She wiped her fingers on the corpse's clothing. "Right, let's get the other one out of the woman."

As we watched the mohican repeating the procedure on the second body, I tipped my head close enough to Ortega to mutter.

"So you know who this one is, as well?"

She jerked around to look at me, whether out of surprise or dislike of my proximity I couldn't be sure. "Yeah, this is Dimi the Twin, too. Ha, pun! The sleeve's registered out of Ulan Bator, which for your information is the black-market downloading capital of Asia. See, Dimi's not a very trusting soul. He likes to have people he can be sure of backing him up. And the circles Dimi mixes in, the only person you can really trust is you."

"Those sound like familiar circles. Is it easy to get yourself copied on Earth?"

Ortega grimaced. "Getting easier all the time. Technology the way it is now, a state-of-the-art resleeving processor fits into a bathroom. Pretty soon it's going to be an elevator. Then a suitcase." She shrugged. "Price of progress."

"About the only way you can get it done on Harlan's World is to file for a stellar-range 'cast, get an insurance copy held for the duration of the trip, and then cancel the transmission at the last minute. Fake a transit certificate, then claim a vital interest for a temporary download from the copy. This guy's off-world and his business is crumbling, that kind of thing. Download once from the original at the transmission station, and again through the insurance company somewhere else. Copy One walks out of the station legally. He just changed his mind about going. Lots of people do. Copy Two never reports back to the insurance company for restorage. Costs a lot of money, though. You've got to bribe a lot of people, steal a lot of machine time to get away with it."

The mohican slipped and cut his thumb on the knife. Ortega rolled her eyes and sighed in a compressed fashion. She turned back to face me.

"It's easier here," she said shortly.

"Yeah? How's it work?"

"It—" She hesitated, as if trying to work out why she was talking to me. "Why do you want to know?"

I grinned at her. "Just naturally nosy, I guess."

●●●

"Okay, Kovacs." She cupped both hands around her coffee mug. "Works like this. One day Mr. Dimitri Kadmin walks into one of the big retrieval and resleeving insurance companies. I mean someone *really* respectable, like Lloyd's or Cartwright Solar, maybe."

"Is that here?" I gestured out at the bridge lights visible beyond the windows of my room. "In Bay City?"

The mohican had given Ortega some odd looks when she stayed behind as the police departed the Hendrix. She saw him off with another admonition to get Kadmin downloaded *rápido*, and then we went upstairs. She barely watched the police cruisers leave.

"Bay City, East Coast, maybe even Europe." Ortega sipped her coffee, wincing at the overload of whiskey she'd asked the Hendrix to dump in it. "Doesn't matter. What matters is the company. Someone established. Someone who's been underwriting since downloading happened. Mr. Kadmin wants to take out an R and R policy, which, after a long discussion about premiums, he does. See, this has got to look good. It's the long con, with the one difference that what we're after here is more than money."

I leaned back against my side of the window frame. The Watchtower suite had been aptly named. All three rooms looked out across the city and the water beyond, either north or westward, and the window shelf in the lounge accounted for about a fifth of the available space, layered with psychedelically colored cushion mats. Ortega and I were seated opposite each other with a clean meter of space between us.

"Okay, so that's one copy. Then what?"

Ortega shrugged. "Fatal accident."

"In Ulan Bator?"

"Right. Dimi runs himself into a power pylon at high speed, falls out of a hotel window, something like that. An Ulan Bator handling agent retrieves the stack, and, for a hefty bribe, makes a copy. In comes Cartwright Solar or Lloyd's with their retrieval writ, freights Dimi D.H. back to their clone bank, and downloads him into the waiting sleeve. Thank you very much, sir. Nice doing business with you."

"Meanwhile . . ."

"Meanwhile the handling agent buys up a black-market sleeve, probably some catatonia case from a local hospital, or a scene-of-the-crime drug victim who's not too physically damaged. The Ulan Bator police do a screaming trade in D.O.A.s. The agent wipes the sleeve's mind, downloads Dimi's copy into it, and the sleeve just walks out of there. Suborbital to the other side of the globe and off to work in Bay City."

"You don't catch these guys too often."

"Almost never. Point is, you've got to catch both copies cold, either dead like this or held on a U.N. indictable offense. Without the U.N. rap, you've got no legal right to download from a living body. And in a no-win situation, the twin just gets its cortical stack blown out through the back of its neck before we can make the bust. I've seen it happen."

"That's pretty severe. What's the penalty for all this?"

"Erasure."

"*Erasure?* You do that here?"

Ortega nodded. There was a small, grim smile playing all around her mouth, but never quite on it. "Yeah, we do that here. Shock you?"

I thought about it. Some crimes in the corps carried the erasure penalty, principally desertion or refusal to obey a combat order, but I'd never seen them applied. It ran counter to the conditioning to cut and run. And on Harlan's World erasure had been abolished a decade before I was born.

"It's kind of old-fashioned, isn't it?"

"You feel bad about what's going to happen to Dimi?"

I ran the tip of my tongue over the cuts on the inside of my mouth. Thought about the cold circle of metal at my neck and shook my head. "No. But does it stop with people like him?"

"There are a few other capital crimes, but they mostly get commuted to a couple of centuries in storage." The look on Ortega's face said she didn't think that was such a great idea.

I put my coffee down and reached for a cigarette. The motions were automatic, and I was too tired to stop them. Ortega waved away the offered pack. Touching my own cigarette to the pack's ignition patch, I squinted at her.

"How old are you, Ortega?"

She looked back at me narrowly. "Thirty-four. Why?"

"Never been D.H.'d, hmm?"

"Yeah, I had psychosurgery a few years back; they put me under for a couple of days. Apart from that, no. I'm not a criminal, and I don't have the money for that kind of travel."

I let out the first breath of smoke. "Kind of touchy about it, aren't you?"

"Like I said, I'm not a criminal."

"No." I thought back to the last time I had seen Virginia Vidaura. "If you were, you wouldn't think two hundred years' dislocation was such an easy rap."

"I didn't say that."

"You didn't have to." I didn't know what had led me to forget that Ortega was the law, but *something* had. Something had been building in the space between the two of us, something like a static charge, something I might have been able to work out if my Envoy intuitions hadn't been so blunted by the new sleeve. Whatever it was, it had just walked out of the room. I drew my shoulders in and pulled harder on the cigarette. I needed sleep.

"Kadmin's expensive, right? With overheads like that, risks like that, he's got to cost."

"About twenty grand a hit."

"Then Bancroft didn't commit suicide."

Ortega raised an eyebrow. "That's fast work, for someone who just got here."

"Oh, come on." I exploded a lungful of smoke at her. "If it was suicide, who the fuck paid out the twenty to have me hit?"

"You're well liked, are you?"

I leaned forward. "No, I'm disliked in a lot of places, but not by anyone with those kind of connections or that kind of money. I'm not classy enough to make enemies at that level. Whoever set Kadmin on me knows I'm working for Bancroft."

Ortega grinned. "Thought you said they didn't call you by name?"

Tired, Takeshi. I could almost see Virginia Vidaura wagging her finger at me. *The Envoy Corps doesn't get taken apart by local law.*

I stumbled on as best I could.

"They knew who I was. Men like Kadmin don't hang around hotels waiting to rip off the tourists. Ortega, come *on.*"

She let my exasperation sink into the silence before she answered me. "So Bancroft was hit, as well? Maybe. So what?"

"So you've got to reopen the inquiry."

"You don't listen, Kovacs." She bent me a smile meant for stopping armed men in their tracks. "The case is closed."

I sagged back against the wall and watched her through the smoke for a while. Finally, I said, "You know, when your cleanup squad arrived tonight, one of them showed me his badge for long enough to actually see it. Quite fancy, close-up. That eagle and shield. All the lettering around it."

She made a get-on-with-it gesture, and I took another puff on my cigarette before I sank the barb in.

"*To protect and serve?* I guess by the time you make lieutenant, you don't really believe that stuff anymore."

Contact. A muscle jumped under one eye, and her cheeks pulled in as if she was sucking on something bitter. She stared at me, and for that moment I thought I might have pushed too far. Then her shoulders slumped and she sighed.

"Ah, go ahead. What the fuck do you know about it anyway? Bancroft's not people, like you and me. He's a fucking Meth."

"A Meth?"

"Yeah. A Meth. You know, *and all the days of Methuselah were nine hundred sixty and nine years.* He's old. I mean, really old."

"Is that a crime, Lieutenant?"

"It should be," Ortega said grimly. "You live that long, things start happening to you. You get too impressed with yourself. Ends up, you think you're God. Suddenly the little people, thirty, maybe forty years old, well, they don't really matter anymore. You've seen whole societies rise and fall, and you start to feel you're standing outside it all, and none of it really matters to you. And maybe you'll start snuffing those little people, just like picking daisies, if they get under your feet."

I looked seriously at her. "You pin anything like that on Bancroft? Ever?"

"I'm not talking about Bancroft." She waved the objection aside impatiently. "I'm talking about his *kind.* They're like the A.I.s. They're a breed apart. They're not human. They deal with humanity the way you and I deal with insect life. Well, when you're dealing with the Bay City police department, having that kind of attitude can sometimes back up on you."

I thought briefly of Reileen Kawahara's excesses and wondered how far off the mark Ortega really was. On Harlan's World, most people could afford to be resleeved at least once, but the point was that unless you were very rich, you had to live out your full span each time and old age, even with antisen treatment, was a wearying business. Second time around was worse because you knew what to expect. Not many had the stamina to do it more than twice. Most people went into voluntary storage after that, with occasional temporary resleevings for family matters, and of course, even those resleevings thinned out as time passed and new generations bustled in without the old ties.

It took a certain kind of person to keep going, to *want* to keep going, life after life, sleeve after sleeve. You had to start out different, never mind what you might become as the centuries piled up.

"So Bancroft gets shortchanged because he's a Meth. Sorry, Laurens, you're an arrogant, long-lived bastard. The Bay City police have got better things to do with its time than take you seriously. That kind of thing."

But Ortega wasn't rising to the bait anymore. She sipped her coffee and made a dismissive gesture. "Look, Kovacs. Bancroft is alive, and whatever the facts of the case he's got enough security to stay that way. No one here is groaning under the burden of a miscarriage of justice. The police department is under-funded, understaffed, and overworked. We don't have the resources to chase Bancroft's phantoms indefinitely."

"And if they're not phantoms?"

Ortega sighed. "Kovacs, I went over that house myself three times with the forensics team. There's no sign of a struggle, no break in the perimeter defenses, and no trace of an intruder anywhere in the security net's records. Miriam Bancroft volunteered to take every state-of-the-art polygraph test there is, and she passed them all without a tremor. She did not kill her husband. No one broke in and killed her husband. Laurens Bancroft killed himself, for reasons best known to himself, and that's all there is to it. I'm sorry you're supposed to prove otherwise, but wishing isn't going to make it fucking so. It's an open-and-shut case."

"And the phone call? The fact Bancroft wasn't exactly going to forget he had remote storage? The fact someone thinks I'm important enough to send Kadmin out here?"

"I'm not going to argue the toss with you on this, Kovacs. We'll interrogate Kadmin and find out what he knows, but for the rest I've been over the ground before and it's starting to bore me. There are people out there who need us a lot worse than Bancroft does. Real-death victims who weren't lucky enough to have remote storage when their stacks were blown out. Catholics getting butchered because their killers know the victims will never come out of storage to put them away." There was a hooded tiredness building up in Ortega's eyes as she ticked the list off on her fingers. "Organic damage cases who don't have the money to get resleeved unless the state can prove some kind of liability against somebody. I wade through this stuff ten hours a day or more, and I'm sorry, I just don't have the sympathy to spare for Mr. Laurens Bancroft with his clones on ice and his magic walls of influence in high places and his fancy lawyers to put us through hoops every time some member of his family or staff wants to slide out from under."

"That happen often, does it?"

"Often enough, but don't look surprised." She gave me a bleak smile. "He's a fucking Meth. They're all the same."

It was a side of her I didn't like, an argument I didn't want to have, and a view of Bancroft I didn't need. And underneath it all, my nerves were screaming for sleep. I stubbed out my cigarette.

"I think you'd better go, Lieutenant. All this prejudice is giving me a headache."

Something flickered in her eyes, something I couldn't read at all. There for a second, then gone. She shrugged, put down the coffee mug, and swung her legs over the side of the shelf. She stretched herself upright, arched her spine until it cracked audibly, and walked to the door without looking back. I stayed where I was, watching her reflection move among the city lights in the window.

At the door, she stopped, and I saw her turn her head.

"Hey, Kovacs."

I looked over at her. "Forget something?"

She nodded her head, mouth clamped in a crooked line, as if acknowledging a point in some game we'd been playing.

"You want an insight? You want somewhere to start? Well, you gave me Kadmin, so I guess I owe you that."

"You don't owe me a thing, Ortega. The Hendrix did it, not me."

"Leila Begin," she said. "Run that by Bancroft's fancy lawyers, see where it gets you."

The door sliced closed and the reflected room held nothing but the lights of the city outside. I stared out at them for a while, lit a new cigarette, and smoked it down to its filter.

Bancroft had not committed suicide, that much was clear. I'd been on the case less than a day, and already I'd had two separate lobbies land on my back. First Kristin Ortega's mannered thugs at the justice facility, then the Vladivostok hit man and his spare sleeve. Not to mention Miriam Bancroft's off-the-wall behavior. Altogether too much muddied water for this to be what it purported to be. Ortega wanted something, whoever had paid Dimitri Kadmin wanted something, and what they wanted, it seemed, was for the Bancroft case to remain closed.

That wasn't an option I had.

"Your guest has left the building," the Hendrix said, jolting me out of my glazed retrospection.

"Thanks," I said absently, stubbing out the cigarette in an ashtray. "Can you lock the door and block the elevators from this floor?"

"Certainly. Do you wish to be advised of any entry into the hotel?"

"No." I yawned like a snake trying to engorge an egg. "Just don't let them up here. And no calls for the next seven and a half hours."

Abruptly it was all I could do to get out of my clothes before the waves of sleep overwhelmed me. I left Bancroft's summer suit draped over a convenient chair and crawled into the massive crimson-sheeted bed. The surface of the bed undulated briefly, adjusting to my body weight and size, then bore me up like water. A faint odor of incense drifted from the sheets.

I made a halfhearted attempt to masturbate, mind churning damply through images of Miriam Bancroft's voluptuous curves, but I kept seeing Sarah's pale body turned to wreckage by the Kalashnikov fire instead.

And sleep dragged me under.

CHAPTEr SEVEN

There are ruins, steeped in shadow, and a bloodred sun going down in turmoil behind distant hills. Overhead soft-bellied clouds panic toward the horizon like whales before the harpoon, and the wind runs addict's fingers through the trees that line the street.

Innenininneninin...

I know this place.

I pick my way between the devastated walls of ruins, trying not to brush against them because, whenever I do, they give out muted gunshots and screams, as if whatever conflict murdered this city has soaked into the remaining stonework. At the same time, I'm moving quite fast, because there is something following me, something that has no such qualms about touching the ruins. I can chart its progress quite accurately by the tide of gunfire and anguish swelling behind me. It is closing. I try to speed up but there is a tightness in my throat and chest that isn't helping matters.

Jimmy de Soto steps out from behind the shattered stub of a tower. I'm not really surprised to see him here, but his ruined face still gives me a jolt. He grins with what's left of his features and puts a hand on my shoulder. I try not to flinch.

"Leila Begin," he says, and nods back to where I have come from. "Run that by Bancroft's fancy lawyer."

"I will," I say, moving past him. But his hand stays on my shoulder, which must mean his arm is stretching out behind me like hot wax. I stop, guilty at the pain that must be causing him, but he's still there at my shoulder. I start moving again.

"Going to turn and fight?" he asks conversationally, drifting along beside me without apparent effort or footing.

"With what?" I say, opening my empty hands.

"Should have armed yourself, pal. Big-time."

"Virginia told us not to fall for the weakness of weapons."

Jimmy de Soto snorts derisively. "Yeah, and look where that stupid bitch ended up. Eighty to a hundred, no remission."

"You can't know that," I say absently, more interested in the sounds of pursuit behind me. "You died years before that happened."

"Oh, come on, who really dies, these days?"

"Try telling that to a Catholic. And anyway, you did die, Jimmy. Irretrievably, as I recall."

"What's a Catholic?"

"Tell you later. You got any cigarettes?"

"Cigarettes? What happened to your arm?"

I break the spiral of non sequiturs and stare down at my arm. Jimmy's got a point. The scars on my forearm have turned into a fresh wound, blood welling up and trickling down into my hand. So of course . . .

I reach up to my left eye and find the wetness below it. My fingers come away bloody.

"Lucky one," Jimmy de Soto says judicially. "They missed the socket."

He should know. His own left socket is a glutted well of gore, all that was left at Innenin when he dug the eyeball out with his fingers. No one ever found out what he was hallucinating at the time. By the time they got Jimmy and the rest of the Innenin beachhead D.H.'d for psychosurgery, the defenders' virus had scrambled their minds beyond retrieval. The program was so virulent that at the time the clinic didn't even dare keep what was left on stack for study. The remains of Jimmy de Soto are on a sealed disk with red DATA CONTAMINANT decals somewhere in a basement at Envoy Corps HQ.

"I've got to do something about this," I say, a little desperately. The sounds awoken from the walls by my pursuer are growing dangerously close. The last of the sun is slipping behind the hills. Blood spills down my arm and face.

"Smell that?" Jimmy asks, lifting his own face to the chilly air around us. "They're changing it."

"What?" But even as I snap the retort, I can smell it, as well. A fresh, invigorating scent, not unlike the incense back at the Hendrix, but subtly different, not quite the heady decadence of the original odor I fell asleep to only . . .

"Got to go," Jimmy says, and I'm about to ask him where when I realize he means me and I'm

Awake.

My eyes snapped open on one of the psychedelic murals of the hotel room. Slim, waiflike figures in kaftans dotted across a field of green grass and yellow and white flowers. I frowned and clutched at the hardened scar tissue on my forearm. No blood. With the realization, I came fully awake and sat up in the big crimson bed. The shift in the smell of incense that had originally nudged me toward consciousness was fully resolved into that of coffee and fresh bread. The Hendrix's olfactory wake-up call. Light was pouring into the dimmed room through a flaw in the polarized glass of the window.

"You have a visitor," the voice of the Hendrix said briskly.

"What time is it?" I croaked. The back of my throat seemed to have been liberally painted with supercooled glue.

"Ten-sixteen, locally. You have slept for seven hours and forty-two minutes."

"And my visitor?"

"Oumou Prescott," the hotel said. "Do you require breakfast?"

I got out of bed and headed for the bathroom. "Yes. Coffee with milk, white meat, well cooked, and fruit juice of some kind. You can send Prescott up."

By the time the door chimed at me, I was out of the shower and padding around in an iridescent blue bathrobe trimmed with gold braid. I collected my breakfast from the service hatch and balanced the tray on one hand while I opened the door.

Oumou Prescott was a tall, impressive-looking African woman, topping my sleeve by a couple of centimeters, her hair braided back with dozens of oval glass beads in seven or eight of my favorite colors, and her cheekbones lined with some sort of abstract tattooing. She stood on the threshold in a pale gray suit and a long black coat turned up at the collar, and looked at me doubtfully.

"Mr. Kovacs."

"Yes, come in. Would you like some breakfast?" I laid the tray on the unmade bed.

"No, thank you. Mr. Kovacs, I am Laurens Bancroft's principal legal representative via the firm of Prescott, Forbes, and Hernandez. Mr. Bancroft informed me—"

"Yes, I know." I picked up a piece of grilled chicken from the tray.

"The point is, Mr. Kovacs, we have an appointment with Dennis Nyman at PsychaSec in—" Her eyes flicked briefly upward to consult a retinal watch. "—thirty minutes."

"I see," I said, chewing slowly. "I didn't know that."

"I've been calling since eight this morning, but the hotel refused to put me through. I didn't realize you would sleep so late."

I grinned at her through a mouthful of chicken. "Faulty research, then. I was only sleeved yesterday."

She stiffened a little at that, but then a professional calm asserted itself. She crossed the room and took a seat on the window shelf.

"We'll be late, then," she said. "I guess you need breakfast."

● ● ●

It was cold in the middle of the bay.

I climbed out of the autocab into watery sunshine and a buffeting wind. It had rained during the night, and there were still a few piles of gray cumulus skulking around inland, sullenly resisting the attempts of a stiff sea breeze to sweep them away. I turned up the collar of my summer suit and made a mental note to buy a coat. Nothing serious, something coming to midthigh with a collar and pockets big enough to stuff your hands in.

Beside me, Prescott was looking unbearably snug inside her coat. She paid off the cab with a swipe of her thumb, and we both stood back as it rose. A welcome rush of warm air from the lift turbines washed over my hands and face. I blinked my eyes against the small storm of grit and dust and saw how Prescott raised one slender arm to do the same. Then the cab was gone, droning away to join the beehive activity in the sky above the mainland. Prescott turned to the building behind us and gestured with one laconic thumb.

"This way."

I pushed my hands into the inadequate pockets of my suit and followed her lead. Bent slightly into the wind, we picked our way up the long, winding steps to PsychaSec Alcatraz.

I'd expected a high-security installation, and I wasn't disappointed. Psycha-Sec was laid out in a series of long, low double-story modules with deeply recessed windows reminiscent of a military command bunker. The only break in this pattern was a single dome at the western end, which I guessed had to house the satellite uplink gear. The whole complex was a pale granite gray and the windows a smoky reflectant orange. There was no holodisplay, or broadcast publicity, in fact nothing to announce we'd got the right place except a sober plaque laser-engraved into the sloping stone wall of the entrance block:

PSYCHASEC S.A.

D.H.F. RETRIEVAL AND SECURE HOLDING

CLONIC RESLEEVING

Above the plaque was a small black sentry eye flanked by heavily grilled speakers. Oumou Prescott raised her arm and waved at it.

"Welcome to PsychaSec Alcatraz," a construct voice said briskly. "Please identify yourself within the fifteen-second security time limit."

"Oumou Prescott and Takeshi Kovacs to see Director Nyman. We have an appointment."

A thin green scanning laser flickered over us both from head to foot and then a section of the wall hinged smoothly back and down forming a passage inside. Glad to get out of the wind, I stepped nimbly into the niche and followed orange runway lights down a short corridor into a reception area, leaving Prescott to bring up the rear. As soon as we stepped off the walkway and into reception, the massive door slab rumbled upright and closed again. Solid security.

Reception was a circular, warmly lit area with banks of seats and low tables set at the cardinal compass points. There were small groups of people seated north and east, conversing in low tones. In the center was a circular desk where a receptionist sat behind a battery of secretarial equipment. No artificial constructs here, this was a real human being, a slim young man barely out of his teens who looked up with intelligent eyes as we approached.

"You can go right through, Ms. Prescott. The director's office is up the stairs and third door on your right."

"Thank you." Prescott took the lead again, turning back briefly to mutter as soon as we were out of earshot of the receptionist.

"Nyman's a bit impressed with himself since this place was built, but he's basically a good person. Try not to let him irritate you."

"Sure."

We followed the receptionist's instructions until, outside the aforementioned door, I had to stop and suppress a snigger. Nyman's door, no doubt in the best possible Earth taste, was pure mirrorwood from top to bottom. After the high-profile security system and flesh-and-blood reception, it seemed about as subtle as the vaginal spittoons at Madame Mi's Wharfwhore Warehouse. My amusement must have been evident because Prescott gave me a frown as she knocked on the door.

"Come."

Sleep had done wonders for the interface between my mind and my new sleeve. Composing my rented features, I followed Prescott into the room.

Nyman was at his desk, ostensibly working at a gray-and-green-colored holodisplay. He was a thin, serious-looking man who affected steel-rimmed external eyelenses to go with his expensively cut black suit and short, tidy hair. His expression, behind the lenses, was slightly resentful. He'd not been happy when Prescott phoned him from the cab to say we would be delayed, but Bancroft had obviously been in touch with him because he accepted the later appointment time with the stiff acquiescence of a disciplined child.

"Since you have requested a viewing of our facilities here, Mr. Kovacs, shall we start? I have cleared my agenda for the next couple of hours, but I do have clients waiting."

Something about Nyman's manner brought Warden Sullivan to mind, but it was an altogether smoother, less embittered Sullivan. I glanced over Nyman's suit and face. Perhaps if the warden had made his career in storage for the super-rich instead of the criminal element, he might have turned out like this.

"Fine."

It got pretty dull after that. PsychaSec, like most D.H.F. depots, wasn't much more than a gigantic set of air-conditioned warehouse shelves. We tramped through basement rooms cooled to the seven to eleven degrees Celsius recommended by the makers of altered carbon, peered at racks of the big thirty-centimeter expanded-format disks, and admired the retrieval robots that ran on wide-gauge rails along the storage walls. "It's a duplex system," Nyman said proudly. "Every client is stored on two separate disks in different parts of the building. Random code distribution, only the central processor can find them both, and there's a lock on the system to prevent simultaneous access to both copies. To do any real damage, you'd have to break in and get past all the security systems twice."

I made polite noises.

"Our satellite uplink operates through a network of no less than eighteen secure clearing orbital platforms, leased in random sequence." Nyman was getting carried away with his own sales pitch. He seemed to have forgotten that neither

Prescott nor myself were in the market for PsychaSec's services. "No orbital is leased for more than twenty seconds at a time. Remote storage updates come in via needlecast, with no way to predict the transmission route."

Strictly speaking, that wasn't true. Given an artificial intelligence of sufficient size and inclination, you'd get it right sooner or later, but this was clutching at straws. The kind of enemies who used A.I.s to get at you didn't need to finish you off with a particle blaster to the head. I was looking in the wrong place.

"Can I get access to Bancroft's clones?" I asked Prescott abruptly.

"From a legal point of view?" Prescott shrugged. "Mr. Bancroft's instructions give you carte blanche as far as I know."

Carte blanche? Prescott had been springing these on me all morning. The words almost had the taste of heavy parchment. It was like something an Alain Marriott character would say in a Settlement years flick.

Well, you're on Earth now. I turned to Nyman, who nodded grudgingly.

"There are some procedures," he said.

We went back up to ground level, along corridors that forcibly reminded me of the resleeving facility at Bay City Central by their very dissimilarity. No rubber-wheeled-gurney tracks here—the sleeve transporters would be air-cushion vehicles—and the corridor walls were decked out in pastel shades. The windows, bunker peepholes from the outside, were framed and corniched in Gaudi-style waves on the inside. At one corner we passed a woman cleaning them by hand. I raised an eyebrow. No end to the extravagance.

Nyman caught the look. "There are some jobs that robot labor just never gets quite right," he said.

"I'm sure."

The clone banks appeared on our left, heavy sealed doors in beveled and sculpted steel counterpointing the ornate windows. We stopped at one, and Nyman peered into the retina scan set beside it. The door hinged smoothly outward, fully a meter thick in tungsten steel. Within was a four-meter-long chamber with a similar door at the far end. We stepped inside, and the outer door swung shut with a soft thud that pushed the air into my ears.

"This is an airtight chamber," Nyman said redundantly. "We will receive a sonic cleansing to ensure that we bring no contaminants into the clone bank. No reason to be alarmed."

A light in the ceiling pulsed on and off in shades of violet to signify that the dust-off was in progress, and then the second door opened with no more sound than the first. We walked out into the Bancroft family vault.

I'd seen this sort of thing before. Reileen Kawahara had maintained a small one for her transit clones on New Beijing, and of course the corps had them in abundance. Still, I'd never seen anything quite like this.

The space was oval, dome ceilinged, and must have extended through both stories of the installation. It was huge, the size of a temple back home. Lighting was low, a womblike orange, and the temperature was blood warm. The clone sacs were everywhere, veined translucent pods of the same orange as the light, suspended from the ceiling by cables and nutrient tubes. The clones were vaguely discernible within, fetal bundles of arms and legs, but fully grown. Or at least, most were; toward the top of the dome I could see smaller sacs where new additions to the stock were being cultured. The sacs were organic, a toughened analog of womb lining, and they would grow with the fetus within to the meter and a half lozenges in the lower half of the vault. The whole crop hung there like an insane mobile, just waiting for some huge sickly breeze to stir it into motion.

Nyman cleared his throat, and both Prescott and I shook off the paralyzed wonder that had gripped us on the threshold.

"This may look haphazard," he said, "but the spacing *is* computer generated."

"I know." I nodded and went closer to one of the lower sacs. "It's fractal derived, right?"

"Ah, yes." Nyman seemed almost to resent my knowledge.

I peered in at the clone. Centimeters away from my face Miriam Bancroft's features dreamed in amniotic fluid beneath the membrane. Her arms were folded protectively across her breasts, and her hands were folded lightly into fists under her chin. Her hair had been gathered into a thick, coiled snake on the top of her head and covered in some kind of web.

"The whole family's here," Prescott murmured at my shoulder. "Husband and wife, and all sixty-one children. Most have only one or two clones, but Bancroft and his wife run to six each. Impressive, huh?"

"Yeah." Despite myself, I had to put out a hand and touch the membrane above Miriam Bancroft's face. It was warm and gave slightly under my hand. There was raised scarring around the entry points of the nutrient feeds and waste pipes, and in tiny pimples where needles had been pushed through to extract tissue samples or provide IV additives. The membrane would give in to such penetrations and heal afterwards.

I turned away from the dreaming woman and faced Nyman.

"This is all very nice, but presumably you don't shell one of these whenever Bancroft comes in here for transit. You must have tanks, as well."

"This way." Nyman gestured us to follow him and went to the back of the chamber where another pressure door was set into the wall. The lowest sacs swayed eerily in the wake of our passage, and I had to duck to avoid brushing against one. Nyman's fingers played a brief tarantella over the keypad of the pressure door, and we went through into a long, low room whose clinical illumination was almost blinding after the womb light of the main vault. A row of eight metallic cylinders not unlike the one I'd woken up in yesterday were ranked along one wall, but where my birthing tube had been unpainted and scarred with the million tiny defacements of frequent use, these units carried a thick gloss of cream paint with yellow trim around the transparent observation plate and the various functional protrusions.

"Full life-support suspension chambers," Nyman said. "Essentially the same environment as the pods. This is where all the resleeving is done. We bring fresh clones through, still in the pod, and load them here. The tank nutrients have an enzyme to break down the pod wall, so the transition is completely trauma-free. Any clinical work is carried out by staff working in synthetic sleeves, to avoid any risk of contamination."

I caught the exasperated rolling of Oumou Prescott's eyes on the periphery of my vision, and a grin twitched at the corner of my mouth.

"Who has access to this chamber?"

"Myself, authorized staff under a day code. And the owners, of course."

I wandered down the line of cylinders, bending to examine the data displays at the foot of each one. There was a Miriam clone in the sixth, and two Naomis at seven and eight.

"You've got the daughter on ice twice?"

"Yes." Nyman looked puzzled, and then slightly superior. This was his chance to get back the initiative he'd lost on the fractal patterning. "Have you not been informed of her current condition?"

"Yeah, she's in psychosurgery," I growled. "That doesn't explain why there's two of her here."

"Well." Nyman darted a glance back at Prescott, as if to say that the divulging of further information involved some legal dimension. The lawyer cleared her throat.

"PsychaSec has instructions from Mr. Bancroft to always hold a spare clone of himself and his immediate family ready for decanting. While Ms. Bancroft is committed to the Vancouver Psychiatric stack, both sleeves are stored here."

"The Bancrofts like to alternate their sleeves," Nyman said knowledgeably. "Many of our clients do; it saves on wear and tear. The human body is capable of quite remarkable regeneration if stored correctly, and of course, we offer a complete package of clinical repair for more major damage. Very reasonably priced."

"I'm sure it is." I turned back from the end cylinder and grinned at him. "Still, not much you can do for a vaporized head, is there?"

There was a brief silence, during which Prescott looked fixedly at a corner of the ceiling and Nyman's lips tightened to almost anal proportions.

"I consider that remark in very poor taste," the director said finally. "Do you have any more *important* questions, Mr. Kovacs?"

I paused next to Miriam Bancroft's cylinder and looked into it. Even through the fogging effect of the observation plate and the gel, there was a sensual abundance to the blurred form within.

"Just one question. Who decides when to alternate the sleeves?"

Nyman glanced across at Prescott as if to enlist legal support for his words. "I am directly authorized by Mr. Bancroft to effect the transfer on every occasion that he is digitized, unless specifically required not to. He made no such request on this occasion."

There was something here, scratching at the Envoy antennae; something some-where *fitted*. It was too early to give it concrete form. I looked around the room.

"This place is entry monitored, right?"

"Naturally." Nyman's tone was still chilly.

"Was there much activity the day Bancroft went to Osaka?"

"No more than usual. Mr. Kovacs, the police have already been through these records. I really don't see what value—"

"Indulge me," I suggested, not looking at him, and the Envoy cadences in my voice shut him down like a circuit breaker.

● ● ●

Two hours later I was staring out of the window of another autocab as it kicked off from the Alcatraz landing quay and climbed over the Bay.

"Did you find what you were looking for?"

I glanced at Oumou Prescott, wondering if she could sense the frustration coming off me. I thought I'd got most of the external giveaways on this sleeve locked down, but I'd heard of lawyers who got empath conditioning to pick up more subliminal clues to their witnesses' state of mind when on the stand. And here, on Earth, it wouldn't surprise me if Oumou Prescott had a full infrared sub-sonic body-and-voice scan package racked into her beautiful ebony head.

The entry data for the Bancroft vault, Thursday 16th of August, was as free of suspicious comings and goings as the Mishima Mall on a Tuesday afternoon. Eight A.M., Bancroft came in with two assistants, stripped off, and climbed into the waiting tank. The assistants left with his clothes. Fourteen hours later his al-ternate clone climbed dripping out of the neighboring tank, collected a towel from another assistant, and went to get a shower. No words exchanged beyond pleasantries. Nothing.

I shrugged. "I don't know. I don't really know what I'm looking for yet."

Prescott yawned. "Total absorb, huh?"

"Yeah, that's right." I looked at her more closely. "You know much about the corps?"

"Bit. I did my articles in U.N. litigation. You pick up the terminology. So what have you absorbed so far?"

"Only that there's a lot of smoke building up around something the authori-ties say isn't burning. You ever meet the lieutenant who ran the case?"

"Kristin Ortega. Of course. I'm not likely to forget her. We were yelling at each other across a desk for the best part of a week."

"Impressions?"

"Of Ortega?" Prescott looked surprised. "Good cop, as far as I know. Got a reputation for being very tough. The Organic Damage Division are the police de-partment's hard men, so earning a reputation like that wouldn't have been easy. She ran the case efficiently enough—"

"Not for Bancroft's liking."

Pause. Prescott looked at me warily. "I said efficiently. I didn't say persistently. Ortega did her job, but—"

"But she doesn't like Meths, right?"

Another pause. "You have quite an ear for the street, Mr. Kovacs."

"You pick up the terminology," I said modestly. "Do you think Ortega would have kept the case open if Bancroft hadn't been a Meth?"

Prescott thought about it for a while. "It's a common enough prejudice," she said slowly, "but I don't get the impression Ortega shut us down because of it. I think she just saw a limited return on her investment. The police department has a promotion system based at least partly on the number of cases solved. No one saw a quick solution to this one, and Mr. Bancroft was alive, so . . ."

"Better things to do, huh?"

"Yes. Something like that."

I stared out the window some more. The cab was flitting across the tops of slender multistory stacks and the traffic-crammed crevices between. I could feel an old fury building in me that had nothing to do with my current problems. Something that had accrued through the years in the corps and the emotional rubble you got used to seeing, like silt on the surface of your soul. *Virginia Vidaura, Jimmy de Soto dying in my arms at Innenin, Sarah* . . . A loser's catalog, any way you looked at it.

I locked it down.

The scar under my eye was itching, and there was the curl of the nicotine craving in my fingertips. I rubbed at the scar. Left the cigarettes in my pocket. At some indeterminate point this morning I'd determined to quit. A thought struck me at random.

"Prescott, you chose this sleeve for me, right?"

"Sorry?" She was scanning through a subretinal projection, and it took her a moment to refocus on me. "What did you say?"

"This sleeve. You chose it, right?"

She frowned. "No, as far as I know, that selection was made by Mr. Bancroft. We just provided the shortlist according to specifications."

"No, he told me his lawyers had handled it. Definitely."

"Oh." The frown cleared away, and she smiled faintly. "Mr. Bancroft has a great many lawyers. Probably he routed it through another office. Why?"

I grunted. "Nothing. Whoever owned this body before was a smoker, and I'm not. It's a real pain in the balls."

Prescott's smile gained ground. "Are you going to give up?"

"If I can find the time. Bancroft's deal is, I crack the case, I can be resleeved no expense spared, so it doesn't really matter long term. I just hate waking up with a throatful of shit every morning."

"Do you think you can?"

"Give up smoking?"

"No. Crack this case."

I looked at her, deadpan. "I don't really have any other option, counselor. Have you read the terms of my employment?"

"Yes. I drew them up." Prescott gave me back the deadpan look, but buried beneath it were traces of the discomfort that I needed to see to stop me reaching across the cab and smashing her nose bone up into her brain with one stiffened hand.

"Well, well," I said, and went back to looking out of the window.

● ● ●

AND MY FIST UP YOUR WIFE'S CUNT WITH YOU WATCHING YOU FUCKING METH MOTHERFUCKER YOU CAN'T

I slipped off the headset and blinked. The text had carried some crude but effective virtual graphics and a subsonic that made my head buzz. Across the desk, Prescott looked at me with knowing sympathy.

"Is it all like this?" I asked.

"Well, it gets less coherent." She gestured at the holograph display floating above the desktop, where representations of the files I was accessing tumbled in cool shades of blue and green. "This is what we call the R and R stack. Rabid and Rambling. Actually, these guys are mostly too far gone to be any real threat, but it's not nice, knowing they're out there."

"Ortega bring any of them in?"

"It's not her department. The Transmission Felony Division catches a few every now and then, when we squawk loudly enough about it, but dissemination technology being the way it is, it's like trying to throw a net over smoke. And even when you do catch them, the worst they'll get is a few months in storage. It's a waste of time. We mostly just sit on this stuff until Bancroft says we can delete it."

"And nothing new in the last six months?"

Prescott shrugged. "The religious lunatics, maybe. Some increased traffic from the Catholics on Resolution 653. Mr. Bancroft has an undeclared influence in the U.N. Court, which is more or less common knowledge. Oh, and some Martian archaeological sect has been screaming about that songspire he keeps in his hall. Apparently last month was the anniversary of their founder's martyrdom by leaky pressure suit. But none of these people have the wherewithal to crack the perimeter defenses at Suntouch House."

I tilted my chair back and stared up at the ceiling. A flight of gray birds angled overhead in a southward-pointing chevron. Their voices were faintly audible, honking to each other. Prescott's office was environment formatted, all six internal surfaces projecting virtual images. Currently her gray metal desk was incongruously positioned halfway down a sloping meadow on which the sun was beginning to decline, complete with a small herd of cattle in the distance and occasional birdsong. The image resolution was some of the best I'd seen.

"Prescott, what can you tell me about Leila Begin?"

The silence that ensued pulled my eyes back down to ground level. Oumou Prescott was staring off into a corner of the field.

"I suppose Kristin Ortega gave you that name," she said slowly.

"Yeah." I sat up. "She said it would give me some insight into Bancroft. In fact, she told me to run it by you to see if you rattled."

Prescott swiveled to face me. "I don't see how this can have any bearing on the case at hand."

"Try me."

"Very well." There was a snap in her voice as she said it, and a defiant look on her face.

"Leila Begin was a prostitute. Maybe still is. Fifty years ago, Bancroft was one of her clients. Through a number of . . . indiscretions, this became known to Miriam Bancroft. The two women met at some function down in San Diego, apparently agreed to go to the bathroom together, and Miriam Bancroft beat the shit out of Leila Begin."

I studied Prescott's face across the table, puzzled. "And that's it?"

"No, that's not it, Kovacs," she said tiredly. "Begin was six months pregnant at the time. She lost the child as a result of the beating. You physically can't fit a spinal stack into a fetus, so that made it real death. Potential three-to-five-decade sentence."

"Was it Bancroft's baby?"

Prescott shrugged. "Debatable. Begin refused to let them do a gene match on the fetus. Said it was irrelevant who the father was. She probably figured the uncertainty was more valuable from a press point of view than a definite no."

"Or she was too distraught?"

"Come on, Kovacs." Prescott jerked a hand irritably at me. "This is an Oakland whore we're talking about."

"Did Miriam Bancroft go into storage?"

"No, and that's where Ortega gets to stick her knife in. Bancroft bought off everybody. The witnesses, the press, even Begin took a payoff in the end. Settled out of court. Enough to get her a Lloyd's cloning policy and take her out of the game. Last I heard, she was wearing out her second sleeve somewhere down in Brazil. But this is half a century ago, Kovacs."

"Were you around?"

"No." Prescott leaned across the desk. "And neither was Kristin Ortega, which makes it kind of sickening to hear her whining on about it. Oh, I had an earful of it, too, when they pulled out of the investigation last month. She never even met Begin."

"I think it might be a matter of principle," I said gently. "Is Bancroft still going to prostitutes on a regular basis?"

"That is none of my concern."

I stuck my finger through the holographic display and watched the colored files distort around the intrusion. "You might have to make it your concern, counselor. Sexual jealousy's a pretty sturdy motive for murder, after all."

"May I remind you that Miriam Bancroft tested negative on a polygraph when asked that question," Prescott said sharply.

"I'm not talking about Mrs. Bancroft." I stopped playing with the display and stared across the desk at the lawyer before me. "I'm talking about the other million available orifices out there and the even larger number of partners or blood relatives who might not relish seeing some Meth fucking them. That's going to have to include some experts on covert penetration, no pun intended, and maybe the odd psychopath or two. In short, someone capable of getting into Bancroft's house and torching him."

Off in the distance, one of the cows lowed mournfully.

"What about it, Prescott?" I waved my hand through the holograph. "Anything in here that begins *For what you did to my girl, daughter, sister, mother, delete as applicable*?"

I didn't need her to answer me. I could see it in her face.

With the sun painting slanting stripes across the desk and birdsong in the trees across the meadow, Oumou Prescott bent to the database keyboard and called up a new, purple oblong of holographic light on the display. I watched as it bloomed and opened like some cubist rendition of an orchid. Behind me, another cow voiced its resigned disgruntlement.

I slipped the headset back on.

CHAPTEr EIGHT

The town was called Ember. I found it on the map about two hundred kilometers north of Bay City on the coast road. There was an asymmetrical yellow symbol in the sea next to it.

"*Free Trade Enforcer,*" Prescott said, peering over my shoulder. "Aircraft carrier. It was the last really big warship anyone ever built. Some idiot ran it aground way back at the start of the Colony years, and the town grew up around the site to cater to the tourists."

"Tourists?"

She looked at me. "It's a big ship."

I rented an ancient ground car from a seedy-looking dealership two blocks down from Prescott's office and drove north over the rust-colored suspension bridge. I needed time to think. The coastal highway was poorly maintained but almost deserted, so I stuck to the yellow line in the center of the road and barreled along at a steady hundred and fifty. The radio yielded a medley of stations whose cultural assumptions were largely above my head, but I finally found a Neo-maoist propaganda DJ memory-wired into some dissemination satellite that nobody had ever bothered to decommission. The mix of high political sentiment and saccharine karaoke numbers was irresistible. The smell of the passing sea blew in through the open window and the road unwound ahead of me, and for a while I forgot about the corps and Innenin and everything that had happened since.

By the time I hit the long curve down into Ember, the sun was going down behind the canted angles of the *Free Trade Enforcer*'s launch deck, and the last of its rays were leaving almost imperceptible pink stains on the surf on either side of the wreck's shadow. Prescott was right. It was a big ship.

I slowed my speed in deference to the rise of buildings around me, wondering idly how anyone could have been stupid enough to steer a vessel that large so close to shore. Maybe Bancroft knew. He'd probably been around then.

Ember's main street ran along the seafront the entire length of the town and was separated from the beach by a line of majestic palm trees and a neo-Victorian railing in wrought iron. There were holograph 'casters fixed to the trunks of the palms, all projecting the same image of a woman's face wreathed with the words SLIPSLIDE—ANCHANA SALOMAO & THE RIO TOTAL BODY THEATER. Small knots of people were out, rubbernecking at the images.

I rolled the ground car along the street in low gear, scanning the facades, and finally found what I was looking for about two-thirds of the way along the front. I coasted past and parked the car quietly about fifty meters up, sat still for a few minutes to see if anything happened, and then, when it didn't, I got out of the car and walked back along the street.

Elliott's Data Linkage Brokerage was a narrow facade sandwiched between an industrial chemicals outlet and a vacant lot where gulls screeched and fought over scraps among the shells of discarded hardware. The door of Elliott's was propped open with a defunct flatscreen monitor and led directly into the operations room. I stepped inside and cast a glance up and down. There were four consoles set in back-to-back pairs, harbored behind a long molded-plastic reception counter. Beyond them, doors led to a glass-walled office. The far wall held a bank of seven monitors with incomprehensible lines of data scrolling down. A ragged gap in the line of screens marked the previous position of the doorstop. There were scars in the paintwork behind where the brackets had resisted extraction. The screen next to the gap had rolling flickers, as if whatever had killed the first one was contagious.

"Help you?"

A thin-faced man of indeterminate age poked his head around the corner of one of the sloping banks of console equipment. There was an unlit cigarette in his mouth and a trailing thread of cable jacked into an interface behind his right ear. His skin was unhealthily pale.

"Yeah, I'm looking for Victor Elliott."

"Out front." He gestured back the way I had come. "See the old guy on the rail? Watching the wreck? That's him."

I looked out into the evening beyond the door and picked out the solitary figure at the rail.

"He owns this place, right?"

"Yeah. For his sins." The datarat cracked a grin and gestured around. "Not much call for him to be in the office, business the way it is."

I thanked him and went back out onto the street. The light was starting to fade now, and Anchana Salomao's holographic face was gaining a new dominance in the gathering gloom. Crossing beneath one of the banners, I came up next to the man on the rail and leaned my own arms on the black iron. He looked around as I joined him and gave me a nod of acknowledgment, then went back to staring at the horizon as if he was looking for a crack in the weld between sea and sky.

"That's a pretty grim piece of parking," I said, gesturing out at the wreck.

It earned me a speculative look before he answered me. "They say it was terrorists." His voice was empty, disinterested, as if he'd once put too much effort into using it and something had broken. "Or sonar failure in a storm. Maybe both."

"Maybe they did it for the insurance," I said.

Elliott looked at me again, more sharply. "You're not from here?" he asked, a fraction more interest edging his tone this time.

"No. Passing through."

"From Rio?" He gestured up at Anchana Salomao as he said it. "You an artist?"

"No."

"Oh." He seemed to consider this for a moment. It was as if conversation was a skill he'd forgotten. "You move like an artist."

"Near miss. It's military neurachem."

He got it then, but the shock didn't seem to go beyond a brief flicker in his eyes. He looked me up and down slowly, then turned back to the sea.

"You come looking for me? You from Bancroft?"

"You might say that."

He moistened his lips. "Come to kill me?"

I took the hardcopy out of my pocket and handed it across to him. "Come to ask you some questions. Did you transmit this?"

He read it, lips moving wordlessly. Inside my head, I could hear the words he was tasting again: . . . *for taking my daughter from me . . . will burn the flesh from your head . . . will never know the hour or the day . . . nowhere safe in this life . . .* It wasn't highly original, but it was heartfelt and articulate in a way that was more worrying than any of the vitriol Prescott had shown me on the Rabid and Rambling stack. It also specified exactly the death Bancroft had suffered. The particle blaster would have charred the outside of Bancroft's skull to a crisp before exploding the superheated contents across the room.

"Yes, that's mine," Elliott said quietly.

"You're aware that someone assassinated Laurens Bancroft last month."

He handed me back the paper. "That so? The way I heard it, the bastard torched his own head off."

"Well, that is a possibility," I conceded, screwing up the paper and tossing it into a refuse-filled trash bin below us on the beach. "But it's not one I'm being paid to take seriously. Unfortunately for you, the cause of death comes uncomfortably close to your prose style there."

"I didn't do it," Elliott said flatly.

"I figured you'd say that. I might even believe you, except that whoever did kill Bancroft got through some very heavy-duty security systems, and you used to be a sergeant in the tactical marines. Now, I knew some tacs back on Harlan's World, and a few of them were wired for covert wet work."

Elliott looked at me curiously. "You a grasshopper?"

"A what?"

"Grasshopper. Offworlder."

"Yeah." If Elliott had ever been afraid of me, it was wearing off fast. I considered playing the Envoy card, but it didn't seem worth it. The man was still talking.

"Bancroft don't need to bring in muscle from offworld. What's your angle on this?"

"Private contractor," I said. "Find the killer."

Elliott snorted. "And you thought it was me."

I hadn't thought that, but I let it go, because the misconception was giving him a feeling of superiority that kept the conversation rolling. Something approaching a spark appeared in his eyes.

"You think I could have got into Bancroft's house? I know I couldn't, because I ran the specs. If there was any way in, I would have taken it a year ago, and you would have found little pieces of him scattered on the lawn."

"Because of your daughter?"

"Yes, because of my daughter." The anger was fueling his animation. "My daughter and all the others like her. She was only a kid."

He broke off and stared out to sea again. After a moment, he gestured at the *Free Trade Enforcer*, where I could now see small lights glimmering around what must be a stage set up on the sloping launch deck. "That was what she wanted. All she wanted. Total Body Theater. Be like Anchana Salomao and Rhian Li. She went to Bay City because she heard there was a connection there, someone who could—"

He jarred to a halt and looked at me. The datarat had called him old, and now for the first time I saw why. In spite of his solid sergeant's bulk and barely swelling waistline, the face was old, carved in the harsh lines of long-term pain. He was on the edge of tears.

"She could have made it, too. She was beautiful."

He was fumbling for something in his pocket. I produced my cigarettes and offered him one. He took it automatically, lit it from the proffered ignition patch on the pack, but he went on fumbling in his pockets until he'd dug out a small kodakristal. I really didn't want to see this, but he activated it before I could say anything, and a tiny cubed image sprang up in the air between us.

He was right. Elizabeth Elliott was a beautiful girl, blonde and athletic and only a few years younger than Miriam Bancroft. Whether she had the driving determination and horselike stamina that you needed in Total Body Theater, the picture didn't show, but she probably could have given it a shot.

The holoshot showed her sandwiched between Elliott and another woman who was an almost perfect older edition of Elizabeth. The three of them had been taken in bright sunlight somewhere with grass, and the picture was marred by a bar of shadow falling from a tree beyond the cast of the recorder across the older woman's face. She was frowning, as if she had noticed the flaw in the composition, but it was a small frown, a fractional chiseling of lines between her brows. A palpable shimmer of happiness overwhelmed the detail.

"Gone," Elliott said, as if he had guessed who my attention was focused on. "Four years ago. You know what dipping is?"

I shook my head. *Local color,* Virginia Vidaura said in my ear. *Soak it up.*

Elliott looked up, for a moment I thought, at the holo of Anchana Salomao, but then I saw that his head was tilted at the sky beyond. "Up there," he said, and jarred to a halt the way he had when he mentioned his daughter's youth.

I waited.

"Up there, you got the comsats. Raining data. You can see it on some virtual maps; it looks like someone's knitting the world a scarf." He looked down at me again, eyes shiny. "Irene said that. Knitting the world a scarf. Some of that scarf is people. Digitized rich folks, on their way between bodies. Skeins of memory and feeling and thought, packaged up by numbers."

Now I thought I knew what was coming, but I kept quiet.

"If you're good, like she was, and you've got the equipment, you can sample those signals. They call them mindbites. Moments in the head of a fashion house princess, the ideas of a particle theorist, memories from a king's childhood. There's a market for this stuff. Oh, the society magazines run edited skullwalks of these sorts of people, but it's all authorized, sanitized. Cut for public consumption. No unguarded moments, nothing that could embarrass anybody or damage popularity, just great big plastic smiles on everything. That ain't what people really want."

I had my doubts about that. The skullwalk magazines were big on Harlan's World, as well, and the only time their consumers protested was when one of the notables they portrayed was caught in some moment of human weakness. Infidelity and abusive language were usually the biggest generators of public outcry. It made sense. Anyone pitiful enough to want to spend so much time outside their own head wasn't going to want to see the same basic human realities reflected in the gilded skulls of those they admired.

"With mindbites, you get everything," Elliott said with a peculiar enthusiasm I suspected was a graft from his wife's opinions. "The doubt, the muck, the humanity. People will pay a fortune for it."

"But it's illegal?"

Elliott gestured back at the shopfront that bore his name. "The data market was down. Too many brokers. Saturated. We had a clone and resleeving policy to pay on both of us, plus Elizabeth. My tac pension wasn't going to be enough. What could we do?"

"How long did she get?" I asked him softly.

Elliott stared out to sea. "Thirty years."

After a while, stare still fixed on the horizon, he said, "I was okay for six months, then I turn on the screen and see some corporate negotiator wearing Irene's body." He half turned toward me and coughed out something that might have been a laugh. "Corporation bought it direct from the Bay City storage facility. Paid five times what I could have afforded. They say the bitch only wears it alternate months."

"Elizabeth know that?"

He nodded once, like an axe coming down. "She got it out of me, one night. I was jack-happy. Been cruising the stacks all day, looking for business. No handle on where I was or what was going on. You want to know what she said?"

"No," I muttered.

He didn't hear me. His knuckles had whitened on the iron railing. "She said *don't worry, Daddy, when I'm rich we'll buy Mummy back.*"

This was getting out of hand.

"Look, Elliott, I'm sorry about your daughter, but from what I hear she wasn't working the kind of places Bancroft goes. Jerry's Biocabins isn't exactly the Houses, is it?"

The ex-tac spun on me without warning, and there was blind murder in his eyes and his crooked hands. I couldn't blame him. All he could see in front of him was Bancroft's man.

But you *can't* jump an Envoy—the conditioning won't let it happen. I saw the attack coming almost before he knew he was going to do it himself, and I had the neurachem of my borrowed sleeve on-line fragments of a second later. He hit low, driving under the guard he thought I'd put up, looking for the body blows that would break up my ribs. The guard wasn't there, and neither was I. Instead, I stepped inside the hooks of his punches, took him off balance with my weight, and tangled one leg amidst his. He stumbled back against the railing, and I drove a cruel elbow uppercut into his solar plexus. His face went gray with the shock. Leaning over, I pinned him to the rail and jammed the fork of my thumb and fingers into his throat.

"That's enough," I snapped, a little unsteadily. The sleeve's neurachem wiring was a rougher piece of work than the corps systems I'd used in the past, and in overdrive, the overwhelming impression was of being slung around in a subcutaneous bag of chicken wire.

I looked down at Elliott.

His eyes were a handbreadth from mine, and despite the grip I had on his throat they were still burning with rage. Breath whistled in his teeth as he clawed after the strength to break my grip and damage me.

I yanked him off the rail and propped him away from me with a cautionary arm.

"Listen, I'm passing no judgments here. I just want to know. What makes you think she has any connection to Bancroft?"

"Because she *told* me, motherfucker." The sentence hissed out of him. "She told me what he'd done."

"And what was that?"

He blinked rapidly, the undischarged rage condensing into tears. "Dirty things," he said. "She said he *needed* them. Badly enough to come back. Badly enough to pay."

Meal ticket. *Don't worry, Daddy, when I'm rich we'll buy Mummy back.* Easy enough mistake to make when you're young. But nothing comes that easy.

"You think that's why she died?"

He turned his head and looked at me as if I was a particularly poisonous species of spider on his kitchen floor.

"She didn't *die*, mister. Someone killed her. Someone took a razor and cut her up."

"Trial transcript says it was a client. Not Bancroft."

"How would they know?" he said dully. "They name a body, who knows who's inside it. Who's paying for it all."

"They find him yet?"

"Biocabin whore's killer? What do you think? It ain't exactly like she worked for the Houses, right?"

"That's not what I meant, Elliott. You say she turned Bancroft in Jerry's, I'll believe you. But you've got to admit it doesn't sound like Bancroft's style. I've met the man, and slumming?" I shook my head. "He doesn't read that way to me."

Elliott turned away.

"Flesh," he said. "What you going to read in a Meth's flesh?"

It was nearly full dark. Out across the water on the sloping deck of the warship, the performance had started. We both stared at the lights for a while, heard the bright snatches of music, like transmissions from a world that we were forever locked out of.

"Elizabeth's still on stack," I said quietly.

"Yeah, so what? Resleeving policy lapsed four years ago, when we sank all the money we had into some lawyer said he could crack Irene's case." He gestured back at the dimly lit frontage of his offices. "I look like the kind of guy's going to come into some money real soon?"

There was nothing to say after that. I left him watching the lights and walked back to the car. He was still there when I drove back past him on the way out of the little town. He didn't look around.

PART TWO

rEACTION
(INTRUSION CONFLICT)

CHAPTEr NINE

I called Prescott from the car. Her face looked mildly irritated as it scribbled into focus on the dusty little screen set into the dashboard.

"Kovacs. Did you find what you were looking for?"

"Still don't really know what I'm looking for," I said cheerfully. "You think Bancroft ever does the biocabins?"

She pulled a face. "Oh, please."

"All right, here's another one. Did Leila Begin ever work biocabin joints?"

"I really have no idea, Kovacs."

"Well, look it up, then. I'll hold." My voice came out stony. Prescott's well-bred distaste wasn't sitting too well beside Victor Elliott's anguish for his daughter.

I drummed my fingers on the wheel while the lawyer went offscreen, and found myself muttering a Millsport fisherman's rap to the rhythm. Outside, the coast slid by in the night, but the scents and sounds of the sea were suddenly all wrong. Too muted, not a trace of belaweed on the wind.

"Here we are." Prescott settled herself back within range of the phone scanner, looking slightly uncomfortable. "Begin's Oakland records show two stints in biocabins, before she got tenure in one of the San Diego Houses. She must have had an entrée, unless it was a talent scout who spotted her out."

Bancroft would have been quite an entrée to anywhere. I resisted the temptation to say it.

"You got an image there?"

"Of Begin?" Prescott shrugged. "Only a 2-D. You want me to send it?"

"Please."

The ancient car phone fizzled a bit as it adjusted to the change of incoming signal, and then Leila Begin's features emerged from the static. I leaned closer, scanning them for the truth. It took a moment or two to find, but it was there.

"Right. Now, can you get me the address of that place Elizabeth Elliott worked? Jerry's Closed Quarters. It's on a street called Mariposa."

"Mariposa and San Bruno," Prescott's disembodied voice came back from behind Leila Begin's full-service pout. "Jesus, it's right under the old expressway. That's *got* to be a safety violation."

"Can you send me a map, route marked through from the bridge?"

"You're going there? Tonight?"

"Prescott, these places don't do a lot of business during the day," I said patiently. "Of course I'm going there tonight."

There was a slight hesitation on the other end of the line.

"It's not a recommended area, Kovacs. You need to be careful."

This time I couldn't be bothered to stifle the snort of amusement. It was like listening to someone tell a surgeon to be careful and not get his hands bloody. She must have heard me.

"I'm sending the map," she said stiffly.

Leila Begin's face blinked out, and a tracery of grid-patterned streets inked themselves into the place she had been. I didn't need her anymore. Her hair had been iridescent crimson, her throat choked with a steel collar, and her eyes made up with startle lines, but it was the lines of the face below it all that stayed with me. The same lines faintly emergent in Victor Elliott's kodakristal of his daughter. The understated but undeniable similarity.

Miriam Bancroft.

●●●

There was rain in the air when I got back to the city, a fine drizzle sifting down from the darkened sky. Parked across the street from Jerry's, I watched the blinking neon CLUB sign through the streaks and beads of water on the windshield of the ground car. Somewhere in the gloom below the concrete bones of the expressway a holo of a woman danced in a cocktail glass, but there was a fault in the 'caster and the image kept fizzling out.

I'd been worried about the ground car drawing attention, but it seemed that I'd come to the right part of town with it. Most of the vehicles around Jerry's were flightless; the only exceptions to the rule were the autocabs that occasionally spiraled down to disgorge or collect passengers and then sprang back up into the aerial traffic flow with inhuman accuracy and speed. With their arrays of red, blue, and white navigation lights they seemed like jeweled visitors from another world, barely touching the cracked and litter-strewn paving while their charges alighted or climbed aboard.

I watched for an hour. The club did brisk business, varied clientele but mostly male. They were checked at the door by a security robot that resembled nothing so much as a concertina'd octopus strung from the lintel of the main entrance. Some had to divest themselves of concealed items, presumably weapons, and one or two were turned away. There were no protests—you can't argue with a robot. Outside, people parked, climbed in and out of cars, and did deals with merchandise too small to make out at this distance. Once, two men started a knife fight in the shadows between two of the expressway's support pillars, but it didn't come to much. One combatant limped off, clutching a slashed arm, and the other returned to the club's interior as if he'd done no more than go out to relieve himself.

I climbed out of the car, made sure it was alarmed, and wandered across the street. A couple of the dealers were seated cross-legged on the hood of a car, shielded from the rain by a static repulsion unit set up between their feet, and they glanced up as I approached.

"Sell you a disk, man? Hot spinners out of Ulan Bator, House quality."

I gave them one smooth sweep, shook my head unhurriedly.

"Stiff?"

Another shake. I reached the robot, paused as its multiple arms snaked down to frisk me, then tried to walk over the threshold as the cheap synth voice said, "Clear." One of the arms prodded me gently back at chest height.

"Do you want cabins or bar?"

I hesitated, pretending to weigh it up. "What's the deal in the bar?"

"Ha ha ha." Someone had programmed a laugh into the robot. It sounded like a fat man drowning in syrup. It cut off abruptly. "The bar is *look*, but don't *touch*. No money down, no hands on. House rule. That applies to other customers, too."

"Cabins," I said, anxious to get away from the mechanical barker's software. The street dealers on the car had been positively warm by comparison.

"Down the stairs, to the left. Take a towel from the pile."

I went down the short metal-railed flight and turned left along a corridor lit from the ceiling by rotating red lights like the ones on the autocabs outside. Incessant junk rhythm music thrashed the air as if this was the ventricle of some massive heart on tetrameth. As promised, there was a pile of fresh white towels in an alcove and beyond it the doors to the cabins. I walked past the first four, two of which were occupied, and stepped into the fifth.

The floor was satin-sheened padding, about two meters by three. If it was stained, it didn't show, because the only illumination came from a single rotating cherry like the ones in the corridor. The air was warm and stale. Under the sweeping shadows cast by the light a battered-looking credit console stood in one corner, stalk painted matte black, red LED digital display at the top. There was a slot for cards and cash. No pad for DNA credit. The far wall was frosted glass.

I'd seen this one coming and drawn a sheaf of currency through an autobank on the way down through the city. I selected one of the large-denomination plasticized notes and fed it into the slot. Punched the commence button. My credit flashed up in LED red. The door hinged smoothly shut behind me, muffling the music, and a body thudded against the frosted glass ahead with an abruptness that made me twitch. The display digits flickered to life. Minimal expenditure so far. I studied the body pressed against the glass. Heavy breasts pressed flat, a woman's profile and the indistinct lines of hips and thighs. Piped moaning came softly through hidden speakers. A voice gusted.

"Do you want to see me see me see me. . . ?"

Cheap echo box on the vocoder.

I pressed the button again. The glass unfrosted, and the woman on the other side became visible. She shifted, side to side, showing herself to me, worked-out body, augmented breasts, leaned forward and licked the glass with the tip of her tongue, breath misting it again. Her eyes locked onto mine.

"Do you want to touch me touch me touch me. . . ?"

Whether the cabins used subsonics or not, I was getting a definite reaction from it all. My penis thickened and stirred. I locked down the throbbing, forced the blood back out and into my muscles the way a combat call would do. I needed to be limp for this scene. I reached for the debit button again. The glass screen slid aside, and she stepped through, like someone coming out of a shower. She moved up to me; one hand slid out, cupping.

"Tell me what you want, honey," she said from somewhere in the base of her throat. The voice seemed hard edged, deprived of the vocoder effect.

I cleared my throat. "What's your name?"

"Anemone. Want to know why they call me that?"

Her hand worked. Behind her, the meter was clicking over softly.

"You remember a girl used to work here?" I asked.

She was working on my belt now. "Honey, any girl *used* to work here ain't going to do for you what I am. Now, how would you—"

"She was called Elizabeth. Her real name. Elizabeth Elliott."

Her hands fell abruptly away, and the mask of arousal slid off her face as if it was greased underneath.

"What the fuck is this? You the Sia?"

"The *what*?"

"Sia. The heat." Her voice was rising. She stepped away from me. "We *had* this, man—"

"No." I took a step toward her, and she dropped into a competent-looking defensive crouch. I backed up again, voice low. "No, I'm her mother."

Taut silence. She glared at me.

"Bullshit. Lizzie's ma's in the store."

"No." I pulled her hand back to my groin. "Feel. There's nothing there. They sleeved me in this, but I'm a woman. I don't, I couldn't . . ."

She unbent fractionally from her crouch, hands tugging almost unwillingly down. "That looks like prime tank flesh to me," she said untrustingly. "You just come out of the store, how come you're not paroled in some bone bag junkie's sleeve?"

"It's not parole." The corps' deep-cover training came rocketing in across my mind like a flight of low-level strike jets, spinning vapor-trail lies on the edge of plausibility and half-known detail. Something inside me tilted with the joy of mission time. "You know what I went down for?"

"Lizzie said mindbites, something—"

"Yeah. Dipping. You know *who* I dipped?"

"No. Lizzie never talked much about—"

"Elizabeth didn't know. And it never came out on the wires."

The heavy-breasted girl put her hands on her hips. "So who—"

I skinned her a smile. "Better you don't know. Someone powerful. Someone with enough pull to unstack me, and give me this."

"Not powerful enough to get you back in something with a pussy, though." Anemone's voice was still doubtful, but the conviction was coming up fast, like a bottleback school under reef water. She *wanted* to believe this fairy-tale mother come looking for her lost daughter. "How come you're cross-sleeved?"

"There's a deal," I told her, gliding near the truth to flesh out the story. "This . . . person . . . gets me out, and I have to do something for them. Something that needs a man's body. If I do it, I get a new sleeve for me and Elizabeth."

"That so? So why you here?" There was an edge of bitterness in her voice that told me her parents would never come to this place looking for her. And that she believed me. I laid the last pieces of the lie.

"There's a problem with resleeving Elizabeth. Someone's blocking the procedure. I want to know who it is, and why. You know who cut her up?"

She shook her head, face turned down.

"A lot of the girls get hurt," she said quietly. "But Jerry's got insurance to cover that. He's real good about it, even puts us into store if it's going to take a long time to heal. But whoever did Lizzie wasn't a regular."

"Did Elizabeth have regulars? Anyone important? Anyone strange?"

She looked up at me, pity showing in the corners of her eyes. I'd played Irene Elliott to the hilt. "Mrs. Elliott, all the people who come here are strange. They wouldn't be here if they weren't."

I made myself wince. "Anyone important?"

"I don't know. Look, Mrs. Elliott, I liked Lizzie. She was real kind to me a coupla times when I got down, but we never got close. She was close with Chloe and—" She paused, and added hurriedly, "Nothing like that, you know, but her and Chloe, and Mac, they used to share things, you know, talk and everything."

"Can I talk to them?"

Her eyes flickered to the corners of the cabin, as if she had just heard an inexplicable noise. She looked hunted.

"It's better if you don't. Jerry, you know, he doesn't like us talking to the public. If he catches us . . ."

I put every ounce of Envoy persuasiveness into stance and tone. "Well, maybe you could ask for me. . . ."

The hunted look deepened, but her voice firmed up.

"Sure. I'll ask around. But not now. You've got to go. Come back tomorrow the same time. Same cabin. I'll stay free for this time. Say you made an appointment."

I took her hand in both of mine. "Thank you, Anemone."

"My name's not Anemone," she said abruptly. "I'm called Louise. Call me Louise."

"Thank you, Louise." I held on to her hand. "Thank you for doing this—"

"Look, I'm not promising anything," she said with an attempt at roughness. "Like I said, I'll ask. That's all. Now, you go. Please."

She showed me how to cancel the remainder of my payment on the credit console, and the door hinged immediately open. No change. I didn't say anything else. I didn't try to touch her again. I walked out through the open door and left her standing there with her arms wrapped around her chest and her head down, staring at the satin-padded floor of the cabin as if she was seeing it for the first time.

Lit in red.

● ● ●

Outside, the street was unchanged. The two dealers were still there, deep in negotiations with a huge Mongol who was leaning on the hood of the car, looking at something between his hands. The octopus arched its arms to let me pass, and I stepped into the drizzle. The Mongol looked up as I passed, and a flinch of recognition passed over his face.

I stopped, turning in midstep, and he dropped his gaze again, muttering something to the dealers. The neurachem came on-line like a shiver of cold water inside. I moved across the space to the car, and the sparse conversation between the three men dried up instantly. Hands slid into pouches and pockets. Something was pushing me, something that had very little to do with the look the Mongol had given me. Something dark that had spread its wings on the low-key misery of the cabin, something uncontrolled that Virginia Vidaura would have bawled me out for. I could hear Jimmy de Soto whispering in my ear.

"You waiting for me?" I asked the Mongol's back, and saw how the muscles in it tensed.

Maybe one of the dealers felt it coming. He held up his exposed hand in a placatory gesture. "Look, man," he began weakly.

I sliced him a glance out of the corner of my eye, and he shut up.

"I said—"

That was when it all came apart. The Mongol pushed himself off the car hood with a roar and swatted at me with an arm the size of a ham. The blow never landed, but even deflecting it, I staggered back a pace. The dealers skinned their weapons, deadly little slabs of black and gray metal that spat and yapped in the rain. I twisted away from the traceries of fire, using the Mongol for cover, and shot a palm heel into his contorted face. Bone crunched and I came around him onto the car while the dealers were still trying to work out where I was. The neurachem made their movements into the pouring of thick honey. One gun-filled fist came tracking toward me, and I smashed the fingers around the metal with a side-flung kick. The owner howled, and the edge of my hand cracked into the other dealer's temple. Both men reeled off the car, one still moaning, the other insensible or dead. I came up into a crouch.

The Mongol took off, running.

I vaulted the roof of the ground car and went after him without thinking. The concrete jarred my feet as I landed, sent splinters of pain lancing up both shins, but the neurachem damped it down instantly and I was only a dozen meters behind. I threw out my chest and sprinted.

Ahead of me, the Mongol bounced around in my field of vision like a combat jet trying to elude pursuing fire. For a man of his size, he was remarkably fast, flitting between the marching support pillars of the expressway and into the shadows a good twenty meters ahead now. I put on speed, wincing at the sharp pains in my chest. Rain slapped at my face.

Fucking cigarettes.

We came out from under the pillars and across a deserted intersection where the traffic lights leaned at drunken angles. One of them stirred feebly, lights changing, as the Mongol passed it. A senile robot voice husked out at me. *Cross now. Cross now. Cross now.* I already had. The echoes followed me beseechingly up the street.

Past the derelict hulks of vehicles that hadn't moved from their curbside resting places in years. Barred and shuttered frontages that might or might not be rolled up for business during daylight hours, steam rising from a grate in the side of the street like something alive. The paving under my feet was slick with the rain and a gray muck distilled from items of decaying garbage. The shoes that had come with Bancroft's summer suit were thin soled and devoid of useful grip. Only the perfect balance of the neurachem kept me upright.

The Mongol cast a glance back over his shoulder as he came level with two parked wrecks, saw I was still there, and broke left across the street as soon as he cleared the last vehicle. I tried to adjust my trajectory and cut him off, crossing the street at an angle before I reached the wrecked cars, but my quarry had timed the trap too well. I was already on the first wreck, and I skidded trying to stop in time. I bounced off the hood of the rusting vehicle into a shopfront shutter. The metal clanged and sizzled; a low-current antiloitering charge stung my hands. Across the street, the Mongol stretched the distance between us by another ten meters.

A wayward speck of traffic moved in the sky above me.

I spotted the fleeing figure on the other side of the street and kicked off from the curb, cursing the impulse that had made me turn down Bancroft's offer of armaments. At this range a beam weapon would have carved the Mongol's legs out from under him easily. Instead, I tucked in behind him and tried to find the lung capacity from somewhere to close up the gap again. Maybe I could panic him into tripping.

That wasn't what happened, but it was close enough. The buildings to our left gave way to wasteland bordered by a sagging fence. The Mongol looked back again and made his first mistake. He stopped, threw himself on the fence, which promptly collapsed, and scrambled over into the darkness beyond. I grinned and followed. Finally, I had the advantage.

Perhaps he was hoping to lose himself in the darkness, or expecting me to twist an ankle over the uneven ground. But the Envoy conditioning squeezed my pupils into instant dilation in the low-light surroundings and mapped my steps over the uneven surface with lightning speed, and the neurachem put my feet there with a rapidity to match. The ground ghosted by beneath me the way it had beneath Jimmy de Soto in my dream. Given a hundred meters of this I was going to overtake my Mongol friend, unless he, too, had augmented vision.

In the event, the wasteland ran out before that, but by then there was barely the original dozen meters between us when we both hit the fence on the far side. He scaled the wire, dropped to the ground, and started up the street while I was still climbing, but then, abruptly, he appeared to stumble. I cleared the top of the fence and swung down lightly. He must have heard me drop, though, because he spun out of the huddle, still not finished clipping together the thing in his hands. The muzzle came up, and I dived for the street.

I hit hard, skinning my hands and rolling. Lightning torched the night where I had been. The stink of ozone washed over me, and the crackle of disrupted air curled in my ears. I kept rolling, and the particle blaster lit up again, charring past my shoulder. The damp street hissed with steam in its wake. I scrambled for cover that wasn't there.

"*Lay down your weapon!*"

A cluster of pulsating lights dropped vertically from above, and the loudspeaker barked down the night like the voice of a robot god. A searchlight exploded in the street and flooded us with white fire. From where I lay, I screwed up my eyes and could just make out the police transport, a regulation crowd-control five meters off the street, lights flashing. The soft storm of its turbines swept flapping wings of paper and plastic up against the walls of nearby buildings and pinned them there like dying moths.

"*Stand where you are!*" the loudspeaker thundered again. "*Lay down your weapon!*"

The Mongol brought his particle blaster around in a searing arc, and the transport bucked as its pilot tried to avoid the beam. Sparks showered off one turbine where the weapon found its mark, and the transport sideslipped badly. Machine rifle fire answered from a mounting somewhere below the vessel's nose, but by that time the Mongol was across the street, had torched down a door, and was gone through the smoking gap.

Screams from somewhere within.

I picked myself slowly up off the ground and watched as the transport settled to within a meter of the ground. An extinguisher canister fumed into life on the smoldering engine canopy and dripped white foam onto the street. Just behind the pilot's window, a hatch whined up and Kristin Ortega stood framed in the opening.

CHAPTEr TEN

The transport was a stripped-down version of the one that had given me the ride out to Suntouch House, and it was noisy in the cabin. Ortega had to shout to make herself heard above the engines.

"We'll put in a sniffer squad, but if he's connected, he can get stuff that'll change his body's chemical signature before dawn. After that, we're down to witness sightings. Stone Age stuff. And in this part of town . . ."

The transport banked, and she gestured down at the warren of streets below. "Look at it. Licktown, they call it. Used to be called Potrero way back. They say it was a nice area."

"So what happened?"

Ortega shrugged in her steel lattice seat. "Economic crisis. You know how it is. One day you own a house, your sleeve policy's paid up, the next you're on the street looking at a single life span."

"That's tough."

"Yeah, isn't it," the detective said dismissively. "Kovacs, what the *fuck* were you doing at Jerry's?"

"Getting an itch scratched," I growled. "Any laws against it?"

She looked at me. "You weren't getting greased in Jerry's. You were barely in there ten minutes."

I lifted my own shoulders and made an apologetic face. "You ever been downloaded into a male body straight out of the tank, you'll know what it's like. Hormones. Things get rushed. Places like Jerry's, performance isn't an issue."

Ortega's lips curved in something approximating a smile. She leaned forward across the space between us.

"Bullshit, Kovacs. Bull. Shit. I accessed what they've got on you at Millsport. Psychological profile. They call it the Kemmerich gradient, and yours is so steep you'd need pitons and rope to get up it. Everything you do, performance is going to be an issue."

"Well." I fed myself a cigarette and ignited it as I spoke. "You know, there's a lot you can do for some women in ten minutes."

Ortega rolled her eyes and waved the comment away as if it was a fly buzzing around her face.

"Right. And you're telling me with the credit you have from Bancroft, Jerry's is the best you can afford?"

"It's not about cost," I said, and wondered if that was the truth of what brought people like Bancroft down to Licktown.

Ortega leaned her head against the window and looked out at the rain. She didn't look at me. "You're chasing leads, Kovacs. You went down to Jerry's to follow up something Bancroft did there. Given time, I can find out what that was, but it'd be easier if you just told me."

"Why? You told me the Bancroft case was closed. What's your interest?"

That brought her eyes back around to mine, and there was a light in them. "My interest is keeping the peace. Maybe you haven't noticed, but every time we meet it's to the sound of heavy-caliber gunfire."

I spread my hands. "I'm unarmed. All I'm doing is asking questions. And speaking of questions. How come you were sitting on my shoulder when the fun started?"

"Just lucky, I guess."

I let that one go. Ortega was tailing me, that much was certain. And that in turn meant there had to be more to the Bancroft case than she was admitting.

"What's going to happen to my car?" I asked.

"We'll have it picked up. Notify the rental company. Someone can come and get it from the impound. Unless you want it."

I shook my head.

"Tell me something, Kovacs. Why'd you rent a ground car? On what Bancroft's paying you, you could have had one of these." She slapped the bulkhead by her side.

"I like to go places on the ground," I said. "You get a better sense of distance that way. And on Harlan's World, we don't go up in the air much."

"Really?"

"Really. Listen, the guy who nearly torched you out of the sky back there—"

"Excuse me?" She cranked up one eyebrow in what by now I was beginning to think of as her trademark expression. "Correct me if I'm wrong, but I think we saved your sleeve back there. You were the one looking down the wrong end of the hardware."

I gestured. "Whatever. He was waiting for me."

"Waiting for you?" Whatever she really thought, Ortega's face was disbelieving. "According to those Stiff dealers we loaded into the wagon, he was buying product. An old customer, they say."

I shook my head. "He was waiting for me. I went to talk to him, he took off."

"Maybe he didn't like your face. One of the dealers, I think it was the one whose skull you cracked, said you were looking jacked up to kill someone." She shrugged again. "They say you started it, and it certainly looks that way."

"In that case, why aren't you charging me?"

"Oh, with what?" She exhaled an imaginary plume of smoke. "Organic damage, surgery reparable, to a pair of Stiff peddlers? Endangering police property?

Breach of the peace in Licktown? Give me a break, Kovacs. This sort of thing goes down every night outside Jerry's. I'm too tired for the paperwork."

The transport tipped, and through the window I could see the dim form of the Hendrix's tower. I'd accepted Ortega's offer of a ride home in much the same spirit as I had the police lift out to Suntouch House—to see where it would take me. Envoy wisdom. Go with the flow, and see what it shows you. I'd no reason to suppose Ortega was lying to me about our destination, but still part of me was surprised to see that tower. Envoys aren't big on trust.

After an initial wrangle with the Hendrix about landing permission, the pilot set us down on a grimy-looking drop pad atop the tower. I could feel the wind tugging at the transport's lightweight body as we landed, and as the hatch unfolded upward, the cold came battering aboard. I got up to go. Ortega stayed where she was, watching me go with a lopsided look that I still couldn't work out. The charge I'd felt last night was back. I could feel the need to say something pressing on me like an impending sneeze.

"Hey, how'd the bust go down on Kadmin?"

She shifted in the seat and stuck out one long leg to rest her boot on the chair I had just vacated. A thin smile.

"Grinding through the machine," she said. "We'll get there."

"Good." I climbed out into the wind and rain, raising my voice. "Thanks for the lift."

She nodded gravely, then tipped her head back to say something to the pilot behind her. The whine of the turbines built, and I ducked hurriedly out from under the hatch as it began to close. As I stepped back, the transport unglued itself and lifted away, lights flashing. I caught a final glimpse of Ortega's face through the rain-streaked cabin window, then the wind seemed to carry the little craft away like an autumn leaf wheeling away and down toward the streets below. In seconds it was indistinguishable from the thousands of other flyers speckling the night sky. I turned and walked against the wind to the drop pad's access staircase. My suit was sodden from the rain. What had possessed Bancroft to outfit me for summer with the scrambled weather systems that Bay City had so far exhibited was beyond me. On Harlan's World, when it's winter, it stays that way long enough for you to make decisions about your wardrobe.

The upper levels of the Hendrix were in darkness relieved only by the occasional glow of dying illuminum tiles, but the hotel obligingly lit my way with neon tubes that flickered on in my path and died out again behind me. It was a weird effect, making me feel as if I was carrying a candle or torch.

"You have a visitor," the hotel said chattily as I got into the elevator and the doors whirred closed.

I slammed my hand against the emergency stop button, raw flesh where I'd skinned my palm stinging. "What?"

"You have a visi—"

"Yeah, I heard." It occurred to me, briefly, to wonder if the A.I. could take offense at my tone. "Who is it, and where are they?"

"She identifies herself as Miriam Bancroft. Subsequent search of the city archives has confirmed sleeve identity. I have allowed her to wait in your room, since she is unarmed and you left nothing of consequence there this morning. Aside from refreshment, she has touched nothing."

Feeling my temper rising, I found focus on a small dent in the metal of the elevator door and made an attempt at calm.

"This is interesting. Do you make arbitrary decisions like this for all your guests?"

"Miriam Bancroft is the wife of Laurens Bancroft," the hotel said reproachfully. "Who in turn is paying for your room. Under the circumstances, I thought it wise not to create unnecessary tensions."

I looked up at the ceiling of the elevator.

"You been checking up on me?"

"A background check is part of the contract I operate under. Any information retained is wholly confidential, unless subpoenaed under U.N. directive 231.4."

"Yeah? So what else you know?"

"Lieutenant Takeshi Lev Kovacs," the hotel said. "Also known as Mamba Lev, One Hand Rending, the Icepick; born Newpest, Harlan's World, 35th May 187, colonial reckoning. Recruited to U.N. Protectorate Forces 11th September 204, selected for Envoy Corps enhancement 31st June 211 during routine screening—"

"All right." Inwardly I was a little surprised at how deep the A.I. had got. Most people's records dry up as soon as the trace goes offworld. Interstellar needlecasts are expensive. Unless the Hendrix had just broken into Warden Sullivan's records, which was illegal. Ortega's comment about the hotel's previous charge sheet drifted back to me. What kind of crimes did an A.I. commit anyway?

"It also occurred to me that Mrs. Bancroft is probably here in connection with the matter of her husband's death, which you are investigating. I thought you would prefer to speak to her if possible, and she was not amenable to waiting in the lobby."

I sighed, and unpinned my hand from the elevator's stop button.

"No, I bet she wasn't."

She was seated in the window, nursing a tall, ice-filled glass and watching the lights of the traffic below. The room was in darkness broken only by the soft glow of the service hatch and the tricolored neon-frame liquor cabinet. Enough to see that she wore some kind of shawl over work trousers and a body-molded leotard. She didn't turn her head when I let myself in, so I advanced across the room into her field of vision.

"The hotel told me you were here," I said. "In case you were wondering why I didn't unsleeve myself in shock."

She looked up at me and shook hair back from her face.

"Very dry, Mr. Kovacs. Should I applaud?"

I shrugged. "You might say thank you for the drink."

She examined the top of her glass thoughtfully for a moment, then flicked her eyes up again.

"Thank you for the drink."

"Don't mention it." I went to the cabinet and surveyed the bottles racked there. A bottle of fifteen-year-old single malt suggested itself. I uncorked it, sniffed at the neck of the bottle, and picked out a tumbler. Keeping my eyes on my hands as they poured, I said, "Have you been waiting long?"

"About an hour. Oumou Prescott told me you'd gone to Licktown, so I guessed you'd be back late. Did you have some trouble?"

I held on to the first mouthful of whiskey, felt it sear the internal cuts where Kadmin had put the boot in, and swallowed hastily. I grimaced.

"Now why would you think that, Mrs. Bancroft?"

She made an elegant gesture with one hand. "No reason. Do you not want to talk about it?"

"Not particularly." I sank into a huge lounger bag at the foot of the crimson bed and sat staring across the room at her. Silence descended. From where I was sitting she was backlit by the window and her face was deep in shadow. I kept my eyes leveled on the faint gleam that might have been her left eye. After a while she shifted in her seat and the ice in her glass clicked.

"Well." She cleared her throat. "What would you like to talk about?"

I waved my glass at her. "Let's start with why you're here."

"I want to know what progress you've made."

"You can get a progress report from me tomorrow morning. I'll file one with Oumou Prescott before I go out. Come *on*, Mrs. Bancroft. It's late. You can do better than that."

For a moment I thought she might leave, the way she twitched. But then she took her glass in both hands, bent her head over it as if in search of inspiration, and after a long moment looked up again.

"I want you to stop," she said.

I let the words sink into the darkened room.

"Why?"

I saw her lips part in the smile, heard the sound her mouth made as it split.

"Why not?" she said.

"Well." I sipped at my drink, sluicing the alcohol around the cuts in my mouth to shut down my hormones. "To begin with, there's your husband. He's made it pretty clear that cutting and running could seriously damage my health. Then there's the hundred thousand dollars. And after that, well, then we get into the ethereal realm of things like promises and my word. And to be honest, I'm *curious*."

"A hundred thousand isn't so much money," she said carefully. "And the Protectorate is big. I could give you the money. Find a place for you to go where Laurens would never find you."

"Yes. That leaves my word, and my curiosity."

She sat forward over her drink. "Let's not pretend, Mr. Kovacs. Laurens didn't contract you, he dragged you here. He locked you into a deal you had no choice but to accept. No one could say you were honor bound."

"I'm still curious."

"Maybe I could satisfy that," she said softly.

I swallowed more whiskey. "Yeah? Did you kill your husband, Mrs. Bancroft?"

She made an impatient gesture. "I'm not talking about your game of detectives. You are . . . curious about other things, are you not?"

"I'm sorry?" I looked at her over the rim of my glass.

Miriam Bancroft pushed herself off the window shelf and set her hips against it. She set down the glass with exaggerated care and leaned back on her hands so that her shoulders lifted. It changed the shape of her breasts, moving them beneath the sheer material of her leotard.

"Do you know what Merge Nine is?" she asked, a little unsteadily.

"Empathin?" I dug the name out from somewhere. Some thoroughly armed robbery crew I knew back on Harlan's World, friends of Virginia Vidaura's. The Little Blue Bugs. They did all their work on Merge Nine. Said it welded them into a tighter team. Bunch of fucking psychos.

"Yes, empathin. Empathin derivatives, tailed with Satyron and Ghedin enhancers. This sleeve—" She gestured down at herself, spread fingers brushing the curves. "—this is state-of-the-art biochemtech, out of the Nakamura Labs. I secrete Merge Nine, when . . . aroused. In my sweat, in my saliva, in my cunt, Mr. Kovacs."

And she came off the shelf, shawl sliding off her shoulders to the floor. It puddled silkenly around her feet, and she stepped over it toward me.

Well, there's Alain Marriott, honorable and strong in all his myriad experia incarnations; and then there's reality. In reality, and whatever it costs, there are some things you don't turn away from.

I met her halfway across the room. Merge Nine was already in the air, in the scent of her body and the water vapor on her breath. I drew in a deep breath and felt the chemical triggers go off like plucked strings in the pit of my stomach. My drink was gone, set aside somewhere, and the hand that had held it was molded around one of Miriam Bancroft's jutting breasts. She drew my head down with hands on either side, and I found it there again, Merge Nine in the beads of sweat webbed in the soft down that ran in a line down her cleavage. I tugged at the seam of the leotard, untrapping the breasts pressed beneath it, tracing and finding one nipple with my mouth.

Above me I felt her mouth gasp open, and knew the empathin was working its way into my sleeve's brain, tripping dormant telepath instincts and sending out feelers for the intense aura of arousal that this woman was generating. Knew, as well, that she would be beginning to taste the flesh of her own breast in my mouth. Once triggered, the empathin rush was like a volleyed tennis ball, building intensity with every rebound from one inflamed sensorium to the other, until the merge reached a climax just short of unbearable.

Miriam Bancroft was beginning to moan now, as we sank to the floor and I moved back and forth between her breasts, rubbing their springy resistance over my face. Her hands had turned hungry, grasping and digging softly with nails at my flanks and the swollen ache between my legs. We scrabbled feverishly at each other's clothing, mouths trembling with the need to fill themselves, and when we had shed everything we wore, the rug beneath us seemed to lay individual strands of heat on our skin. I settled over her, and my stubble rasped faintly over the sprung smoothness of her belly, my mouth making wet Os on its path downward. Then there was the deep salt taste as my tongue tracked down the creases of her cunt, soaking up Merge Nine with her juices and coming back to press and flick at the tiny bud of her clitoris. Somewhere, at the other end of the world, my penis was pulsing in her hand. A mouth closed over the head and sucked gently.

Blending, our climaxes built rapidly and with unerring concurrence, and the mixed signals of the Merge Nine union blurred until I could find no distinction between the excruciating tautness of the prick between her fingers and the pressure of my own tongue somewhere indistinct up beyond its feasible reach inside her. Her thighs clamped around my head. There was a grunting sound, but whose throat it came from I was no longer aware. Separateness melted away into mutual sensory overload, tension building layer after layer, peak after peak, and then suddenly she was laughing at the warm, salty splash over her face and fingers and I was clamped against her corkscrewing hips as her own simultaneous crest swept her away.

For a while there was trembling release, in which the slightest movement, the sliding of flesh against flesh, brought sobbing spasms from us both. Then, gift of the long period my sleeve had been in the tank, the sweaty images of Anemone pressed against the glass of the biocabin, my penis twitched and began to tighten again. Miriam Bancroft nudged at it with her nose, ran the tip of her tongue along and around it, licking off the stickiness until it was smooth and taut against her cheek, then swung around and straddled me. Reaching back for balance and hold, she sank down, impaling herself on the shaft with a long, warm groan. She leaned over me, breasts swinging, and I craned and sucked hungrily at the elusive globes. My hands came up to grasp her thighs where they were spread on either side of my body.

And then the motion.

The second time took longer, and the empathin lent it an air that was more aesthetic than sexual. Taking her cue from the signals gusting out of my sensorium, Miriam Bancroft settled into a slow churning motion while I watched her taut belly and outthrust breasts with detached lust. For no reason I could discern, the Hendrix piped a slow, deep ragga beat in from the corners of the room, and a lighting effect patterned the ceiling above us with swirling blotches of red and purple. When the effect tilted and the swirling stars came to dapple our bodies, I felt my mind tilting with it, and my perceptions slid sideways out of focus. There was only the grinding of Miriam Bancroft's hips over me, and fragmented glimpses of her body and face wrapped in colored light. When I came, it was a distant explosion that seemed to have more to do with the woman shuddering to a halt astride me than with my own sleeve.

Later, as we lay side by side, hands milking each other through further inconclusive peaks and troughs, she said, "What do you think of me?"

I looked down the length of my body to what her hand was doing, and cleared my throat.

"Is that a trick question?"

She laughed, the same throaty cough that I had warmed to in the chart room at Suntouch House.

"No. I want to know."

"Do you care?" It was not said harshly, and somehow the Merge Nine leached it of its brutal overtones.

"You think that's what it is to be a Meth?" The word sounded strange on her lips, as though she were not talking about herself. "You think we don't care about anything young?"

"I don't know," I said truthfully. "It's a point of view that I've heard. Living three hundred years is bound to change your perspectives."

"Yes, it does." Her breath caught slightly as my fingers slid inside her. "Yes, like that. But you don't stop caring. You see it all sliding past you. And all you want to do is grab on, hold on to something, to stop it all from draining away."

"Is that right?"

"Yes, it is. So what do you think of me?"

I leaned over her and looked at the young woman's body she inhabited, the fine lines of her face, and the old, old eyes. I was still stoned on the Merge Nine, and I couldn't find a flaw anywhere in her. She was the most beautiful thing I had ever seen. I gave up the struggle for objectivity and bowed my head to kiss her on one breast.

"Miriam Bancroft, you are a wonder to behold, and I would willingly trade my soul to possess you."

She staved off a chuckle. "I'm serious. Do you like me?"

"What kind of a question—"

"I'm serious." The words were grounded deeper than the empathin. I pulled in some control and looked her in the eyes.

"Yes," I said simply. "I like you."

Her voice lowered into her throat. "Do you like what we did?"

"Yes, I like what we did."

"Do you want more?"

"Yes, I want more."

She sat up to face me. The milking motions of her hand grew harder, more demanding. Her voice hardened to match. "Say it again."

"I want more. Of you."

She pushed me down with a hand flat on my chest and leaned over me. I was growing back to somewhere near a full erection. She started to time her strokes, slow and sharp.

"Out west," she murmured, "about five hours away by cruiser, there's an island. It's mine. No one goes there, there's a fifty-kilometer exclusion umbrella, satellite patrolled, but it's beautiful. I've built a complex there, with a clone bank and a resleeving facility." Her voice got that uneven edge in it again. "I sometimes decant the clones. Sleeve copies of myself. To play. Do you understand what I'm offering you?"

I made a noise. The image she had just planted, of being the focus for a pack of bodies like this one, all orchestrated by the same mind, tightened the last notches on my hard-on, and her hand slid up and down its full length as if machined there.

"What was that?" She leaned over me, brushing her nipples across my chest.

"How long," I managed, through the coiling and uncoiling of my stomach muscles, through the flesh and mist tones of the Merge Nine, "is this fun park invitation good for?"

She grinned then, a grin of pure lechery.

"Unlimited rides," she said.

"But for a limited period only, right?"

She shook her head. "No, you don't understand me. This place is mine. All of it, the island, the sea around it, everything on it, is mine. I can keep you there as long as you care to stay. Until you tire of it."

"That might take a long time."

"No." There was a hint of sadness in the way she shook her head this time, and her gaze fell a little. "No, it won't."

The pistoning grip on my penis slackened fractionally. I groaned and grabbed at her hand, forcing it back into motion. The move seemed to rekindle her, and she went to work again in earnest, speeding up and slowing down, bending to feed me her breasts or supplement her strokes with sucking and licking. My time perception spiraled out of sight to be replaced with an endless gradient of sensation that sloped upward, excruciatingly slowly, toward a peak I could hear myself begging for in drugged tones somewhere far away.

As the orgasm loomed, I was vaguely aware through the Merge Nine link that she was sinking fingers into herself, rubbing with an uncontrolled desire completely at odds with the calculation with which she manipulated me. Fine-tuned by the empathin, she brought on her own peak a few seconds before mine, and as I started to come, she smeared her own juices hard over my face and thrashing body.

Whiteout.

And when I came to, much later, with the Merge Nine crash laid across me like a lead weight, she was gone like a fever dream.

CHAPTEr ELEVEN

When you have no friends, and the woman you slept with last night has left you with a screaming head and without a word, you have a limited number of options. When I was younger I used to go out looking for squalid brawls in the streets of Newpest. This got a couple of people stabbed, neither of them me, and led in turn to my apprenticeship in one of the Harlan's World gangs, Newpest chapter. Later on I upgraded this kind of retreat by joining the military: brawling with a purpose, and with more extensive weaponry, but as it turned out, just as squalid. I don't suppose I should have been as surprised as I was—the only thing the Marine Corps recruiters had really wanted to know was how many fights I had won.

These days I've evolved a slightly less destructive response to general chemical malaise. When a forty-minute swim in the Hendrix's underground pool failed to dispel either the longing for Miriam Bancroft's torrid company or the Merge Nine hangover, I did the only thing I felt equipped for. I ordered painkillers from room service, and went shopping.

Bay City had already settled into the swing of the day by the time I finally hit the streets, and the commercial center was choked with pedestrians. I stood on the edges for a couple of minutes, then dived in and began to look in windows.

A blonde marine sergeant with the unlikely name of Serenity Carlyle taught me to shop, back on the World. Prior to that I had always employed a technique best described as precision purchase. You identify your target, you go in, get it, and come out. You can't get what you want, cut your losses and get out equally fast. Over the period that we spent together, Serenity weaned me off this approach and sold me her philosophy of consumer grazing.

"Look," she told me one day in a Millsport coffeehouse. "Shopping—actual, physical shopping—could have been phased out centuries ago if they'd wanted it that way."

"They who?"

"People. Society." She waved a hand impatiently. "Whoever. They had the capacity back then. Mail order, virtual supermarkets, automated debiting systems. It could have been done and it never happened. What does that tell you?"

At twenty-two years old, a Marine Corps grunt via the street gangs of Newpest, it told me nothing. Carlyle took in my blank look and sighed.

"It tells you that people *like* shopping. That it satisfies a basic, acquisitive need at a genetic level. Something we inherited from our hunter-gatherer ancestors. Oh, you've got automated convenience shopping for basic household items, mechanical food distribution systems for the marginalized poor. But you've also got a massive proliferation of commercial hives and speciality markets in food and crafts that people physically have to *go to*. Now why would they do that, if they didn't enjoy it?"

I probably shrugged, maintaining my youthful cool.

"Shopping is physical interaction, exercise of decision-making capacity, sating of the desire to acquire, and an impulse to more acquisition, a scouting urge. It's so basically fucking human when you think about it. You've got to learn to love it, Tak. I mean you can cross the whole archipelago on a hover; you never even need to get wet. But that doesn't take the basic pleasure out of swimming, does it? Learn to shop *well*, Tak. Get flexible. Enjoy the uncertainty."

Enjoyment wasn't exactly what I was feeling at the moment, but I stuck with it and I stayed flexible, true to Serenity Carlyle's creed. I started out vaguely looking for a heavy-duty waterproof jacket, but the thing that finally pulled me into a shop was a pair of all-terrain walking boots.

The boots were followed by loose black trousers and a crossover insulated top with enzyme seals that ran all the way from waist to a tight crew neck. I'd seen variations on the outfit a hundred times on the streets of Bay City so far. Surface assimilation. It would do. After brief hungover reflection, I added a defiant red silk bandanna across my forehead, Newpest gang style. It wasn't exactly assimilative, but it went with the vaguely mutinous irritation that had been rising in me since yesterday. I dumped Bancroft's summer suit in a trash bin on the street outside and left the shoes beside it.

Before I left it, I searched through the jacket pockets and came up with two cards—the doctor at Bay City Central and Bancroft's armorer.

Larkin and Green proved to be the names not of two gunsmiths but of two streets that intersected on a leafy slope called Russian Hill. The autocab had some visitor's blurb about the area, but I skipped it. LARKIN AND GREEN— ARMORERS SINCE 2203 was a discreet corner facade, extending less than a half-dozen meters along each street, but bordered by blinded units that looked as if they had probably been annexed. I pushed through well-cared-for wooden doors into the cool, oil-smelling interior.

Inside, the place reminded me of the chart room at Suntouch House. There was space, and light flooding in from two stories of tall windows. The upper floor had been removed and replaced with a wide gallery on four sides overlooking the ground level. The walls were hung with flat display cases, and the space under the gallery overhang hosted heavy, glass-topped trolleys that performed the same function. There was the faint tang of an ambient modifier in the air, scent of old trees under the gun oil, and the floor under my newly booted feet was carpeted.

A black steel face appeared over the gallery rail. Green photoreceptors burned in place of eyes. "May I be of assistance, sir?"

"I'm Takeshi Kovacs. I'm here from Laurens Bancroft," I said, tipping my head back to meet the mandroid's gaze. "I'm looking for some hardware."

"Of course, sir." The voice was smoothly male and devoid of any sales subsonics I could detect. "Mr. Bancroft told us to expect you. I am with a client, but I shall be down presently. Please make yourself at home. There are chairs to your left and a refreshments cabinet. Please help yourself."

The head disappeared, and a murmured conversation I had vaguely registered when I came in was resumed. I located the refreshments cabinet, found it stocked with alcohol and cigars, and closed it hurriedly. The painkillers had taken the edge off the Merge Nine hangover, but I was in no fit state for further abuse. With a light shock, I realized I'd gone through the day so far without a cigarette. I wandered over to the nearest display case and looked in at a selection of samurai swords. There were date tickets attached to the scabbards. Some of them were older than me.

The next case held a rack of brown and gray projectile weapons that seemed to have been grown rather than machined. The barrels sprouted from organically curved wrappings that flared gently back to the stock. These, too, were dated back into the last century. I was trying to decipher the curled engraving on a barrel, when I heard a metallic tread on the staircase behind me.

"Has sir found anything to his liking?"

I turned to face the approaching mandroid. Its entire body was the same polished gunmetal, molded into the muscle configuration of an archetypal human male. Only the genitals were absent. The face was long and thin, fine featured enough to hold attention despite its immobility. The head was carved into furrows to represent thick, back-combed hair. Stamped across the chest was the almost eroded legend MARS EXPO 2076.

"Just looking," I said, and gestured back at the guns. "Are these made of wood?"

The green photoreceptor gaze regarded me gravely. "That is correct, sir. The stocks are a beech hybrid. They are all handmade weapons. Kalashnikov, Purdey, and Beretta. We stock all the European houses here. Which was sir interested in?"

I looked back. There was a curious poetry to the forms, something slung partway between functional bluntness and organic grace, something that cried out to be cradled. To be used.

"They're a bit ornate for me. I had in mind something a little more practical."

"Certainly, sir. Can we assume sir is not a novice in this field?"

I grinned at the machine. "We can assume that."

"Then perhaps sir would care to tell me what his preferences in the past have been."

"Smith and Wesson eleven-millimeter magnum. Ingram 40 flechette gun. Sunjet particle thrower. But that wasn't in this sleeve."

The green receptors glowed. No comment. Perhaps it hadn't been programmed for light conversation with Envoys.

"And what exactly is sir looking for in this sleeve?"

I shrugged. "Something subtle. Something not. Projectile weapons. And a blade. The heavy one needs to be something like the Smith."

The mandroid became quite still. I could almost hear the whirring of data retrieval. I wondered briefly how a machine like this had come to wind up here. It had clearly not been designed for the job. On Harlan's World, you don't see many mandroids. They're expensive to build, compared to a synthetic or even a clone, and most jobs that require a human form are better done by those organic alternatives. The truth is that a robot human is a pointless collision of two disparate functions: artificial intelligence, which really works better strung out on a mainframe, and hard-wearing, hazard-proof bodywork, which most cyberengineering firms designed to spec for the task at hand. The last robot I'd seen on the World was a gardening crab.

The photoreceptors brightened slightly, and the thing's posture unlocked. "If sir would care to come this way, I believe I have the right combination."

I followed the machine through a door that blended so well with the decor of the back wall that I hadn't seen it and down a short corridor. Beyond was a long, low room whose unpainted plaster walls were lined with raw fiberglass packing cases. There were a number of people working quietly at points up and down the room. The air carried the businesslike rattle of hardware in practiced hands. The mandroid led me to a small, gray-haired man dressed in grease-streaked coveralls who was stripping down an electromag bolt thrower as if it were a roast chicken. He looked up as we approached.

"Chip?" He nodded at the machine and ignored me.

"Clive, this is Takeshi Kovacs. He's a friend of Mr. Bancroft, looking for equipment. I'd like you to show him the Nemex and a Philips gun, and then pass him on to Sheila for a blade weapon."

Clive nodded again and set aside the electromag.

"This way," he said.

The mandroid touched my arm lightly. "Should sir require anything further, I shall be in the showroom."

It bowed fractionally and left. I followed Clive along the rows of packing cases to where a variety of handguns were laid out on piles of plastic confetti. He selected one and turned back to me with it in his hands.

"Second series Nemesis X," he said, holding out the gun. "The Nemex. Manufactured under license for Mannlicher-Schoenauer. Fires a jacketed slug with a customized propellant called Druck 31. Very powerful, very accurate. The magazine takes eighteen shells in a staggered clip. Bit bulky but worth it in a firefight. Feel the weight."

I took the weapon and turned it over in my hands. It was a big, heavy-barreled pistol, slightly longer than the Smith & Wesson but well balanced. I swapped it hand to hand for a while, getting the feel of it, squinted down the sight. Clive waited beside me patiently.

"All right." I handed it back. "And something subtle?"

"Philips squeeze gun." Clive reached into an open packing case and dug inside the confetti until he came up with a slim gray pistol almost half the size of the Nemex. "A solid steel load. Uses an electromagnetic accelerator. Completely silent, accurate up to about twenty meters. No recoil, and you've got a reverse field option on the generator that means the slugs can be retrieved from the target afterwards. Takes ten."

"Batteries?"

"Specs are for between forty and fifty discharges. After that, you're losing muzzle velocity with every shot. You get two replacement batteries included in the price and a recharging kit compatible with household power outlets."

"Do you have a firing range? Somewhere I can try these out?"

"Out the back. But both these babies come with a virtual combat practice disk, and that's perfect parity between virtual and actual performance. Warranty guarantees it."

"All right, fine." Collecting on a guarantee like that might prove a slow process if some cowboy used the resulting unhandiness to put a bullet through your skull. No telling when you might get resleeved, if at all. But by now the ache in my head was beginning to get through the painkillers. Maybe target practice wasn't the thing right at that moment. I didn't bother asking the price either. It wasn't my money I was spending. "Ammunition?"

"Comes in boxes of five, both guns, but you get a free clip with the Nemex. Sort of a promotion for the new line. That going to be enough?"

"Not really. Give me two five-packs for both guns."

"Ten clips each?" There was a dubious respect in Clive's voice. Ten clips is a lot of ammunition for a handgun, but I'd discovered that there were times when being able to fill the air with bullets was worth a lot more than actually hitting anything. "And you wanted a blade, right?"

"That's right."

"Sheila!" Clive turned away down the long room and called out to a tall woman with crewcut blonde hair who was sitting cross-legged on a crate with her hands in her lap and the matte-gray of a virtual set masking her face. She looked around when she heard her name, remembered the mask, and tipped it off, blinking. Clive waved at her, and she uncoiled herself from the crate, swaying slightly from the shift back to reality as she got up.

"Sheila, this guy's looking for steel. You want to help him out?"

"Sure." The woman reached out a lanky arm. "Name's Sheila Sorenson. What kind of steel you looking for?"

I matched her grip. "Takeshi Kovacs. I need something I can throw in a hurry, but it's got to be small. Something I can strap to a forearm."

"All right," she said amiably. "Want to come with me? You finished here?"

Clive nodded at me. "I'll take this stuff out to Chip, and he'll package it up for you. You want it for delivery or carryout?"

"Carryout."

"Thought so."

Sheila's end of the business turned out to be a small rectangular room with a couple of silhouette cork targets on one wall and an array of weapons ranging from stilettos to machetes hung on the other three. She selected a flat black knife with a gray metal blade about fifteen centimeters long and took it down.

"Tebbit knife," she said inconsequentially. "Very nasty."

And with every appearance of casualness she turned and unleashed the weapon at the left-hand target. It skipped through the air like something alive and buried itself in the silhouette's head. "Tantalum steel alloy blade, webbed carbon hilt. There's a flint set in the pommel for weighting, and of course you can bash them over the head with that if you don't get them with the sharp end."

I stepped across to the target and freed the knife. The blade was narrow and honed to a razor's edge on each side. A shallow gutter ran down the center, delineated with a thin red line that had tiny, intricate characters etched into it. I tilted the weapon in an attempt to read the engraving, but it was in a code I didn't recognize. Light glinted dully off the gray metal.

"What's this?"

"What?" Sheila moved to stand beside me. "Oh, yeah. Bioweapon coding. The runnel is coated with C-381. Produces cyanide compounds on contact with hemoglobin. Well away from the edges, so if you cut yourself there's no problem, but if you sink it in anything with blood . . ."

"Charming."

"Told you it was nasty, didn't I." There was pride in her voice.

"I'll take it."

Back out on the street, weighed down with my purchases, it occurred to me I'd need a jacket after all, if only to conceal the newly acquired arsenal. I cast a glance upward in search of an autocab and decided instead that there was enough sun in the sky to justify walking. I thought, at last, that my hangover was beginning to recede.

I was three blocks down the hill before I realized I was being tailed.

It was the Envoy conditioning, stirring sluggishly to life in the wake of the Merge Nine, that told me. Enhanced proximity sense, the faintest shiver, and a figure in the corner of my eye once too often. This one was good. In a more crowded part of town I might have missed it, but here the pedestrians were too thin on the ground to provide much camouflage.

The Tebbit knife was strapped to my left forearm in a soft leather sheath with neural spring-load, but neither of the guns were accessible without making it obvious that I'd spotted my shadow. I debated trying to lose the tail, but abandoned the idea almost as soon as it occurred to me. It wasn't my town, I felt sludgy with chemicals, and anyway I was carrying too much. Let whoever it was come shopping with me. I picked up my pace a little and worked my way gradually down into the commercial center, where I found an expensive thigh-length red and blue wool coat with Inuit-inspired totem pole figures chasing each other in lines across it. It wasn't quite what I'd had in mind, but it was warm and had numerous capacious pockets. Paying for it at the shop's glass front, I managed to catch a glimpse of my tail's face. Young, Caucasian, dark hair. I didn't know him.

The two of us crossed Union Square, pausing to take in another Resolution 653 demonstration that had stalled in a corner and was gradually wearing thin. The chants wavered, people drifted away, and the metallic bark of the PA system was beginning to sound plaintive. There was a good chance I could have slipped away in the crowd, but by now I couldn't be bothered. If the tail had been going to do anything other than watch, he'd had his chance back in the leafy seclusion of the hills. There was too much going on here for a hit. I steered my way through the remnants of the demonstration, brushing aside the odd leaflet, and then headed south toward Mission Street and the Hendrix.

On my way down Mission, I stepped inadvertently into the cast radius of a street seller. Instantly, my head flooded with images. I was moving along an alley full of women whose clothing was designed to display more than they would have shown of themselves naked. Boots that turned legs into slices of consumer flesh above the knee, thighs with arrow-shaped bands pointing the way, structural support lifting and pressing breasts out for view, heavy rounded pendants nestling glanlike in sweat-beaded cleavages. Tongues flickered out, licked across lips painted cherry red or tomb black, teeth bared in challenge.

A tide of cool swept in across me, erasing the sweaty need and turning the posturing bodies into an abstract expression of womanhood. I found myself tracking angles and the circumferences of bulges like a machine, mapping the geometry of flesh and bone as if the women were a species of plant.

Betathanatine. The Reaper.

Final offspring of an extended chemical family engineered for near-death research projects early in the millennium, betathanatine brought the human body as close to flat-line status as was feasible without gross cellular damage. At the same time, control stimulants in the Reaper molecule induced a clinical functioning of intellect, which had enabled researchers to go through artificially induced death experiences without the overwhelming sense of emotion and wonder that might mar their data perception. Used in smaller doses, Reaper produced a depth of cool indifference to such things as pain, arousal, joy, and grief. All the detachment that men had pretended for centuries before the naked female form was there for the taking, in capsule. It was almost custom built for the male adolescent market.

It was also an ideal military drug. Riding the Reaper, a Godwin's Dream renouncer monk could torch a village full of women and children and feel nothing but fascination for the way the flames melted flesh from bone.

The last time I'd used betathanatine had been in street battles on Sharya. A full dose, designed to bring body temperature down to room normal and slow my heart to a fractional rate. Tricks to beat the antipersonnel detectors on Sharyan spider tanks. With no register on infrared, you could get up close, scale a leg, and crack the hatches with termite grenades. Concussed by the shockwave, the crew usually slaughtered as easily as newborn kittens.

"Got Stiff, man," a hoarse voice said redundantly. I blinked away the broadcast and found myself looking at a pale Caucasian face beneath a gray cowl. The broadcast unit sat on his shoulder, tiny red active lights winking at me like bat eyes. On the World there are very tight laws regulating the use of direct-to-head dissemination, and even accidental broadcasts can generate the same kind of violence as spilling someone's drink in a wharf-front bar. I shot out one arm and shoved the dealer hard in the chest. He staggered against a shopfront.

"Hey—"

"Don't piss in my head, friend. I don't like it."

I saw his hand snake down to a unit at his waist and guessed what was coming. Retargeting, I got the soft of his eyes under my stiffened fingers . . .

And was face-to-face with a hissing mound of wet membranous flesh nearly two meters tall. Tentacles writhed at me, and my hand was reaching into a phlegm-streaked hollow framed with thick black cilia. My gorge rose and my throat closed up. Riding out a shudder of revulsion, I pushed into the seething cilia and felt the slimy flesh give.

"You want to go on seeing, you'll unplug that shit," I said tightly.

The mound of flesh vanished, and I was back with the dealer, fingers still pressed hard onto the upper curves of his eyeballs.

"All right, man, all right." He held up his hands, palms out. "You don't want the stuff, don't buy it. I'm just trying to make a living here."

I stepped back and gave him the space to get off the shopfront he was pinned to.

"Where I come from, you don't go into people's heads on the street," I offered by way of explanation. But he'd already sensed my retreat from the confrontation, and he just made a gesture with his thumb that I assumed was obscene.

"I give a fuck where you're from? Fucking grasshopper? Get out of my face."

I left him there, wondering idly as I crossed the street if there was any moral difference between him and the genetic designers who had built Merge Nine into Miriam Bancroft's sleeve.

I paused on a corner and bent my head to kindle a cigarette.

Midafternoon. My first of the day.

CHAPTEr TWELVE

As I dressed in front of the mirror that night, I suffered the hard-edged conviction that someone else was wearing my sleeve and that I had been reduced to the role of a passenger in the observation car behind the eyes.

Psychoentirety rejection, they call it. Or just fragmenting. It's not unusual to get some tremors, even when you're an experienced sleeve changer, but this was the worst case I'd had for years. For long moments, I was literally terrified to have a detailed thought, in case the man in the mirror noticed my presence. Frozen, I watched him adjust the Tebbit knife in its neurospring sheath, pick up the Nemex and the Philips gun one by one and check the load of each weapon. The slug guns had both come equipped with cheap fibergrip holsters that enzyme-bonded to clothing wherever they were pressed. The man in the mirror settled the Nemex under his left arm where it would be hidden by his jacket and stowed the Philips gun in the small of his back. He practiced snatching the guns from their holsters a couple of times, throwing them out at his reflection, but there was no need. The virtual practice disks had lived up to Clive's promises. He was ready to kill someone with either weapon.

I shifted behind his eyes.

Reluctantly, he stripped off the guns and the knife and laid them once more on the bed. Then he stood for a while until the unreasonable feeling of nakedness had passed.

The weakness of weapons, Virginia Vidaura had called it, and from day one in Envoy training it was considered a cardinal sin to fall into it.

A weapon—any weapon—is a tool, she told us. Cradled in her arms was a Sunjet particle gun. *Designed for a specific purpose, just as any tool is, and only useful in that purpose. You would think a man a fool to carry a force hammer with him everywhere simply because he is an engineer. And as it is with engineers, so it is doubly with Envoys.*

In the ranks, Jimmy de Soto coughed his amusement. At the time he was speaking for most of us. Ninety percent of Envoy intake came up through the Protectorate's conventional forces, where weaponry generally held a status somewhere between that of toy and personal fetish. U.N. marines went everywhere armed, even on furlough.

Virginia Vidaura heard the cough and caught Jimmy's eye.

"Mr. de Soto. You do not agree."

Jimmy shifted, a little abashed at how easily he had been picked out. "Well, ma'am. My experience has been that the more punch you carry, the better account you give of yourself."

There was a faint of ripple of assent through the ranks. Virginia Vidaura waited until it subsided.

"Indeed," she said, and held out the particle thrower in both hands. "This . . . device punches somewhat. Please come here and take it."

Jimmy hesitated a little, but then pushed his way to the front and took the weapon. Virginia Vidaura fell back so that Jimmy was center stage before the assembled trainees, and stripped off her corps jacket. In the sleeveless coveralls and spacedeck slippers, she looked slim and very vulnerable.

"You will see," she said loudly, "that the charge setting is at Test. If you hit me, it will result in a small first-degree burn, nothing more. I am at a distance of approximately five meters. I am unarmed. Mr. de Soto, would you care to attempt to mark me? On your call."

Jimmy looked startled, but he duly brought the Sunjet up to check the setting, then lowered it and looked at the woman opposite him.

"On your call," she repeated.

"*Now,*" he snapped.

It was almost impossible to follow. Jimmy was swinging the Sunjet as the word left his mouth, and in approved firefight fashion, he cut the charge loose before the barrel even reached the vertical. The air filled with the particle thrower's characteristic angry crackle. The beam licked out. Virginia Vidaura was not there. Somehow she had judged the angle of the beam to perfection and ducked away from it. Somehow else, she had closed the five-meter gap by half and the jacket in her right hand was in motion. It wrapped around the barrel of the Sunjet and jerked the weapon aside. She was on Jimmy before he realized what had happened, batting the particle thrower away across the training room floor, tripping and tumbling him, and bringing the heel of one palm gently to rest under his nose.

The moment stretched and then broke as the man next to me pursed his lips and blew out a long, low whistle. Virginia Vidaura bowed her head slightly in the direction of the sound, then bounced to her feet and helped Jimmy up.

"A weapon is a tool," she repeated, a little breathlessly. "A tool for killing and destroying. And there will be times when, as an Envoy, you must kill and destroy. Then you will choose and equip yourself with the tools that you need. But remember the weakness of weapons. They are an extension—*you* are the killer and destroyer. You are whole, with or without them."

Shrugging his way into the Inuit jacket, he met his own eyes in the mirror once more. The face he saw looking back was no more expressive than the mandroid at Larkin and Green. He stared impassively at it for a moment, then lifted one hand to rub at the scar under the left eye. A final glance up and down and I left the room with the sudden, cold resurgence of control flooding through my nerves. Riding down in the elevator, away from the mirror, I forced a grin.

Got the frags, Virginia.

Breathe, she said. *Move. Control.*

And we went out into the street. The Hendrix offered me a courteous good evening as I stepped through the main doors, and across the street my tail emerged from a teahouse and drifted along parallel to me. I walked for a couple of blocks, getting the feel of the evening and wondering whether to lose him. The halfhearted sunlight had persisted for most of the day and the sky was more or less unclouded, but it still wasn't warm. According to a map I'd called up from the Hendrix, Licktown was a good dozen and a half blocks south. I paused on a corner, signaled an autocab down from the prowl lane above, and saw my tail doing the same as I climbed aboard.

He was beginning to annoy me.

The cab curved away southward. I leaned forward and passed a hand over the visitor's blurb panel.

"Welcome to Urbline Services," a smooth female voice said. "You are linked to the Urbline central data stack. Please state the information you require."

"Are there any unsafe areas in Licktown?"

"The zone designated Licktown is generally considered to be unsafe in its entirety," the data stack said blandly. "However, Urbline Services guarantees carriage to any destination within the Bay City limits and—"

"Yeah. Can you give me a street reference for the highest incidence of violent criminality in the Licktown area?"

There was a brief pause while the datahead went down rarely used channels.

"Nineteenth Street, the blocks between Missouri and Wisconsin show fifty-three incidences of organic damage over the last year. One hundred seventy-seven prohibited substance arrests, one hundred twenty-two with incidence of minor organic damage, two hun—"

"That's fine. How far is it from Jerry's Closed Quarters, Mariposa and San Bruno?"

"Straight-line distance is approximately one kilometer."

"Got a map?"

The console lit up with a street grid, complete with location crosshairs for Jerry's and the names of the streets fired in green. I studied it for a couple of moments.

"All right. Drop me there. Nineteenth and Missouri."

"As part of our customer charter, it is my duty to warn you that this is not an advisable destination."

I sat back and felt the grin creeping back onto my face, unforced this time. "Thanks."

The cab set me down, without further protest, at the cross of Nineteenth and Missouri. I glanced around as I climbed out and grinned again. *Inadvisable destination* had been a typical machine understatement.

Where the streets I'd chased the Mongol through the night before were deserted, this part of Licktown was alive, and its inhabitants made Jerry's clientele look almost salubrious. As I paid off the autocab, a dozen heads swiveled to focus on me, none of them wholly human. I could almost feel mechanical photomultiplier eyes ratcheting in from a distance on the currency I'd chosen to pay with, seeing the notes in ghostly luminescent green, canine-augmented nostrils twitching with the scent of my hotel bath gel, the whole crowd picking up the blip of wealth on their street sonar like the trace of a bottleback shoal on a Millsport skipper's screen.

The second cab was spiraling down behind me. An unlit alley beckoned, less than a dozen meters away. I'd barely stepped into it when the first of the locals made their play.

"You looking for something, tourist?"

There were three of them, the lead vocalist a two-and-a-half-meter giant naked to the waist with what looked like Nakamura's entire muscle-graft sales for the year wrapped around his arms and trunk. There were red illuminum tattoos under the skin of his pectorals so his chest looked like a dying coal fire, and a glans-headed cobra reared up the ridged muscle of his stomach from his waistline. The hands that hung open at his sides were tipped with filed talons. His face was seamed with scar tissue from the Freak Fights he had lost, and there was a cheap prosthetic magnilens screwed into one eye. His voice was surprisingly soft and sad sounding.

"Come slumming, maybe," the figure on the giant's right said viciously. He was young and slim and pale with long, fine hair falling across his face, and there was a twitchiness about his stance that said cheap neurachem. He would be the fastest.

The third member of the welcoming committee said nothing, but lips peeled back from a canine snout to show transplanted predator teeth and an unpleasantly long tongue. Below the surgically augmented head, the body was male human beneath tightly strapped leather.

Time was shortening. My tail would be paying off his cab, getting his bearings. If he'd decided to take the risk. I cleared my throat.

"I'm just passing through. You're wise, you'll let me. There's a citizen landing back there you'll find easier to take."

There was a brief, disbelieving pause. Then the giant reached for me. I brushed away his hand, fell back a step, and wove a rapid pattern of obvious killing strikes into the air between us. The trio froze, the canine augment snarling. I drew breath.

"Like I said, you're wise you'll let me pass."

The giant was ready to let it go. I could see it in his broken face. He'd been a fighter long enough to spot combat training, and the instincts of a lifetime in the ring told him when the balance was tipped. His two companions were younger and knew less about losing. Before he could say anything, the pale kid with the neurachem lashed out with something sharp, and the augment went for my right arm. My own neurachem, already ticking over and probably more pricey, was faster. I took the kid's arm and broke it at the elbow, twisting him around on his own pain and into his two companions. The augment ducked around him, and I kicked out, connecting hard with nose and mouth. A yelp and he went down. The kid dropped to his knees, keening and nursing his shattered elbow. The giant surged forward and fetched up with the stiffened fingers of my right hand a centimeter from his eyes.

"Don't," I said quietly.

The kid moaned on the ground at our feet. Behind him, the canine augment lay where the kick had thrown him, twitching feebly. The giant crouched between them, big hands reaching as if to comfort. He looked up at me, mute accusation for something in his face.

I backed away down the alley about a dozen meters, then turned and sprinted. Let my tail work his way through that and catch me up.

The alley made a right-angle turn before spilling out onto another crowded street. I turned the corner and let my speed run down so that I emerged into the street at a fast walk. Turning left, I shouldered my way into the midst of the crowd and started looking for street signs.

Outside Jerry's, the woman was still dancing, imprisoned in the cocktail glass. The club sign was alight, and business seemed, if anything, to be brisker than the previous night. Small knots of people came and went beneath the flexing arms of the door robot, and the dealers I'd injured during the fight with the Mongol had been replaced several times over.

I crossed the street and stood before the robot while it patted me down, and the synth voice said, "Clear. Do you want cabins or bar?"

"What's the deal in the bar?"

"Ha ha ha," went the laugh protocol. "The bar is *look*, but don't *touch*. No money down, no hands on. House rule. That applies to other customers, too."

"Cabins."

"Down the stairs, to the left. Take a towel from the pile."

Down the stairs, along the corridor lit in rotating red, past the towel alcove and the first four closed cabin doors. Blood-deep thunder of the junk rhythm in the air. I closed the fifth door behind me, fed a few notes to the credit console for appearances' sake, and stepped up to the frosted glass screen.

"Louise?"

The curves of her body thudded against the glass, breasts flattened. The cherry light in the cabin flung stripes of light across her.

"Louise, it's me. Irene. Lizzie's mother."

A smear of something dark between the breasts, across the glass. The neurachem leapt alive inside me. Then the glass door hinged open and the girl's body sagged off its inner surface into my arms. A wide-muzzled gun appeared over her shoulder, pointed at my head.

"Right there, fucker," a tight voice said. "This is a toaster. You do one wrong thing, it'll take your head off your chest and turn your stack to solder."

I froze. There was an urgency in the voice that wasn't far off panic. Very dangerous.

"That's it." The door behind me opened, gusting the pulse of the music in the corridor, and a second gun muzzle jammed into my back. "Now you put her down, real slow, and stand back."

I lowered the body in my arms gently onto the satin-padded floor and stood up again. Bright white light sprang up in the cabin, and the revolving cherry blinked pinkly twice and went out. The door behind me thudded shut on the music while before me, a tall, blond man in close-fitting black advanced into the room, knuckles whitened on the trigger of his particle blaster. His mouth was compressed and the whites of his eyes were flaring around stimulant-blasted pupils. The gun in my back bore me forward and the blond kept coming until the muzzle of the blaster was smearing my lower lip against my teeth.

"Now who the *fuck* are you?" he hissed at me.

I turned my head aside far enough to open my mouth. "Irene Elliott. My daughter used to work here."

The blond stepped forward, gun muzzle tracing a line down my cheek and under my chin.

"You're lying to me," he said softly. "I've got a friend out at the Bay City Justice Facility, and he tells me Irene Elliott's still on stack. See, we checked out the bag of shit you sold this cunt."

He kicked at the inert body on the floor, and I peered down out of the corner of my nearest eye. In the harsh white light the marks of torture were livid on the girl's flesh.

"Now I want you to think real carefully about your next answer, whoever you are. Why are you asking after Lizzie Elliott?"

I slid my eyes back over the barrel of the blaster to the clenched face beyond. It wasn't the expression of someone who'd been dealt in. Too scared.

"Lizzie Elliott's my daughter, you piece of shit, and if your friend up at the city store had any real access, you'd know why the record still says I'm on stack."

The gun in my back shoved forward more sharply, but unexpectedly the blond seemed to relax. His mouth flexed in a rictus of resignation. He lowered the blaster.

"All right," he said. "Deek, go and get Oktai."

Someone at my back slipped out of the cabin. The blond waved his gun at me. "You. Sit down in the corner." His tone was distracted, almost casual.

I felt the gun taken out of my back and moved to obey. As I settled onto the satin floor, I weighed the odds. With Deek gone, there were still three of them. The blond; a woman in what looked to me like a synthetic Asian-skinned sleeve, toting the second particle blaster whose imprint I could still feel in my spine; and a large black man whose only weapon appeared to be an iron pipe. Not a chance. These were not the street sharks I'd faced down on Nineteenth Street. There was a cold, embodied purpose about them, a kind of cheap version of what Kadmin had had back at the Hendrix.

For a moment I looked at the synthetic woman and wondered, but it couldn't be. Even if he'd somehow managed to slip the charges Kristin Ortega had talked about and got himself resleeved, Kadmin was on the inside. He knew who had hired him, and who I was. The faces peering at me from around the bio-cabin, on their own admission, knew nothing.

Let's keep it that way.

My gaze crept across to Louise's battered sleeve. It looked as if they had cut slits in the skin of her thighs and then forced the wounds apart until they tore. Simple, crude, and very effective. They would have made her watch while they did it, compounding the pain with terror. It's a gut-swooping experience seeing that happen to your body. On Sharya, the religious police used it a lot. She'd probably need psychosurgery to get over the trauma.

The blond saw where my eyes had gone and offered me a grim nod, as if I'd been an accomplice to the act.

"Want to know why her head's still on, huh?"

I looked bleakly across the room at him. "No. You look like a busy man, but I guess you'll get around to it."

"No need," he said casually, enjoying his moment. "Old Anemone's Catholic. Third or fourth generation, the girls tell me. Sworn affidavit on disk, full Vow of Abstention filed with the Vatican. We take on a lot like that. Real convenient sometimes."

"You talk too much, Jerry," the woman said.

The blond's eyes flared whitely at her, but whatever retort he was mustering behind the curl of his lip quieted as two men, presumably Deek and Oktai, pushed into the tiny room on another wave of junk rhythm from the corridor. My eyes measured Deek and placed him in the same category—*muscle*—as the pipe wielder, then switched to his companion, who was staring steadily at me. My heart twitched. Oktai was the Mongol.

Jerry jerked his head in my direction.

"This him?" he asked.

Oktai nodded slowly, a savage grin of triumph etched across his broad face. His massive hands were clenching and unclenching at his sides. He was working through an extreme of hate so deep it was choking him. I could see the bump where someone had inexpertly repaired his broken nose with tissue weld, but that didn't seem like enough to warrant the fury I was watching.

"All right, Ryker." The blond leaned forward a little. "You want to change your story? You want to tell me why you're breaking my balls down here?"

He was talking to me.

Deek spat into a corner of the room.

"I don't know," I said clearly, "what the fuck you are talking about. You turned my daughter into a prostitute, and then you killed her. And for that, I'm going to kill you."

"I doubt you'll get the chance for that," Jerry said, crouching opposite me and looking at the floor. "Your daughter was a stupid, starstruck little cunt who thought she could put a lock on me and—"

He stopped and shook his head disbelievingly.

"The fuck am I talking to? I *see* you standing there, and still I'm buying this shit. You're good, Ryker, I'll give you that." He sniffed. "Now. I'm going to ask you one more time, nicely. Maybe see if we can cut a deal. After that I'm going to send you to see some very sophisticated friends of mine. You understand what I'm saying?"

I nodded once, slowly.

"Good. So here it comes, Ryker. What are you doing in Licktown?"

I looked into his face. Small-time punk with delusions of connection. I wasn't going to learn anything here.

"Who's Ryker?"

The blond lowered his head again and looked at the floor between my feet. He seemed unhappy about what was going to happen next. Finally he licked his lips, nodded slightly to himself, and made a brushing gesture across his knees as he stood up.

"All right, tough guy. But I want you to remember you had the choice." He turned to the synthetic woman. "Get him out of here. I want no traces. And tell them he's n-wired to the eyes; they'll get nothing out of him in this sleeve."

The woman nodded and gestured me to my feet with her blaster. She prodded Louise's corpse with the toe of one boot. "And this?"

"Get rid of it. Milo, Deek, go with her."

The pipe wielder shoved his weapon into his waistband and stooped to shoulder the corpse as if it were a bundle of kindling. Deek, close behind, slapped it affectionately on one bruised buttock.

The Mongol made a noise in his throat. Jerry glanced across at him with faint distaste. "No, not you. They're going places I don't want you to see. Don't worry, there'll be a disk."

"Sure, man," Deek said over his shoulder. "We'll bring it right back across."

"All right, that's enough," the woman said roughly, moving to face me. "Let's have an understanding here, Ryker. You got neurachem, so do I. And this is a high-impact chassis. Lockheed-Mitoma test pilot specs. You can't damage me worth a jack. And I'll be happy to burn your guts out if you even look at me wrong. They don't care what state you're in where we're going. That clear, Ryker?"

"My name's not Ryker," I said irritably.

"Right."

We went through the frosted glass door, into a tiny space that held a makeup table and shower stall, and out onto a corridor parallel to the one at the front of the booths. Here the lighting was unambiguous, there was no music, and the corridor gave onto larger, partially curtained dressing rooms where young men and women slumped smoking or just staring into space like untenanted synthetics. If any of them saw the little procession go past, they gave no indication. Milo went ahead with the corpse, Deek took up position at my back, and the synthetic woman brought up the rear, blaster held casually at her side. My last glimpse of Jerry was a proprietorial figure standing with hands on hips in the corridor behind us. Then Deek cuffed me across the side of the head, and I turned to face the front again. Louise's dangling, mutilated legs preceded me out into a gloomy covered parking area, where a pure black lozenge of aircar awaited us.

The synthetic cracked the vehicle's trunk open and waved the blaster at me. "Plenty of room. Make yourself comfortable."

I climbed into the trunk and discovered she was right. Then Milo tipped Louise's corpse in with me and slammed the lid down, leaving the two of us in darkness together. I heard the dull clunk of other doors opening and closing elsewhere, and then the whispering of the car's engines and the faint bump as we lifted from the ground.

The journey was quick, and smoother than a corresponding surface trip would have been. Jerry's friends were driving carefully—you don't want to be pulled down by a bored patrolman for unsignaled lane change when you've got passengers in the trunk. It might almost have been pleasantly womblike there in the dark, but for the faint stench of feces from the corpse. Louise had voided her bowels during the torture.

I spent most of the journey feeling sorry for the girl, and worrying at the Catholic madness like a dog with a bone. This woman's stack was utterly undamaged. Financial considerations aside, she could be brought back to life on the spin of a disk. On Harlan's World she'd be temporarily resleeved for the court hearing, albeit probably in a synthetic, and once the verdict came down there'd be a Victim Support supplement from the state added to whatever policy her family already held. Nine cases out of ten, that was enough money to ensure resleeving of some sort. Death, where is thy sting?

I didn't know if they had V.S. supplements on Earth. Kristin Ortega's angry monologue two nights ago seemed to suggest not, but at least there was the potential to bring this girl back to life. Somewhere on this fucked-up planet, some guru had ordained otherwise, and Louise, alias Anemone, had queued up with how many others to ratify the insanity.

Human beings. Never figure them out.

The car tilted and the corpse rolled unpleasantly against me as we spiraled down. Something wet seeped through the leg of my trousers. I could feel myself starting to sweat with the fear. They were going to decant me into some flesh with none of the resistance to pain that my current sleeve had. And while I was imprisoned there, they could do whatever they liked to that sleeve, up to and including physically killing it.

And then they would start again, in a fresh body.

Or, if they were really sophisticated, they could jack my consciousness into a virtual matrix similar to the ones used in psychosurgery, and do the whole thing electronically. Subjectively there'd be no difference, but there what might take days in the real world could be done in as many minutes.

I swallowed hard, using the neurachem while I still had it to stifle the fear. As gently as I could, I pushed Louise's cold embrace away from my face and tried not to think about the reason she had died.

The car touched down and rolled along the ground for a few moments before it stopped. When the trunk cracked open again, all I could see was the roof of another covered parking lot strung with illuminum bars.

They took me out with professional caution, the woman standing well back, Deek and Milo to the sides giving her a clear field of fire. I clambered awkwardly over Louise and out onto a floor of black concrete. Scanning the gloom covertly, I saw about a dozen other vehicles, nondescript, registration bar codes illegible at this distance. A short ramp at the far end led up to what must be the landing pad. Indistinguishable from a million other similar installations. I sighed, and as I straightened up, I felt the damp on my leg again. I glanced down at my clothes. There was a dark stain of something on my thigh.

"So where are we?" I asked.

"End of the line's where you are," Milo grunted, lifting Louise out. He looked at the woman. "This going to the usual place?"

She nodded, and he set off across the parking lot toward a set of double doors. I was moving to follow when a jerk of the woman's blaster brought me up short.

"Not you. That's the chute—the easy way out. We got people want to talk to you before you get to go down the chute. You go this way."

Deek grinned and produced a small weapon from his back pocket. "That's right, Mr. Badass Cop. You go this way."

They marched me through another set of doors into a commercial-capacity elevator, which, according to the flashing LED display on the wall, sank two dozen levels before we stopped. Throughout the ride, Deek and the woman stood in opposite corners of the car, guns leveled. I ignored them and watched the digit counter.

When the doors opened there was a medical team waiting for us with a strap-equipped gurney. My instincts screamed at me to try and jump them, but I held myself immobile while the two pale-blue-clad men came forward to hold my arms and the female medic shot me in the neck with a hypodermic spray. There was an icy sting, a brief rush of cold, and then the corners of my vision disappeared in webbings of gray. The last thing I saw clearly was the incurious face of the medic as she watched me lose consciousness.

CHAPTEr THIrTEEN

I awoke to the sound of the *ezan* being called somewhere nearby, poetry turned querulous and metallic in the multiple throats of a mosque's loudspeakers. It was a sound I'd last heard in the skies over Zihicce on Sharya, and it had been shortly followed by the shrill aerial scream of marauder bombs. Above my head, light streamed down through the latticed bars of an ornate window. There was a dull, bloated feeling in my guts that told me my period was due.

I sat up on the wooden floor and looked down at myself. They'd sleeved me in a woman's body, young, no more than twenty years old, with copper-sheened skin and a heavy bell of black hair that, when I put my hands to it, felt lank and dirty with the onset of the period. My skin was faintly greasy, and from somewhere I got the idea that I had not bathed in a while. I was clothed in a rough khaki shirt several sizes too big for my sleeve, and nothing else. Beneath it, my breasts felt swollen and tender. I was barefoot.

I got up and went to the window. There was no glass but it was well above my new head height, so I hauled myself up on the bars and peered out. A sun-drenched landscape of poorly tiled roofs stretched away as far as I could see, forested with listing receptor aerials and ancient satellite dishes. A cluster of minarets speared the horizon off to the left, and an ascending aircraft trailed a line of white vapor somewhere beyond. The air that blew through was hot and humid.

My arms were beginning to ache, so I lowered myself back down to the floor and padded across the room to the door. Predictably, it was locked.

The *ezan* stopped.

Virtuality. They'd tapped into my memories and come up with this. I'd seen some of the most unpleasant things in a long career of human pain on Sharya. And the Sharyan religious police were as popular in interrogation software as Angin Chandra had been in pilot porn. And now, on this harsh virtual Sharya, they'd sleeved me in a woman.

Drunk one night, Sarah had told me *Women are the race, Tak. No two ways about it. Male is just a mutation with more muscle and half the nerves. Fighting, fucking machines.* My own cross-sleevings had born that theory out. To be a woman was a sensory experience beyond the male. Touch and texture ran deeper, an interface with environment that male flesh seemed to seal out instinctively. To a man, skin was a barrier, a protection. To a woman, it was an organ of contact.

That had its disadvantages.

In general, and maybe because of this, female pain thresholds ran higher than male, but the menstrual cycle dragged them down to an all-time low once a month.

No neurachem. I checked.

No combat conditioning, no reflex of aggression.

Nothing.

Not even callouses on the young flesh.

The door banged open, and I jumped. Fresh sweat sprang out on my skin. Two bearded men with eyes of hot jet came into the room. They were both dressed in loose linen for the heat. One held a role of adhesive tape in his hands, the other a small blowtorch. I flung myself at them, just to unlock the freezing panic reflex and gain some measure of control over the built-in helplessness.

The one with the tape fended off my slim arms and backhanded me across the face. It floored me. I lay there, face numb, tasting blood. One of them yanked me back to my feet by an arm. Distantly, I saw the face of the other, the one who had hit me, and tried to focus on him.

"So," he said. "We begin."

I lunged for his eyes with the nails of my free arm. The Envoy training gave me the speed to get there, but I had no control and I missed. Two of my nails drew blood on his cheek. He flinched and jumped back.

"Bitch cunt," he said, lifting a hand to the claw mark and examining the blood on his fingers.

"Oh, please," I managed, out of the unnumbed side of my mouth. "Do we have to have the script, too? Just because I'm *wearing* this—"

I jammed to a halt. He looked pleased. "*Not* Irene Elliott, then," he said. "We progress."

This time he hit me just under the rib cage, driving all the breath out of my body and paralyzing my lungs. I folded over his arm like a coat and slid off onto the floor, trying to draw breath. All that came out was a faint creaking sound. I twisted on the floorboards while, somewhere high above me, he retrieved the adhesive tape from the other man and unsnapped a quarter-meter length. It made an obscene tearing sound, like skin coming off. Shredding it free with his teeth, he squatted beside me and taped my right wrist to the floor above my head. I thrashed as if galvanized, and it took him a moment to immobilize my other arm long enough to repeat the process. An urge to scream that wasn't mine surfaced, and I fought it down. Pointless. Conserve your strength.

The floor was hard and uncomfortable against the soft skin of my elbows. I heard a grating sound and turned my head. The second man was drawing up a pair of stools from the side of the room. While the one who had beaten me taped my legs apart, the spectator sat down on one of the stools, produced a pack of cigarettes, and shook one out. Grinning broadly at me, he put it in his mouth and reached down for the blowtorch. When his companion stepped back to admire his handiwork, he offered him the pack. It was declined. The smoker shrugged, ignited the blowtorch, and tilted his head to light up from it.

"You will tell us," he said, gesturing with the cigarette and pluming smoke into the air above me, "everything you know about Jerry's Closed Quarters and Elizabeth Elliott."

The blowtorch hissed and chuckled softly to itself in the quiet room. Sunlight poured in through the high window and brought with it, infinitely faintly, the sounds of a city full of people.

They started with my feet.

● ● ●

The screaming runs on and on, higher and louder than I ever believed a human throat could render, shredding my hearing. Traceries of red streak across my vision.

Innenininnenininnenin . . .

Jimmy de Soto staggers into view, Sunjet gone, gory hands plastered to his face. The shrieks peal out from his stumbling figure, and for a moment I can almost believe it's his contamination alarm that's making the noise. I check my own shoulder meter reflexively, then the half-submerged edge of an intelligible word rises through the agony and I know it's him.

He is standing almost upright, a clear-cut sniper target even in the chaos of the bombardment. I throw myself across the open ground and knock him into the cover of a ruined wall. When I roll him onto his back to see what's happened to his face, he's still screaming. I pull his hands away from his face by main force, and the raw socket of his left eye gapes up at me in the murk. I can still see fragments of the eye's mucous casing on his fingers.

"Jimmy, Jimmy, what the fuck . . ."

The screaming sandpapers on and on. It's taking all my strength to prevent him going back for the other undamaged eye as it wallows in its socket. My spine goes cold as I realize what's happening.

Viral strike.

I stop yelling at Jimmy and bawl down the line.

"Medic! Medic! Stack down! Viral strike!"

And the world caves in as I hear my own cries echoed up and down the Innenin beachhead.

● ● ●

After a while, they leave you alone, curled around your wounds. They always do. It gives you time to think about what they have done to you, more importantly what else they have not yet done. The fevered imagining of what is still to come is almost as potent a tool in their hands as the heated irons and blades themselves.

When you hear them returning, the echo of footsteps induces such fear that you vomit up what little bile you have left in your stomach.

●●●

Imagine a satellite blowup of a city on mosaic, 1:10,000 scale. It'll take up most of a decent interior wall, so stand well back. There are certain obvious things you can tell at a glance. Is it a planned development, or did it grow organically, responding to centuries of differing demand? Is it or was it ever fortified? Does it have a seaboard? Look closer, and you can learn more. Where the major thoroughfares are likely to be, if there is an IP shuttleport, if the city has parks. You can maybe, if you're a trained cartographer, even tell a little about the movements of the inhabitants. Where the desirable areas of town are, what the traffic problems are likely to be, and if the city has suffered any serious bomb damage or riots recently.

But there are some things you will never know from that picture. However much you magnify and reel in detail, it can't tell you if crime is generally on the increase, or what time the citizens go to bed. It can't tell you if the mayor is planning to tear down the old quarter, if the police are corrupt, or what strange things have been happening at Number Fifty-one, Angel Wharf. And the fact that you can break down the mosaic into boxes, move it around, and reassemble it elsewhere makes no difference. Some things you will only ever learn by going into that city and talking to the inhabitants.

Digital human storage hasn't made interrogation obsolescent, it's just brought back the basics. A digitized mind is only a snapshot. You don't capture individual thoughts any more than a satellite image captures an individual life. A psychosurgeon can pick out major traumas on an Ellis model and make a few basic guesses about what needs to be done, but in the end she's still going to have to generate a virtual environment in which to counsel her patient, and go in there and do it. Interrogators, whose requirements are so much more specific, have an even worse time.

What D.H.S. *has* done is make it possible to torture a human being to death, and then start again. With that option available, hypnotic and drug-based questioning went out the window long ago. It was too easy to provide the necessary chemical or mental counterconditioning in those for whom this sort of thing was a hazard of their trade.

There's no kind of conditioning in the known universe that can prepare you for having your feet burnt off. Or your nails torn out.

Cigarettes stubbed out on your breasts.

A heated iron inserted into your vagina.

The pain. The humiliation.
The damage.

●●●

Psychodynamics / Integrity training.
Introduction.
The mind does interesting things under extreme stress. Hallucination, displacement, retreat. Here in the corps, you will learn to use them all, not as blind reactions to adversity, but as moves in a game.

●●●

The red-hot metal sinks into flesh, parting the skin like polyethylene. The pain consumes, but worse is seeing it happen. Your scream, once disbelief, is by now gruesomely familiar in your ears. You know it won't stop them, but you still scream, begging—

●●●

"Some fucking game, eh, pal?"

Jimmy grinning up at me from his death. Innenin is still around us, but that can't be. He was still screaming when they took him away. In reality—

His face changes abruptly, turns somber.

"You keep reality out of this; there's nothing for you there. Stay removed. Have they done her any structural harm?"

I wince. "Her feet. She can't walk."

"Motherfuckers," he says matter-of-factly. "Why don't we just tell them what they want to know?"

"We don't know what they want to know. They're after this guy Ryker."

"Ryker, who the fuck's he?"

"I don't know."

He shrugs. "So spill about Bancroft. Or you still feeling honor bound or something?"

"I think I already spilled. They don't buy it. It's not what they want to hear. These are fucking amateurs, man. Meatpackers."

"You keep screaming it, they got to believe it sooner or later."

"That isn't the fucking point, Jimmy. When this is over, it doesn't matter who I am, they're going to put a bolt through my stack and sell the body off for spare parts."

"Yeah." Jimmy puts one finger into his empty eye socket and scratches absently at the clotted gore within. "See your point. Well, in a construct situation, what you got to do is get to the next screen somehow. Right?"

●●●

During the period on Harlan's World known, with typical grim humor, as the Unsettlement, guerrillas in the Quellist Black Brigade were surgically implanted with a quarter kilo of enzyme-triggered explosive that would, on demand, turn the surrounding fifty square meters and anything in it to ash. It was a tactic that met with questionable success. The enzyme in question was fury related, and the conditioning required for arming the device was patchy. There were a number of involuntary detonations.

Still, no one ever volunteered to interrogate a member of the Black Brigade. Not after the first one, anyway. Her name—

●●●

You thought they could do nothing worse, but now the iron is inside you and they are letting it heat up slowly, giving you time to think about it. Your pleading is babbled—

●●●

As I was saying . . .

Her name was Iphigenia Deme, Iffy to those of her friends who had not yet been slaughtered by Protectorate Forces. Her last words, strapped to the interrogation table downstairs at Number Eighteen, Shimatsu Boulevard, are reputed to have been: *That's fucking enough!*

The explosion brought the entire building down.

●●●

That's fucking enough.

●●●

I jackknifed awake, the last of my screams still shrilling inside me, hands scrabbling to cover remembered wounds. Instead, I found young, undamaged flesh beneath crisp linen, a faint rocking motion, and the sound of small waves lapping nearby. Above my head was a sloping wooden ceiling and a porthole through which low-angled sunlight flooded. I sat up in the narrow bunk, and the sheet fell away from my breasts. The coppery upper slopes were smooth and unscarred, the nipples intact.

Back to start.

Beside the bed was a simple wooden chair with a white T-shirt and canvas trousers folded neatly over it. There were rope sandals on the floor. The tiny cabin held nothing else of interest apart from another bunk, the twin of mine, whose covers were thrown carelessly back, and a door. A bit crude, but the message was clear. I slipped into the clothes and walked out onto the sunlit deck of a small fishing boat.

"Aha, the dreamer." The woman seated in the stern of the skiff clapped her hands together as I emerged. She was about ten years older than the sleeve I was wearing, and darkly handsome in a suit cut from the same linen as my trousers. There were espadrilles on her bare feet and wide-lensed sunglasses over her eyes. In her lap was a sketch pad shaded with what looked like a cityscape. As I stood there, she set it aside and stood up to greet me. Her movements were elegant, self-assured. I felt gawky by comparison.

I looked over the side at the blue water.

"What is it this time?" I said with forced lightness. "Feed me to the sharks?"

She laughed, showing perfect teeth. "No, that won't be necessary at this stage. All I want to do is talk."

I stood loose limbed, staring at her. "So talk."

"Very well." The woman folded herself gracefully back onto the seat at the stern. "You have . . . involved yourself in matters that are clearly not your affair, and you have suffered as a result. My interest is, I think, identical to yours. That is, to avoid further unpleasantness."

"My interest is in seeing you die."

A small smile. "Yes, I'm sure it is. Even a virtual death would probably be very satisfying. So, at this point, let me point out that the specifics for this construct include fifth-dan Shotokan proficiency."

She extended a hand to show me the callouses on her knuckles. I shrugged.

"Moreover, we can always return to the way things were earlier." She pointed out over the water, and following her arm, I saw the city she had been sketching on the horizon. Squinting into the reflected sunlight, I could make out the minarets. I almost managed to smile at the cheap psychology of it. A boat. The sea. Escape. These boys had bought their programming off the rack.

"I don't want to go back there," I said truthfully.

"Good. Then tell us who you are."

I tried not to let the surprise show on my face. The deep-cover training awoke, spinning lies. "I thought I had."

"What you have said is somewhat confused, and you . . . curtailed the interrogation by stopping your own heart. You are not Irene Elliott, that much is certain. You do not appear to be Elias Ryker, unless he has undergone substantial retraining. You claim a connection with Laurens Bancroft, and also to be an offworlder, a member of the Envoy Corps. This is not what we expected."

"I bet it isn't," I muttered.

"We do not wish to be involved in matters that do not concern us."

"You already are involved. You've abducted and tortured an Envoy. You got any idea what the corps will do to you for that? They'll hunt you down and feed your stacks to the E.M.P. All of you. Then your families, then your business associates, then *their* families, and then anyone else who gets in the way. By the time they've finished, you won't even be a memory. You don't fuck with the corps and live to write songs about it. They'll *eradicate* you."

It was a colossal bluff. The corps and I had not been on speaking terms for at least a decade of my subjective lifetime, and the best part of a century of objective time. But throughout the Protectorate, the Envoys were a threat that could be dealt across the table to anyone up to and including a planetary president with the same assurance that small children in Newpest are threatened with the Patchwork Man.

"It was my understanding," the woman said quietly, "that the Envoy Corps were banned from operations on Earth unless U.N. mandated. Perhaps you have as much to lose by revelation as anyone else?"

Mr. Bancroft has an undeclared influence in the U.N. Court, which is more or less common knowledge. Oumou Prescott's words came back to me, and I leapt to parry.

"Perhaps *you* would like to take that up with Laurens Bancroft and the U.N. Court," I suggested, folding my arms.

The woman looked at me for a while. The wind ruffled my hair, bringing with it the faint rumble of the city. Finally she said, "You are aware we could erase your stack and break down your sleeve into pieces so small there would be no trace. There would, effectively, be nothing to find."

"They'd find you," I said, with the confidence that a strand of truth in the lie provides. "You can't hide from the corps. They'll find you whatever you do. About the only thing you can hope for now is to try to cut a deal."

"What deal?" she asked woodenly.

In the fractions of a second before I spoke, my mind went into overdrive, measuring the tilt and power of every syllable chosen before it was launched. This was the escape window. There wouldn't be another chance.

"There's a biopirate operation moving stolen military custom through the West Coast," I said carefully. "They're being fronted by places like Jerry's."

"And they called the Envoys?" The woman's tone was scornful. "For biopirates? Come on, Ryker. Is that the best you can do?"

"I'm not Ryker," I snapped. "This sleeve's a cover. Look, you're right. Nine times out of ten, this stuff doesn't touch us. The Envoys weren't designed to take on criminality at that level. But these people have taken some items they should never have touched. Rapid-response diplomatic bioware. Stuff they should never even have seen. Someone's pissed off about it—and I mean at U.N. presidium level—so they called us in."

The woman frowned. "And the deal?"

"Well, first of all you cut me loose, and no one talks about this to anybody. Let's call it a professional misunderstanding. And then you open some channels for me. Name some names. Black clinic like this, the information circulates. That might be worth something to me."

"As I said before, we do not wish to involve ourselves—"

I came off the rail, letting just enough anger bleed through. "Don't fuck with me, pal. You *are* involved. Like it or not, you took a big bite of something that didn't concern you, and now you're going to either chew it or spit it out. Which is it going to be?"

Silence. Only the sea breeze between us, the faint rocking of the boat.

"We will consider this," the woman said.

Something happened to the glinting light on the water. I shifted my gaze out past the woman's shoulder and saw how the brightness unstitched itself from the waves and scribbled into the sky, magnifying. The city whited out as if from a nuclear flash; the edges of the boat faded, as if into a sea mist. The woman opposite went with it. It became very quiet.

I raised a hand to touch the mist where the parameters of the world ended, and my arm seemed to move in slow motion. There was a static hiss like rain building under the silence. The ends of my fingers turned transparent, then white like the minarets of the city under the flash. I lost the power of motion, and the white crept up my arm. The breath stopped in my throat; my heart paused in midbeat. I was

Not.

CHAPTEr FOUrTEEN

I woke once more, this time to a rough numbness in the surface of my skin, like the feeling your hands get just after you've rinsed them clean of detergent or turpentine, but spread throughout the body. Reentry into a male sleeve. It subsided rapidly as my mind adjusted to the new nervous system. The faint chill of air-conditioning on exposed flesh. I was naked. I reached up with my left hand and touched the scar under my eye.

They'd put me back.

Above me the ceiling was white and set with powerful spotlights. I propped myself up on my elbows and looked around. Another faint chill, this one internal, coasted through me as I saw that I was in an operating theater. Across the room from where I lay stood a polished steel surgical platform complete with runnels for the blood and the folded arms of the autosurgeon suspended spiderlike above. None of the systems were active, but there were small screens blinking the word STANDBY on the walls and on a monitor unit beside me. I leaned closer to the display and saw a function checklist scrolling down repeatedly. They had been programming the autosurgeon to take me apart.

I was swinging myself off the waiting tray when the door cracked open and the synthetic woman came in with a pair of medics in tow. The particle blaster was stowed at her hip, and she was carrying a recognizable bundle.

"Clothes." She flung them at me with a scowl. "Get dressed."

One of the medics laid a hand on her arm. "Procedure calls for—"

"Yeah," the woman sneered. "Maybe he'll sue us. You don't think this place is up to a simple De- and Re-, maybe I'll talk to Ray about moving our business through someone else."

"He's not talking about the resleeve," I observed, pulling on my trousers. "He wants to check for interrogation trauma."

"Who asked you?"

I shrugged. "Suit yourself. Where are we going?"

"To talk to someone," she said shortly, and turned back to the medics. "If he is who he says he is, trauma isn't going to be an issue. And if he isn't, he's coming right back here anyway."

I continued dressing as smoothly as I could. Not out of the fire yet, then. My crossover tunic and jacket were intact, but the bandanna was gone, which annoyed me out of all proportion. I'd only bought it a few hours ago. No watch, either. Deciding not to make an issue of it, I press-sealed my boots and stood up.

"So who are we going to see?"

The woman gave me a sour look. "Someone who knows enough to check out your shit. And then, personally, I think we'll be bringing you back here for orderly dispersal."

"When this is over," I said evenly, "maybe I can persuade one of our squads to pay you a visit. In your real sleeve, that is. They'll want to thank you for your support."

The blaster came out of its sheath with a soft strop and was under my chin. I barely saw it happen. My recently resleeved senses scrabbled for a reaction, eons too late. The synthetic woman leaned close to the side of my face.

"Don't you ever threaten me, you piece of shit," she said softly. "You got these clowns scared; they're anchored in place, and they think you're carrying the weight to sink them. That doesn't work with me. Got it?"

I looked at her out of the corner of my eye, the best I could manage with my head jammed up by the gun.

"Got it," I said.

"Good," she breathed, and removed the blaster. "You check out with Ray, I'll line up and apologize with everybody else. But until then you're just another potential wipeout gibbering for your stack."

We went at a rapid pace down corridors that I tried to memorize and into an elevator identical to the one that had delivered me to the clinic. I counted the floors off again, and when we stepped out into the parking area my eyes jerked involuntarily to the door that they had taken Louise through. My recollections of time during the torture were hazy—the Envoy conditioning was deliberately curtaining off the experience to avert the trauma—but even if it had gone on a couple of days, that was about ten minutes real time. I'd probably only been in the clinic an hour or two maximum, and Louise's body might still be waiting for the knife behind that door, her mind still stacked.

"Get in the car," the woman said laconically.

This time my ride was a larger, more elegant machine reminiscent of Bancroft's limousine. There was already a driver in the forward cabin, liveried and shaven headed with the bar code of his employer printed above his left ear. I'd seen quite a few of these on the streets of Bay City, and wondered why anyone would submit to it. On Harlan's World no one outside the military would be seen dead with authorization stripes. It was too close to the serfdom of the Settlement years for comfort.

A second man stood by the rear cabin door, an ugly-looking machine pistol dangling negligently from his hand. He, too, had the shaven skull and the bar code. I looked hard at it as I passed him and got into the rear cabin. The synthetic woman leaned down to talk to the chauffeur, and I cranked up the neurachem to eavesdrop.

". . . head in the clouds. I want to be there before midnight."

"No problem. Coastal's running light tonight and—"

One of the medics slammed the door shut on me, and the solid clunk at max amplification nearly blew my eardrums. I sat in silence, recovering, until the woman and the machine pistoleer opened the doors on either side and climbed in next to me.

"Close your eyes," the woman said, producing my bandanna. "I'm going to blindfold you for a few minutes. If we do let you go, these guys aren't going to want you knowing where to find them."

I looked around at the windows. "These look polarized to me anyway."

"Yeah, but no telling how good that neurachem is, huh? Now hold still."

She knotted the red cloth with practiced efficiency and spread it a little to cover my whole field of vision. I settled back in the seat.

"Couple of minutes. You just sit quiet and no peeking. I'll tell you when."

The car boosted up and presumably out because I heard the drumming of rain against the bodywork. There was a faint smell of leather from the upholstery, which beat the odor of feces on the inbound journey, and the seat I was in molded itself supportively to my form. I seemed to have moved up in the order of things.

Strictly temporary, man. I smiled faintly as Jimmy's voice echoed in the back of my skull. He was right. A couple of things were clear about whoever we were going to see. This was someone who didn't want to come to the clinic, who didn't even want to be seen near it. That bespoke respectability, and with it power, the power to access offworld data. Pretty soon they were going to know that the Envoy Corps was an empty threat, and very shortly after that I was going to be dead. Really dead.

That kind of dictates the action, pal.

Thanks, Jimmy.

After a few minutes the woman told me to take off the blindfold. I pushed it up onto my forehead and retied it there in its customary position. At my side, the muscle with the machine pistol smirked. I gave him a curious look.

"Something funny?"

"Yeah." The woman spoke without turning her gaze from the city lights beyond the window. "You look like a fucking idiot."

"Not where I come from."

She turned to look at me pityingly. "You aren't where you come from. You're on Earth. Try behaving like it."

I looked from one to the other of them, the pistoleer still smirking, the synthetic with the expression of polite contempt, then shrugged and reached up with both hands to untie the bandanna. The woman went back to watching the lights of the city sink below us. The rain seemed to have stopped.

I chopped down savagely from head height, left and right. My left fist jarred into the pistoleer's temple with enough force to break the bone, and he slumped sideways with a single grunt. He never even saw the blow coming. My right arm was still in motion.

The synthetic whipped around, probably faster than I could have struck, but she misread me. Her arm was raised to block and cover her head, and I was under the guard, reaching. My hand closed on the blaster at her belt, knocked out the safety, and triggered it. The beam seethed into life, cutting downward, and a large quantity of the woman's right leg burst open in wet ropes of flesh before the blowback circuits cut the blast. She howled, a cry more of rage than of pain, and then I dragged the muzzle of the weapon up, triggering another blast diagonally across her body. The blaster carved a channel a handbreadth wide right through her and into the seat behind. Blood exploded across the cabin.

The blaster cut out again, and the cabin went suddenly dim as the flaring of the beam weapon stopped. Beside me, the synthetic woman bubbled and sighed, and then the section of her torso that the head was attached to sagged away from the left side of the body. Her forehead came to rest against the window she had been looking out of. It looked oddly as if she was cooling her brow on the rain-streaked glass. The rest of the body sat stiffly upright, the massive sloping wound cauterized clean by the beam. The mingled stink of cooked meat and fried synthetic components was everywhere.

"Trepp? *Trepp?*" It was the chauffeur's intercom squawking. I wiped blood out of my eyes and looked at the screen set in the forward bulkhead.

"She's dead," I told the shocked face, and held up the blaster. "They're both dead. And you're next, if you don't get us on the ground right now."

The chauffeur rallied. "We're five hundred meters above the bay, friend, and I'm flying this car. What do you propose doing about that?"

I selected a midpoint on the wall between the two cabins, knocked out the blowback cutout on the blaster, and shielded my face with one hand.

"Hey, what are you—"

I fired through into the driver's compartment on tight focus. The beam punched a molten hole about a centimeter wide, and for a moment it rained sparks backwards into the cabin as the armoring beneath the plastic resisted. Then the sparks died as the beam broke through, and I heard something electrical short out in the forward compartment. I stopped firing.

"The next one goes right through your seat," I promised. "I've got friends who'll resleeve me when they fish us out of the bay. You I'll carve into steaks right through this fucking wall, and even if I miss your stack, they'll have a hard time finding which part of you it's inside. Now fucking *get me on the ground.*"

The limousine banked abruptly to one side, losing altitude. I sat back a little amidst the carnage and cleaned more blood off my face with one sleeve.

"That's good," I said more calmly. "Now set me down near Mission Street. And if you're thinking about signaling for help, think about this. If there's a fire-fight, you die first. Got it? You die first. I'm talking about real death. I'll make sure I burn out your stack if it's the last thing I do before they take me down."

His face looked back at me on the screen, pale. Scared, but not scared enough. Or maybe scared of someone else. Anyone who bar-codes their employees isn't likely to be the forgiving type, and the reflex of long-held obedience through hierarchy is usually enough to overcome fear of a combat death. That's how you fight wars, after all—with soldiers who are more afraid of stepping out of line than they are of dying on the battlefield.

I used to be like that myself.

"How about this?" I offered rapidly. "You violate traffic protocol putting us down. The Sia turn up, bust you, and hold you. You say nothing. I'm gone and they've got nothing on you outside of a traffic misdemeanor. Your story is you're just the driver, your passengers had a little disagreement in the backseat, and then I hijacked you to the ground. Meanwhile, whoever you work for bails you out *rápido*, and you pick up a bonus for not cracking in virtual holding."

I watched the screen. His expression wavered, and he swallowed hard. Enough carrot, time for the stick. I locked the blowback circuit on again, lifted the blaster so he could see it, and fitted it to the nape of Trepp's neck.

"I'd say you're getting a bargain."

At point-blank range, the blaster beam vaporized spine, stack, and everything around it. I turned back to the screen.

"Your call."

The driver's face convulsed, and the limo started to lose height raggedly. I watched the flow of traffic through the window, then leaned forward and tapped on the screen.

"Don't forget that violation, will you?"

He gulped and nodded. The limo dropped vertically through stacked lanes of traffic and bumped hard along the ground, to a chorus of furious collision-alert screeches from the vehicles around us. Through the window I recognized the street I'd cruised with Curtis the night before. Our pace slowed somewhat.

"Crack the nearside door," I said, tucking the blaster under my jacket. Another jerky nod and the door in question clunked open, then hung ajar. I swiveled, kicked it wide, and heard police sirens wailing somewhere above us. My eyes met the driver's on the screen for a moment, and I grinned.

"Wise man," I said, and threw myself out of the coasting vehicle.

The pavement hit me in the shoulder and back as I rolled amidst startled cries from passing pedestrians. I rolled twice, hit hard against a stone frontage, and climbed cautiously to my feet. A passing couple stared at me, and I skinned my teeth in a smile that made them hurry on, finding interest in other shopfronts.

A stale blast of displaced air washed over me as a traffic cop's cruiser dropped in the wake of the offending limo. I stayed where I was, giving back the diminishing handful of curious looks from passersby who had seen my unorthodox arrival. Interest in me was waning, in any case. One by one the stares slipped away, drawn by the flashing lights of the police cruiser, now hovering menacingly above and behind the stationary limo.

"Turn off your engines and remain where you are," the airborne speaker system crackled.

A crowd started to knot up as people hurried past me, jostling and trying to see what was going on. I leaned back on the frontage, checking myself for damage from the jump. By the feel of the fading numbness in my shoulder and across my back, I'd done it right this time.

"Raise your hands above your head and step away from your vehicle," came the metallic voice of the traffic cop.

Over the bobbing heads of the spectators, I made out the driver, easing himself out of the limo in the recommended posture. He looked relieved to be alive. For a moment I caught myself wondering why that kind of standoff wasn't more popular in the circles I moved in.

Just too many death wishes all around, I guess.

I backstepped a few meters in the mix of the crowd, then turned and slipped away into the brightly lit anonymity of the Bay City night.

CHAPTEr FIFTEEN

The personal, as everyone's so fucking fond of saying, is political. So if some idiot politician, some power player, tries to execute policies that harm you or those you care about, take it personally. Get angry. The Machinery of Justice will not serve you here—it is slow and cold, and it is theirs, hardware and soft-. Only the little people suffer at the hands of Justice; the creatures of power slide out from under with a wink and a grin. If you want justice, you will have to claw it from them. Make it personal. Do as much damage as you can. Get your message across. That way you stand a far better chance of being taken seriously next time. Of being considered dangerous. And make no mistake about this: being taken seriously, being considered dangerous, marks the difference—the only difference in their eyes— between players and little people. Players they will make deals with. Little people they liquidate. And time and again they cream your liquidation, your displacement, your torture and brutal execution with the ultimate insult that it's just business, it's politics, it's the way of the world, it's a tough life, and that it's nothing personal. Well, fuck them. Make it personal.

QUELLCRIST FALCONER
Things I Should Have Learned by Now
Volume II

There was a cold blue dawn over the city by the time I got back to Licktown, and everything had the wet gunmetal sheen of recent rain. I stood in the shadow of the expressway pillars and watched the gutted street for any hint of movement. There was a feeling I needed, but it wasn't easy to come by in the cold light of the rising day. My head was buzzing with rapid data assimilation, and Jimmy de Soto floated around in the back of my mind like a restless demon familiar.

Where are you going, Tak?

To do some damage.

The Hendrix hadn't been able to give me anything on the clinic I'd been taken to. From Deek's promise to the Mongol to bring a disk of my torture right back across, I supposed that the place had to be on the other side of the Bay, probably in Oakland, but that in itself wasn't much help, even for an A.I. The whole Bay Area appeared to be suffused with illegal biotech activity. I was going to have to retrace my steps the hard way.

Jerry's Closed Quarters.

Here the Hendrix had been more helpful. After a brief skirmish with some low-grade counterintrusion systems, it laid out the biocabin club's entrails for me on the screen in my room. Floor plan, security staffing, timetables, and shifts. I slammed through it in seconds, fueled by the latent rage from my interrogation. With the sky beginning to pale in the window behind me, I fitted the Nemex and the Philips gun in their holsters, strapped on the Tebbit knife, and went out to do some interrogating of my own.

I'd seen no sign of my tail when I let myself into the hotel, and he didn't seem to be around when I left, either. Lucky for him, I guess.

Jerry's Closed Quarters by dawn light.

What little cheap erotic mystique had clung to the place by night was gone now. The neon and holosigns were bleached out, pinned on the building like a garish brooch on an old gown. I looked bleakly at the dancing girl, still trapped in the cocktail glass, and thought of Louise, alias Anemone, tortured to a death her religion would not let her come back from.

Make it personal.

The Nemex was in my right hand like a decision taken. As I walked toward the club, I worked the slide action on it, and the metallic snap was loud in the quiet morning air. A slow, cold fury was beginning to fill me up now.

The door robot stirred as I approached, and its arms came up in a warding-off gesture.

"We're closed, friend," the synth voice said.

I leveled the Nemex at the lintel and shot out the robot's brain dome. The casing might have stopped smaller-caliber shells, but the Nemex slugs smashed the unit to pieces. Sparks fireworked abruptly and the synth voice shrieked. The concertina octopus arms thrashed spastically, then went slack. Smoke curled from the shattered lintel housing.

Cautiously, I prodded one dangling tentacle aside with the Nemex, stepped through, and met Milo coming upstairs to find out what the noise was about. His eyes widened as he saw me.

"You. What—"

I shot him through the throat, watched him flap and tumble down the steps, and then, as he struggled to get back on his feet, shot him again in the face. As I went down the stairs after Milo a second heavy appeared in the dimly lit space below me, took one shocked look at Milo's corpse, and went for a clumsy-looking blaster at his belt. I nailed him twice through the chest before his fingers touched the weapon.

At the bottom of the stairs I paused, unholstered the Philips gun left-handed, and stood in silence for a moment, letting the echoes of the gunfire die away in my ears. The heavy artillery rhythm that I'd come to expect of Jerry's was still playing, but the Nemex had a loud voice. On my left was the pulsing red glow of the corridor that led to the cabins, on the right a spiderweb holo with a variety of pipes and bottles trapped in it and the word BAR illuminumed onto flat black doors beyond. The data in my head said a minimal security presence for the cabins—three at most, more likely down to two at this time of the morning. Milo and the nameless heavy on the stairs down, leaving one more possible. The bar was soundproofed, wired into a separate sound system, and running between two and four armed guards who doubled as bar staff.

Jerry the cheapskate.

I listened, cranking up the neurachem. From the corridor that led left, I heard one of the cabin doors open stealthily and then the soft scrape of someone sliding their feet along the ground in the mistaken belief that it would make less noise than walking. Keeping my eyes fixed on the bar doors to my right, I stuck the Philip's gun around the corner to the left and, without bothering to look, sewed a silent scribble of bullets across the red-lit air in the corridor. The weapon seemed to sigh them out like branches blowing in a breeze. There was a strangled grunt, and then the thud and clatter of a body and weapon hitting the floor.

The doors to the bar remained closed.

I eased my head around the angle of the wall and in the stripes of red thrown by the rotating lights saw a stocky-looking woman in combat fatigues clutching at her side with one arm and clawing after a fallen handgun with the other. I stepped quickly across to the weapon and kicked it well out of her reach, then knelt beside her. I must have scored multiple hits; there was blood on her legs, and her shirt was drenched in it. I laid the muzzle of the Philips gun against her forehead.

"You work security for Jerry?"

She nodded, eyes flaring white around her irises.

"One chance. Where is he?"

"Bar," she hissed through her teeth, fighting back the pain. "Table. Back corner."

I nodded, stood up, and sighted carefully between her eyes.

"Wait, you—"

The Philips gun sighed.

Damage.

I was in the midst of the spiderweb holo, reaching for the bar doors, when they swung open and I found myself face-to-face with Deek. He had even less time to react to the phantom before him than Milo had. I tipped him the tiniest of formal bows, barely an inclination of my head, and then let go of the fury inside me and shot him repeatedly at waist height with both Nemex and Philips gun. He staggered back through the doors under the multiple impacts, and I followed him in, still firing.

It was a wide space, dimly lit by angled spots and the subdued orange guide lights of the dancers' runway, now abandoned. Along one wall, cool blue light shone up from behind the bar, as if it was fronting an obscure downward staircase to paradise. Behind was racked with the pipes, jack-ins, and bottles on offer.

The keeper of this angel's hoard took one look at Deek, reeling backwards with his hands sunk in his ruined guts, and went for the holdout below the bar at a speed that was truly semidivine.

I heard the dropped glass shatter, threw out the Nemex, and hammered him back against the displayed wares on the wall like an impromptu crucifixion. He hung there a moment, curiously elegant, then turned and clawed down a racket of bottles and pipes on his way to the floor. Deek went down, too, still moving, and a dim, bulky-looking form leaning against the edge of the runway leapt forward, clearing a handgun from the waist. I left the Nemex focused on the bar—no time to turn and aim—and snapped off a shot from the Philips gun, half-raised. The figure grunted and staggered, losing his weapon and slumping against the runway. My left arm raised, straightened, and the head shot punched him back onto the dance platform.

The Nemex echoes were still dying in the corners of the room.

By now I had sight of Jerry. He was ten meters away, surging to his feet behind a flimsy table when I leveled the Nemex. He froze.

"Wise man." The neurachem was singing like wires, and there was an adrenaline grin hanging crazily off my face. My mind rattled through the count. One shell left in the Philips gun, six in the Nemex. "Leave your hands right there, and sit the rest of you down. You twitch a finger and I'll take it off at the wrist."

He sank back into his seat, face working. Peripheral scan told me there was no one else moving in the room. I stepped carefully over Deek, who had rolled into a fetal ball around the damage in his gut and was giving out a deep, agonized wailing. Keeping the Nemex focused on the table in front of Jerry's groin, I dropped my other arm until the Philips gun was pointing straight down and pulled the trigger. The noise from Deek stopped.

At this, Jerry erupted.

"Are you *fucking crazy, Ryker? Stop it! You can't—*"

I jerked the Nemex barrel at him, and either that or something in my face shut him up. Nothing stirred behind the curtains at the end of the runway, nothing behind the bar. The doors stayed closed. Crossing the remaining distance to Jerry's table, I kicked one of the chairs around backwards and then straddled it, facing him.

"You, Jerry," I said evenly, "need to listen to people occasionally. I've told you, my name is not Ryker."

"Whoever the fuck you are, I'm connected." There was so much venom on the face before me it was a wonder Jerry didn't choke on it. "I'm jacked into the fucking machine, you get me? This. All this. You're going to fucking pay. You're going to wish—"

"I'd never met you," I finished for him. I stowed the empty Philips gun back in its fibergrip holster. "Jerry, I already wish I'd never met you. Your sophisticated friends were sophisticated enough for that. But I notice they didn't tell you I was back on the street. Not so tight with Ray these days, is that it?"

I was watching his face, and the name didn't register. Either he was very cool under fire, or he genuinely wasn't fishing in the senior fleet. I tried again.

"Trepp's dead," I said casually. His eyes moved, just a fraction. "Trepp, and a few others. Want to know why you're still alive?"

His mouth tightened, but he said nothing. I leaned over the table and pushed the barrel of the Nemex up against his left eye.

"I asked you a question."

"Fuck you."

I nodded and settled back onto my seat. "Hard man, huh? So I'll tell you. I need some answers, Jerry. You can start by telling me what happened to Elizabeth Elliott. That should be easy; I figure you carved her up yourself. Then I want to know who Elias Ryker is, who Trepp works for, and where the clinic is that you sent me to."

"Fuck you."

"You don't think I'm serious? Or are you just hoping the cops are going to show up and save your stack?" I fished the commandeered blaster out of my pocket left-handed and drew a careful bead on the dead security guard on the runway. The range was short and the beam torched his head off in a single explosion. The stench of charred flesh rolled across the room to us. Keeping one eye on Jerry, I played the beam around a little until I was sure I'd destroyed everything from the shoulders up, then snapped the weapon off and lowered it. Jerry stared at me over the table.

"You piece of shit, he only *worked security for me!*"

"That's just become a proscribed profession, as far as I'm concerned. Deck and the rest are going the same way. And so are you, unless you tell me what I want to know." I lifted the beam weapon. "One chance."

"All right." The crack was audible in his voice. "All right, all right. Elliott tried to put a lock on a customer; she got some big-name Meth come slumming down here, reckoned she'd got enough shit to twist him. Stupid cunt tried to make me a partnership deal; she figured I could lean on this Meth guy. No fucking clue what she was dealing with."

"No." I looked stonily at him across the table. "I guess not."

He caught the look. "Hey, man, I know what you're thinking, but it ain't like that. I tried to warn her off, so she went direct. Direct to a fucking Meth. You think I wanted this place ripped down and me buried under it? I had to deal with her, man. Had to."

"You iced her?"

He shook his head. "I made a call," he said in a subdued voice. "That's how it works around here."

"Who's Ryker?"

"Ryker's a—" He swallowed. "A cop. Used to work Sleeve Theft, then they upped him to the Organic Damage Division. He was fucking that Sia cunt, the one came out here the night you crocked Oktai."

"Ortega?"

"Yeah, Ortega. Everybody knew it; they say that's how he got the transfer. That's why we figured you were, he was, back on the street. When Deek saw you talking to Ortega we figured she'd accessed someone, done a deal."

"Back on the street? Back from where?"

"Ryker was dirty, man." Now the flow had started, it was coming in full flood. "He RD'd a couple of sleevedealers, up in Seattle—"

"RD?"

"Yeah, RD'd." Jerry looked momentarily nonplussed, as if I'd just queried the color of the sky.

"I'm not from here," I said patiently.

"RD. Real death. He pulped them, man. Couple of other guys went down, stack intact, so Ryker paid off some dipper to register the lot of them Catholic. Either the input didn't take, or someone at OrgDam found out. He got the double-barrel. Two hundred years, no remission. Word is, Ortega headed up the squad that took him down."

Well, well. I waved the Nemex encouragingly.

"That's it, man. All I got. It's off the wire. Street talk. Look, Ryker never shook this place down, even back when he worked ST. I run a clean house. I never even met the guy."

"And Oktai?"

Jerry nodded vigorously. "That's it, Oktai. Oktai used to run spare-part deals out of Oakland. You, I mean, Ryker used to shake him down all the time. Beat him half to death couple of years back."

"So Oktai comes running to you—"

"That's it. He's, like, crazy, saying Ryker must be working some scam down here. So we run the cabin tapes, get you talking to—"

Jerry dried up as he saw where we were heading. I gestured again with the gun.

"That's fucking it." There was an edge of desperation in his voice.

"All right." I sat back a little and patted my pockets for cigarettes, remembered I had none. "You smoke?"

"Smoke? Do I look like a fucking idiot?"

I sighed. "Never mind. What about Trepp? She looked a little upmarket for your cred. Who'd you borrow her from?"

"Trepp's an indie. Contract hire for whoever. She does me favors sometimes."

"Not anymore. You ever see her real sleeve?"

"No. Wire says she keeps it on ice in New York most of the time."

"That far from here?"

" 'Bout an hour, suborbital."

By my reckoning that put her in the same league as Kadmin. Global muscle, maybe interplanetary, too. The Senior Fleet.

"So who's the wire say she's working for now?"

"I don't know."

I studied the barrel of the blaster as if it were a Martian relic. "Yeah, you do." I looked up and offered him a bleak smile. "Trepp's gone. Unstacked, the works. You don't need to worry about selling her out. You need to worry about me."

He stared defiantly at me for a couple of moments, then looked down.

"I heard she was doing stuff for the Houses."

"Good. Now, tell me about the clinic. Your sophisticated friends."

The Envoy training should have been keeping my voice even, but maybe I was getting rusty, because Jerry heard something there. He moistened his lips.

"Listen, those are dangerous people. You got away; you'd better just leave it at that. You got no idea what they—"

"I've got a pretty good idea, actually." I pointed the blaster into his face. "The clinic."

"Christ, they're just people I know. You know, business associates. They can use the spare parts, sometimes, and I—" He changed tack abruptly as he saw my face. "They do stuff for me sometimes. It's just business."

I thought of Louise, alias Ancmone, and the journey we'd taken together. I felt a muscle beneath my eye twitch, and it was all I could do not to pull the trigger there and then. I dug up my voice, instead, and used it. It sounded more like a machine than the door robot had.

"We're going for a ride, Jerry. Just you and me, to visit your business associates. And don't fuck with me. I've already figured out it's over the other side of the bay. And I've got a good memory for places. You steer me wrong, and I'll RD you on the spot. Got it?"

From his face I judged that he did.

But just to make sure, on the way out of the club I stopped beside each corpse and burnt its head off down to the shoulders. The burning left an acrid stench that followed us out of the gloom and into the early morning street like a ghost of rage.

●●●

There's a village up on the north arm of the Millsport archipelago where, if a fisherman survives drowning, he is required to swim out to a low reef about half a kilometer from shore, spit into the ocean beyond, and return. Sarah's from there, and once, holed up in a cheap swamp hotel, hiding from heat both physical and figurative, she tried to explain the rationale. It always sounded like macho bullshit to me.

Now, marching down the sterile white corridors of the clinic once again, with the muzzle of my own Philips gun screwed into my neck, I began to have some understanding of the strength it must take to wade back into that water. I'd had cold shivers since we went down in the elevator for the second time, Jerry holding the gun on me from behind. After Innenin, I'd more or less forgotten what it was like to be genuinely afraid, but virtualities were a notable exception. There, you had no control, and literally anything could happen.

Again and again.

They were rattled at the clinic. The news of Trepp's barbecue ride must have reached them by now, and the face that Jerry had spoken to on the screen at the discreetly appointed front door had gone death white at the sight of me.

"We thought—"

"Never mind that," Jerry snapped. "Open the fucking door. We've got to get this piece of shit off the street."

The clinic was part of an old turn-of-the-millennium block that someone had renovated in neoindustrial style, doors painted with heavy black and yellow chevrons, facades draped in scaffolding, and balconies hung with fake cabling and hoists. The door before us divided along the upward points of the chevrons and slid noiselessly apart. With a last glance at the early morning street, Jerry thrust me inside.

The entrance hall was also neoind, more scaffolding along the walls, and patches of exposed brickwork. A pair of security guards were waiting at the end. One of them put out a hand as we approached, and Jerry swung on him, snarling.

"I don't need any fucking help. You're the wipeouts who let this mother-fucker go in the first place."

The two guards exchanged a glance, and the extended grasp turned into a placatory gesture. They conveyed us to an elevator door that proved to be the same commercial-capacity shaft I'd ridden down from the parking lot on the roof last time. When we came out at the bottom, the same medical team was waiting, sedating implements poised. They looked edgy, tired. Butt end of the night shift. When the same nurse moved to hypo me, Jerry brought out the snarl again. He had it down to perfection.

"Never fucking mind that." He screwed the Philips gun harder into my neck. "He isn't going anywhere. I want to see Miller."

"He's in surgery."

"Surgery?" Jerry barked a laugh. "You mean he's watching the machine make pick-and-mix. All right, Chung, then."

The team hesitated.

"What? Don't tell me you got all your consultants working for a living this morning."

"No, it's . . ." The man nearest me gestured. "It's not procedure, taking him in awake."

"Don't fucking tell me about procedure." Jerry did a good impression of a man about to explode with fury. "Was it procedure to let this piece of shit get out and wreck my place after I sent him over here? Was that fucking procedure? *Was it?*"

There was silence. I looked at the blaster and Nemex, shoved into Jerry's waistband, and measured the angles. Jerry took a renewed grip on my collar and ground the gun under my jaw once again. He glared at the medics and spoke with a kind of gritted calm.

"He ain't moving. Got it? There isn't time for this bullshit. We are going to see Chung. Now, *move.*"

They bought it. Anyone would have. You pile on the pressure, and most people fall back on response. They give in to the higher authority, or the man with the gun. These people were tired and scared. We double-timed it down the corridors. Past the operating theater I had woken up in, or one like it. I caught a glimpse of figures gathered around the surgery platform, the autosurgeon moving spiderlike above them. We were a dozen paces further along when someone stepped into the corridor behind us.

"Just a moment." The voice was cultured, almost leisurely, but it brought the medics and Jerry up short. We turned to face a tall, blue-smocked figure wearing bloodstained spray-on surgical gloves and a mask, which he now unpinned with one fastidious thumb and forefinger. The visage beneath was blandly handsome, blue eyes in a tan-complexioned, square-jawed face, this year's Competent Male, courtesy of some upmarket cosmetic salon.

"Miller," Jerry said.

"What exactly is going on here? Courault—" The tall man turned to the female medic. "—You know better than to bring subjects through here unsedated."

"Yes, sir. Mr. Sedaka insisted that there was no risk involved. He said he was in a hurry to see Director Chung."

"I don't care how much of a hurry he's in." Miller swung on Jerry, eyes narrowing with suspicion. "Are you insane, Sedaka? What do you think this is, the visitors' gallery? I've got clients in there. Recognizable faces. Courault, sedate this man immediately."

Oh, well. No one's lucky forever.

I was already moving. Before Courault could lift the hypospray from her hip sack, I yanked both the Nemex and the blaster from Jerry's waistband and spun, firing. Courault and her two colleagues went down, multiply injured. Blood splattered on antiseptic white behind them. Miller had time for one outraged yell, and then I shot him in the mouth with the Nemex. Jerry was just backing away from me, the unloaded Philips gun still dangling from his hand. I threw up the blaster.

"Look, I did my fucking best. I—"

The beam cut loose and his head exploded.

In the sudden quiet that followed, I retraced my steps to the doors of the surgery and pushed through them. The little knot of figures, immaculately suited to a man and woman, had left the table on which a young female sleeve was laid out, and were gaping at me behind forgotten surgical masks. Only the auto-surgeon continued working unperturbed, making smooth incisions and cauterizing wounds with abrupt little sizzlings. Indistinct lumps of raw red poked out of an array of small metal dishes collected at the subject's head. It looked unnervingly like the start of some arcane banquet.

The woman on the table was Louise.

There were five men and women in the theater, and I killed them all while they stared at me. Then I shot the autosurgeon to pieces with the blaster and raked the beam over the rest of the equipment in the room. Alarms sirened into life from every wall. In the storm of their combined shrieking, I went around and inflicted real death on everyone there.

Outside, there were more alarms and two of the medical crew were still alive. Courault had succeeded in crawling a dozen meters down the corridor in a broad trail of her own blood, and one of her male colleagues, too weak to escape, was trying to prop himself up against the wall. The floor was slippery under him, and he kept sliding back down. I ignored him and went after the woman. She stopped when she heard my footsteps, twisted her head to look around, and then began to crawl again, frantically. I stamped a foot down between her shoulders to make her stop and then kicked her onto her back.

We looked at each other for a long moment while I remembered her impassive face as she had put me under the night before. I lifted the blaster for her to see.

"Real death," I said, and pulled the trigger.

I walked back to the remaining medic, who had seen and was now scrabbling desperately backwards away from me. I crouched down in front of him. The screaming of the alarms rose and fell over our heads like lost souls.

"Jesus Christ," he moaned as I pointed the blaster at his face. "Jesus Christ. I only *work* here."

"Good enough," I told him.

The blaster was almost inaudible against the alarms.

Working rapidly, I took care of the third medic in similar fashion, dealt with Miller a little more at length, stripped Jerry's headless corpse of its jacket, and tucked the garment under my arm. Then I scooped up the Philips gun, tucked it into my waistband, and left. On my way out along the screaming corridors of the clinic, I killed every person I met, and melted their stacks to slag.

Personal.

The police were landing on the roof as I let myself out of the front door and walked unhurriedly down the street. Under my arm, Miller's severed head was beginning to seep blood through the lining of Jerry's jacket.

PART THREE

ALLIANCE
(APPLICATION UPGRADE)

CHAPTEr SIXTEEN

It was quiet and sunny in the gardens at Suntouch House, and the air smelled of mown grass. From the tennis courts came the faint popping of a game in progress, and once I heard Miriam Bancroft's voice raised in excitement. Flash of tanned legs beneath a flaring white skirt and a puff of shell-pink dust where the driven ball buried itself in the back of her opponent's court. There was a polite ripple of applause from the seated figures watching. I made my way down toward the courts, flanked by heavily armed security men with blank faces.

The players were taking a game break when I arrived, feet planted wide in front of their seats, heads down. As my feet crunched on the gravel surround, Miriam Bancroft looked up through tangled blonde hair and met my eye. She said nothing, but her hands worked at the handle of her racket and a smile split her lips. Her opponent, who also glanced up, was a slim young man with something about him that suggested he might genuinely be as young as his body. He looked vaguely familiar.

Bancroft was seated at the middle of a row of deck chairs, Oumou Prescott on his right and a man and woman I'd never met on his left. He didn't get up when I reached him; in fact, he barely looked at me. One hand gestured to the seat next to Prescott.

"Sit down, Kovacs. It's the last game."

I twitched a smile, resisting the temptation to kick his teeth down his throat, and folded myself into the deck chair. Oumou Prescott leaned across to me and murmured behind her hand.

"Mr. Bancroft has had some unwanted attention from the police today. You are being less . . . subtle . . . than we had hoped."

"Just warming up," I muttered back.

By some prior agreed time limit, Miriam Bancroft and her opponent shrugged off their towels and took up position. I settled back and watched the play, eyes mostly on the woman's taut body as it surged and swung within the white cotton, remembering how it looked unclothed, how it had writhed against me. Once, just before a service, she caught me looking at her, and her mouth bent in fractional amusement. She was still waiting for an answer from me, and now she thought she had it. When the match finished, in a flurry of hard-fought but visibly inevitable points, she came off court glowing.

She was talking to the man and woman I didn't know when I approached to offer my congratulations. She saw me coming and turned to include me in the little group.

"Mr. Kovacs." Her eyes widened the slightest bit. "Did you enjoy watching?"

"Very much," I said truthfully. "You're quite merciless."

She tipped her head to one side and began to towel her sweat-soaked hair with one hand. "Only when required," she said. "You won't know Nalan or Joseph, of course. Nalan, Joseph, this is Takeshi Kovacs, the Envoy Laurens hired to look into his murder. Mr. Kovacs is from offworld. Mr. Kovacs, this is Nalan Ertekin, chief justice of the U.N. Supreme Court, and Joseph Phiri from the Commission of Human Rights."

"Delighted." I made a brief formal bow to both of them. "You're here to discuss Resolution 653, I imagine."

The two officials exchanged a glance, then Phiri nodded. "You're very well informed," he said gravely. "I've heard a lot about the Envoy Corps, but still I'm impressed. How long have you been on Earth, exactly?"

"About a week," I exaggerated, hoping to play down the usual paranoia elected officials exhibit around Envoys.

"A week, yes. Impressive indeed." Phiri was a heavyset black man, apparently in his fifties, with hair that was graying a little and careful brown eyes. Like Dennis Nyman, he affected external eyewear, but where Nyman's steely lenses had been designed to enhance the planes of his face, this man wore the glasses to deflect attention. They were heavy framed and gave him the appearance of a forgetful cleric, but behind the lenses, the eyes missed nothing.

"And are you making progress with your investigation?" This was Ertekin, a handsome Arab woman a couple of decades younger than Phiri, and therefore likely on at least her second sleeve. I smiled at her.

"Progress is difficult to define, your honor. As Quell would have it, *they come to me with progress reports, but all I see is change, and bodies burnt.*"

"Ah, you are from Harlan's World, then," Ertekin said politely. "And do you consider yourself a Quellist, Mr. Kovacs?"

I let the smile become a grin. "Sporadically. I'd say she had a point."

"Mr. Kovacs has been quite busy, in fact," Miriam Bancroft said hurriedly. "I imagine he and Laurens have a lot to discuss. Perhaps it might be better if we left them to these matters."

"Yes, of course." Ertekin inclined her head. "Perhaps we'll talk again later."

The three of them drifted over to commiserate with Miriam's opponent, who was ruefully stowing his racket and towels in a bag; but for all Miriam's diplomatic steerage, Nalan Ertekin did not seem unduly concerned to make her escape. I felt a momentary glimmer of admiration for her. Telling a U.N. executive—in effect, an officer of the Protectorate—that you're a Quellist is a bit like confessing to ritual slaughter at a vegetarian dinner; it's not really the done thing.

I turned to find Oumou Prescott at my shoulder.

"Shall we?" she said grimly, and pointed up toward the house. Bancroft was already striding ahead. We went after him at what I thought was an excessive pace.

"One question," I managed, between breathing. "Who's the kid? The one Mrs. Bancroft crucified."

Prescott flicked me an impatient glance.

"Big secret, huh?"

"No, Mr. Kovacs, it is not a secret, large or otherwise. I merely think you might do better occupying your mind with other matters than the Bancrofts' houseguests. If you must know, the other player was Marco Kawahara."

"Was it, indeed." Accidentally, I'd slipped into Phiri's speech patterns. Chalk up a double strike for personality. "So that's where I've seen his face before. Takes after his mother, doesn't he?"

"I really wouldn't know," Prescott said dismissively. "I have never met Ms. Kawahara."

"Lucky you."

Bancroft was waiting for us in an exotic conservatory pinned to the seaward wing of the house. The glass walls were a riot of alien colors and forms, among which I picked out a young mirrorwood tree and numerous stands of martyrweed. Bancroft was standing next to one of the latter, spraying it carefully with a white metallic dust. I don't know much about martyrweed beyond its obvious uses as a security device, so I had no idea what the powder was.

Bancroft turned as we came in. "Please keep your voices reasonably low." His own voice was curiously flat in the sound-absorbent environment. "Martyrweed is highly sensitive at this stage of development. Mr. Kovacs, I assume you are familiar with it."

"Yeah." I glanced at the vaguely hand-shaped cups of the leaves, with the central crimson stains that had given the plant its name. "You sure these are mature?"

"Fully. On Adoracion, you'll have seen them larger, but I had Nakamura tailor these for indoor use. This is as secure as a Nilvibe cabin and—" He gestured to a trio of steel-frame chairs beside the martyrweed. "—a great deal more comfortable."

"You wanted to see me," I said impatiently. "What about?"

For just a moment that black iron stare bent on me with the full force of Bancroft's three and a half centuries, and it was like locking gazes with a demon. For that second, the Meth soul was looking out and I saw reflected in those eyes all the myriad ordinary single lives that they had watched die, like the pale flickerings of moths at a flame. It was an experience I'd had only once before, and that was when I'd taken issue with Reileen Kawahara. I could feel the heat on my wings.

Then it was gone, and there was only Bancroft, moving to seat himself and setting the powder spray aside on an adjacent table. He looked up and waited to see if I would sit down, as well. When I did not, he steepled his fingers and frowned. Oumou Prescott hovered between us.

"Mr. Kovacs, I am aware that by the terms of our contract I agreed to meet all reasonable expenses in this investigation, but when I said that, I did not expect to be paying for a trail of willful organic damage from one side of Bay City to another. I have spent most of this morning buying off both the West Coast triads and the Bay City police, neither of whom were very well disposed toward me even before you started this carnage. I wonder if you realize how much it is costing me just to keep you alive and out of storage."

I looked around at the conservatory and shrugged.

"I imagine you can afford it."

Prescott flinched. Bancroft allowed himself the splinter of a smile.

"Perhaps, Mr. Kovacs, I no longer wish to afford it."

"Then pull the fucking plug." The martyrweed trembled visibly at the sudden change in tone. I didn't care. Abruptly, I was no longer in the mood for playing the Bancrofts' elegant games. I was tired. Discounting the brief period of unconsciousness at the clinic, I had been awake for over thirty hours, and my nerves were raw from the continual use of the neurachem system. I had been in a firefight. I had escaped from a moving aircar. I had been subjected to interrogation routines that would have traumatized most human beings for a lifetime. I had committed multiple combat murders. And I had been in the act of crawling into bed when the Hendrix let Bancroft's curt summons through the call block I'd requested, quote, "in the interests of maintaining good client relations and so assuring continued guest status." Someday, someone was going to have to overhaul the hotel's antique service-industry idiolect; I had weighed the idea of doing it myself with the Nemex when I got off the phone, but my irritation at the hotel's enslaved responses to guest holding was overridden by the anger I felt toward Bancroft himself. It was that anger that had stopped me ignoring the call and going to bed anyway, and propelled me out to Suntouch House dressed in the same rumpled clothes I had been wearing since the previous day.

"I beg your pardon, Mr. Kovacs?" Oumou Prescott was staring at me. "Are you suggesting—"

"No, I'm not, Prescott. I'm threatening." I switched my gaze back to Bancroft. "I didn't ask to join this fucking Noh dance. You dragged me here, Bancroft. You pulled me out of the store on Harlan's World, and you jacked me into Elias Ryker's sleeve just to piss Ortega off. You sent me out there with a few vague hints and watched me stumble around in the dark, cracking my shins on your past misdemeanors. Well, if you don't want to play anymore, now that the current's running a little hard, that's fine with me. I'm through risking my stack for a piece of shit like you. You can just put me back in the box, and I'll take my chances a hundred and seventeen years from now. Maybe I'll get lucky, and whoever wants you toasted will have wiped you off the face of the planet by then."

I'd had to check my weapons at the main gate, but I could feel the dangerous looseness of the Envoy combat mode stealing over me as I spoke. If the Meth demon came back and got out of hand, I was going to choke the life out of Bancroft there and then just for the satisfaction.

Curiously, what I said seemed only to make him thoughtful. He heard me out, inclined his head as if in agreement, then turned to Prescott.

"Ou, can you drop out for a while? There are some things that Mr. Kovacs and I need to discuss in private."

Prescott looked dubious. "Shall I post someone outside?" she queried, with a hard glance at me. Bancroft shook his head.

"I'm sure that won't be necessary."

Prescott left, still looking dubious, while I struggled not to admire Bancroft's cool. He'd just heard me say I was happy to go back into storage, he'd been reading my body count all morning, and still he thought he had my specs down tight enough to know whether I was dangerous or not.

I took a seat. Maybe he was right.

"You've got some explaining to do," I said evenly. "You can start with Ryker's sleeve, and go on from there. Why'd you do it, and why conceal it from me?"

"Conceal it?" Bancroft's brows arched. "We barely discussed it."

"You told me you'd left the sleeve selection to your lawyers. You were at pains to stress that. But Prescott insists you made the selection yourself. You should have briefed her a bit better on the lies you were going to tell."

"Well." Bancroft made a gesture of acceptance. "A reflexive caution, then. One tells the truth to so few people in the end, it becomes a habit. But I had no idea it would matter to you so much. After your career in the corps, and your time in storage, I mean. Do you usually exhibit this much interest in the past history of the sleeves you wear?"

"No, I don't. But ever since I arrived, Ortega's been all over me like anticontaminant plastic. I thought it was because she had something to hide. Turns out, she's just trying to protect her boyfriend's sleeve while he's in the store. Incidentally, did you bother to find out why Ryker was on stack?"

This time Bancroft's open-handed motion was dismissive. "A corruption charge. Unjustified organic damage, and attempted falsification of personality detail. I understand it wasn't his first offense."

"Yeah, that's right. In fact, he was well known for it. Well known and very unpopular, especially around places like Licktown, which is where I've been the last couple of days, following the trail of your dripping dick. But we'll come back to that. I want to know why you did it. Why am I wearing Ryker's sleeve?"

Bancroft's eyes flared momentarily at the insult, but he really was too good a player to rise to it. Instead, he shot his right cuff in a displacement gesture I recognized from Diplomatic Basic, and smiled faintly.

"Really, I had no idea it would prove inconvenient. I was looking to provide you with suitable armor, and the sleeve carries—"

"Why Ryker?"

There was a beat of silence. Meths were not people you interrupted lightly, and Bancroft was having a hard time dealing with the lack of respect. I thought about the tree beyond the tennis courts. No doubt Ortega, had she been there, would have cheered.

"A move, Mr. Kovacs. Merely a move."

"A move? Against Ortega?"

"Just so." Bancroft settled back into his seat. "Lieutenant Ortega made her prejudices quite clear the moment she stepped into this house. She was unhelpful in the extreme. She lacked respect. It was something that I remembered, an account to be adjusted. When the shortlist Oumou provided me with included Elias Ryker's sleeve, and listed Ortega as paying the tank mortgage, I saw the move as almost karmic. It dictated itself."

"A little childish for someone your age, don't you think?"

Bancroft inclined his head. "Perhaps. But then, do you recall a General Mac-Intyre of Envoy Command, resident of Harlan's World, who was found gutted and decapitated in his private jet a year after the Innenin massacre?"

"Vaguely." I sat, cold, remembering. But if Bancroft could play the control game, so could I.

"Vaguely?" Bancroft raised an eyebrow. "I'd have thought a veteran of Innenin could scarcely fail to recall the death of the commander who presided over the whole debacle, the man many claim was actually guilty by negligence of all those real deaths."

"MacIntyre was exonerated of all blame by the Protectorate Court of Inquiry," I said quietly. "Do you have a point to make?"

Bancroft shrugged. "Only that it seems his death was a revenge killing, despite the verdict handed down by the court, a pointless act, in fact, since it could not bring back those who died. Childishness is a common enough sin amongst humans. Perhaps we should not be so quick to judge."

"Perhaps not." I stood up and went to stand at the door of the conservatory, looking out. "Well, then don't feel that I'm sitting in judgment, but why exactly didn't you tell me you spent so much time in whorehouses?"

"Ah, the Elliott girl. Yes, Oumou has told me about this. Do you seriously think her father had something to do with my death?"

I turned back. "Not now, no. I seriously believe he had nothing to do with your death, in fact. But I've wasted a lot of time finding that out."

Bancroft met my eye calmly. "I'm sorry if my briefing was inadequate, Mr. Kovacs. It is true, I spend some of my leisure time in purchased sexual release, both real and virtual. Or, as you so elegantly put it, whorehouses. I'd not considered it especially important. Equally, I spend part of my time in small-scale gambling. And occasionally null-gravity knife fighting. All of these things could make me enemies, as indeed could most of my business interests. I didn't feel that your first day in a new sleeve on a new world was the time for a line-by-line explanation of my life. Where would I expect to begin? Instead, I told you the background of the crime and suggested that you talk to Oumou. I didn't expect you to take off after the first clue like a heatseeker. Nor did I expect you to lay waste to everything that got in your way. I was told the Envoy Corps had a reputation for *subtlety*."

Put like that, he had a point. Virginia Vidaura would have been furious. She probably would have been right behind Bancroft, waiting to deck me for gross lack of finesse. But then, neither she nor Bancroft had been looking into Victor Elliott's face the night he told me about his family. I swallowed a sharp retort and marshaled what I knew, trying to decide how much to let go of.

"Laurens?"

Miriam Bancroft was standing just outside the conservatory, a towel draped around her neck and her racquet under one arm.

"Miriam." There was a genuine deference in Bancroft's tone, but little else that I could determine.

"I'm taking Nalan and Joseph out to *Hudson's Raft* for a scuba lunch. Joseph's never done it before, and we've talked him into it." She glanced from Bancroft to myself and back. "Will you be coming with us?"

"Maybe later," Bancroft said. "Where will you be?"

Miriam shrugged. "I hadn't really thought about it. Somewhere on the starboard decks. Benton's, maybe?"

"Fine. I'll catch up with you. Spear me a kingfish if you see one."

"Aye aye." She touched the blade of one hand to the side of her head in a ludicrous salute that made both of us smile unexpectedly. Miriam's gaze quivered and settled on me. "Do you like seafood, Mr. Kovacs?"

"Probably. I've had very little time to exercise my tastes on Earth, Mrs. Bancroft. So far I've eaten only what my hotel has to offer."

"Well, once you've developed a taste for it," she said significantly, "maybe we'll see you, as well?"

"Thank you, but I doubt it."

"Well," she repeated brightly, "try not to be too much longer, Laurens. I'll need *some* help keeping Marco off Nalan's back. He's fuming, by the way."

Bancroft grunted. "The way he played today, I'm not surprised. I thought for a while he was doing it deliberately."

"Not the last game," I said, to no one in particular.

The Bancrofts focused on me, he unreadably, she with her head tipped to one side and a sudden wide smile that made her look unexpectedly childlike. For a moment I met her gaze, and one hand rose to touch her hair with what seemed like fractional uncertainty.

"Curtis will be bringing the limousine around," she said. "I'll have to go. It was a pleasure to see you again, Mr. Kovacs."

We both watched her stride away across the lawn, her tennis skirt tilting back and forth. Even allowing for Bancroft's apparent indifference to his wife as a sexual being, Miriam's wordplay was steering fractionally too close to the wind for my liking. I had to plug the silence with something.

"Tell me something, Bancroft," I said with my eyes still on the receding figure. "No disrespect intended, but why does someone who's married to her, who's chosen to stay married, spend his time in, quote, purchased sexual release?"

I turned casually back and found him watching me without expression. He said nothing for several seconds, and when he spoke, his voice was carefully bland.

"Have you ever come in a woman's face, Kovacs?"

Culture shock is something they teach you to lock down very early on in the corps, but just occasionally a blast gets through the armor and the reality around you feels like a jigsaw that won't quite fit together. I barely chopped off my stare before it got started. This man, older than the entire human history of my planet, was asking me this question. It was as if he'd asked me had I ever played with water pistols.

"Uh. Yes. It, uh, it happens if—"

"A woman you paid?"

"Well, sometimes. Not especially. I—" I remembered his wife's abandoned laughter as I exploded into and around her mouth, come trickling down over her knuckles like foam from a popped champagne bottle. "I don't really remember. It's not a special fetish of mine, and—"

"Nor of mine," the man in front of me snapped, with rather too much emphasis. "I choose it merely as an example. There are things, desires, in all of us that are . . . better suppressed. Or at least, that cannot be expressed in a civilized context."

"I'd hardly counterpose civilization with spilling semen."

"You come from another place," Bancroft said broodingly. "A brash, young, colonial culture. You can have no concept of how the centuries of tradition have molded us here on Earth. The young of spirit, the adventurous, all left on the ships in droves. They were encouraged to leave. Those who stayed were the stolid, the obedient, the limited. I watched it happen, and at the time I was glad, because it made carving out an empire so much easier. Now I wonder if it was worth the price we paid. Culture fell in on itself, grappled after norms to live by, settled for the old and familiar. Rigid morality, rigid law. The U.N. declarations fossilized into global conformity. There was a—" He gestured. "—a sort of supracultural straitjacket, and with an inherent fear of what might be born from the colonies, the Protectorate arose while the ships were still in flight. When the first of them made planetfall, their stored peoples woke into a prepared tyranny."

"You talk as if you stood outside it. With this much vision, you still can't fight your way free?"

Bancroft smiled thinly. "Culture is like a smog. To live within it, you must breathe some of it in and, inevitably, be contaminated. And in any case, what does *free* mean in this context? Free to spill semen on my wife's face and breasts?

Free to have her masturbate in front of me, to share the use of her flesh with other men and women? Two hundred and fifty years is a long time, Mr. Kovacs, time enough for a very long list of dirty, degrading fantasies to infest the mind and titillate the hormones of each fresh sleeve you wear, while all the time your finer feelings grow purer and more rarified. Do you have any concept of what happens to emotional bonds over such a period?"

I opened my mouth, but he held up his hand for silence and I let him have it. It's not every day you get to hear the outpourings of a soul centuries old, and Bancroft was in full flow.

"No," he answered his own question. "How could you? Just as your culture is too shallow to appreciate what it is to live on Earth, your life experience cannot possibly encompass what it is to love the same person for two hundred and fifty years. In the end, if you endure, if you beat the traps of boredom and complacency, in the end what you are left with is not love. It is almost veneration. How then to match that respect, that veneration, with the sordid desires of whatever flesh you are wearing at the time? I tell you, you cannot."

"So instead you vent yourself on prostitutes?"

The thin smile returned. "I am not proud of myself, Mr. Kovacs. But you do not live this long without accepting yourself in every facet, however distasteful. The women are there. They satisfy a market need, and are recompensed accordingly. And in this way I purge myself."

"Does your wife know this?"

"Of course. And has for a very considerable time. Oumou informs me that you are already aware of the facts regarding Leila Begin. Miriam has calmed down a lot since then. I'm sure she has . . . adventures of her own."

"How sure?"

Bancroft made an irritated gesture. "Is this relevant? I don't have my wife monitored, if that's what you mean, but I know her. She has her appetites to contend with just as I do."

"And this doesn't bother you?"

"Mr. Kovacs, I am many things, but I am not a hypocrite. It is the flesh, nothing more. Miriam and I understand this. And now, since this line of questioning doesn't seem to be leading anywhere, can we please get back on track? In the absence of any guilt on the part of Elliott, what else do you have?"

I made a decision then that came up from levels of instinct way below conscious thought. I shook my head. "There's nothing yet."

"But there will be?"

"Yes. You can write Ortega off to this sleeve, but there's still Kadmin. He wasn't after Ryker. He knew me. Something's going on."

Bancroft nodded in satisfaction. "Are you going to speak to Kadmin?"

"If Ortega lets me."

"Meaning?"

"Meaning the police will have run whatever satellite footage they've got over

Oakland this morning, which means they can probably identify me leaving the clinic. There must have been something overhead at the time. I don't suppose they'll be at their most cooperative."

Bancroft permitted himself another of his splintered smiles. "Very astute, Mr. Kovacs. But you need have nothing to fear on that count. The Wei Clinic— what little you left of it—is reluctant to either release internal video footage or press charges against anyone. They have more to fear in any investigation than you do. Of course, whether they choose to seek more private reprisals is, shall we say, a more protracted question."

"And Jerry's?"

A shrug. "The same. With the proprietor dead, a managing interest has stepped in."

"Very tidy."

"I'm glad you appreciate it." Bancroft got to his feet. "As I said, it has been a busy morning, and negotiations are by no means at an end. I would be grateful if you could limit your depredations somewhat in the future. It has been . . . costly."

Getting to my feet, just for a moment I had the traceries of fire at Innenin across the back of my vision, the screaming deaths heard at a level that was bone deep, and suddenly Bancroft's elegant understatement rang sickly and grotesque, like the antiseptic words of General MacIntyre's damage reports . . . *for securing the Innenin beachhead, a price well worth paying* . . . Like Bancroft, MacIntyre had been a man of power, and like all men of power, when he talked of prices worth paying, you could be sure of one thing.

Someone else was paying.

CHAPTEr SEVENTEEN

The Fell Street station was an unassuming block done out in a style I assumed must be Martian Baroque. Whether it had been planned that way as a police station or taken over after the fact was difficult to decide. The place was, potentially, a fortress. The mock-eroded rubystone facings and hooded buttresses provided a series of natural niches in which were set high, stained-glass windows edged by the unobtrusive nubs of shield generators. Below the windows, the abrasive red surface of the stonework was sculpted into jagged obstructions that caught the morning light and turned it bloody. I couldn't tell whether the steps up to the arched entrance were deliberately uneven or just well worn.

Inside, stained light from a window and a peculiar calm fell on me simultaneously. Subsonics, I guessed, casting a glance around at the human flotsam waiting submissively on the benches. If these were arrested suspects, they had been rendered remarkably unconcerned by something and I doubted it would be the Zen Populist murals that someone had commissioned for the hall. I crossed the patch of colored light cast by the window, picked my way through small knots of people conversing in lowered tones more appropriate to a library than a holding center, and found myself at a reception counter. A uniformed cop, presumably the desk sergeant, blinked kindly back at me—the subsonics were obviously getting to him, as well.

"Lieutenant Ortega," I told him. "Organic Damage."

"Who shall I say it is?"

"Tell her it's Elias Ryker."

Out of the corner of my eye, I saw another uniform turn at the sound of the name, but nothing was said. The desk sergeant spoke into his phone, listened, then turned back to me.

"She's sending someone down. Are you armed?"

I nodded and reached under my jacket for the Nemex.

"Please surrender the weapon carefully," he added with a gentle smile. "Our security software is a little touchy, and it's apt to stun you if you look like you're pulling something."

I slowed my movements to frame advance, dumped the Nemex on the desk, and set about unstrapping the Tebbit knife from my arm. When I was finished, the sergeant beamed beatifically at me.

"Thank you. It'll all be returned to you when you leave the building."

The words were barely out of his mouth when two of the mohicans appeared through a door at the back of the hall and directed themselves rapidly toward me. Their faces were painted with identical glowers that the subsonics apparently made little impact on in the short time it took them to reach me. They went for an arm apiece.

"I wouldn't," I told them.

"Hey, he's not under arrest, you know," the desk sergeant said pacifically. One of the mohicans jerked a glance at him and snorted in exasperation. The other one just stared at me the whole time as if he hadn't eaten red meat recently. I met the stare with a gentle smile. Following the meeting with Bancroft I had gone back to the Hendrix and slept for almost twenty hours. I was rested, neurachemically alert, and feeling a cordial dislike of authority of which Quell herself would have been proud.

It must have shown. The mohicans abandoned their attempts to paw me, and the three of us rode up four floors in silence broken only by the creak of the ancient elevator.

Ortega's office had one of the stained-glass windows, or more precisely the bottom half of one, before it was bisected horizontally by the ceiling. Presumably the remainder rose missilelike from the floor of the office above. I began to see some evidence for the original building having been converted to its present use. The other walls of the office were environment formatted with a tropical sunset over water and islands. The combination of stained glass and sunset meant that the office was filled with a soft orange light in which you could see the drifting of dust motes.

The lieutenant was seated behind a heavy wooden desk as if caged there. Chin propped on one cupped hand, one shin and knee pressed hard against the edge of the desk, she was brooding over the scrolldown of an antique laptop when we came through the door. Aside from the machine, the only items on the desktop were a battered-looking heavy-caliber Smith & Wesson and a plastic cup of coffee, heating tab still unpulled. She dismissed the mohicans with a nod.

"Sit down, Kovacs."

I glanced around, saw a frame chair under the window, and hooked it up to the desk. The late-afternoon light in the office was disorienting.

"You work the night shift?"

Her eyes flared. "What kind of crack is that?"

"Hey, nothing." I held up my hands and gestured at the low light. "I just thought you might have cycled the walls for it. You know, it's ten o'clock in the morning outside."

"Oh, that." Ortega grunted, and her eyes swiveled back down to the screen display. It was hard to tell in the tropical sunset, but I thought they might be gray-green, like the sea around the maelstrom. "It's out of synch. The department got it cheap from someplace in El Paso–Juárez. Jams up completely sometimes."

"That's tough."

"Yeah, sometimes I'll just turn it off, but the neons are—" She looked up abruptly. "What the fuck am I—Kovacs, do you know how close you are to a storage rack right now?"

I made a span of my right index finger and thumb, and looked at her through it. "About the width of a testimony from the Wei Clinic, was what I heard."

"We can put you there, Kovacs. Seven forty-three yesterday morning, walking out the front door larger than life."

I shrugged.

"And don't think your Meth connections are going to keep you organic forever. There's a Wei Clinic limo driver telling interesting stories about hijack and real death. Maybe he'll have something to say about you."

"Impound his vehicle, did you?" I asked casually. "Or did Wei reclaim it before you could run tests?"

Ortega's mouth compressed into a hard line.

I nodded. "Thought so. And the driver will say precisely zero until Wei springs him, I imagine."

"Listen, Kovacs. I keep pushing, something's got to give. It's a matter of time, motherfucker. Strictly that."

"Admirable tenacity," I said. "Shame you didn't have some of that for the Bancroft case."

"There is no fucking Bancroft case."

Ortega was on her feet, palms hard down on the desktop, eyes slitted in rage and disgust. I waited, nerves sprung in case Bay City police stations were as prone to accidental suspect injury as some others I had known. Finally, the lieutenant drew a deep breath and lowered herself joint by joint back into her seat. The anger had smoothed off her face, but the disgust was still there, caught in the fine lines at the corners of her eyes and the set of her wide mouth. She looked at her nails.

"Do you know what we found at the Wei Clinic yesterday?"

"Black-market spare parts? Virtual torture programs? Or didn't they let you stay that long?"

"We found seventeen bodies with their cortical stacks burnt out. Unarmed. Seventeen dead people. Really dead."

She looked up at me again, the disgust still there.

"You'll have to pardon my lack of reaction," I said coldly. "I saw a lot worse when I was in uniform. In fact, I *did* a lot worse when I was fighting the Protectorate's battles for them."

"That was war."

"Oh, *please.*"

She said nothing. I leaned forward across the desk.

"And don't tell me those seventeen bodies are what you're on fire about, either." I gestured at my own face. "This is your problem. You don't like the idea of someone carving this up."

She sat silent for a moment, thinking, then reached into a drawer of the desk and took out a pack of cigarettes. She offered them to me automatically, and I shook my head with clenched determination.

"I quit."

"Did you?" There was genuine surprise in her voice, as she fed herself a cigarette and lit it. "Good for you. I'm impressed."

"Yeah, Ryker should be pleased, too, when he gets off stack."

She paused behind the veil of smoke, then dropped the pack back into the drawer and palm-heeled it shut.

"What do you want?" she asked flatly.

● ● ●

The holding racks were five floors down in a double-story basement where it was easier to regulate temperatures. Compared to PsychaSec, it was a toilet.

"I don't see that this is going to change anything," Ortega said as we followed a yawning technician along the steel gantry to slot 3089b. "What's Kadmin going to tell you that he hasn't told us?"

"*Look.*" I stopped and turned to face her, hands spread and held low. On the narrow gantry we were uncomfortably close. Something chemical happened, and the geometries of Ortega's stance seemed suddenly fluid, dangerously tactile. I felt my mouth dry up.

"I—" she said.

"3089b," the technician called, hefting the big, thirty-centimeter disk out of its slot. "This the one you wanted, Lieutenant?"

Ortega pushed hurriedly past me. "That's it, Micky. Can you set us up with a virtual?"

"Sure." Micky jerked a thumb at one of the spiral staircases collared in at intervals along the gantry. "You want to go down to Five, slap on the 'trodes. Take about five minutes."

"The point is," I said, as the three of us clattered down the steel steps, "you're the Sia. Kadmin knows you; he's been dealing with you all his professional life. It's part of what he does. I'm an unknown. If he's never been extrasystem, the chances are he's never met an Envoy before. And they tell nasty stories about the corps most places I've been."

Ortega gave me a skeptical look over her shoulder. "You're going to *frighten* him into a statement? Dimitri Kadmin? I don't think so."

"He'll be off balance, and when people are off balance they give things away. Don't forget, this guy's working for someone who wants me dead. Someone who *is* scared of me, at least superficially. Some of that may rub off on Kadmin."

"And this is supposed to convince me that someone murdered Bancroft after all?"

"Ortega, it doesn't matter whether you believe it or not. We've been through

Ortega appeared beside me, at first a pale pencil sketch of a woman, all flickering lines and diffident shading. As I watched, pastel colors raced through her, and her movements grew more defined. She was turning to speak to me, one hand reaching into the pocket of her jacket. I waited and the final gloss of color popped out onto her surfaces. She produced her cigarettes.

"Smoke?"

"No thanks, I—" Realizing the futility of worrying about virtual health, I accepted the pack and shook one out. Ortega lit us both with her lighter, and the first bite of smoke in my lungs was ecstasy.

I looked up at the geometric sky. "Is this standard?"

"Pretty much." Ortega squinted into the distance. "Resolution looks a bit higher than usual. Think Micky's showing off."

Kadmin scribbled into existence on the other side of the table. Before the virtual program had even colored him in properly, he became aware of us and folded his arms across his chest. If my appearance in the cell was putting him off balance as hoped, it didn't show.

"Again, Lieutenant?" he said when the program had rendered him complete. "There is a U.N. ruling on maximum virtual time for one arrest, you know."

"That's right, and we're still a long way off it," Ortega said. "Why don't you sit down, Kadmin."

"No, thank you."

"I said sit, motherfucker." There was an abrupt undercurrent of steel in the cop's voice, and magically Kadmin blinked off and reappeared seated at the table. His face betrayed a momentary flash of rage at the displacement, but then it was gone and he unfolded his arms in an ironic gesture.

"You're right, it's so much more comfortable like this. Won't you both join me?"

We took our seats in the more conventional way, and I stared at Kadmin as we did it. It was the first time I'd seen anything quite like it.

He was the Patchwork Man.

Most virtual systems recreate you from self-images held in the memory, with a commonsense subroutine to prevent your delusions from impinging too much. I generally come out a little taller and thinner in the face than I usually am. In this case, the system seemed to have scrambled a myriad different perceptions from Kadmin's presumably long list of sleeves. I'd seen it done before, as a technique, but most of us grow rapidly attached to whatever sleeve we're living in, and that form blanks out previous incarnations. We are, after all, evolved to relate to the physical world.

The man in front of me was different. His frame was that of a Caucasian Nordic, topping mine by nearly thirty centimeters, but the face was at odds. It began African, broad and deep ebony, but the color ended like a mask under the eyes, and the lower half was divided along the line of the nose, pale copper on the left, corpse white on the right. The nose was both fleshy and aquiline and mediated well between the top and bottom halves of the face, but the mouth was a mismatch of left and right sides that left the lips peculiarly twisted. Long straight black hair was combed manelike back from the forehead, shot through on one side with pure white. The hands, immobile on the metal table, were equipped with claws similar to the ones I'd seen on the giant Freak Fighter in Licktown, but the fingers were long and sensitive. He had breasts, impossibly full on a torso so overmuscled. The eyes, set in jet skin, were a startling pale green. Kadmin had freed himself from conventional perceptions of the physical. In an earlier age, he would have been a shaman; here, the centuries of technology had made him more. An electronic demon, a malignant spirit that dwelled in altered carbon and emerged only to possess flesh and wreak havoc.

He would have made a fine Envoy.

"I take it I don't have to introduce myself," I said quietly.

Kadmin grinned, revealing small teeth and a delicate pointed tongue. "If you're a friend of the lieutenant, you don't have to do anything you don't want to here. Only the slobs get their virtuality edited."

"Do you know this man, Kadmin?" Ortega asked.

"Hoping for a confession, Lieutenant?" Kadmin threw back his head and laughed musically. "Oh, the crudity! This man? This woman, maybe? Or, yes, even a dog could be trained to say as much as he has said, given the right tranquilizers, of course. They do tend to go pitifully insane when you decant them if not. But, yes, even a dog. We sit here, three silhouettes carved from electronic sleet in the Difference Storm, and you talk like a cheap period drama. Limited vision, Lieutenant, limited vision. Where is the voice that said altered carbon would free us from the cells of our flesh? The vision that said we would be *angels*."

"You tell me, Kadmin. You're the one with the exalted professional standing." Ortega's tone was detached. She system-magicked a long scroll of printout into one hand and glanced idly down it. "Pimp, triad enforcer, virtual interrogator in the corporate wars—it's all quality work. Me, I'm just some dumb cop can't see the light."

"I'm not going to quarrel with you there, Lieutenant."

"Says here you were a wiper for MeritCon a while back, scaring archaeologue miners off their claims in Syrtis Major. Slaughtering their families by way of incentive. Nice job." Ortega tossed the printout back into oblivion. "We've got you cold, Kadmin. Digital footage from the hotel surveillance system, verifiable simultaneous sleeving, both stacks on ice. That's an erasure mandatory, and even if your lawyers dance it down to Compliance at Machine Error, the sun's going to be a red dwarf by the time they let you off stack."

Kadmin smiled. "Then what are you here for?"

"Who sent you?" I asked him softly.

"The Dog speaks!

Is it a wolf I hear,
Howling his lonely communion
With the unpiloted stars,
Or merely the self-importance and servitude
In the bark of a dog?

How many millennia did it take,
Twisting and torturing
The pride from the one
To make a tool,
The other?"

I inhaled smoke and nodded. Like most Harlanites, I knew Quell's *Poems and Other Prevarications* more or less by heart. It was taught in schools in lieu of the later and weightier political works, most of which were still deemed too radical to be put in the hands of children. This wasn't a great translation, but it captured the essence. More impressive was the fact that anyone not actually from Harlan's World could quote such an obscure volume.

I finished it for him.

"And how do we measure the distance from spirit to spirit?
And who do we find to blame?"

"Have you come seeking blame, Mr. Kovacs?"

"Among other things."

"How disappointing."

"You expected something else?"

"No," Kadmin said with another smile. "Expectation is our first mistake. I meant, how disappointing for you."

"Maybe."

He shook his great piebald head. "Certainly. You will take no names from me. If you seek blame, I will have to bear it for you."

"That's very generous, but you'll remember what Quell said about lackeys."

"Kill them along the way, but count your bullets, for there are more worthy targets." Kadmin chuckled deep inside himself. "Are you threatening me in monitored police storage?"

"No. I'm just putting things into perspective." I knocked ash off my cigarette and watched it sparkle out of existence before it reached the floor. "Someone's pulling your strings; that's who I'm going to wipe. You're nothing. You I wouldn't waste spit on."

Kadmin tipped his head back as a stronger tremor ran through the shifting lines in the sky, like cubist lightning. It reflected in the dull sheen on the metal table and seemed to touch his hands for a moment. When he looked down at me again, it was with a curious light in his eyes.

"I was not asked to kill you," he said tonelessly. "Unless your abduction proved inconvenient. But now I will."

Ortega was on him as the last syllable left his mouth. The table blinked out of existence, and she kicked him backwards off the chair with one booted foot. As he rolled back to his feet, the same boot caught him in the mouth and floored him again. I ran my tongue around the almost healed gashes inside my own mouth, and felt a distinct lack of sympathy.

Ortega dragged Kadmin up by the hair, the cigarette in her hand replaced by a vicious-looking blackjack courtesy of the same system magic that had eliminated the table.

"I hear you right?" she hissed. "You making threats, fuckhead?"

Kadmin bared his teeth in a bloodstained grin.

"Police brutal—"

"That's right, motherfucker." Ortega hit him across the cheek with the blackjack. The skin split. "Police brutality in a monitored police virtuality. Sandy Kim and WorldWeb One would have a field day, wouldn't they. But you know what? I reckon your lawyers aren't going to want to run this particular tape."

"Leave him alone, Ortega."

She seemed to remember herself then, and stepped back. Her face twitched and she drew a deep breath. The table blinked back, and Kadmin was suddenly sitting upright again, mouth undamaged.

"You, too," he said quietly.

"Yeah, sure." There was contempt in Ortega's voice, at least half of it directed at herself, I guessed. She made a second effort to bring her breathing back under control, rearranged her clothing unnecessarily. "Like I said, going to be a cold day in hell by the time you get the chance. Maybe I'll wait for you."

"Whoever sent you worth this much, Kadmin?" I wondered softly. "You going down silent out of contractual loyalty, or are you just scared shitless?"

For answer, the composite man folded his arms across his chest and stared through me.

"You through, Kovacs?" Ortega asked.

I tried to meet Kadmin's distant gaze. "Kadmin, the man I work for has a lot of influence. This could be your last chance to cut a deal."

Nothing. He didn't even blink.

I shrugged. "I'm through."

"Good," Ortega said grimly. "Because sitting downwind of this piece of shit is beginning to eat away at my usually tolerant nature." She waggled her fingers in front of his eyes. "Be seeing you, fuckhead."

At that, Kadmin's eyes turned up to meet hers, and a small, peculiarly unpleasant smile twisted his lips.

We left.

●●●

Back on the fourth floor, the walls of Ortega's office had reverted to a dazzling high noon over beaches of white sand. I screwed up my eyes against the glare while Ortega trawled through a desk drawer and came up with her own and a spare pair of sunglasses.

"So what did you learn from that?"

I fitted the lenses uncomfortably over the bridge of my nose. They were too small. "Not much, except that little gem about not having orders to wipe me. Someone wanted to talk to me. I'd pretty much guessed that anyway, else he could have just blown my stack out all over the lobby of the Hendrix. Still, means someone wanted to cut a deal of their own, outside of Bancroft."

"Or someone wanted to interrogate the guts out of you."

I shook my head. "About what? I'd only just arrived. Doesn't make any sense."

"The corps? Unfinished business?" Ortega made little flicking motions with her hand as if she were dealing me the suggestions. "Maybe a grudge match?"

"No. We went through this one when we were yelling at each other the other night. There are people who'd like to see me wiped, but none of them live on Earth, and none of them swing the kind of influence to go interstellar. And there's nothing I know about the corps that isn't in a low-wall database somewhere. And anyway, it's just too much of a fucking coincidence. No, this is about Bancroft. Someone wanted in on the program."

"Whoever had him killed?"

I tipped my head down to look at her directly over the sun lenses. "You believe me, then."

"Not entirely."

"Oh, come *on*."

But Ortega wasn't listening. "What I want to know," she brooded, "is why he rewrote his codes at the end. You know, we've sweated him nearly a dozen times since we downloaded him Sunday night. That's the first time he's come close to even admitting he was there."

"Even to his lawyers?"

"We don't know what he says to them. They're big-time sharks, out of Ulan Bator and New York. That kind of money carries a scrambler into all privy virtual interviews. We get nothing on tape but static."

I raised a mental eyebrow. On Harlan's World, all virtual custody was monitored as a matter of course. Scramblers were not permitted, no matter how much money you were worth.

"Speaking of lawyers, are Kadmin's here in Bay City?"

"Physically, you mean? Yeah, they've got a deal with a Marin County practice. One of their partners is renting a sleeve here for the duration." Ortega's lip curled. "Physical meetings are considered a touch of class these days. Only the cheap firms do business down the wires."

"What's this suit's name?"

There was a brief pause while she hung on to the name. "Kadmin's a spinning item right now. I'm not sure we go this far."

"Ortega, we go all the way. That was the deal. Otherwise I'm back to risking Elias's fine features with some more maximal-push investigation."

She was silent for a while.

"Rutherford," she said finally. "You want to talk to Rutherford?"

"Right now, I want to talk to anyone. Maybe I didn't make things clear earlier. I'm working cold here. Bancroft waited a month and a half before he brought me in. Kadmin's all I've got."

"Keith Rutherford's a handful of engine grease. You won't get any more out of him than you did Kadmin downstairs. And anyway, how the fuck am I supposed to introduce you, Kovacs? 'Hi, Keith, this is the ex-Envoy loose cannon your client tried to wipe on Sunday. He'd like to ask you a few questions.' He'll close up faster than an unpaid hooker's hole."

She had a point. I thought about it for a moment, staring out to sea.

"All right," I said slowly. "All I need is a couple of minutes' conversation. How about you tell him I'm Elias Ryker, your partner from Organic Damage. I practically am, after all."

Ortega took off her lenses and stared at me.

"Are you trying to be funny?"

"No. I'm trying to be practical. Rutherford's sleeving in from Ulan Bator, right?"

"New York," she said tightly.

"New York. Right. So he probably doesn't know anything about you or Ryker."

"Probably not."

"So what's the problem?"

"The problem is, Kovacs, that I don't like it."

There was more silence. I dropped my gaze into my lap and let out a sigh that was only partially manufactured. Then I took off my own sunglasses and looked up at her. It was all there on plain display. The naked fear of sleeving and all that it entailed; paranoid essentialism with its back to the wall.

"Ortega," I said gently. "I'm not him. I'm not trying to be hi—"

"You couldn't even come close," she snapped.

"All we're talking about is a couple of hours' make-believe."

"Is that all?"

She said it in a voice like iron, and she put her sunglasses back on with such brusque efficiency that I didn't need to see the tears welling up in the eyes behind the mirror lenses.

"All right," she said finally, clearing her throat. "I'll get you in. I don't see the point, but I'll do it. Then what?"

"That's a little difficult to say. I'll have to improvise."

"Like you did at the Wei Clinic?"

I shrugged noncommittally. "Envoy techniques are largely reactive. I can't react to something until it happens."

"I don't want another bloodbath, Kovacs. It looks bad on the city stats."

"If there's violence, it won't be me that starts it."

"That's not much of a guarantee. Haven't you got *any* idea what you're going to do?"

"I'm going to talk."

"Just talk?" She looked at me disbelievingly. "That's all?"

I fitted my ill-fitting sunglasses back over my face.

"Sometimes that's all it takes," I said.

CHAPTEr EIGHTEEN

I met my first lawyer when I was fifteen. He was a harried-looking juvenile-affray expert who defended me, not unhandily, in a minor organic damage suit involving a Newpest police officer. He bargained them down with a kind of myopic patience to Conditional Release and eleven minutes of virtual psychiatric counseling. In the hall outside the juvenile court, he looked into my probably infuriatingly smug face and nodded as if his worst fears about the meaning of his life were being confirmed. Then he turned on his heel and walked away. I forget his name.

My entry into the Newpest gang scene shortly afterwards precluded any more such legal encounters. The gangs were web smart, wired up, and already writing their own intrusion programs or buying them from kids half their age in return for low-grade virtual porn ripped off the networks. They didn't get caught easily, and in return for this favor the Newpest heat tended to leave them alone. Intergang violence was largely ritualized and excluded other players most of the time. On the odd occasion that it spilled over and affected civilians, there would be a rapid and brutal series of punitive raids that left a couple of lead gang heroes in the store and the rest of us with extensive bruising. Fortunately I never worked my way up the chain of command far enough to get put away, so the next time I saw the inside of a courtroom was the Innenin inquiry.

The lawyers I saw there had about as much in common with the man who had defended me at fifteen as automated machine rifle fire has with farting. They were cold, professionally polished, and well on their way up a career ladder that would ensure that despite the uniforms they wore, they would never have to come within a thousand kilometers of a genuine firefight. The only problem they had, as they cruised sharkishly back and forth across the cool marble floor of the court, was in drawing the fine differences between war—mass murder of people wearing a uniform not your own; justifiable loss—mass murder of your own troops, but with substantial gains; and criminal negligence—mass murder of your own troops, without appreciable benefit. I sat in that courtroom for three weeks listening to them dress it like a variety of salads, and with every passing hour the distinctions, which at one point I'd been pretty clear on, grew increasingly vague. I suppose that proves how good they were.

After that, straightforward criminality came as something of a relief.

"Something bothering you?" Ortega glanced sideways at me as she brought the unmarked cruiser down on a shelving pebble beach below the split-level, glass-fronted offices of Prendergast Sanchez, attorneys-at-law.

"Just thinking."

"Try cold showers and alcohol. Works for me."

I nodded and held up the minuscule bead of metal I had been rolling between my finger and thumb. "Is this legal?"

Ortega reached up and killed the primaries. "More or less. No one's going to complain."

"Good. Now, I'm going to need verbal cover to start with. You do the talking; I'll just shut up and listen. Take it from there."

"Fine. Ryker was like that, anyway. Never used two words if one would do it. Most of the time with the scumbags, he'd just look at them."

"Sort of a Micky Nozawa type, huh?"

"*Who?*"

"Never mind." The rattle of upthrown pebbles on the hull died away as Ortega cut the engines to idle. I stretched in my seat and threw open my side of the hatch. Climbing out, I saw an overburly figure coming down the meandering set of wooden steps from the split level. Looked like grafting. A blunt-looking gun was slung over his shoulder, and he wore gloves. Probably not a lawyer.

"Go easy," Ortega said, suddenly at my shoulder. "We have jurisdiction here. He isn't going to start anything."

She flashed her badge as the muscle jumped the last step to the beach and landed on flexed legs. You could see the disappointment on his face as he saw it.

"Bay City police. We're here to see Rutherford."

"You can't park that here."

"I already have," Ortega told him evenly. "Are we going to keep Mr. Rutherford waiting?"

There was a prickly silence, but she'd gauged him correctly. Contenting himself with a grunt, the muscle gestured us up the staircase and followed at prudent shepherding distance. It took a while to get to the top, and I was pleased to see when we arrived that Ortega was considerably more out of breath than I was. We went across a modest sundeck made from the same wood as the stairs and through two sets of automatic plate-glass doors into a reception area styled to look like someone's lounge. There were rugs on the floor, knitted in the same patterns as my jacket, and empathist prints on the walls. Five single armchairs provided parking.

"Can I help you?"

This was a lawyer, no question about it. A smoothly groomed blonde woman in a loose skirt and jacket tailored to fit the room, hands resting comfortably in her pockets.

"Bay City police. Where's Rutherford?"

The woman flickered a glance sideways at our escort and, having received the nod, did not bother to demand identification.

"I'm afraid Keith is occupied at the moment. He's in virtual with New York."

"Well, get him out of virtual, then," Ortega said with dangerous mildness.

"And tell him the officer who arrested his client is here to see him. I'm sure he'll be interested."

"That may take some time, Officer."

"No, it won't."

The two women locked gazes for a moment, and then the lawyer looked away. She nodded to the muscle, who went back outside still looking disappointed.

"I'll see what I can do," she said glacially. "Please wait here."

We waited, Ortega at the floor-to-ceiling window, staring down at the beach with her back to the room, and myself prowling the artwork. Some of it was quite good. With the separately ingrained habits of working in monitored environments, neither of us said anything for the ten minutes it took to produce Rutherford from the inner sanctum.

"Lieutenant Ortega." The modulated voice reminded me of Miller's at the clinic, and when I looked up from a print over the fireplace, I saw much the same kind of sleeve. Maybe a little older, with slightly craggier patriarchal features designed to inspire instant respect in jurors and judges alike, but the same athletic frame and off-the-rack good looks. "To what do I owe this unexpected . . . visit? Not more harassment, I hope."

Ortega ignored the allegation. "Detective Sergeant Elias Ryker," she said, nodding at me. "Your client just admitted to one count of abduction and made a first-degree organic-damage threat under monitor. Care to see the footage?"

"Not particularly. Care to tell me why you're here?"

Rutherford was good. He'd barely reacted; barely, but enough to catch it out of the corner of my eye. My mind went into overdrive.

Ortega leaned on the back of an armchair. "For a man defending a mandatory-erasure case, you're showing a real lack of imagination."

Rutherford sighed theatrically. "You have called me away from an important link. I assume you do have something to say."

"Do you know what third-party retroassociative complicity is?" I asked the question without turning from the print, and when I did look up, I had Rutherford's complete attention.

"I do not," he said stiffly.

"That's a pity, because you and the other partners of Uzala Bennett are right in the firing line if Kadmin rolls over. But of course, if that happens—" I spread my hands and shrugged. "—it'll be open season. In fact, it may already be."

"All right, that's enough." Rutherford's hand rose decisively to a remote summons emitter pinned to his lapel. Our escort was on his way. "I don't have time to play games with you. There is no statute by that name, and this is getting perilously close to harassment."

I raised my voice. "Just wanted to know which side you want to be on when the program crashes, Rutherford. There is a statute. U.N. indictable offense, last handed down fourth of May 2207. Look it up. I had to go back a long way to dig this one up, but it'll take all of you down in the end. Kadmin knows it; that's why he's cracking."

Rutherford smiled. "I don't think so, Detective."

I repeated my shrug. "Shame. Like I said, look it up. Then decide which side you want to play for. We're going to need inside corroboration, and we're prepared to pay for it. If it isn't you, Ulan Bator's stuffed with lawyers who'll give blow jobs for the chance."

The smile wavered fractionally.

"That's right, think about it." I nodded at Ortega. "You can get me at Fell Street, same as the lieutenant here. Elias Ryker, offworld liaison. I'm promising you, this is going to go down, whatever happens, and when it does, I'll be a good person to know."

Ortega took the cue like she'd been doing it all her life. Like Sarah would have done. She unleaned herself from the chair back and made for the door.

"Be seeing you, Rutherford," she said laconically, as we stepped back out onto the deck. The muscle was there, grinning widely and flexing his hands at his sides. "And you, don't even think about it."

I contented myself with the silent look that I had been told Ryker used to such great effect and followed my partner down the stairs.

●●●

Back in the cruiser, Ortega snapped on a screen and watched identity data from the bug scroll down.

"Where'd you put it?"

"Print over the fireplace. Corner of the frame."

She grunted. "They'll sweep it out of there in nothing flat, you know. And none of it's admissible as evidence, anyway."

"I know. You've told me that twice already. That's not the point. If Rutherford rattled, he'll jump first."

"You think he rattled?"

"A little."

"Yeah." She glanced curiously at me. "So what the fuck is third-party retroassociative complicity?"

"No idea. I made it up."

Her eyebrow went up. "No shit?"

"Convinced you, huh? Know what, you could have given me a polygraph test while I was spinning it, and I would have convinced that, too. Basic Envoy tricks. Course, Rutherford will know that as soon as he looks it up, but it's already served its purpose."

"Which is what?"

"Provide the arena. Tell lies, you keep your opponent off balance. It's like fighting on unfamiliar ground. Rutherford was rattled, but he smiled when I told him this stuff was why Kadmin was acting up." I looked up through the windshield at the house above, formulating the scrapings of intuition into understanding. "He was fucking relieved when I said that. I don't suppose normally he would have given that much away, but the bluff had him running scared, and him knowing better than me about something was that little ray of stability he needed. And that means he knows another reason why Kadmin changed behavior. He knows the real reason."

Ortega grunted approvingly. "Pretty good, Kovacs. You should have been a cop. You notice his reaction when I told him the good news about what Kadmin had done? He wasn't surprised at all."

"No. He was expecting it. Or something like it."

"Yeah." She paused. "This really what you used to do for a living?"

"Sometimes. Diplomatic missions, or deep-cover stuff. It wasn't—"

I fell silent as she elbowed me in the ribs. On the screen, a series of coded sequences were unwinding like snakes of blue fire.

"Here we go. Simultaneous calls—he must be doing this in virtual to save time. One, two, three—that one's New York, must be to update the senior partners, and oops."

The screen flared and went abruptly dark.

"They found it," I said.

"They did. The New York line probably has a sweeper attached, flushes out the call vicinity on connection."

"Or one of the others does."

"Yeah." Ortega punched up the screen's memory and stared at the call codes. "They're all three routed through discreet clearing. Take us a while to locate them. You want to eat?"

• • •

Homesickness isn't something a veteran Envoy should confess to. If the conditioning hasn't already ironed it out of you, the years of sleeving back and forth across the Protectorate should have. Envoys are citizens of that elusive state, Here and Now, a state that jealously admits of no dual nationalities. The past is relevant only as data.

Homesickness was what I felt as we stepped past the kitchen area of the *Flying Fish*, and the aroma of sauces I had last tasted in Millsport hit me like a friendly tentacle. Teriyaki, frying tempura, and the undercurrent of miso. I stood wrapped in it for a moment, remembering that time. A ramen bar Sarah and I had skulked in while the heat from the Gemini Biosys gig died down, eyes hooked to newsnet broadcasts and a corner videophone with a smashed screen that was supposed to ring, anytime now. Steam on the windows and the company of taciturn Millsport skippers.

And back beyond that, I remembered the moth-battered paper lanterns outside Watanabe's on a Newpest Friday night. My teenage skin slick with sweat from the jungle wind blowing out of the south and my eyes glittering with tetrameth in one of the big wind-chime mirrors. Talk, cheaper than the big bowls of ramen, about Big Scores and yakuza connections, tickets north and beyond, new sleeves and new worlds. Old Watanabe had sat out on the deck with us, listening to it all but never commenting, just smoking his pipes and glancing from time to time in the mirror at his own Caucasian features—always with mild surprise, it seemed to me.

He never told us how he'd got that sleeve, just as he never denied or confirmed the rumors about his escapades with the Marine Corps, the Quell Memorial Brigade, the Envoys, whatever. An older gang member once told us he'd seen Watanabe face down a roomful of Seven Percent Angels with nothing but his pipe in his hands, and some kid from the swamp towns once came up with a fuzzy slice of newsreel footage he claimed was from the Settlement wars. It was only 2-D, hurriedly shot just before an assault team went over the top, but the sergeant being interviewed was subtitled Watanabe, Y, and there was something about the way he tilted his head when questioned that had us all crowing recognition at the screen. But then, Watanabe was a common enough name, and come to that, the guy who said he'd seen the Angels face-down was also fond of telling us how he'd slept with a Harlan family heiress when she came slumming, and none of us believed *that*.

Once, on a rare evening when I was both straight and alone at Watanabe's, I swallowed enough of my adolescent pride to ask the old man for his advice. I'd been reading U.N. armed forces promotional literature for weeks, and I needed someone to push me one way or the other.

Watanabe just grinned at me around the stem of his pipe. "I should advise you?" he asked. "Share with you the wisdom that brought me to this?"

We both looked around the little bar and the fields beyond the deck.

"Well, uh, yes."

"Well, uh, *no*," he said firmly, and resumed his pipe.

"Kovacs?"

I blinked and found Ortega in front of me, looking curiously into my eyes.

"Something I need to know about?"

I smiled faintly and glanced around at the kitchen's shining steel counters. "Not really."

"It's good food," she said, misinterpreting the look.

"Well, let's get some, then."

She led me out of the steam and onto one of the restaurant's gantries. The *Flying Fish* was, according to Ortega, a decommissioned aerial minesweeper that some oceanographic institute had bought up. The institute was now either defunct or had moved on and the bayward-facing facility had been gutted, but someone had stripped the *Flying Fish*, rerigged her as a restaurant, and cabled her five hundred meters above the decaying facility buildings. Periodically the whole vessel was reeled gently back down to earth to disgorge its sated customers and take on fresh. There was a queue around two sides of the docking hangar when we arrived, but Ortega jumped it with her badge, and when the airship came floating down through the open roof of the hangar, we were the first aboard.

I settled cross-legged onto cushions at a table that was secured to the blimp's hull on a metal arm and thus did not touch the gantry at all. The gantry was cordoned with the faint haze of a power screen that kept the temperature decent and the gusting wind to a pleasant breeze. Around me the hexagonal grating floor allowed me an almost uninterrupted view past the edge of the cushions to the sea a kilometer below. I shifted uneasily. Heights had never been my strong point.

"Used to use it for tracking whales and stuff," Ortega said, gesturing sideways at the hull. "Back before places like this could afford the satellite time. Course, with Understanding Day, the whales were suddenly big money for anyone who could talk to them. You know they've told us almost as much about the Martians as four centuries of archaeologues on Mars itself. Christ, they remember them coming here. Race memory, that is."

She paused. "I was born on Understanding Day," she added inconsequentially.

"Really?"

"Yep. January ninth. They named me Kristin after some whale scientist in Australia, worked on the original translation team."

"Nice."

Who she was really talking to caught up with her. She shrugged, abruptly dismissive. "When you're a kid you don't see it that way. I wanted to be called Maria."

"You come here often?"

"Not often. But I figured anyone out of Harlan's World would like it."

"Good guess."

A waiter arrived and carved the menu into the air between us with a holotorch. I glanced briefly down the list and selected one of the ramen bowls at random. Something vegetarian.

"Good choice," Ortega said. She nodded at the waiter. "I'll have the same. And juice. You want anything to drink?"

"Water."

Our selections flared briefly in pink, and the menu disappeared. The waiter pocketed the holotorch at his breast with a snappy gesture and withdrew. Ortega looked around her, seeking neutral conversation.

"So, uh—you got places like this in Millsport?"

"On the ground, yes. We're not big on aerial stuff."

"No?" She raised her customary eyebrow. "Millsport's an archipelago, isn't it? I would have thought airships were—"

"An obvious solution to the real estate shortage? Right as far as that goes, but I think you're forgetting something." I flicked my eyes skywards. "We Are Not Alone."

It clicked. "The orbitals? They're hostile?"

"Mmm. Let's say capricious. They tend to shoot down anything airborne that masses more than a helicopter. And since no one's ever been able to get close enough to decommission one of them—or even get aboard, come to that—we have no way of knowing what their exact programming parameters are. So we just play it safe, and don't go up in the air much."

"Must make IP traffic tough."

I nodded. "Well, yeah. Course, there isn't much traffic anyway. No other habitable planets in the system, and we're still too busy exploiting the World to bother about terraforming. Few exploration probes, and maintenance shuttles to the platforms. Bit of exotic-element mining, that's about it. And there are a couple of launch windows down around the equator toward evening and one crack-of-dawn slot up on the pole. It looks like a couple of orbitals must have crashed and burned, way back when, left holes in the net." I paused. "Or maybe someone shot them down."

"Someone? You mean, someone, not the Martians?"

I spread my hands. "Why not? Everything they've ever found on Mars was razed or buried. Or so well disguised we spent decades looking right at it before we even realized it was there. It's the same on most of the settled worlds. All the evidence points to some kind of conflict out there."

"But the archaeologues say it was a civil war, a colonial war."

"Yeah, right." I folded my arms and sat back. "The archaeologues say what the Protectorate tells them to say, and right now it's fashionable to deplore the tragedy of the Martian domain tearing itself apart and sinking via barbarism into extinction. Big warning for the inheritors. Don't rebel against your lawful rulers, for the good of all civilization."

Ortega looked nervously around her. Conversation at some of the nearer tables had skittered and jarred to a halt. I gave the spectators a wide smile.

"Do you mind if we talk about something else?" Ortega asked uncomfortably.

"Sure. Tell me about Ryker."

The discomfort vanished into an icy stillness. Ortega put her hands flat on the table in front of her and looked at them.

"No, I don't think so," she said eventually.

"Fair enough." I watched cloud formations shimmer in the haze of the power screen for a while, and avoided looking down at the sea below me. "But I think you want to really."

"How very male of you."

The food arrived, and we ate in silence broken only by the traditional slurping. Despite the Hendrix's perfectly balanced autochef breakfast, I discovered I was ravenous. The food had triggered a hunger in me deeper than the needs of my stomach. I was draining the dregs of my bowl before Ortega had got halfway through hers.

"Food okay?" she asked ironically as I sat back.

I nodded, trying to wipe away the skeins of memory associated with the ramen, but unwilling to bring the Envoy conditioning on-line and spoil the sated feeling in my belly. Looking around at the clean metal lines of the dining gantry and the sky beyond, I was as close to totally contented as I had been since Miriam Bancroft left me drained in the Hendrix.

Ortega's phone shrilled. She unpocketed it and answered, still chewing her last mouthful.

"Yeah? Uh-huh. Uh-huh, good. No, we'll go." Her eyes flickered briefly to mine. "That so? No, leave that one, too. It'll keep. Yeah, thanks, Zak. Owe you one."

She stowed the phone again and resumed eating.

"Good news?"

"Depends on your point of view. They traced the two local calls. One to a fightdrome over in Richmond, place I know. We'll go down and take a look."

"And the other call?"

Ortega looked up at me from her bowl, chewed, and swallowed. "The other number was a residential discreet. Bancroft residence. Suntouch House. Now what, exactly, do you make of that?"

CHAPTEr NINETEEN

O rtega's fightdrome was an ancient bulk carrier, moored up in the north end of the bay, alongside acres of abandoned warehouses. The vessel must have been over half a kilometer long with six clearly discernible cargo cells between stem and stern. The one at the rear appeared to be open. From the air, the body of the carrier was a uniform orange that I assumed was rust.

"Don't let it fool you," Ortega grunted as we circled. "They've polymered the hull a quarter meter thick all over. Take a shaped charge to sink it now."

"Expensive."

She shrugged. "They've got the backing."

We landed on the quay. Ortega killed the motors and leaned across me to peer up at the ship's superstructure, which at a glance appeared to be deserted. I pushed myself back into the seat a little, discomforted in equal parts by the pressure of the lithe torso in my lap and my slightly overfull stomach. She felt the movement, seemed suddenly to realize what she was doing, and pulled herself abruptly upright again.

"No one home," she said awkwardly.

"So it seems. Shall we go and have a look?"

We got out into the customary blanket-snap of wind off the bay and made for a tubular aluminum gangway that led onto the vessel near the stern. It was uncomfortably open ground, and I crossed it with an eye constantly sweeping the railed and craned lines of the ship's deck and bridge tower. Nothing stirred. I squeezed my left arm lightly against my side to check that the fibergrip holster hadn't slipped down, as the cheaper varieties often did after a couple of days' wear. With the Nemex I was tolerably sure I could air out anyone shooting at us from the rail.

In any event it wasn't necessary. We reached the end of the gangway without incident. A slim chain was fixed across the open entrance with a hand-lettered sign hung on it.

PANAMA ROSE
FIGHT TONIGHT—22.00
GATE PRICE DOUBLE

I lifted the rectangle of thin metal and looked at the crude lettering dubiously.

"Are you *sure* Rutherford called here?"

"Like I said before, don't let it fool you." Ortega was unhooking the chain. "Fighter chic. Crude's the in-thing. Last season it was neon signs, but even that's not cool enough now. Place is fucking globally hyped. Only about three or four like it on the planet. There's no coverage allowed in the arenas. No holos, not even televisuals. You coming, or what?"

"Weird." I followed her down the tubular corridor, thinking of the Freak Fights I'd gone to when I was younger. On Harlan's World, all fights were broadcast. They got the highest-viewing figures of any transmitted entertainment online. "Don't people like watching this sort of stuff?"

"Yeah, of course they do." Even with the distortion of the echoing corridor, I could hear Ortega's lip curling in the tone of her voice. "Never get enough of it. That's how this scam works. See, first they set up the Creed—"

"Creed?"

"Yeah, Creed of Purity or some such shit. Didn't anyone ever tell you it's rude to interrupt? Creed goes, you want to see the fight, you go see it in the flesh. That's *better* than watching it on the Web. More classy. So, limited audience seating, sky-high demand. That makes the tickets very sexy, which makes them very expensive, which makes them even more sexy, and whoever thought of it just rides that spiral up through the roof."

"Smart."

"Yeah, smart."

We came to the end of the gangway and stepped out again onto a wind-whipped deck. On either side of us the roofing of two of the cargo cells swelled smoothly to waist height like two enormous steel blisters on the ship's skin. Beyond the rear swelling, the bridge towered blankly into the sky, seeming entirely unconnected with the hull we were standing on. The only motion came from the chains of a loading crane ahead of us that the wind had set swinging fractionally.

"The last time I was out here," Ortega said, raising her voice to compete with the wind, "was because some dipshit newsprick from WorldWeb One got caught trying to walk recording implants into a title fight. They threw him into the bay. After they'd removed the implants with a pair of pliers."

"Nice."

"Like I said, it's a classy place."

"Such flattery, Lieutenant. I hardly know how to respond."

The voice coughed from rusty-looking loudspeaker horns set on two-meter-high stalks along the rail. My hand flew to the Nemex butt, and my vision cycled out to peripheral scan with a rapidity that hurt. Ortega gave me an almost imperceptible shake of the head and looked up at the bridge. The two of us swept the superstructure for movement in opposite directions, coordinating unconsciously. Under the immediacy of the tension, I felt a warm shiver of pleasure at that unlooked-for symmetry.

"No, no. Over here," the metallic voice said, this time relegated to the horns to the stern. As I watched, the chains on one of the rear loading cranes grated into motion and began to run, presumably hauling something up from the open cell in front of the bridge. I left my hand on the Nemex. Overhead, the sun was breaking through the cloud cover.

The chain ended in a massive iron hook, in the crook of which stood the speaker, one hand still holding a prehistoric microphone, the other gripped lightly around the rising chain. He was dressed in an inappropriate-looking gray suit that flapped in the wind, leaning out from the chain at a fastidious angle, hair glinting in a wandering shaft of sunlight. I narrowed my eyes to confirm. Synthetic. Cheap synthetic.

The crane swung out over the curved cover of the cargo cell, and the synth alighted elegantly on the top, looking down on us.

"Elias Ryker," he said, and his voice was not much smoother than the tannoy had been. Someone had done a real cut-rate job on the vocal chords. He shook his head. "We thought we'd seen the last of you. How short the legislature's memory."

"Carnage?" Ortega lifted a hand to shade against the sudden sunlight. "That you?"

The synthetic bowed faintly and stowed the mike inside his jacket. He began to pick his way down the sloping cell cover.

"Emcee Carnage, at your service, officers. And pray what have we done to offend today?"

I said nothing. From the sound of it, I was supposed to know this Carnage, and I didn't have enough to work with at the moment. Remembering what Ortega had told me, I fixed the approaching synth with a blank stare, and hoped I was being sufficiently Ryker-like.

The synthetic reached the edge of the cell cover and jumped down. Up close, I saw that it wasn't only the vocal chords that were crude. This body was so far from the one Trepp had been using when I torched her, it was barely deserving of the same name. I wondered briefly if it was some kind of antique. The black hair was coarse and enameled looking, the face slack silicoflesh, the pale blue eyes clearly logo'd across the white. The body looked solid, but a little too solid, and the arms were slightly wrong, reminiscent of snakes rather than limbs. The hands at the ends of the cuffs were smooth and lineless. The synth offered one featureless palm, as if for inspection.

"Well?" he asked gently.

"Routine check, Carnage," Ortega said, helping me out. "Been some bomb threats on tonight's fight. We're here to have a look."

Carnage laughed, jarringly. "As if you cared."

"Well, like I said," Ortega answered evenly. "It's routine."

"Oh well, you'd better come along then." The synthetic sighed and nodded at me. "What's the matter with him? Did they lose his speech functions in the stack?"

We followed him toward the back of the ship and found ourselves skirting the pit formed by the rolled-back cover of the rearmost cargo cell. I glanced down inside and saw a circular white fighting ring, walled on four sides by slopes of steel and plastic seating. Banks of lighting equipment were strung above, but there were none of the spiky spherical units I associated with telemetry. In the center of the ring, someone was kneeling, painting a design on the mat by hand, and looked up as we passed.

"Thematic," Carnage said, seeing where I was looking. "Means something in Arabic. This season's fights are all themed around Protectorate police actions. Tonight it's Sharya. Right Hand of God Martyrs versus Protec Marines. Hand-to-hand, no blades over ten centimeters."

"Bloodbath, in other words," Ortega said.

The synth shrugged. "What the public wants, the public pays for. I understand it *is* possible to inflict an outright mortal wound with a ten-centimeter blade. Just very difficult. A real test of skill, they say. This way."

We went down a narrow companionway into the body of the ship, our own footsteps clanging around us in the tight confines.

"Arenas first, I presume," Carnage shouted above the echoes.

"No, let's see the tanks first," Ortega suggested.

"Really?" It was hard to tell with the low-grade synthetic voice, but Carnage seemed to be amused. "Are you quite sure it's a bomb you're looking for, Lieutenant? It seems to me the arena would be the obvious place to—"

"Got something to hide, Carnage?"

The synthetic turned back to look at me for a moment, quizzically. "No, not at all, Detective Ryker. The tanks it is, then. Welcome to the conversation, by the way. Was it cold on stack? Of course, you probably never expected to be there yourself."

"That's enough," Ortega interposed herself. "Just take us to the tanks and save the small talk for tonight."

"But of course. We aim to cooperate with law enforcement. As a legally incorporated—"

"Yeah, yeah." Ortega waved the verbiage away with weary patience. "Just take us to the fucking tanks."

I reverted to my dangerous stare.

We rode to the tank area in a dinky little electromag train that ran along one side of the hull, through two more converted cargo cells equipped with the same fighting rings and banks of seats but this time covered over with plastic sheeting. At the far end, we disembarked and stepped through the customary sonic cleansing lock. A great deal dirtier than PsychaSec's facilities, ostensibly made of black iron, the heavy door swung outward to reveal a spotlessly white interior.

"At this point we dispense with image," Carnage said carelessly. "Bare-bones low-tech is all very well for the audience, but behind the scenes, well." He gestured around at the gleaming facilities. "You can't make an omelette without a little oil in the pan."

The forward cargo section was huge and chilly, the lighting gloomy, the technology aggressively massive. Where Bancroft's low-lit womb mausoleum at Psycha-Sec had spoken in soft, cultured tones of the trappings of wealth, where the resleeving room at Bay City Storage Facility had groaned minimal funding for minimal deservers, the *Panama Rose*'s body bank was a brutal growl of power. The storage tubes were racked on heavy chains like torpedoes on either side of us, jacked into a central monitor system at one end of the hold via thick black cables that twisted across the floor like pythons. The monitor unit itself squatted heavily ahead of us like an altar to some unpleasant spider god. We approached it on a metal jetty raised a quarter meter above the frozen writhings of the data cables. Behind it to left and right, set into the far wall, were the square glass sides of two spacious decanting tanks. The right-hand tank already held a sleeve, floating backlit and tethered cruciform by monitor lines.

It was like walking into the Andric cathedral in Newpest.

Carnage walked to the central monitor, turned, and spread his arms rather like the sleeve above and behind him.

"Where would you like to start? I *assume* you've brought sophisticated bomb-detection equipment with you."

Ortega ignored him. She took a couple of steps closer to the decanting tank and looked up into the wash of cool green light it cast down into the gloom. "This one of tonight's whores?" she asked.

Carnage sniffed. "In not so many words, it is. I do wish you'd understand the difference between what they peddle in those greasy little shops down the coast, and this."

"So do I," Ortega told him, eyes still upward on the body. "Where'd you get this one from, then?"

"How should I know?" Carnage made a show of studying the plastic nails on his right hand. "Oh, we have the bill of sale somewhere, if you *must* look. By the look of him, I'd say this one's out of Nippon Organics, or one of the Pacific Rim combines. Does it really matter?"

I went to the wall and stared up at the floating sleeve. Slim, hard looking, and brown, with the delicately lifted Japanese eyes on the shelf of unscalably high cheekbones, a thick, straight drift of impenetrably black hair like seaweed in the tank fluid. Gracefully flexible with the long hands of an artist, but muscled for speed combat. It was the body of a tech ninja, the body I'd dreamed about having at fifteen, on dreary rain-filled days in Newpest. It wasn't far off the sleeve they'd given me to fight the Sharya war in. It was a variation on the sleeve I'd bought with my first big payoff in Millsport, the sleeve I'd met Sarah in.

It was like looking at myself under glass. The self I'd built somewhere in the coils of memory that trail all the way back to childhood. Suddenly I stood, exiled into Caucasian flesh, on the wrong side of the mirror.

Carnage came up to me and slapped the glass. "You approve, Detective Ryker?" When I said nothing, he went on. "I'm sure you do, someone with your appetite for, well, brawling. The specs are quite remarkable. Reinforced chassis, the bones are all culture-grown marrow alloy jointed with polybond ligamenting, carbon-reinforced tendons, Khumalo neurachem—"

"Got neurachem," I said, for something to say.

"I know all about your neurachem, Detective Ryker." Even through the poor-quality voice, I thought I could hear a soft, sticky delight. "The fightdrome scanned your specs when you were on stack. There was some talk of buying you up, you know. Physically, I mean. It was thought your sleeve could be used in a humiliation bout. Faked, of course, we would never dream of the actual thing here. That would be, well, *criminal.*" Carnage paused dramatically. "But then it was decided that humiliation fights were not the, uh, the spirit of the establishment. A lowering of tone, you understand. Not a real contest. Shame really, with all the friends you've made, it would have been a big crowd puller."

I wasn't really listening to him, but it dawned on me that Ryker was being insulted, and I pivoted away from the glass to fix Carnage with what seemed like an appropriate glare.

"But I digress," the synthetic went on smoothly. "What I meant to say is that your neurachem is to this system as my voice is to that of Anchana Salomao. *This*—" He gestured once more at the tank. "—is *Khumalo* neurachem, patented by Cape Neuronics only last year. A development of almost spiritual proportions. There are no synaptic chemical amplifiers, no servo chips or implanted wiring. The system is grown in, and it responds *directly to thought.* Consider that, Detective. No one offworld has it yet. The U.N. is thought to be considering a ten-year colonial embargo, though I myself doubt the efficacy of such—"

"Carnage." Ortega drifted in behind him, impatiently. "Why haven't you decanted the other fighter yet?"

"But we are, Lieutenant." Carnage waved one hand at the rack of body tubes on the left. From behind them came the sound of prowling heavy machinery. I peered into the gloom and made out a big automated forklift unit rolling down the rows of containers. As we watched, it locked to a stop and bright directed lighting sprang up on its frame. The forks reached and clamped on a tube, extracting it from the chained cradle while smaller servos disconnected the cabling from it. Separation complete, the machine withdrew slightly, swiveled about, and trundled back along the rows toward the empty decanting tank.

"The system is entirely automated," Carnage said superfluously.

Below the tank, I now noticed a line of three circular openings, like the forward discharge ports of an IP dreadnought. The forklift rose up a little on hydraulic pistons and loaded the tube it was carrying smoothly into the center port.

The tube fit snugly, the visible end rotating through about ninety degrees before a steel baffle slammed down over it. Its task completed, the forklift sank back down on its hydraulics, and its engines died.

I watched the tank.

It seemed like a while, but in fact probably took less than a minute. A hatch broke open in the floor of the tank, and a silvery shoal of bubbles erupted upward. Drifting after them came the body. It bobbed fetally for a moment, turning this way and that in the eddies caused by the air, then its arms and legs began to unfold, aided by the gently tugging monitor wires secured at wrist and ankle. It was bigger boned than the Khumalo sleeve, blocky and more heavily muscled, but similar in color. A strong-boned, hawk-nosed visage tipped lazily toward us as the thin wires pulled it upright.

"Sharyan Right Hand of God martyr," Carnage said beamingly. "Not really, of course, but the race type's accurate and it's got an authentic Will of God enhanced response system." He nodded at the other tank. "The marines on Sharya were multiracial, but there were enough Jap types there to make it believable."

"Not much of a contest, is it," I said. "State-of-the-art neurachem against century-old Sharyan biomech."

Carnage grinned with his slack silicoflesh face. "Well, that will depend on the fighters. I'm told the Khumalo system takes a bit of getting used to, and to be honest it isn't always the best sleeve that wins. It's more about psychology. Endurance, pain tolerance . . ."

"Savagery," Ortega added. "Lack of empathy."

"Things like that," the synthetic agreed. "That's what makes it exciting, of course. If you'd care to come tonight, Lieutenant, Detective, I'm sure I can find you a couple of remaindered seats near the back."

"You'll be commentating," I surmised, already hearing the specs-rich vocabulary that Carnage used come tumbling out over the loudspeaker, the killing ring drenched in focused white light, the roaring, surging crowd in the darkened seating, the smell of sweat and bloodlust.

"Of course I will." Carnage's logo'd eyes narrowed. "You haven't been away so long, you know."

"Are we going to look for these bombs?" Ortega said loudly.

It took us over an hour to go over the hold, looking for imaginary bombs, while Carnage looked on with poorly veiled amusement. Up above, the two sleeves destined for slaughter in the arena looked down on us from their green-lit glass-sided wombs, and their presences weighed no less heavily for their closed eyes and dreaming visages.

CHAPTER TWENTY

O rtega dropped me on Mission Street as evening was falling over the city. She'd been withdrawn and monosyllabic on the flight back from the fightdrome, and I guessed the strain of reminding herself I was not Ryker was beginning to take a toll. But when I made a production out of brushing off my shoulders as I got out of the cruiser, she laughed impulsively.

"Stick around the Hendrix tomorrow," she said. "There's someone I want you to talk to, but it'll take a while to set up."

"Fair enough." I turned to go.

"Kovacs."

I turned back. She was leaning across to look up and out of the open door at me. I put an arm on the uplifted door wing of the cruiser and looked down. There was a longish pause during which I could feel my blood beginning to adrenalize gently.

"Yes?"

She hesitated a moment longer, then said, "Carnage was hiding something back there, right?"

"From the amount he talked, I'd say yes."

"That's what I thought." She prodded hurriedly at the control console, and the door began to slide back down. "See you tomorrow."

I watched the cruiser lift into the sky and sighed. I was reasonably sure that going to Ortega openly had been a good move, but I hadn't expected it to be so messy. However long she and Ryker had been together, the chemistry must have been devastating. I remembered reading somewhere how the initial pheromones of attraction between bodies appeared to undergo a form of encoding the longer said bodies were in proximity, binding them increasingly close. None of the biochemists interviewed appeared to really understand the process, but there had been some attempts to play with it in labs. Speeding up or interrupting had met with mixed results, one of which was empathin and its derivatives.

Chemicals. I was still reeling from the cocktail of Miriam Bancroft, and I didn't need this. I told myself, in no uncertain terms, *I didn't need this.*

Up ahead, over the heads of the evening's scattered pedestrians, I saw the holographic bulk of the left-handed guitar player outside the Hendrix. I sighed again and started walking.

Halfway up the block, a bulky automated vehicle rolled past me, hugging the curb. It looked pretty much like the robocrawlers that cleaned the streets of Millsport, so I paid no attention to it as it drew level. Seconds later, I was drenched in the machine's imagecast.

. . . from the Houses from the Houses from the Houses from the Houses from the Houses from the Houses . . .

The voices groaned and murmured, male, female, overlaid. It was like a choir in the throes of orgasm. The images were inescapable, varying across a broad spectrum of sexual preference. A whirlwind of fleeting sensory impressions.

Genuine . . .

Uncut . . .

Full-sense repro . . .

Tailored . . .

As if to prove this last, the random images thinned out into a stream of heterosex combinations. They must have scanned my response to the blur of options and fed directly back to the broadcast unit. Very high tech.

The flow ended with a phone number in glowing numerals and an erect penis in the hands of a woman with long dark hair and a crimson-lipped smile. She looked into the lens. I could feel her fingers.

Head in the Clouds, she breathed. *This is what it's like. Maybe you can't afford to come up here, but you can certainly afford this.*

Her head dipped; her lips slid down over the penis. Like it was happening to me. Then the long black hair curtained in from either side and inked the image out. I was back on the street, swaying, coated in a thin sheen of sweat. The autocaster grumbled away down the street behind me, some of the more streetwise pedestrians skipping sharply sideways out of its 'cast radius.

I found I could recall the phone number with gleaming clarity.

The sweat cooled rapidly to a shiver. I flexed my shoulders and started walking, trying not to notice the knowing looks of the people around me. I was almost into a full stride again when a gap opened in the strollers ahead and I saw the long, low limousine parked outside the Hendrix's front doors.

Jangling nerves sent my hand leaping toward the holstered Nemex before I recognized the vehicle as Bancroft's. Forcing out a deep breath, I circled the limousine and ascertained that the driver's compartment was empty. I was still wondering what to do when the rear compartment hatch cracked open and Curtis unfolded himself from the seating inside.

"We need to talk, Kovacs," he said in a man-to-man sort of voice that put me on the edge of a slightly hysterical giggle. "Decision time."

I looked him up and down, reckoned from the tiny eddies in his stance and demeanor that he was chemically augmented at the moment, and decided to humor him.

"Sure. In the limo?"

" 'S cramped in there. How about you ask me up to your room?"

My eyes narrowed. There was an unmistakable hostility in the chauffeur's voice, and a just as unmistakable hard-on pressing at the front of his immaculate chinos. Granted, I had a similar, if detumescing, lump of my own, but I remembered distinctly that Bancroft's limo had shielding against the street 'casts. This was something else.

I nodded at the hotel entrance.

"Okay, let's go."

The doors parted to let us in, and the Hendrix came to life.

"Good evening, sir. You have no visitors this evening—"

Curtis snorted. "Disappointed, hah, Kovacs."

"—nor any calls since you left." The hotel continued smoothly. "Do you wish this person admitted as a guest?"

"Yeah, sure. You got a bar we can go to?"

"I *said* your *room*," Curtis growled behind me, then yelped as he barked his shin on one of the lobby's low, metal-edged tables.

"The Midnight Lamp bar is located on this floor," the hotel said doubtfully. "But it has not been used for a considerable time."

"I said—"

"Shut up, Curtis. Didn't anyone ever tell you not to rush a first date? The Midnight Lamp is fine. Fire it up for us."

Across the lobby, adjacent to the check-in console, a wide section of the back wall slid grudgingly aside, and lights flickered on in the space beyond. With Curtis making sneering sounds behind me, I went to the opening and peered down a short flight of steps into the Midnight Lamp bar.

"This'll do fine. Come on."

Someone overliteral in imagination had done the interior decoration of the Midnight Lamp bar. The walls, themselves psychedelic whirls of midnight blues and purples, were festooned with a variety of clock faces showing either the declared hour or a few minutes to, interwoven with every form of lamp known to man, from clay prehistoric to enzyme-decay light canisters. There was indented bench seating along both walls, clock-face tables, and in the center of the room a circular bar in the shape of a countdown dial. A robot composed entirely of clocks and lamps waited immobile just beside the dial's twelve mark.

It was all the more eerie for the complete absence of any other customers, and as we made our way toward the waiting robot, I could feel Curtis's earlier mood quiet a little.

"What will it be, gentlemen?" the machine said unexpectedly, from no apparent vocal outlet. Its face was an antique white analog clock with spider-thin baroque hands and the hours marked off in Roman numerals. A little unnerved, I turned back to Curtis, whose face was showing signs of unwilling sobriety.

"Vodka," he said shortly. "Subzero."

"And a whiskey. Whatever it is I've been drinking out of the cabinet in my room. At room temperature, please. Both on my tab."

The clock face inclined slightly, and one multijointed arm swung up to select glasses from an overhead rack. The other arm, which ended in a lamp with a forest of small spouts, trickled the requested spirits into the glasses.

Curtis picked up his glass and threw a generous portion of the vodka down his throat. He drew breath hard through his teeth and made a satisfied growling noise. I sipped at my own glass a little more circumspectly, wondering how long it had been since liquid last flowed through the bar's tubes and spigots. My fears proved unfounded, so I deepened the sip and let the whiskey melt its way down into my stomach.

Curtis banged down his glass.

"*Now* you ready to talk?"

"All right, Curtis," I said slowly, looking into my drink. "I imagine you have a message for me."

"Sure have." His voice was cranked to snapping point. "The lady says, you going to take her very generous offer, or not. Just that. I'm supposed to give you time to make up your mind, so I'll finish my drink."

I fixed my gaze on a Martian sand lamp hanging from the opposite wall. Curtis's mood was beginning to make some sense.

"Muscling in on your territory, am I?"

"Don't push your luck, Kovacs." There was a desperate edge to the words. "You say the wrong thing here, and I'll—"

"You'll what?" I set my glass down and turned to face him. He was less than half my subjective age, young and muscled and chemically wound up in the illusion that he was dangerous. He reminded me so much of myself at the same age it was maddening. I wanted to shake him. "You'll *what*?"

Curtis gulped. "I was in the provincial marines."

"What as, a pinup?" I went to push him in the chest with one stiffened hand, then dropped it, ashamed. I lowered my voice. "Listen, Curtis. Don't do this to us both."

"You think you're pretty fucking tough, don't you?"

"This isn't about tough, C-urtis." I'd almost called him kid. It seemed as if part of me wanted the fight after all. "This is about two different species. What did they teach you in the provincial marines? Hand-to-hand combat? Twenty-seven ways to kill a man with your hands? Underneath it all you're still a man. I'm an Envoy, Curtis. It's not the same."

He came for me anyway, leading with a straight jab that was supposed to distract me while the following roundhouse kick scythed in from the side at head height. It was a skull cracker if it landed, but it was hopelessly overdramatic. Maybe it was the chemicals he'd dressed up in that night. No one in their right mind throws kicks above waist height in a real fight. I ducked the jab and the kick in the same movement and grabbed his foot. A sharp twist and Curtis tipped, staggered, and landed spread-eagled on the bartop. I smashed his face against the unyielding surface and held him there with my hand knotted in his hair.

"See what I mean?"

He made muffled noises and thrashed impotently about while the clock-faced bartender stood immobile. Blood from his broken nose was streaked across the bar's surface. I studied the patterns it had made while I brought my breathing back down. The lock I had on my conditioning was making me pant. Shifting my grip to his right arm, I jerked it up high into the small of his back. The thrashing stopped.

"Good. Now you keep still or I'll break it. I'm not in the mood for this." As I spoke, I was feeling rapidly through his pockets. In the inner breast pouch of his jacket I found a small plastic tube. "Aha. So what little delights have we got tubing around your system tonight? Hormone enhancers, by the look of that hard-on." I held the tube up to the dim light and saw thousands of tiny crystal slivers inside it. "Military format. Where did you get this stuff, Curtis? Discharge freebie from the marines, was it?" I recommenced my search and came up with the delivery system—a tiny skeletal gun with a sliding chamber and a magnetic coil. Tip the crystals into the breech and close it, the magnetic field aligns them and the accelerator spits them out at penetrative speed. Not so different from Sarah's shard pistol. For battlefield medics, they were a hardy and consequently very popular alternative to hyposprays.

I hauled Curtis to his feet and shoved him away from me. He managed to stay on his feet, clutching at his nose with one hand and glaring at me.

"You want to tip your head back to stop that," I told him. "Go ahead, I'm not going to hurt you again."

"Botherfucker!"

I held up the crystals and the little gun. "Where did you get these?"

"Suck by prick, Kovacs." Curtis tipped his head back fractionally, despite himself, trying to keep me in view at the same time. His eyes rolled in their sockets like a panicked horse's. "I'b dot tellig you a fuckig thig."

"Fair enough." I put the chemicals back on the bar and regarded him gravely for a couple of seconds. "Then let me tell you something instead. When they make an Envoy, do you want to know what they do? They burn out every evolved violence limitation instinct in the human psyche. Submission signal recognition, pecking-order dynamics, pack loyalties. It all goes, tuned out a neuron at a time; and they replace it with a conscious will to harm."

He stared back at me in silence.

"Do you understand me? It would have been easier to kill you just then. It would have been easier. I had to stop myself. That's what an Envoy is, Curtis. A reassembled human. An artifice."

The silence stretched. There was no way to know if he was taking it in or not. Thinking back to Newpest a century and a half ago, and the young Takeshi Kovacs, I doubted he was. At his age, the whole thing would have sounded like a dream of power come true.

I shrugged. "In case you hadn't guessed already, the answer to the lady's question is no. I'm not interested. There, that should make you happy, and it only cost you a broken nose to find out. If you hadn't dosed yourself to the eyes, it might not even have cost that much. Tell her thank you very much, the offer is appreciated, but there's too much going on here to walk away from. Tell her I'm starting to enjoy it."

There was a slight cough from the entrance to the bar. I looked up and saw a suited, crimson-haired figure on the stairs.

"Am I interrupting something?" the mohican inquired. The voice was slow and relaxed. Not one of the heavies from Fell Street.

I picked up my drink from the bar. "Not at all, officer. Come on down and join the party. What'll you have?"

"Overproof rum," the cop said, drifting over to us. "If they've got it. Small glass."

I raised a finger at the clock face. The bartender produced a square-cut glass from somewhere and filled it with a deep-red liquid. The mohican ambled past Curtis, sparing him a curious glance on the way, and apprehended the drink with a long arm.

"Appreciated." He sipped at the drink and inclined his head. "Not bad. I'd like a word with you, Kovacs. In private."

We both glanced at Curtis. The chauffeur glared back at me with hate-filled eyes, but the new arrival had defused the confrontation. The cop jerked his head in the direction of the exit. Curtis went, still clutching his wounded face. The cop watched him out of sight before he turned back to me.

"You do that?" he asked casually.

I nodded. "Provoked. Things got a bit out of hand. He thought he was protecting someone."

"Well, I'm glad he ain't protecting me."

"Like I said, it got a bit out of hand. I overreacted."

"Hell, you don't need to explain yourself to me." The cop leaned on the bar and looked around him with frank interest. I recalled his face now. Bay City Storage. The one with the quick-tarnishing badge. "He feels aggrieved enough, he can press charges, and we'll play back some more of this place's memory."

"Got your warrant, then?" I put the question with a lightness I didn't feel.

"Almost. Always takes a while with the legal department. Fucking A.I.s. Look, I wanted to apologize for Mercer and Davidson, the way they were at the station. They act like a brace of dickheads sometimes, but they're fundamentally okay."

I waved my glass laterally. "Forget it."

"Good. I'm Rodrigo Bautista, detective sergeant. Ortega's partner most of the time." He drained his glass and grinned at me. "*Loosely* attached, I should point out."

"Noted." I signaled the bartender for refills. "Tell me something. You guys all go to the same hairdresser, or is it some kind of team bonding thing?"

"Same hairdresser." Bautista shrugged sorrowfully. "Old guy up on Fulton. Ex-con. Apparently mohicans were cool back when they threw him in the store. It's the only goddamn style he knows, but he's a nice old guy and he's cheap. One of us started going there few years back; he gave us discounts. You know how it is."

"But not Ortega?"

"Ortega cuts her own hair." Bautista made a what-can-you-do gesture. "Got a little holocast scanner, says it improves her spatial coordination or some such shit."

"Different."

"Yeah, she is." Bautista paused reflectively, gaze soaking up the middle distance. He sipped absently at his freshened drink. "It's her I'm here about."

"Uh-oh. Is this going to be a friendly warning?"

Bautista pulled a face. "Well, it's going to be friendly, whatever you call it. I ain't looking for a broken nose."

I laughed despite myself. Bautista joined me with a gentle smile.

"Thing is, it's tearing her up you walking around with that face on. She and Ryker were real close. She's been paying the sleeve mortgage a year now, and on a lieutenant's pay that ain't an easy thing to do. Never figured on an overbid like that fucker Bancroft pulled. After all, Ryker ain't exactly young, and he never was a beauty."

"Got neurachem," I pointed out.

"Oh, sure. Got neurachem." Bautista waved an arm with largesse. "You tried it yet?"

"Couple of times."

"Like dancing flamenco in a fishing net, right?"

"It's a little rough," I admitted.

This time we both laughed. When it cranked down, the cop focused on his glass again. His face grew serious.

"I ain't trying to lean on you. All I'm saying is, go easy. This ain't exactly what she needs right now."

"Me either," I said feelingly. "This isn't even my fucking planet."

Bautista looked sympathetic, or maybe just slightly drunk. "Harlan's World's a lot different from this, I guess."

"You guess right. Look, I don't mean to be unsubtle, but hasn't anyone pointed out to Ortega that Ryker's as gone for good as it gets without real death? She's not looking to wait two hundred years for him, is she?"

The cop looked at me through narrowed eyes. "You heard about Ryker, huh?"

"I know he's down for the double-barrel. I know what he went down for."

Bautista got something in his eyes then that looked like shards of old pain. It can't be much fun talking about your corrupt colleagues. For a moment I regretted what I'd said.

Local color. Soak it up.

"You want to sit down?" the cop said unhappily, casting around for bar stools that had evidently been removed at some stage. "Over in the booths, maybe? This'll take a while to tell."

We settled at one of the clock-face tables, and Bautista fumbled in his pocket for cigarettes. I twitched, but when he offered me one I shook my head. Like Ortega, he looked surprised.

"I quit."

"In that sleeve?" Bautista's eyebrows lifted respectfully behind a veil of fragrant blue smoke. "Congratulations."

"Thanks. You were going to tell me about Ryker."

"Ryker." The cop jetted smoke out of his nostrils and sat back. "Was working with the Sleeve Theft boys until a couple of years ago. They're quite a sophisticated bunch compared to us. It ain't so easy to steal a whole sleeve intact, and that breeds a smarter class of criminal. There's some crossover of jurisdiction with Organic Damage, mostly when they start breaking down the bodies. Places like the Wei Clinic."

"Oh?" I said neutrally.

Bautista nodded. "Yeah, someone saved us an awful lot of time and effort over there yesterday. Turned the place into a spare-parts sale. But I guess you wouldn't know anything about that."

"Must have happened as I was walking out the door."

"Yeah, well, anyway. Back in the winter of '09, Ryker was chasing down some random insurance fraud, you know the stuff, where resleeve policy clones turn out to be empty tanks and no one knows where the bodies went. It split wide open and turns out the bodies are being used for some dirty little war down south. High-level corruption. It bounced all the way up to U.N. presidium level and back. A few token heads roll, and Ryker gets to be a hero."

"Nice."

"In the short term, yeah. The way it works around here, heroes get a very high profile, and they went the whole program for Ryker. Interviews on World-Web One, highly publicized fling with Sandy Kim even. Bylines in the faxes. Before it all could tail off, Ryker grabbed his chance. Put in for a transfer to OrgDam. He'd worked with Ortega a couple of times before—like I said, we overlap here and there—so he knew the program. No way could the department turn him down, especially with some bullshit speech he made about wanting to go where he could make a difference."

"And did he? Make a difference, I mean?"

Bautista puffed out his cheeks. "He was a good cop. Maybe. A month in, you could have asked Ortega that question, but then the two of them hooked up and her judgment went all to pieces."

"You don't approve?"

"Hey, what's to approve? You feel that way about someone, you go with it. It just makes it tough to get any objectivity on this thing. When Ryker fucked up, Ortega was bound to side with him."

"Did she?" I took our empty glasses to the bar and got them refilled, still talking. "I thought she brought him in."

"Where'd you hear that?"

"Talk. Not a massively reputable source. It's not true, then?"

"Nah. Some of the street slime like to talk it up that way. I think the idea of us ratting each other out makes them cream their pants. What happened was, Internal Affairs took Ryker down in her apartment."

"Ohhh."

"Yeah, ain't that a laser up the ass." Bautista looked up at me as I handed him his new drink. "She never let it show, you know. Just went right to work against the I.A.D. charges."

"From what I heard, they had him cold."

"Yeah, your source got that bit right." The mohican looked into his glass pensively, as if unsure he should go on. "Ortega's theory was that Ryker was set up by some high-ranking asshole who took a fall back in '09. And it's true he upset a lot of people."

"But you don't buy it?"

"I'd like to. Like I said, he was a good cop. But like I also said, Sleeve Theft was dealing to a smarter class of criminal, and that meant you had to be careful. Smart criminals have smart lawyers, and you can't bounce them around whenever you feel like it. Organic Damage handles everyone, from the scum on up. Generally we get a bit more leeway. That was what you, sorry, what Ryker wanted when he transferred. The leeway." Bautista tipped back his glass and set it down with a throat-clearing noise. He looked at me steadily. "I think Ryker got carried away."

"Blam, blam, blam?"

"Something like that. I've seen him interrogate before; he's right on the line most of the time. One slip." There was an old terror in Bautista's eyes now. The fear he lived with every day. "With some of these turds, it's real easy to lose your cool. So easy. I think that's what happened."

"My source says he RD'd two and left another two with their stacks still intact. That sounds pretty fucking careless."

Bautista jerked his head affirmatively. "What Ortega says. But it won't wash. See, it all went down in a black clinic up in Seattle. The two intacts made it out of the building breathing, grabbed a cruiser, and flew. Ryker put a hundred twenty-four holes in that cruiser when it lifted. Not to mention the surrounding traffic. The intacts ditched in the Pacific. One of them died at the controls, the other one in the impact. Sank in a couple of hundred meters of water. Ryker was out of his jurisdiction, and the Seattle cops ain't all that keen on out-of-town badges shooting up the traffic, so the retrieval teams never let him close to the bodies.

"Everyone was real surprised when the stacks came up Catholic, and someone at the Seattle P.D. wasn't buying. Dig a little bit deeper and it turns out the reasons-of-conscience decals are fake. Dipped in by someone real careless."

"Or in a real hurry."

Bautista snapped his fingers and pointed a finger across the table at me. He was definitely a little drunk now. "There you go. The way I.A.D. read it, Ryker'd screwed up letting the witnesses escape, and his only hope was to slap a do-not-disturb sign on their stacks. Course, when they did bring back the intacts, they both swore blind that Ryker had turned up without a warrant, bluffed and then smashed his way into the clinic, and when they wouldn't answer his questions, started playing Who's Next with a plasma gun."

"Was it true?"

"About the warrant? Yeah. Ryker had no business being up there in the first place. About the rest? Who knows?"

"What did Ryker say?"

"He said he didn't do it."

"Just that?"

"Nah, it was a long story. He'd gone up on a tip, bluffed himself inside just to see how far he could push it, and suddenly they were shooting at him. Claims he might have taken someone out but probably not with a head shot. Claims the clinic must have brought in two sacrificial employees and torched them before he arrived. Claims he knows nothing about any dipping that went on." Bautista shrugged blearily. "They found the dipper, and he said Ryker paid him to do it. Polygraph tested. But he also says Ryker called him up, didn't do it face-to-face. Virtual link."

"Which can be faked. Easily."

"Yeah." Bautista looked pleased. "But then, this guy says he's done work for Ryker before, this time face-to-face, and he polygraphed out on that, too. Ryker knows him, that's indisputable. And then, of course, I.A.D. wanted to know why Ryker didn't take any backup with him. They got witnesses in the street who said Ryker was like a maniac, shooting blind trying to bring the cruiser down. Seattle P.D. didn't take too kindly to that, like I said."

"A hundred and twenty-four holes," I muttered.

"Yep. That's a lot of holes. Ryker wanted to bring those two intacts down pretty badly."

"It *could* have been a setup."

"Yeah, it could have been." Bautista sobered up a little, and his voice got angry. "Could have been a lot of things. But the fact is that you—*shit,* sorry—the fact is that *Ryker* went too far out, and when the branch broke, there was no one there to catch him."

"So Ortega buys the setup story, stands by Ryker, and fights I.A.D. all the way down, and when they lose . . ." I nodded to myself. "When they lose, she picks up the sleeve mortgage to keep Ryker's body out of the city auction room. And goes looking for fresh evidence?"

"Got it in one. She's already lodged an appeal, but there's a minimum two-year elapse from start of sentence before she can get the disk spinning." Bautista let go of a gut-deep sigh. "Like I said, it's tearing her up."

We sat quietly for a while.

"You know," Bautista said finally. "I think I'm going to go. Sitting here talking about Ryker to Ryker's face is getting a little weird. I don't know how Ortega copes."

"Just part of living in the modern age," I told him, knocking back my drink.

"Yeah, I guess. You'd think I'd have a handle on it by now. I spend half my life talking to victims wearing other people's faces. Not to mention the scumbags."

"So which do you make Ryker for? Victim or scumbag?"

Bautista frowned. "That ain't a nice question. Ryker was a good cop who made a mistake. That don't make him a scumbag. Don't make him a victim, either. Just makes him someone who screwed up. Me, I only live about a block away from that myself."

"Sure. Sorry." I rubbed at the side of my face. Envoy conversations weren't supposed to slip like that. "I'm a little tired. That block you live on sounds familiar. I think I'm going to go to bed. You want another drink before you go, help yourself. It's on my tab."

"No thanks." Bautista drained what was left in his glass. "Old cop's rule. Never drink alone."

"Sounds like I should have been an old cop." I stood up, swaying a little. Ryker may have been a death-wish smoker, but he didn't have much tolerance for alcohol. "You can see yourself out okay, I guess."

"Sure." Bautista got up to go and made about a half-dozen paces before he turned back. He frowned with concentration. "Oh, yeah. Goes without saying, I was never here, right."

I gestured him away. "You were never here," I assured him.

He grinned bemusedly, and his face looked suddenly very young. "Right. Good. See you around, probably."

"See you."

I watched him out of sight, then, regretfully, let the ice-cold processes of Envoy control trickle down through my befuddled senses. When I was unpleasantly sober again, I picked up Curtis's drug crystals from the bar and went to talk to the Hendrix.

CHAPTEr TWENTY-ONE

"You know anything about synamorphesterone?"

"Heard of it." Ortega dug absently at the sand with the toe of one boot. It was still damp from the tide's retreat, and our footprints welled soggily behind us. In either direction the curve of the beach was deserted. We were alone apart from the gulls that wheeled in geometric formations high overhead.

"Well, since we're waiting, you want to fill me in?"

"Harem drug." When I looked blank, Ortega puffed out her cheeks impatiently. She was acting like someone who hadn't slept well.

"I'm not from here."

"You were on Sharya, you told me."

"Yeah. In a military capacity. There wasn't all that much time for cultural awareness. We were too busy killing people."

This last wasn't quite true. Following the sack of Zihicce, the Envoys had been steeped in the mechanics of engineering a regime compliant to the Protectorate. Troublemakers were rooted out, cells of resistance infiltrated and then crushed, collaborators plugged into the political edifice. In the process we'd learned quite a lot about local culture.

I'd asked for an early transfer out.

Ortega shaded her eyes and scanned the beach in both directions. Nothing stirred. She sighed. "It's a male response enhancer. Boosts aggression, sexual prowess, confidence. On the street in the Middle East and Europe they call it Stallion, in the south it's Toro. We don't get much of it here; street mood's more ambient. Which I'm glad about. From what I hear, it can be very nasty. You run across some last night?"

"Sort of." This was pretty much what I'd learned from the Hendrix database last night, but more concise and with less chemistry. And Curtis's behavior ran the checklist of symptoms and side effects like a model. "Suppose I wanted to get hold of some of this stuff, where could I pick it up? Easily, I mean."

Ortega gave me a sharp look, and picked her way back up the beach onto dryer sand. "Like I said, we don't get much of it here," she said in time with her labored, sinking footsteps. "You'd have to ask around. Someone with better than local connections. Or get it synthesized locally. But I don't know. With designer hormones, that's likely to be more expensive than just buying it in from down south."

She paused at the crest of the dune and looked around again.

"Where the hell is she?"

"Maybe she's not coming," I suggested morosely. I hadn't slept all that well myself. Most of the night after Rodrigo Bautista's departure had been spent brooding over the uncooperatively jagged pieces of the Bancroft jigsaw and fighting off the urge to smoke. My head seemed barely to have hit the pillow when the Hendrix buzzed me awake with Ortega's call. It was still obscenely early in the morning.

"She'll come," Ortega said. "The link's booked through to her personal pickup. Call's probably delayed at incoming security. We've been in here only about ten seconds, real time."

I shivered in the cold wind from offshore and said nothing. Overhead, the gulls repeated their geometry. The virtuality was cheap, not designed for long stay.

"Got any cigarettes?"

I was seated in the cold sand, smoking with a kind of mechanical intensity, when something moved on the extreme right of the bay. I straightened up and narrowed my eyes, then laid a hand on Ortega's arm. The motion resolved itself into a plume of sand or water, ripped into the air by a fast-moving surface vehicle that was tearing around the curve of the beach toward us.

"Told you she'd come."

"Or someone would," I muttered, getting to my feet and reaching for the Nemex, which was, of course, not there. Not many virtual forums allowed firearms in their constructs. Instead, I brushed sand from my clothes and moved down the beach, still trying to rid myself of the brooding feeling that I was wasting my time here.

The vehicle was close enough now to be visible, a dark dot at the front of the pluming wake. I could hear its engine, a shrill whine over the melancholy carping of the gulls. I turned to Ortega, who was watching the approaching craft impassively at my side.

"Bit excessive for a phone call, isn't it?" I said nastily.

Ortega shrugged and spun her cigarette away into the sand. "Money doesn't automatically mean taste," she said.

The speeding dot became a stubby, finned one-man ground jet, painted iridescent pink. It was plowing along through the shallow surf at the water's edge, flinging water and wet sand indiscriminately behind it, but a few hundred meters away the pilot must have seen us, because the little craft veered out across the deeper water and cut a spray tail twice its own height toward us.

"*Pink?*"

Ortega shrugged again.

The ground jet beached about ten meters away and shuddered to a halt, ripped-up gobbets of wet sand splattering down around it. When the storm of its arrival had died, a hatch was flung back and a black-clad, helmeted figure clambered out. That the figure was a woman was abundantly clear from the formfitting flight suit, a suit that ended in boots inlaid with curling silver tracery from heel to toe.

I sighed and followed Ortega up to the craft.

The woman in the flight suit jumped down into the shallow water and splashed up to meet us, tugging at the seals on her helmet. As we met, the helmet came off and long, coppery hair spilled out over the suit's shoulders. The woman put her head back and shook out the hair, revealing a wide-boned face with large, expressive eyes the color of flecked onyx, a delicately arched nose, and a generously sculpted mouth.

The old, ghostly hint of Miriam Bancroft's beauty this woman had once owned had been scrubbed out utterly.

"Kovacs, this is Leila Begin," Ortega said formally. "Ms. Begin, this is Takeshi Kovacs, Laurens Bancroft's retained investigator."

The large eyes appraised me frankly.

"You're from offworld?" she asked me.

"That's correct. Harlan's World."

"Yes, the lieutenant mentioned it." There was a well-designed huskiness to Leila Begin's voice, and an accent that suggested she was unused to speaking Amanglic. "I can only hope that means you have an open mind."

"Open to what?"

"The truth." Begin gave me a surprised look. "Lieutenant Ortega tells me you are interested in the truth. Shall we walk?"

Without waiting for a response, she set off parallel with the surf. I exchanged a glance with Ortega, who gestured with her thumb but showed no signs of moving herself. I hesitated for a couple of moments, then went after Begin.

"What's all this about the truth?" I asked, catching her up.

"You have been retained to discover who killed Laurens Bancroft," she said intensely, without looking around. "You wish to know the truth of what transpired the night he died. Is this not so?"

"You don't think it was suicide, then?"

"Do you?"

"I asked first."

I saw a faint smile cross her lips. "No. I don't."

"Let me guess. You're pinning it on Miriam Bancroft."

Leila Begin stopped and turned on one of her ornate heels. "Are you mocking me, Mr. Kovacs?"

There was something in her eyes that drained the irritable amusement out of me on the spot. I shook my head.

"No, I'm not mocking you. But I'm right, aren't I?"

"Have you met Miriam Bancroft?"

"Briefly, yes."

"You found her charming, no doubt."

I shrugged evasively. "A bit abrasive at times, but generally, yes. Charming would do it."

Begin looked me in the eyes. "She is a psychopath," she said seriously.

She resumed walking. After a moment I followed her.

"*Psychopath*'s not a narrow term anymore," I said carefully. "I've heard it applied to whole cultures on occasion. It's even been applied to me once or twice. Reality is so flexible these days, it's hard to tell who's disconnected from it and who isn't. You might even say it's a pointless distinction."

"Mr. Kovacs." There was an impatient note in the woman's voice now. "Miriam Bancroft assaulted me when I was pregnant, and murdered my unborn child. She was aware that I was pregnant. She acted with intention. Have you ever been seven months pregnant?"

I shook my head. "No."

"That is too bad. It's an experience we should all be required to go through at least once."

"Kind of hard to legislate."

Begin looked at me sidelong. "In that sleeve, you look like a man acquainted with loss, but that's the surface. Are you what you appear, Mr. Kovacs? Are you acquainted with loss? Irretrievable loss, we're discussing. Are you acquainted with that?"

"I think so," I said, more stiffly than I'd intended.

"Then you will understand my feelings about Miriam Bancroft. On Earth, cortical stacks are fitted after birth."

"Where I come from, too."

"I lost that child. No amount of technology will bring it back."

I couldn't tell if the rising tide of emotion in Leila Begin's voice was real or contrived, but I was losing focus. I cut back to start.

"That doesn't give Miriam Bancroft a motive for killing her husband."

"Of course it does." Begin favored me with the sidelong glance again, and there was another bitter smile on her face. "I was not an isolated incident in Laurens Bancroft's life. How do you think he met me?"

"In Oakland, I heard."

The smile blossomed into a hard laugh. "Very euphemistic. Yes, he certainly met me in Oakland. He met me on what they used to call the Meat Rack. Not a very classy place. Laurens needed to degrade, Mr. Kovacs. That's what made him hard. He'd been doing it for decades before me, and I don't see why he would have stopped afterwards."

"So Miriam decides, suddenly, enough's enough and ventilates him?"

"She's capable of it."

"I'm sure she is." Begin's theory was as full of holes as a captured Sharyan deserter, but I wasn't about to elaborate the details of what I knew to this woman. "You harbor no feelings about Bancroft himself, I suppose? Good or bad."

The smile again. "I was a whore, Mr. Kovacs. A good one. A good whore feels what the client wants her to feel. There's no room for anything else."

"You telling me you can shut your feelings down just like that?"

"You telling me you can't?" she retorted.

"All right, what did Laurens Bancroft want you to feel?"

She stopped and faced me slowly. I felt uncomfortably as if I had just slapped her. Her face had gone masklike with remembrance.

"Animal abandonment," she said finally. "And then abject gratitude. And I stopped feeling them both as soon as he stopped paying me."

"And what do you feel now?"

"Now?" Leila Begin looked out to sea, as if testing the temperature of the breeze against what was inside her. "Now I feel nothing, Mr. Kovacs."

"You agreed to talk to me. You must have had a reason."

Begin made a dismissive gesture. "The lieutenant asked me to."

"Very public spirited of you."

The woman's gaze came back to me. "You know what happened after my miscarriage?"

"I heard you were paid off."

"Yes. Unpleasant sounding, isn't it? But that's what happened. I took Bancroft's money and I shut up. It was a lot of money. But I didn't forget where I came from. I still get back to Oakland two or three times a year. I know the girls who work the Rack now. Lieutenant Ortega has a good name there. Many of the girls owe her. You might say I am paying off some favors."

"And revenge on Miriam Bancroft doesn't come into it?"

"What revenge," Leila Begin laughed her hard little laugh again. "I am giving you information because the lieutenant has asked me to. You won't be able to do anything to Miriam Bancroft. She is a Meth. She is untouchable."

"No one's untouchable. Not even Meths."

Begin looked at me sadly.

"You are not from here," she said. "And it shows."

●●●

Begin's call had been routed through a Caribbean linkage broker, and the virtual time rented out of a Chinatown forum provider. *Cheap,* Ortega told me on the way in, *and probably as secure as anywhere. Bancroft wants privacy, he spends half a million on discretion systems. Me, I just go talk where no one's listening.*

It was also cramped. Slotted in between a pagoda-shaped bank and a steamy-windowed restaurant frontage, space was at a premium. The reception area was reached by filing up a narrow steel staircase and along a gantry pinned to one wing of the pagoda's middle tier. A lavish seven or eight square meters of fused sand flooring under a cheap glass viewdome provided prospective clients with a waiting area, natural light, and two pairs of seats that looked as if they had been torn out of a decommissioned jetliner. Adjacent to the seats, an ancient Asian woman sat behind a battery of secretarial equipment, most of which appeared to be switched off, and guarded a flight of access steps into the bowels of the building. Down below, it was all hairpin corridors racked with cable conduits and piping. Each length of corridor was lined with the doors of the service cubicles. The 'trode couches were set into the cubicles at a sharp upright angle to economize on floor space and surrounded on all sides by blinking, dusty-faced instrument panels. You strapped yourself in, 'troded up, and then tapped the code number given to you at reception into the arm of the couch. Then the machine came and got your mind.

Returning from the wide-open horizon of the beach virtuality was a shock. Opening my eyes on the banks of instrumentation just above my head, I suffered a momentary flashback to Harlan's World. Thirteen years old and waking up in a virtual arcade after my first porn format. A low-ratio forum where two minutes of real time got me an experiential hour and a half in the company of two pneumatically breasted playmates whose bodies bore more resemblance to cartoons than real women. The scenario had been a candy-scented room of pink cushions and fake fur rugs with windows that gave poor resolution onto a nighttime cityscape. When I started running with the gangs and making more money, the ratio and resolution went up, and the scenarios got more imaginative, but the thing that never changed was the stale smell and the tackiness of the 'trodes on your skin when you surfaced afterwards between the cramped walls of the coffin.

"Kovacs?"

I blinked and reached for the straps. Shouldering my way out of the cubicle, I found Ortega already waiting in the pipe-lined corridor.

"So what do you think?"

"I think she's full of shit." I raised my hands to forestall Ortega's outburst. "No, listen, I buy Miriam Bancroft as scary. I've got no argument with that. But there are about half a hundred reasons why she doesn't fit the bill. Ortega, you polygraphed her, for fuck's sake."

"Yeah, I know." Ortega followed me down the corridor. "But that's what I've been thinking about. You know, she volunteered to take that test. I mean, it's witness mandatory anyway, but she was demanding it practically as soon as I got to the scene. No weeping-partner shit, not even a tear, she just slammed into the incident cruiser and asked for the wires."

"So?"

"So I'm thinking about that stuff you pulled with Rutherford. You said if they polygraphed you while you were doing that, you wouldn't register, now—"

"Ortega, that's Envoy conditioning. Pure mind discipline. It's not physical. You can't buy stuff like that off the rack at SleeveMart."

"Miriam Bancroft wears state-of-the-art Nakamura. They use her face and body to sell the stuff—"

"Does Nakamura do something that'll beat a police polygraph?"

"Not officially."

"Well, there you—"

"Don't be so fucking obtuse. You never heard of custom biochem?"

I paused at the foot of the stairs up to reception and shook my head. "I don't buy it. Torch her husband with a weapon only she and he have access to. No one's that stupid."

We went upstairs, Ortega at my heels.

"Think about it, Kovacs. I'm not saying it was premeditated—"

"And what about the remote storage? It was a pointless crime—"

"—not saying it was even rational, but you've got to—"

"—got to be someone who didn't know—"

"Fuck! Kovacs!"

Ortega's voice, up a full octave.

We were into the reception zone by now. Still two clients waiting on the left, a man and a woman deep in discussion of a large paper-wrapped package. On the right a peripheral flicker of crimson where there should have been none. I was looking at blood.

The ancient Asian receptionist was dead, throat cut with something that glinted metallic deep within the wound around her neck. Her head rested in a shiny pool of her own blood on the desk in front of her.

My hand leapt for the Nemex. Beside me, I heard the snap as Ortega chambered the first slug in her Smith & Wesson. I swung toward the two waiting clients and their paper-wrapped package.

Time turned dreamlike. The neurachem made everything impossibly slow, separate images drifting to the floor of my vision like autumn leaves.

The package had fallen apart. The woman was holding a compact Sunjet, the man a machine pistol. I cleared the Nemex and started firing from the hip.

The door to the gantry burst open, and another figure stood in the opening, brandishing a pistol in each fist.

Beside me, Ortega's Smith & Wesson boomed and blew the new arrival back through the door like a reversed film sequence of his entrance.

My first shot ruptured the headrest of the woman's seat, showering her with white padding. The Saberlite sizzled, the beam went wide. The second slug exploded her head and turned the drifting white flecks red.

Ortega yelled in fury. She was still firing—upward, my peripheral sense told me. Somewhere above us, her shots splintered glass.

The machine gunner had struggled to his feet. I registered the bland features of a synth and put a pair of slugs into him. He staggered back against the wall, still raising the gun. I dived for the floor.

The dome above our heads smashed inward. Ortega yelled something and I rolled sideways. A body tumbled bonelessly head over feet onto the ground next to me.

The machine pistol cut loose, aimless. Ortega yelled again and flattened herself on the floor. I rolled upright on the lap of the dead woman and shot the synthetic again, three times in rapid succession. The gunfire choked off.

Silence.

I swung the Nemex left and right, covering the corners of the room and the front door. The jagged edges of the smashed dome above. Nothing.

"Ortega?"

"Yeah, fine." She was sprawled on the other side of the room, propping herself up on one elbow. There was a tightness in her voice that belied her words. I swayed to my feet and made my way across to her, footsteps crunching on broken glass.

"Where's it hurt?" I demanded, crouching to help her sit up.

"Shoulder. Fucking bitch got me with the Sunjet."

I stowed the Nemex and looked at the wound. The beam had carved a long diagonal furrow across the back of Ortega's jacket and clipped through the left shoulder pad at the top. The meat beneath the pad was cooked, seared down to the bone in a narrow line at the center.

"Lucky," I said with forced lightness. "You hadn't ducked, it would have been your head."

"I wasn't ducking, I was fucking falling over."

"Good enough. You want to stand up?"

"What do you think?" Ortega levered herself to her knees on her uninjured arm and then stood. She grimaced at the movement of her jacket against the wound. "*Fuck,* that stings."

"I think that's what the guy in the doorway said."

Leaning on me, she turned to stare, eyes centimeters away. I deadpanned it, and the laughter broke across her face like a sunrise. She shook her head.

"Jesus, Kovacs, you are one sick motherfucker. They teach you to tell postfirefight jokes in the corps or is it just you?"

I guided her toward the exit. "Just me. Come on, let's get you some fresh air."

Behind us, there was a sudden flailing sound. I jerked around and saw the synthetic sleeve staggering upright. Its head was smashed and disfigured where my last shot had torn the side of the skull off, and the gun hand was spasmed open at the end of a stiff, bloodstreaked right arm, but the other arm was flexing, hand curling into a fist. The synth stumbled against the chair, righted itself, and came toward us, dragging its right leg.

I drew the Nemex and pointed it.

"Fight's over," I advised.

The slack face grinned at me. Another halting step. I frowned.

"For Christ's sake, Kovacs." Ortega was fumbling for her own weapon. "Get it over with."

I snapped off a shot, and the shell punched the synth backwards onto the glass-strewn floor. It twisted a couple of times, then lay still but breathing sluggishly. As I watched it, fascinated, a gurgling laugh arose from its mouth.

"That's fucking enough," it coughed, and laughed again. "Eh, Kovacs? That's fucking enough."

The words held me in shock for the space of a heartbeat, then I wheeled and made for the door, dragging Ortega with me.

"Wha—"

"Out. Get the fuck out." I thrust her through the door ahead of me and grabbed the railing outside. The dead pistoleer lay twisted on the walkway ahead. I shoved Ortega again, and she vaulted the body awkwardly. Slamming the door after me, I followed her at a run.

We were almost to the end of the gantry when the dome behind us detonated in a geyser of glass and steel. I distinctly heard the door come off its hinges behind us, and then the blast picked us both up like discarded coats and threw us down the stairs into the street.

CHAPTEr TWENTY-TWO

The police are more impressive by night.

First of all, you've got the flashing lights casting dramatic color into everyone's faces, grim expressions steeped alternately in criminal red and smoky blue. Then there's the sound of the sirens on the night, like an elevator ratcheting down the levels of the city, the crackling voices of the comsets, somehow brisk and mysterious at the same time, the coming and going of dimly lit, bulky figures and snatches of cryptic conversation, the deployed technology of law enforcement for wakened bystanders to gape at, the lack of anything else going on to provide a vacuum backdrop. There can be absolutely nothing to see beyond this, and people will still watch for hours.

Nine o'clock on a workday morning, it's a different matter. A couple of cruisers turned up in response to Ortega's call, but their lights and sirens were barely noticeable above the general racket of the city. The uniformed crews strung incident barriers at either end of the street and shepherded customers out of the neighboring businesses, while Ortega persuaded the bank's private security not to arrest me as a possible accessory to the bombing. There was a bounty on terrorists, apparently. A crowd of sorts developed, beyond the almost invisible hazing of the barriers, but it seemed mostly composed of irate pedestrians trying to get past.

I sat the whole thing out on the curb opposite, checking over the superficial injuries I'd acquired on my short flight down from the gantry to the street. Mostly, it was bruising and abrasions. The shape of the forum provider's reception area had channeled most of the blast directly upward through the roof, and that was the route the bulk of the shrapnel had taken, as well. We'd been very lucky.

Ortega left the clutch of uniformed officers gathered outside the bank and strode across the street toward me. She had removed her jacket, and there was a long white smear of tissue weld congealing over her shoulder wound. She held her discarded shoulder holster dangling in one hand, and her breasts moved beneath the thin cotton of a white T-shirt that bore the legend YOU HAVE THE RIGHT TO REMAIN SILENT—WHY DON'T YOU TRY IT FOR A WHILE? She seated herself next to me on the curb.

"Forensic wagon's on the way," she said inconsequentially. "You reckon we'll get anything useful out of the wreckage?"

I looked at the smoldering ruin of the dome and shook my head.

"There'll be bodies, maybe even stacks intact, but those guys were just local street muscle. All they'll tell you is that the synth hired them, probably for half a dozen ampules of tetrameth each."

"Yeah, they were kind of sloppy, weren't they?"

I felt a smile ghost across my lips. "Kind of. But then I don't think they were even supposed to get us."

"Just keep us busy till your pal blew up, huh?"

"Something like that."

"The way I figure it, the detonator was wired into his vital signs, right? You snuff him and, boom, he takes you with him. Me, too. And the cheap hired help."

"And wipes out his own stack and sleeve." I nodded. "Tidy, isn't it."

"So what went wrong?"

I rubbed absently at the scar under my eye. "He overestimated me. I was supposed to kill him outright, but I missed. Probably would have killed himself at that stage, but I messed up his arm trying to stop the machine pistol." *In my mind's eye the gun drops from splayed fingers and skitters across the floor.* "Blew it way out of his reach, as well. He must have been lying there, willing himself to die when he heard us leaving. Wonder what make of synth he was using."

"Whoever it was, they can have an endorsement from me any day of the week," Ortega said cheerfully. "Maybe there'll be something left for forensics after all."

"You know who it was, don't you?"

"He called you Kov—"

"It was Kadmin."

There was a short silence. I watched the smoke curling up from the ruined dome. Ortega breathed in, out.

"Kadmin's in the store."

"Not anymore he isn't." I glanced sideways at her. "You got a cigarette?"

She passed me the pack wordlessly. I shook one out, fitted it into the corner of my mouth, touched the ignition patch to the end, and drew deeply. The movements happened as one, reflex conditioned over years like a macro of need. I didn't have to consciously do anything. The smoke curling into my lungs was like a breath of the perfume you remember an old lover wearing.

"He knew me." I exhaled. "And he knew his Quellist history, too. *That's fucking enough* is what a Quellist guerrilla called Iffy Deme said when she died under interrogation during the Unsettlement on Harlan's World. She was wired with internal explosives, and she brought the house down. Sound familiar? Now who do we know who can swap Quell quotes like a Millsport native?"

"He's in the fucking store, Kovacs. You can't get someone out of the store without—"

"Without an A.I. With an A.I., you can do it. I've seen it done. Core command on Adoracion did it with our prisoners of war, like that." I snapped my fingers. "Like hooking elephant rays off a spawning reef."

"As easy as that?" Ortega said ironically.

I sucked down some more smoke and ignored her. "You remember when we were in virtual with Kadmin, we got that lightning effect across the sky?"

"Didn't see it. No, wait, yeah. I thought it was a glitch."

"It wasn't. It touched him. Reflected in the table. That's when he promised to kill me." I turned toward her and grinned queasily. The memory of Kadmin's virtual entity was clear and monstrous. "You want to hear a genuine first-generation Harlan's World myth? An offworld fairy story?"

"Kovacs, even with an A.I., they'd need—"

"Want to hear the story?"

Ortega shrugged, winced, and nodded. "Sure. Can I have my cigarettes back?"

I tossed her the pack and waited while she kindled the cigarette. She plumed smoke out across the street. "Go on, then."

"Right. Where I come from originally, Newpest, used to be a textile town. There's a plant on Harlan's World called belaweed, grows in the sea and on most shorelines, too. Dry it out, treat it with chemicals, and you can make something like cotton from it. During the Settlement Newpest was the belacotton capital of the World. Conditions in the mills were pretty bad even back then, and when the Quellists turned everything upside down it got worse. The belacotton industry went into decline, and there was massive unemployment, unrelieved poverty, and fuck-all the Unsettlers could do about it. They were revolutionaries, not economists."

"Same old song, huh?"

"Well, familiar tune anyway. Some pretty horrible stories came out of the textile slums around that time. Stuff like the Threshing Sprites, the Cannibal of Kitano Street."

Ortega drew on her cigarette and widened her eyes. "Charming."

"Yeah, well, bad times. So you get the story of Mad Ludmila the seamstress. This is one they used to tell to kids to make them do their chores and come home before dark. Mad Ludmila had a failing belacotton mill and three children who never helped her out. They used to stay out late playing the arcades across town and sleep all day. So one day, the story goes, Ludmila flips out."

"She wasn't already mad, then?"

"No, just a bit stressed."

"You called her Mad Ludmila."

"That's what the story's called."

"But if she wasn't mad at the beginning—"

"Do you want to hear this story or not?"

Ortega's mouth quirked at the corner. She waved me on with her cigarette.

"*The story goes,* one evening as her children were getting ready to go out, she spiked their coffee with something, and when they were semiconscious, but still aware, mind you, she drove them out to Mitcham's Point and threw them into the threshing tanks one by one. They say you could hear the screams right across the swamp."

"Mm-hmm."

"Of course, the police were suspicious—"

"Really?"

"—but they couldn't prove anything. Couple of the kids had been into some nasty chemicals, they were jerking around with the local yakuza, no one was really surprised when they disappeared."

"Is there a point to this story?"

"Yeah. See, Ludmila got rid of her fucking useless children, but it didn't really help. She still needed someone to man the curing vats, to haul the belaweed up and down the mill stairs, and she was still broke. So what did she do?"

"Something gory, I imagine."

I nodded. "What she did, she picked the bits of her mangled kids out of the thresher and stitched them into a huge three-meter-tall carcass. And then, on a night sacred to the dark powers, she invoked a Tengu to—"

"A what?"

"A Tengu. It's a sort of mischief maker—a demon, I guess you'd call it. She invoked the Tengu to animate the carcass, and then she stitched it in."

"What, when it wasn't looking?"

"Ortega, it's a fairy story. She stitched the soul of the Tengu inside, but she promised to release it if it served her will nine years. Nine's a sacred number in the Harlanite pantheons, so she was as bound to the agreement as the Tengu. Unfortunately—"

"Ah."

"—Tengu are not known for their patience, and I don't suppose old Ludmila was the easiest person to work for, either. One night, not a third of the way through the contract, the Tengu turned on her and tore her apart. Some say it was Kishimo-jin's doing, that she whispered terrible incitements into the Tengu's ear at—"

"Kishimo Gin?"

"Kishimo-jin, the divine protectress of children. It was her revenge on Ludmila for the death of the children. That's one version. There's another that—" I picked up Ortega's mutinous expression out of the corner of my eye and hurried on. "Well, anyway. The Tengu tore her apart, but in so doing, it locked itself into the spell and was condemned to remain imprisoned in the carcass. And now, with the original invoker of the spell dead, and worse still, betrayed, the carcass began to rot. A piece here, a piece there, but irreversibly. And so the Tengu was driven to prowling the streets and mills of the textile quarter, looking for fresh meat to replace the rotting portions of its body. It always killed children, because the parts it needed to replace were child sized, but however many times it sewed new flesh to the carcass—"

"It'd learned to sew, then?"

"Tengu are multitalented. However many times it replaced itself, after a few days the new portions began to putrefy, and it was driven out once more to hunt. In the Quarter they call it the Patchwork Man."

I fell silent. Ortega mouthed a silent O, then slowly exhaled smoke through it. She watched the smoke dissipate, then turned to face me.

"Your mother tell you that story?"

"Father. When I was five."

She looked at the end of her cigarette. "Nice."

"No. He wasn't. But that's another story." I stood up and looked down the street to where the crowd was massed at one of the incident barriers. "Kadmin's out there, and he's out of control. Whoever he was working for, he's working for himself now."

"How?" Ortega spread her hands in exasperation. "Okay, an A.I. could tunnel into the Bay City P.D. stack. I'll buy that. But we're talking about microsecond intrusion here. Any longer and it'd ring bells from here to Sacramento."

"Microsecond's all it needed."

"But Kadmin isn't *on* stack. They'd need to know when he was being spun, and they'd need a fix. They'd need—"

She stopped as she saw it coming.

"Me," I finished for her. "They'd need me."

"But you—"

"I'm going to need some time to sort this out, Ortega." I spun my cigarette into the gutter and grimaced as I tasted the inside of my own mouth. "Today, maybe tomorrow, too. Check the stack. Kadmin's gone. If I were you, I'd keep your head down for a while."

Ortega pulled a sour face. "You telling me to go undercover in my own city?"

"Not telling you to do anything." I pulled out the Nemex and ejected the half-spent magazine with actions almost as automatic as the smoking had been. The clip went into my jacket pocket. "I'm giving you the state of play. We'll need somewhere to meet. Not the Hendrix. And not anywhere you can be traced to, either. Don't tell me, just write it down." I nodded at the crowd beyond the barriers. "Anybody down there with decent implants could have this conversation focused and amped."

"Jesus." She blew out her cheeks. "That's technoparanoia, Kovacs."

"Don't tell me that. I used to do this for a living."

She thought about it for a moment, then produced a pen and scribbled on the side of the cigarette pack. I fished a fresh magazine from my pocket and jacked it into the Nemex, eyes still scanning the crowd.

"There you go." Ortega tossed me the pack. "That's a discreet destination code. Feed it to any taxi in the Bay Area and it'll take you there. I'll be there tonight, tomorrow night. After that, it's back to business as usual."

I caught the pack left-handed, glanced briefly at the numbers, and put it away in my jacket. Then I snapped the slide on the Nemex to chamber the first slug and stuffed the pistol back into its holster.

"Tell me that when you've checked the stack," I said, and started walking.

CHAPTEr TWENTY-THrEE

I walked south.

Over my head, autocabs wove in and out of the traffic with programmed hyperefficiency and swooped occasionally to ground level in attempts to stimulate custom. The weather above the traffic flow was on the change, gray cloud cover racing in from the west and occasional spots of rain hitting my cheek when I looked up. I left the cabs alone. *Go primitive,* Virginia Vidaura would have said. With an A.I. gunning for you, your only hope is to drop out of the electronic plane. Of course, on a battlefield that's a lot more easily done. Plenty of mud and chaos to hide in. A modern city—unbombed—is a logistical nightmare for this kind of evasion. Every building, every vehicle, every street is jacked into the web, and every transaction you make tags you for the data hounds.

I found a battered-looking currency dispenser and replenished my thinning sheaf of plasticized notes from it. Then I backed up two blocks and went east until I found a public phone booth. I searched through my pockets, came up with a card, settled the call 'trodes on my head, and dialed.

There was no image. No sound of connection. This was an internal chip. The voice spoke brusquely out of a blank screen.

"Who is this?"

"You gave me your card," I said. "In case of anything major. Well, now it seems there's something pretty fucking major we need to talk about, Doctor."

There was an audible click as she swallowed, just once, and then her voice was there again, level and cool. "We should meet. I assume you don't want to come to the facility."

"You assume right. You know the red bridge?"

"The Golden Gate, it's called," she said dryly. "Yes, I'm familiar with it."

"Be there at eleven. Northbound highway. Come alone."

I cut the connection. Redialed.

"Bancroft residence. With whom do you wish to speak?" A severely suited woman with a hairstyle reminiscent of Angin Chandra's pilot cuts arrived on the screen a fraction after she started speaking.

"Laurens Bancroft, please."

"Mr. Bancroft is in a conference at present."

That made it even easier. "Fine. When he's available, can you tell him Takeshi Kovacs called."

"Would you like to speak to Mrs. Bancroft. She has left instructions that—"

"No," I said rapidly. "That won't be necessary. Please tell Mr. Bancroft that I shall be out of contact for a few days, but that I will call him from Seattle. That's all."

I cut the connection and checked my watch. There was about an hour and forty minutes left of the time I'd given myself to be on the bridge. I went looking for a bar.

●●●

I'm stacked, backed up and I'm fifth dan
And I'm not afraid of the Patchwork Man

The small coin of urchin rhyme gleamed up at me from the silted bed of my childhood.

But I was afraid.

●●●

The rain still hadn't set in when we got onto the approach road to the bridge, but the clouds were massing sullenly above and the windshield was splattered with heavy droplets too few to trigger the truck's wipers. I watched the rust-colored structure looming up ahead through the distortion of the exploded raindrops and knew I was going to get soaked.

There was no traffic on the bridge. The rust-colored suspension towers rose like the bones of some incalculably huge dinosaur above deserted asphalt lanes and side gantries lined with unidentifiable detritus.

"Slow down," I told my companion as we passed under the first tower, and the heavy vehicle braked with uncalled-for force. I glanced sideways. "Take it easy. I told you, this is a no-risk gig. I'm just meeting someone."

Graft Nicholson gave me a bleary look from the driver's seat, and a breath of stale alcohol came with it.

"Yeah, sure. You hand out this much plastique on drivers every week, right? Just pick them out of Licktown bars for charity?"

I shrugged. "Believe what you want. Just keep your speed down. You can drive as fast as you like after you let me out."

Nicholson shook his tangled head. "This is fucked, man—"

"There. Standing on the walkway. Drop me there." There was a solitary figure leaning on the rail up ahead, apparently contemplating the view of the bay. Nicholson frowned with concentration and hunched the vastly outsize shoulders for which, presumably, he was named. The battered truck drifted sedately but not quite smoothly across two lanes and came to a bumpy halt beside the right-hand barrier.

I jumped down, glanced around for bystanders, saw none, and pulled myself back up on the open door.

"All right now, listen. It's going to be at least two days till I get to Seattle, maybe three, so you just hole up in the first hotel the city-limits datastack has to offer, and you wait for me there. Pay cash, but book in under my name. I'll contact you between ten and eleven in the morning, so be in the hotel at those times. The rest of the time, you can do what you like. I figure I gave you enough cash not to get bored."

Graft Nicholson bared his teeth in a knowing leer that made me feel slightly sorry for anyone working in the Seattle leisure industry that week. "Don't worry 'bout me, man. Old Graft knows how to grab a good time by the titties."

"I'm glad. Just don't get too comfortable. We may need to move it in a hurry."

"Yeah, yeah. What about the rest of the plastique, man?"

"I told you. You'll get paid when we're done."

"And what about if you don't show up in three days?"

"In that case," I said pleasantly, "I'll be dead. That happens, it'd be better to drop out of sight for a few weeks. They're not going to waste time looking for you. They find me, they'll be happy."

"Man, I don't think I'm—"

"You'll be fine. See you in three days." I dropped back to the ground, slammed the truck door, and banged on it twice. The engine rumbled into drive, and Nicholson pulled the truck back out into the middle of the highway.

Watching him go, I wondered briefly if he'd actually go to Seattle at all. I'd given him a sizable chunk of credit, after all, and even with the promise of a second payment if he followed instructions, the temptation would still be to double back somewhere up the coast and head straight back to the bar I'd picked him out of. Or he might get jumpy, sitting in the hotel waiting for a knock on the door, and skip before the three days were up. I couldn't really blame him for these potential betrayals, since I had no intention of turning up myself. Whatever he did was fine by me.

In systems evasion, you must scramble the enemy's assumptions, Virginia said in my ear. *Run as much interference as you can without breaking pace.*

"A friend of yours, Mr. Kovacs?" The doctor had come to the barrier and was watching the car recede.

"Met him in a bar," I said truthfully, climbing over to her side and making for the rail. It was the same view I'd seen when Curtis brought me back from Suntouch House the day of my arrival. In the gloomy, prerain light the aerial traffic glimmered above the buildings across the bay like a swarm of fireflies. Narrowing my eyes, I could make out detail on the island of Alcatraz, the gray-walled and orange-windowed bunker of PsychaSec S.A. Beyond lay Oakland. At my back, the open sea, and to north and south a solid kilometer of empty bridge. Reasonably sure that nothing short of tactical artillery could surprise me here, I turned back to look at the doctor.

She seemed to flinch as my gaze fell on her.

"What's the matter?" I asked softly. "Medical ethics pinching a little?"

"It was not my idea—"

"I know that. You just signed the releases, turned a blind eye, that kind of thing. So who was it?"

"I don't know," she said not quite steadily. "Someone came to see Sullivan. An artificial sleeve. Asian, I think."

I nodded. Trepp.

"What were Sullivan's instructions?"

"Virtual net locater, fitted between the cortical stack and neural interface." The clinical details seemed to give her strength. Her voice firmed up. "We did the surgery two days before you were freighted. Microscalpeled into the vertebrae along the line of the original stack incision, and plugged it with graft tissue. No show under any kind of sweep outside virtual. You'd have to run a full neuro-electrical to find it. How did you guess?"

"I didn't have to guess. Someone used it to locate and lever a contract killer out of the Bay City police holding stack. That's Aiding and Abetting. You and Sullivan are both going down for a couple of decades minimum."

She looked pointedly up and down the empty bridge. "In that case, why aren't the police here, Mr. Kovacs?"

I thought about the rap sheet and military records that must have come to Earth with me, and what it must feel like standing here alone with someone who had done all those things. What it must have taken to come out here alone. Slowly, a reluctant smile crept out of one corner of my mouth.

"All right, I'm impressed," I said. "Now tell me how to neutralize the damn thing."

She looked at me seriously, and the rain began to fall. Heavy drops, dampening the shoulders of her coat. I felt it in my hair. We both glanced up and I cursed. A moment later she stepped closer to me and touched a heavy broach on one wing of her coat. The air above us shimmered, and the rain stopped falling on me. Looking up again, I saw it exploding off the dome of the repulsion field over our heads. Around our feet, the paving darkened in splotches and then uniformly, but a magic circle around our feet stayed dry.

"To actually remove the locater will require microsurgery similar to its placement. It can be done, but not without a full micro-op theater. Anything less, and you run the risk of damaging the neural interface, or even the spinal nerve canals."

I shifted a little, uncomfortable at our proximity. "Yeah, I figured."

"Well, then you've probably also *figured*," she said, burlesquing my accent, "that you can enter either a scrambling signal or a mirror code into the stack receiver to neutralize the broadcast signature."

"If you've got the original signature."

"If, as you say, you have the original signature." She reached into her pocket and produced a small, plastic-sheathed disk, weighed it in her palm for a moment, and then held it out to me. "Well, now you have."

I took the disk and looked at it speculatively.

"It's genuine. Any neuroelectrical clinic will confirm that for you. If you have doubts, I can recommend—"

"Why are you doing this for me?"

She met my eye, without flinching this time. "I'm not doing it for you, Mr. Kovacs. I am doing this for myself."

I waited. She looked away for a moment, across the Bay. "I am not a stranger to corruption, Mr. Kovacs. No one can work for long in a justice facility and fail to recognize a gangster. The synthetic was one of a type. Warden Sullivan has had dealings with these people as long as I have had tenure at Bay City. Police jurisdiction ends outside our doors, and administration salaries are not high."

She looked back at me. "I have never taken payment from these people, nor, until now, had I acted on their behalf. But equally, I have never stood against them. It has been very easy to bury myself in my work and pretend not to see what goes on."

"*The human eye is a wonderful device,*" I quoted from *Poems and Other Prevarications* absently. "*With a little effort, it can fail to see even the most glaring injustice.*"

"Very aptly put."

"It's not mine. So how come you did the surgery?"

She nodded. "As I said, until now I had managed to avoid actual contact with these people. Sullivan had me assigned to Offworld Sleeving because there wasn't much of it, and the favors he did were all local. It made it easier for both of us. He's a good manager in that respect."

"Shame I came along then."

"Yes, it presented a problem. He knew it'd look odd if I was taken off the procedure for one of his more compliant medics, and he didn't want any waves. Apparently this was *something big*." She placed the same derisive stress on the words as she had on my *figured* earlier. "These people were jacked in at high level, and everything had to be smooth. But he wasn't stupid; he had a rationale all ready for me."

"Which was?"

She gave me another candid look. "That you were a dangerous psychopath. A killing machine turned rabid. And that, whatever the reasons, it wouldn't be a good idea to have you swimming the dataflows untagged. No telling where you could needlecast to once you're out of the real world. And I bought it. He showed me the files they have on you. Oh, he wasn't stupid. No. *I* was."

I thought of Leila Begin and our talk of psychopaths on the virtual beach. Of my own flippant responses.

"Sullivan wouldn't be the first person to call me a psychopath. And you wouldn't be the first person to buy it, either. The Envoys, well, it's . . ." I shrugged and looked away. "It's a label. Simplification for public consumption."

"They say a lot of you turned. That twenty percent of the serious crime in the Protectorate is caused by renegade Envoys. Is it true?"

"The percentage?" I stared away through the rain. "I wouldn't know. There are a lot of us out there, yes. There's not much else to do once you've been discharged from the corps. They won't let you into anything that might lead to a position of power or influence. On most worlds you're barred from holding public office. Nobody trusts Envoys, and that means no promotion. No prospects. No loans, no credit."

I turned back to her. "And the stuff we've been trained to do is so close to crime, there's almost no difference. Except that crime is easier. Most criminals are stupid; you probably know that. Even the organized syndicates are like kid gangs compared to the corps. It's easy to get respect. And when you've spent the last decade of your life jacking in and out of sleeves, cooling out on stack, and living virtual, the threats that law enforcement has to offer are pretty bland."

We stood together in silence for a while.

"I'm sorry," she said finally.

"Don't be. Anyone reading those files on me would have—"

"That isn't what I meant."

"Oh." I looked down at the disk in my hands. "Well, if you were looking to atone for something, I'd say you just have. And take it from me, no one stays totally clean. The only place you get to do that is on stack."

"Yes. I know."

"Yeah, well. There is just one more thing I'd like to know."

"Yes?"

"Is Sullivan at Bay City Central right now?"

"He was when I went out."

"And what time is he likely to leave this evening?"

"It's usually around seven." She compressed her lips. "What are you going to do?"

"I'm going to ask him some questions," I said truthfully.

"And if he won't answer them?"

"Like you said, he's not stupid." I put the disk into my jacket pocket. "Thank you for your help, Doctor. I'd suggest you try not to be around the facility at seven tonight. And thank you."

"As I said, Mr. Kovacs, I am doing this for myself."

"That's not what I meant, Doctor."

"Oh."

I placed one hand lightly on her arm, then stepped away from her and so back out into the rain.

CHAPTEr TWENTY-FOUr

The wood of the bench had been worn by decades of occupants into a series of comfortable, buttock-shaped depressions, and the arms were similarly sculpted. I molded myself lengthwise into the curves, cocked my boots on the bench end nearest the doors I was watching, and settled down to read the graffiti etched into the wood. I was soaked from the long walk back across town, but the hall was pleasantly heated and the rain rattled impotently on the long transparent panels of the tilted roof high above my head. After a while, one of the dog-sized cleaning robots came to wipe away my muddy footprints from the fused glass paving. I watched it idly until the job was done and the record of my arrival on the bench was totally erased.

It would have been nice to think my electronic traces could be wiped in the same way, but that kind of escape belonged to the legendary heroes of another age.

The cleaning robot trundled off, and I went back to the graffiti. Most of it was Amanglic or Spanish, old jokes that I'd seen before in a hundred similar places—CABRON MODIFICADO! and ABSENT WITHOUT SLEEVE!, the old crack THE ALTERED NATIVE WAS HERE!!—but high on the bench's backrest and chiseled upside down, like a tiny pool of inverted calm in all the rage and desperate pride, I found a curious haiku in kanji:

Pull on the new flesh like borrowed gloves
And burn your fingers once again.

The author must have been hanging over the back of the bench when he cut it into the wood, but still each character was executed with elegant care. I gazed at the calligraphy for what was probably a long time, while memories of Harlan's World sang in my head like high-tension cables.

A sudden burst of crying over to my right jolted me out of the reverie. A young black woman and her two children, also black, were staring at the stooped, middle-aged white man standing before them in tattered U.N. surplus fatigues. Family reunion. The young woman's face was a mask of shock—it hadn't hit her properly yet—and the smaller child, probably no more than four, just didn't get it at all. She was looking right through the white man, mouth forming the repeated question *where's daddy, where's daddy?* The man's features were glistening in the rainy light from the roof; he looked like he'd been crying since they dragged him out of the tank.

I rolled my head to an empty quadrant of the hall. My own father had walked right past his waiting family and out of our lives when he was resleeved. We never even knew which one he was, although I sometimes wonder if my mother didn't catch some splinter of recognition in an averted gaze, some echo of stance or gait as he passed. I don't know if he was too ashamed to confront us, or more likely too set up with the luck of drawing a sleeve sounder than his own alcohol-wrecked body had been, and already plotting a new course for other cities and younger women. I was ten at the time. The first I knew about it was when the attendants ushered us out of the facility just short of locking up for the night. We'd been there since noon.

The chief attendant was an old man, conciliatory and very good with kids. He put his hand on my shoulder and spoke kindly to me before leading us out. To my mother, he made a short bow and murmured something formal that allowed her to keep the dam of her self-control intact.

He probably saw a few like us every week.

I memorized Ortega's discreet destination code, for something to do with my mind, then shredded that panel of the cigarette pack and ate it.

My clothes were almost dried through by the time Sullivan came through the doors leading out of the facility and started down the steps. His thin frame was cloaked in a long gray raincoat, and he wore a brimmed hat, something I hadn't seen any of so far in Bay City. Framed in the V between my propped feet and reeled into close-up with the neurachem, his face looked pale and tired. I shifted a little on the bench and brushed the holstered Philips gun with the tips of my fingers. Sullivan was coming straight toward me, but when he saw my form sprawled on the bench, he pursed his mouth with disapproval and altered course to avoid what he presumably took for a derelict cluttering up the facility. He passed without giving me another glance.

I gave him a few meters start and then swung silently to my feet and went after him, slipping the Philips gun out of its holster under my coat. I caught up just as he reached the exit. As the doors parted for him, I shoved him rudely in the small of the back and stepped quickly outside in his wake. He was swinging back to face me, features contorted with anger, as the doors started to close.

"What do you think you're—" The rest of it died on his lips as he saw who I was.

"Warden Sullivan," I said affably, and showed him the Philips gun under my jacket. "This is a silent weapon, and I'm not in a good mood. Please do exactly as I tell you."

He swallowed. "What do you want?"

"I want to talk about Trepp, among others. And I don't want to do it in the rain. Let's go."

"My car is—"

"A really bad idea." I nodded. "So let's walk. And, Warden Sullivan, if you so much as blink at the wrong person, I'll shoot you in half. You won't see the gun; no one will. But it'll be there just the same."

"You're making a mistake, Kovacs."

"I don't think so." I tipped my head toward the diminished ranks of parked vehicles in the lot. "Straight through, and left into the street. Keep going till I tell you to stop."

Sullivan started to say something else, but I jerked the barrel of the Philips gun at him and he shut up. Sideways at first, he made his way down the steps to the parking lot and then, with occasional backward glances, across the uneven ground toward the sagging double gate that had rusted open on its runners what looked like centuries ago.

"Eyes front," I called across the widening gap between us. "I'm still back here; you don't need to worry about that."

Out on the street, I let the gap grow to about a dozen meters and pretended complete dissociation from the figure ahead of me. It wasn't a great neighborhood, and there weren't many people out walking in the rain. Sullivan was an easy target for the Philips gun at double the distance.

Five blocks on, I spotted the steamed-up windows of the noodlehouse I was looking for. I quickened my pace and came up on Sullivan's streetside shoulder.

"In here. Go to the booths at the back and sit down."

I made a single sweep of the street, saw no one obvious, and followed Sullivan inside.

The place was almost empty, the daytime diners long departed and the evening not yet cranked up. Two ancient Chinese women sat in a corner with the withered elegance of dried bouquets, heads nodding together. On the other side of the restaurant four young men in pale silk suits lounged dangerously and toyed with expensive-looking chunks of hardware. At a table near one of the windows, a fat Caucasian was working his way through an enormous bowl of chow mein and simultaneously flicking over the pages of a holoporn comic. A video screen set high on one wall gave out coverage of some incomprehensible local sport.

"Tea," I said to the young waiter who came to meet us, and seated myself opposite Sullivan in the booth.

"You aren't going to get away with this," he said unconvincingly. "Even if you kill me, really kill me, they'll check the most recent resleevings and backtrack to you sooner or later."

"Yeah, maybe they'll even find out about the unofficial surgery this sleeve had before I arrived."

"That bitch. She's going to—"

"You're in no position to be making threats," I said mildly. "In fact, you're in no position to do anything except answer my questions and hope I believe you. Who told you to tag me?"

Silence, apart from the game coverage from the set on the wall. Sullivan stared sullenly at me.

"All right, I'll make it easy for you. Simple yes or no. An artificial called Trepp came to see you. Was this the first time you'd had dealings with her?"

"I don't know what you're talking about."

With measured anger, I backhanded him hard across the mouth. He collapsed sideways against the wall of the booth, losing his hat. The conversation of the young men in silk stopped abruptly, then resumed with great animation as I cut them a sideways glance. The two old women got stiffly to their feet and filed out through a back entrance. The Caucasian didn't even look up from his holo-porn. I leaned across the table.

"Warden Sullivan, you're not taking this in the spirit it's intended. I am very concerned to know who you sold me to. I'm not going to go away, just because you have some residual scruples about client confidentiality. Believe me, they didn't pay you enough to hold out on me."

Sullivan sat back up, wiping at the blood trickling from the corner of his mouth. To his credit, he managed a bitter smile with the undamaged portion of his lips.

"You think I haven't been threatened before, Kovacs?"

I examined the hand I'd hit him with. "I think you've had very little experience of personal violence, and that's going to be a disadvantage. I'm going to give you the chance to tell me what I want to know here and now. After that we go somewhere with soundproofing. Now, who sent Trepp?"

"You're a thug, Kovacs. Nothing but—"

I snapped folded knuckles across the table and into his left eye. It made less noise than the slap. Sullivan grunted in shock and reeled away from the blow, cowering into the seat. I watched impassively until he recovered. Something cold was rising in me, something born on the benches of the Newpest Justice Facility and tempered with the years of pointless unpleasantness I had been witness to. I hoped Sullivan wasn't as tough as he was trying to appear, for both our sakes. I leaned close again.

"You said it, Sullivan. I'm a thug. Not a respectable criminal like you. I'm not a Meth, not a businessman. I have no vested interests, no social connections, no purchased respectability. It's just me, and you're in my way. So let's start again. Who sent Trepp?"

"He doesn't know, Kovacs. You're wasting your time."

The woman's voice was light and cheerful, pitched a little loud to carry from the door where she stood, hands in the pockets of a long black coat. She was slim and pale with close-cropped dark hair and a poise to the way she stood that bespoke combat skills. Beneath the coat she wore a gray quilted tunic that looked impact resistant and matching work trousers tucked into ankle boots. A single silver earring in the shape of a discarded 'trode cable dangled from her left ear. She appeared to be alone.

I lowered the Philips gun slowly, and without acknowledging that it had ever been trained on her she took the cue to advance casually into the restaurant. The young men in silk watched her every step of the way, but if she was aware of their gazes, she gave no sign. When she was about five paces from our booth, she gave me a look of inquiry and began to lift her hands slowly out of her pockets. I nodded, and she completed the movement, revealing open palms and fingers set with rings of black glass.

"Trepp?"

"Good guess. You going to let me sit down?"

I waved the Philips gun at the seat opposite, where Sullivan was cupping both hands to his eye. "If you can persuade your associate here to move over. Just keep your hands above the table."

The woman smiled and inclined her head. She glanced at Sullivan, who was already squeezing up to the wall to make space for her, and then, keeping her hands poised at her sides, she swung herself elegantly in beside him. The economy of motion was so tight that her pendant earring barely shifted. Once seated, she pressed both hands palm down on the table in front of her.

"That make you feel safer?"

"It'll do," I said, noticing that the black glass rings, like the earring, were a body joke. Each ring showed, X-ray like, a ghostly blue section of the bones in the fingers beneath. Trepp's style, at least, I could get to like.

"I didn't tell him anything," Sullivan blurted.

"You didn't know anything worth a jack," Trepp said disinterestedly. She hadn't even turned to look at him. "Lucky for you I turned up, I'd say. Mr. Kovacs doesn't look like someone ready to take *don't know* for an answer. Am I right?"

"What do you want, Trepp?"

"Come to help out." Trepp glanced up as something rattled in the restaurant. The waiter had arrived bearing a tray with a large teapot and two handleless cups. "You order this?"

"Yeah. Help yourself."

"Thanks, I love this stuff." Trepp waited while the waiter deposited everything, then busied herself with the teapot. "Sullivan, you want a cup, too? Hey, bring him another cup, would you. Thanks. Now, where was I?"

"You'd come to help out," I said pointedly.

"Yeah." Trepp sipped at the green tea and looked at me over the rim of the cup. "That's right. I'm here to clarify things. See, you're trying to hammer the information out of Sullivan here. And he doesn't know fuck-all. His contact was me, so here I am. Talk to me."

I looked at her levelly. "I killed you last week, Trepp."

"Yeah, so they tell me." Trepp set down the teacup and looked critically at her own fingerbones. "Course, I don't remember that. In fact, I don't even know you, Kovacs. Last thing I remember was putting myself into the tank about a month back. Everything after that's gone. The me you torched in that cruiser, she's dead. That wasn't me. So, no hard feelings, huh?"

"No remote storage, Trepp?"

She snorted. "Are you kidding? I make a living doing this, same as you, but not that much. Anyway, who needs that remote shit? The way I figure it, you fuck up, you've got to pay some kind of tab for it. I fucked up with you, right?"

I sipped my own tea and played back the fight in the aircar, considering the angles. "You were a little slow," I conceded. "A little careless."

"Yeah, careless. I got to watch that. Wearing artificials makes you that way. Very anti-Zen. I got a *sensei* in New York, it drives him up the fucking wall."

"That's too bad," I said patiently. "You want to tell me who sent you now?"

"Hey, better than that. You're invited to meet the Man." She nodded at my expression. "Yeah, Ray wants to talk to you. Same as last time, except this is a voluntary ride. Seems coercion doesn't work too well with you."

"And Kadmin? He's in on this, as well?"

Trepp drew breath in through her teeth. "Kadmin's, well, Kadmin's a bit of a side issue right now. Bit of an embarrassment really. But I think we can deal on that, as well. I really can't tell you too much more now." She shuttled her glance sideways at Sullivan, who was beginning to sit up and pay attention. "It's better if we go someplace else."

"All right." I nodded. "I'll follow you out. But let's have a couple of ground rules before we go. One, no virtuals."

"Way ahead of you there." Trepp finished her tea and started to get up from the table. "My instructions are to convey you directly to Ray. In the flesh."

I put a hand on her arm and she stopped moving abruptly.

"Two. No surprises. You tell me exactly what's going to happen well before it does. Anything unexpected, and you're likely to be disappointing your *sensei* all over again."

"Fine. No surprises." Trepp produced a slightly forced smile that told me she wasn't accustomed to being grabbed by the arm. "We're going to walk out of the restaurant and catch a taxi. That all right by you?"

"Just so long as it's empty." I released her arm and she resumed motion, coming fluidly upright, hands still well away from her sides. I reached into my pocket and tossed a couple of plastic notes at Sullivan. "You stay here. If I see your face come through the door before we're gone, I'll put a hole in it. Tea's on me."

As I followed Trepp to the door, the waiter arrived with Sullivan's teacup and a big white handkerchief, presumably for the warden's smashed lip. Nice kid. He practically tripped over himself trying to stay out of my way, and the look he gave me was mingled disgust and awe. In the wake of the icy fury that had possessed me earlier, I sympathized more than he could have known.

The young men in silk watched us go with the dead-eyed concentration of snakes.

Outside, it was still raining. I turned up my collar and watched as Trepp produced a transport pager and waved it casually back and forth above her head. "Be a minute," she said, and gave me a curious sidelong glance. "You know who that place belongs to?"

"I guessed."

She shook her head. "Triad noodlehouse. Hell of a place for an interrogation. Or do you just like living dangerously?"

I shrugged. "Where I come from, criminals stay out of other people's fights. They're a gutless lot, generally. Much more likely to get interference from a solid citizen."

"Not around here. Most solid citizens around here are a little too solid to get involved in a brawl on some stranger's behalf. The way they figure it, that's what the police are for. You're from Harlan's World, right?"

"That's right."

"Maybe it's that Quellist thing, then. You reckon?"

"Maybe."

An autocab came spiraling down through the rain in response to the pager. Trepp stood aside at the open hatch and made an irony of demonstrating the empty compartment within. I smiled thinly.

"After you."

"Suit yourself." She climbed aboard and moved over to let me in. I settled back on the seat opposite her and watched her hands. When she saw where I was looking, she grinned and spread her arms cruciform along the back of the seat. The hatch hinged down, shedding rain in sliding sheets.

"Welcome to Urbline Services," the cab said smoothly. "Please state your destination."

"Airport," Trepp said, lounging back in her seat and looking for my reaction. "Private carriers' terminal."

The cab lifted. I looked past Trepp at the rain on the rear window. "Not a local trip, then," I said tonelessly.

She brought her arms in again, hands held palm upward. "Well, we figured you wouldn't go virtual, so now we have to do it the hard way. Suborbital. Take about three hours."

"Suborbital?" I drew a deep breath and touched the holstered Philips gun lightly. "You know, I'm going to get really upset if someone asks me to check this hardware before we fly."

"Yeah, we figured that, too. Relax, Kovacs, you heard me say private terminal. This is a custom flight, just for you. Carry a fucking tactical nuke on board if you like. Okay?"

"Where are we going, Trepp?"

She smiled.

"Europe," she said.

CHAPTEr TWENTY-FIVE

Wherever it was in Europe that we landed, the weather was better. We left the blunt, windowless suborbital sitting on the fused glass runway, and walked to the terminal building through glinting sunlight that was a physical pressure on my body, even through my jacket. The sky above was an uncompromising blue from horizon to horizon, and the air felt hard and dry. According to the pilot's time check, it was still only midafternoon. I shrugged my way out of the jacket.

"Should be a limo waiting for us," Trepp said over her shoulder.

We passed, without formality, into the terminal and across a zone of microclimate where palms and other less recognizable tropicalia made a bid for the massive glass ceiling. A misty rain drifted down from sprinkler systems, rendering the air pleasantly damp after the aridity outside. Along the aisles set between the trees, children played and squalled, and old people sat dozily on wrought iron benches in a seemingly impossible coexistence. The middle generations were gathered in knots at coffee stands, talking with more gesticulation than I'd seen in Bay City and seemingly oblivious to the factors of time and schedule that govern most terminal buildings.

I adjusted the jacket across my shoulder to cover my weapons as much as possible and followed Trepp into the trees. It wasn't quick enough to beat the gaze of two security guards standing under a palm nearby, or that of a little girl scuffing her toes along the side of the aisle toward us. Trepp made a sign to the security as they stiffened, and they fell back into the previous relaxed postures with nods. Clearly, we were expected. The little girl wasn't so easily bought; she stared up at me with wide eyes until I made a pistol out of my fingers and shot her with noisy sound effects. Then she showed her teeth in a huge grin and hid behind the nearest bench. I heard her shooting me in the back all the way along the aisle.

Outside again, Trepp steered me past a mob of taxis to where an anonymous black cruiser was idling in a no-waiting zone. We climbed into air-conditioned cool and pale-gray automold seating.

"Ten minutes," she promised, as we rose into the air. "What did you think of the microclimate?"

"Very nice."

"Got them all over the airport. Weekends, people come out from the center to spend the day here. Weird, huh?"

I grunted and watched the window as we banked over the whorled settlement patterns of a major city. Further out, a dusty-looking plain stretched to the horizon and the almost painful blue of the sky. To the left, I could make out the rise of mountains.

Trepp seemed to pick up on my disinclination to talk, and she busied herself with a phone jack that she plugged in behind the ear with the ironic pendant. Another internal chip. Her eyes closed as she began the call, and I was left with the peculiar feeling of aloneness that you get when someone's using one of those things.

Alone was fine with me.

The truth was that I'd been a poor traveling companion for Trepp for most of the journey. In the cabin of the subship I'd been steadfastly withdrawn despite Trepp's obvious interest in my background. Finally she gave up trying to extract anecdotes about Harlan's World and the corps and tried instead to teach me a couple of card games she knew. Impelled by some ghost of cultural politeness, I reciprocated, but two isn't an ideal number for cards and neither of our hearts were in it. We landed in Europe in silence, each flipping through our own selection from the jet's media stack. Despite Trepp's apparent lack of concern on the subject, I was having a hard time forgetting the circumstances of our last trip together.

Below us, the plain gave way to increasingly green uplands and then one valley in particular where the forested crags seemed to close around something man-made. As we started to descend, Trepp unjacked herself with a flutter of eyelids that meant she hadn't bothered to disconnect the chip synapses first—strictly advised against by most manufacturers, but maybe she was showing off. I barely noticed. Most of me was absorbed in the thing we were landing beside.

It was a massive stone cross, larger than any I'd seen before and weather stained with age. As the cruiser spiraled down toward its base and then beyond, I realized that whoever had built the monument had set it on a huge central buttress of rock so it gave the impression of a titanic broadsword sunk into the earth by some retired warrior god. It was entirely in keeping with the dimensions of the mountains around it, as if no human agency could possibly have put it there. The stepped terraces of stone and ancillary buildings below the buttress, themselves monumental in size, shrank almost to insignificance under the brooding presence of this single artifact.

Trepp was watching me with a glitter in her eyes.

The limo settled on one of the stone expanses, and I climbed out, blinking up through the sun at the cross.

"This belong to the Catholics?" I hazarded.

"Used to." Trepp started toward a set of towering steel doors in the rock ahead. "Back when it was new. It's private property now."

"How come?"

"Ask Ray." Now it was Trepp who seemed uninterested in conversation. It was almost as if something in the vast structure was calling a different part of her character into ascendancy. She drifted to the doors as if attracted there by magnetism.

As we reached the portals, they yawned slowly open with a dull hum of powered hinges and stopped with an aperture of two meters between them. I gestured at Trepp, and she stepped over the threshold with a shrug. Something big moved spiderlike down the walls in the dimness to either side of the entrance. I slipped a hand to the butt of the Nemex, knowing as I did that it was futile. We were in the land of the giants now.

Skeletal gun barrels the length of a man's body emerged from the gloom, as the two robot sentry systems sniffed us over. I judged the caliber about the same as the Hendrix's lobby defense system, and relinquished the Nemex. With a vaguely insectile chittering, the automated killing units drew back and spidered back up the walls to their roosting points. At the base of the two alcoves they lived in, I could make out massive iron angels with swords.

"Come on." Trepp's voice was unnaturally loud in the cathedral hush. "You think we wanted to kill you, we would have brought you all the way here?"

I followed her down a flight of stone steps and into the main body of the chamber. We were in a huge basilica that must run the length of the rock buttress beneath the cross and whose ceiling was lost in gloom high above us. Up ahead was another set of steps, leading onto a raised and slightly narrower section where the lighting was stronger. As we reached it, I saw that the roof here was vaulted with the stone statues of hooded guardians, their hands resting on thick broadswords and their lips curled into faintly contemptuous smiles below their hoods.

I felt my own lips twist in fractional response, and my thoughts were all of high-yield explosives.

At the end of the basilica, gray things were hanging in the air. For a moment I thought I was looking at a series of shaped monoliths embedded in a permanent force field, and then one of the gray things shifted slightly in a stray current of the chilly air, and I suddenly knew what they were.

"Are you impressed, Takeshi-san?"

The voice, the elegant Japanese in which I was addressed, hit me like cyanide. My breathing locked up momentarily with the force of my emotions, and I felt a jagged current go though the neurachem system as it responded. I allowed myself to turn toward the voice, slowly. Somewhere under my eye, a muscle twitched with the suppressed will to do violence.

"Ray," I said, in Amanglic. "I should have fucking seen this one on the launch pad."

Reileen Kawahara stepped from a doorway to one side of the circular chamber where the basilica ended, and made an ironic bow. She followed me into Amanglic flawlessly.

"Perhaps you should have seen it coming, yes," she mused. "But if there's a single thing that I like about you, Kovacs, it is your endless capacity to be surprised. For all your war-veteran posturing, you remain at core an innocent. And in these times, that is no mean achievement. How do you do it?"

"Trade secret. You'd have to be a human being to understand it."

The insult fell unregarded. Kawahara looked down at the marbled floor as if she could see it lying there.

"Yes, well, I believe we've been over this ground before."

My mind fled back to New Beijing and the cancerous power structures that Kawahara's interests had created there, the discordant screams of the tortured that I had come to associate with her name.

I stepped closer to one of the gray envelopes and slapped it. The coarse surface gave under my hand, and the thing swung a little on its cables. Something shifted sluggishly within.

"Bullet-proof, right?"

"Mm-hmm." Kawahara tipped her head to one side. "Depends on the bullet, I would say. But impact resistant, certainly."

I manufactured a laugh from somewhere. "Bullet-proof womb lining! Only you, Kawahara. Only you would need to bullet-proof your clones, and then bury them under a mountain."

She stepped forward into the light then, and the force of my hate came up and hit me in the pit of the stomach as I looked at her. Reileen Kawahara claimed upbringing among the contaminated slums of Fission City, Western Australia, but if it was true, she had long ago left behind any trace of her origins. The figure opposite me had the poise of a dancer, a balance of body that was subtly attractive without calling forth any immediate hormonal response, and the face above was elfin and intelligent. It was the sleeve she had worn on New Beijing, custom cultured and untouched by implants of any kind. Pure organism, elevated to the level of art. Kawahara had garbed it in black, stiff tulip-petaled skirts cupping her lower body to midcalf and a soft silk blouse settled over her torso like dark water. The shoes on her feet were modeled on spacedeck slippers but with a modest heel, and her auburn hair was short and winged back from the clean-boned face. She looked like the inhabitant of a screen ad for some slightly sexy investment fund.

"Power is habitually buried," she said. "Think of the Protectorate bunkers on Harlan's World. Or the caverns the Envoy Corps hid you in while you were made over in their image. The essence of control is to remain hidden from view, is it not?"

"Judging by the way I've been led around the last week, I'd say yes. Now do you want to get on with this pitch?"

"Very well." Kawahara glanced aside at Trepp, who wandered away into the gloom, neck craned up at the ceiling like a tourist. I looked around for a seat and found none. "You are aware, no doubt, that I recommended you to Laurens Bancroft."

"He mentioned it."

"Yes, and had your hotel proved slightly less psychotic, matters would never have got as far out of hand as they have. We could have had this conversation a week ago and saved everyone a lot of unnecessary pain. It was not my intention for Kadmin to harm you. His instructions were to bring you here alive."

"There's been a change of program," I said, walking along the curve of the end chamber. "Kadmin's not following his instructions. He tried to kill me this morning."

Kawahara made a gesture of irritation. "I know that. That's why you've been brought here."

"Did you spring him?"

"Yes, of course."

"He was going to roll over on you?"

"He told Keith Rutherford that he felt he was not deployed to his best advantage in holding. That it would be hard to honor his contract with me in such a position."

"Subtle."

"Wasn't it. I never can resist sophisticated negotiation. I feel he earned the reinvestment."

"So you beaconed in on me, hooked him out, and beamed him over to Carnage for resleeving, right?" I felt in my pockets and found Ortega's cigarettes. In the grim twilight of the basilica, the familiar pack was like a postcard from another place. "No wonder the *Panama Rose* didn't have his second fighter decanted when we got there. He'd probably only just finished sleeving Kadmin. That motherfucker walked out of there in a Right Hand of God Martyr."

"About the same time you were coming aboard," Kawahara agreed. "In fact, I understand he was posing as a menial and you walked right past him. I'd rather you didn't smoke in here."

"Kawahara, I'd rather you died of an internal hemorrhage, but I don't suppose you'll oblige me." I touched my cigarette to the ignition patch and drew it to life, remembering. The man knelt in the ring. I played it back slowly. On the deck of the fightdrome ship, peering down at the design being painted onto the killing floor. The upturned face as we passed. Yes, he'd even smiled. I grimaced at the memory.

"You're being a lot less courteous than befits a man in your situation." I thought that underneath the cool I could detect a ragged edge in her voice. Despite her much vaunted self-control, Reileen Kawahara wasn't much better at coping with disrespect than Bancroft, General MacIntyre, or any other creature of power I'd had dealings with. "Your life is in danger, and I am in a position to safeguard it."

"My life's been in danger before," I told her. "Usually as a result of some piece of shit like you making large-scale decisions about how reality ought to be run. You've already let Kadmin get too close for my comfort. In fact, he probably used your fucking virtual locater to do it."

"I sent him," Kawahara gritted, "to collect you. Again, he disobeyed me."

"Didn't he just." I rubbed reflexively at the bruise on my shoulder. "So why should I believe you can do any better next time?"

"Because you know I can." Kawahara came across the center of the chamber, ducking her head to avoid the leathery gray clone sacs, and intercepting my path around the perimeter. Her face was taut with anger. "I am one of the seven most powerful human beings in this solar system. I have access to powers that the U.N. field commander general would kill for."

"This architecture's going to your head, Reileen. You wouldn't even have found *me* if you hadn't been keeping tabs on Sullivan. How the fuck are you going to find Kadmin?"

"Kovacs, Kovacs." There was a definite trembling in her laugh, as if she was fighting off an urge to put her thumbs through my eye sockets. "Do you have any idea what happens on the streets of any given city on Earth if I put out a search on someone? Do you have *any idea* how easy it would be to snuff you out here and now?"

I drew deliberately on the cigarette and plumed the smoke out at her. "As your faithful retainer Trepp said, not ten minutes ago, why bring me here just to snuff me out? You want something from me. Now what is it?"

She breathed in through her nose, hard. A measure of calm seeped onto her face, and she stepped back a couple of paces, turned away from the confrontation.

"You're right, Kovacs. I want you alive. If you disappear now, Bancroft's going to get the wrong message."

"Or the right message." I scuffed absently at engraved lettering on the stone beneath my feet. "Did you torch him?"

"No." Kawahara looked almost amused. "He killed himself."

"Yeah, right."

"Whether you believe it or not is immaterial to me, Kovacs. What I want from you is an end to the investigation. A tidy end."

"And how do you suggest I achieve that?"

"I don't care. Make something up. You're an Envoy, after all. Convince him. Tell him you think the police verdict was correct. Produce a culprit, if you must." A thin smile. "I do not include myself in that category."

"If you didn't kill him, if he torched his own head off, why should you care what happens? What's your interest in this?"

"That isn't under discussion here."

I nodded slowly. "And what do I get in return for this tidy ending?"

"Apart from the hundred thousand dollars?" Kawahara tilted her head quizzically. "Well, I understand you've been made a very generous recreational offer by other parties. And for my part, I will keep Kadmin off your back by whatever means necessary."

I looked down at the lettering beneath my feet and thought it through, link by link.

"Francisco Franco," Kawahara said, mistaking the direction of my gaze for focused interest. "Petty tyrant a long time back. He built this place."

"Trepp said it belonged to the Catholics."

Kawahara shrugged. "Petty tyrant with delusions of religion. Catholics get on well with tyranny. It's in the culture."

I glanced around, ostensibly casual, scanning for robot security systems. "Yeah, looks like it. So let me get this straight. You want me to sell Bancroft a parabolic full of shit, in return for which you'll call off Kadmin, who you set on me in the first place. That's the deal?"

"That, as you put it, is the deal."

I took one last lungful of smoke, savored it, and exhaled.

"You can go fuck yourself, Kawahara." I dropped my cigarette on the engraved stonework and ground it out with my heel. "I'll take my chances with Kadmin, and let Bancroft know you probably had him killed. So. Change your mind about letting me live now?"

My hands hung open at my sides, twitching to be filled with the rough woven bulk of handgun butts. I was going to put three Nemex shells through Kawahara's throat, at stack height, then put the gun in my mouth and blow my own stack apart. Kawahara almost certainly had remote storage anyway, but fuck it, you've got to make a stand somewhere. And a man can stave off his own death wish for only so long.

It could have been worse. It could have been Innenin.

Kawahara shook her head regretfully. She was smiling. "Always the same, Kovacs. *Full of sound and fury, signifying nothing.* Romantic nihilism. Haven't you learned *anything* since New Beijing?"

"There are some arenas so corrupt that the only clean acts possible are nihilistic."

"Oh, that's Quell, isn't it? Mine was Shakespeare, but then I don't expect colonial culture goes back that far, does it?" She was still smiling, poised like a total body theater gymnast about to launch into her aria. For a moment I suffered the almost hallucinatory conviction that she was going to break into a little dance, choreographed to a junk rhythm beat from speakers hidden in the dome above us.

"Takeshi, where did you get this belief that everything can be resolved with such brute simplicity? Surely not from the Envoys? Was it the Newpest gangs? The thrashings your father gave you as a child? Did you really think I would allow you to force my hand? Did you really think I would have come to the table this empty-handed? Think about it. You know me. Did you really believe it would be this easy?"

The neurachem settled within me. I bit it back, hung from the moment like a parachutist braced in the jump hatch.

"All right," I said evenly. "Impress me."

"Gladly." Kawahara reached into the breast pocket of her liquid black blouse. She produced a tiny holofile and flicked it into active with a thumbnail. As the images evolved in the air above the unit, she passed it to me. "A lot of the detail is legalistic, but you will, of course, recognize the salient points."

I took the little sphere of light as if it were a poisonous flower. The name hit me at once, leaping out of the print—

. . . SARAH SACHILOWSKA . . .

—and then the contract terminology, like a building coming down on me in slow motion.

. . . RELEASED INTO PRIVATE STORAGE . . .

. . . PROVISION FOR VIRTUAL CUSTODY . . .

. . . UNLIMITED PERIOD . . .

. . . SUBJECT TO REVIEW AT U.N. DISCRETION . . .

. . . UNDER VESTED AUTHORITY OF THE BAY CITY JUSTICE FACILITY . . .

The knowledge coursed sickly through me. I should have killed Sullivan when I had the chance.

"Ten days." Kawahara was watching my reactions closely. "That's how long you have to convince Bancroft the investigation is over, and to walk away. After that, Sachilowska goes into virtual at one of my clinics. There's a whole new generation of virtual interrogation software out there, and I will personally see to it that she pioneers the lot."

The holofile hit the marble floor with a brittle crack. I lurched at Kawahara, lips peeling back from my teeth. There was a low growling coming up through my throat that had nothing to do with any combat training I had ever undergone, and the Nemex was forgotten as my hands crooked into talons. I knew what her blood was going to taste like.

The cold barrel of a gun touched down on my neck before I got halfway.

"I'd advise against that," Trepp said in my ear.

Kawahara came and stood closer to me. "Bancroft isn't the only one who can buy troublesome criminals off colonial stacks. The Kanagawa Justice Facility was overjoyed when I came to them two days later with a bid for Sachilowska. The way they see it, if you're D.H.F.'d offworld, the chances of you ever having enough money to buy a needlecast back again are pretty slim. And of course, they get paid for the privilege of waving you good-bye. It must seem too good to be true. I imagine they're hoping it's the start of a trend." She fingered the lapel of my jacket thoughtfully. "And in fact, the way the virtuals market is at the moment, it might be a trend worth starting."

The muscle under my eye jumped violently.

"I'll kill you," I whispered. "I'll rip your fucking heart out and eat it. I'll bring this place down around you—"

Kawahara leaned in until our faces were almost touching. Her breath smelled faintly of mint and oregano. "No, you won't," she said. "You'll do exactly as I say, and you'll do it within ten days. Because if you don't, your friend Sachilowska will be starting her own private tour of hell without redemption."

She stepped back and lifted her hands. "Kovacs, you should be thanking whatever deities they've got on Harlan's World that I'm not some kind of sadist. I mean, I've given you an either/or. We could just as easily be negotiating exactly how much agony I put Sachilowska through. I mean, I could start now. That would give you an incentive to wrap things up speedily, wouldn't it? Ten days in most virtuals adds up to about three or four years. You were in the Wei Clinic; do you think she could stand three years of that? I think she'd probably go insane, don't you?"

The effort it cost me to contain my hate was like a rupture down behind my eyeballs and into my chest. I forced the words out.

"Terms. How do I know you'll release her?"

"Because I give you my word." Kawahara let her arms fall to her sides. "I believe you've had some experience of its validity in the past."

I nodded slowly.

"Subsequent to Bancroft's acceptance that the case is closed, and your own disappearance from view, I will D.H.F. Sachilowska back to Harlan's World to complete her sentence." Kawahara bent to pick up the holofile I'd dropped and held it up. She tipped it deftly a couple of times to flick through the pages. "I think you can see here that there is a reversal clause written into the contract. I will of course forfeit a large proportion of the original fee paid, but under the circumstances, I'm prepared to do that." She smiled faintly. "But please bear in mind that a reversal can work in both directions. What I return, I can always buy again. So if you were considering skulking in the undergrowth for a while and then running back to Bancroft, please abandon the idea now. This is a hand that you cannot win."

The gun barrel lifted away from my neck, and Trepp stepped back. The neurachem held me upright like a paraplegic's mobility suit. I stared numbly at Kawahara.

"Why the fuck did you do all this?" I whispered. "Why involve me at all, if you didn't want Bancroft to find his answers?"

"Because you are an Envoy, Kovacs." Kawahara spoke slowly, as if talking to a child. "Because if anybody can convince Laurens Bancroft that he died by his own hand, it is you. And because I knew you well enough to predict your moves. I arranged to have you brought to me almost as soon as you arrived, but the hotel intervened. And then, when chance brought you to the Wei Clinic I endeavored to bring you here once again."

"I bluffed my way out of the Wei Clinic."

"Oh, yes. Your biopirate story. You really think you sold them that second-rate experia rubbish? Be reasonable, Kovacs. You might have backed them up a couple of steps while they thought about it, but the reason, the *only* reason, you got out of the Wei Clinic intact was because I told them to send you that way." She shrugged. "But then you insisted upon escaping. It has been a messy week, and I blame myself as much as anyone else. I feel like a behaviorist who has designed her rat's maze poorly."

"All right." I noted vaguely that I was trembling. "I'll do it."

"Yes. Of course you will."

I searched for something else to say, but it felt as if I had been clinically drained of the potential for resistance. The cold of the basilica seemed to be creeping into my bones. I mastered the trembling with an effort and turned to go. Trepp moved silently forward to join me. We had gone about a dozen steps when Kawahara called out behind me.

"Oh, Kovacs—"

I turned as if in a dream. She was smiling.

"If you do manage to wrap it up cleanly, and very quickly, I might consider some kind of cash incentive. A bonus, so to speak. Negotiable. Trepp will give you a contact number."

I turned away again, numb to a degree I hadn't felt since the smoking ruins of Innenin. Vaguely, I felt Trepp clap me on the shoulder.

"Come on," she said companionably. "Let's get out of here."

I followed her out under the soul-bruising architecture, beneath the sneering smiles of the hooded guardians, and I knew that from among her gray-wombed clones, Kawahara was watching me all the way with a similar smile. It seemed to take forever to leave the hall, and when the huge steel portals cracked open to reveal the outside world, the light that spilled inward was an infusion of life that I grabbed at like a drowning man. All at once, the basilica was a vertical, a cold depth of ocean out of which I was reaching for the sun on the rippled surface. As we left the shadows, my body sucked up the warmth on offer as if it were solid sustenance. Very gradually, the shivering began to leave me.

But as I walked away, beneath the brooding power of the cross, I could still feel the presence of the place like a cold hand on the nape of my neck.

CHAPTEr TWENTY-SIX

That night was a blur. Later, when I tried to get it back, even Envoy recall would give me only fragments.

Trepp wanted a night on the town. The best nightlife in Europe, she maintained, was only minutes away, and she had all the right addresses.

I wanted my thought processes stopped dead in their tracks.

●●●

We started in a hotel room on a street I could not pronounce. Some tetrameth analog fired through the whites of our eyes by needlespray. I sat passively in a chair by the window and let Trepp shoot me up, trying to not think about Sarah and the room in Millsport. Trying not to think at all. Two-tone holographics outside the window cast Trepp's concentrated features in shades of red and bronze, a demon in the act of sealing the pact. I felt the insidious tilt at the corners of perception as the tetrameth went barreling along my synapses, and when it was my turn to do Trepp I almost got lost in the geometries of her face. This was very good stuff. . . .

●●●

There were murals of the Christian hell, flames leaping like clawed fingers over a procession of screaming, naked sinners. At one end of the room, where the figures on the walls seemed to blend with the denizens of the bar in smoke and noise, a girl danced on a rotating platform. A cupped petal of black glass scythed around with the platform, and each time it passed between audience and dancer, the girl was gone and a skeleton danced grinning in her place.

"This place is called All Flesh Will Perish," Trepp yelled above the noise as we forced our way in through the crowd. She pointed to the girl and then to the black glass rings on her fingers. "Where I got the idea for these. Great effect, isn't it."

I got drinks, quickly.

●●●

The human race has dreamed of heaven and hell for millennia. Pleasure or pain unending, undiminished, and uncurtailed by the strictures of life or death. Thanks to virtual formatting, these fantasies can now exist. All that is needed is an industrial-capacity power generator. We have indeed made hell—and heaven—on earth.

"Sounds a bit epic, Angin Chandra's outward-bound valediction-to-the-people sort of thing," Trepp shouted. "But I take your point."

Evidently the words that had been running through my mind were also running out of my mouth. If it was a quote, I didn't know where it was from. Certainly not a Quellism; she would have slapped anyone making that kind of speech.

"Thing is," Trepp was still yelling, "you've got ten days."

●●●

Reality tilts, flows sideways in gobs of flame-colored light. Music. Motion and laughter. The rim of a glass under my teeth. A warm thigh pressed against my own, which I think is Trepp's, but when I turn, another woman with long straight black hair and crimson lips is grinning at me. Her look of open invitation reminds me vaguely of something I've seen recently—

●●●

Street scene:

Tiered balconies on either side, tongues of light and sound splashed out onto pavements from the myriad tiny bars, the street itself knotted with people. I walked beside the woman I had killed last week and tried to hold up my end of a conversation about cats.

There was something I had forgotten. Something clouded.

Something impor—

"You can't fucking believe something like that," Trepp burst out. Or in, into my skull at the moment I had almost crystalized what I—

Was she doing it deliberately? I couldn't even remember what it was I'd believed so strongly about cats a moment ago.

●●●

Dancing, somewhere.

●●●

More 'meth, eye-shot on a street corner, leaning against a wall. Someone walked past, called something out to us. I blinked and tried to look.

"Fuck, hold still, will you!"

"What'd she say?"

Trepp peeled back my eyelids again, frowning with concentration.

"Called us both beautiful. Fucking junkie, probably after a handout."

• • •

In a wood-paneled toilet somewhere, I stared into a fragmented mirror at the face I was wearing as if it had committed a crime against me. Or as if I was waiting for someone else to emerge from behind the seamed features. My hands were braced on the filthy metal basin below, and the epoxy strips bonding the thing to the wall emitted minute tearing sounds under my weight.

I had no idea how long I'd been there.

I had no idea where there was. Or how many theres we had already been through tonight.

None of this seemed to matter because . . .

The mirror didn't fit its frame; there were pointed jags dug into the plastic edges, holding the star-shaped center precariously in place.

Too many edges, I muttered to myself. None of this fucking fits together.

The words seemed significant, like an accidental rhythm and rhyme in ordinary speech. I didn't think I'd ever be able to repair this mirror. I was going to cut my fingers to shreds, just trying. Fuck that.

I left Ryker's face in the mirror and staggered back out to a table piled high with candles, where Trepp was sipping at a long ivory pipe.

• • •

"Micky Nozawa? Are you serious?"

"Fuck, yes." Trepp nodded vigorously. "*The Fist of the Fleet,* right? Seen it four times at least. New York experia chains get a lot of imported colonial stuff. It's getting to be quite chic. That bit where he takes the harpoonist out with the flying kick. You feel it right down to the bone, the way he delivers that fucking kick. Beautiful. Poetry in motion. Hey, you know he did some holoporn stuff when he was younger."

"Bullshit. Micky Nozawa never did porn. He didn't need to."

"Who said anything about need? The couple of bimbettes he was playing around with, I would have played around with them for free."

"Bull. Shit."

"I swear to God. That sleeve with the sort of Caucasian nose and eyes, the one he wrote off in that cruiser wreck. Real early stuff."

• • •

There was a bar, where the walls and ceiling were hung with absurd hybrid musical instruments and the shelves behind the bar were stacked solid with antique bottles, intricately worked statuettes, and other nameless junk. The noise level was comparatively low, and I was drinking something that didn't taste as if it was doing my system too much immediate harm. There was a faint musk in the air and small trays of sweetmeats on the tables.

"Why the fuck do you do it?"

"What?" Trepp shook her head muzzily. "Keep cats? I like ca—"

"Work for fucking Kawahara. She's a fucking abortion of a human being, a fucked-up Meth cunt not worth the slag of a stack, why do you—"

Trepp grabbed the arm I was gesturing with, and for a moment I thought there was going to be violence. The neurachem surged soggily.

Instead, she took the arm and draped it affectionately over her own shoulders, pulling my face closer to her own. She blinked owlishly at me.

"Listen."

There was a longish pause. I listened, while Trepp frowned with concentration, took a long slug from her glass, and set it down with exaggerated care. She wagged a finger at me.

"Judge not lest ye be judged," she slurred.

●●●

Another street, sloping downward. Walking was suddenly easier.

Above, the stars were out in force, clearer than I had seen them all week in Bay City. I lurched to a halt at the sight, looking for the Horned Horse.

Something. Wrong here.

Alien. Not a single pattern I recognized. A cold sweat broke along the insides of my arms, and suddenly the clear points of fire seemed like an armada from the Outside, massing for a planetary bombardment. The Martians returned. I thought I could see them moving ponderously across the narrow slice of sky above us. . . .

"Whoa." Trepp caught me as I fell, laughing. "What you looking for up there, grasshopper?"

Not my sky.

●●●

It's getting bad.

In another toilet, painfully brightly lit, I'm trying to stuff some powder Trepp gave me up my nose. My nasal passages are already seared dry, and it keeps falling back down, as if this body has definitively had enough. A cubicle flushes behind me, and I glance up into the big mirror.

Jimmy de Soto emerges from the cubicle, combat fatigues smudged with Innenin mud. In the hard bathroom light, his face is looking particularly bad.

"All right, pal?"

"Not especially." I scratch at the inside of my nose, which is beginning to feel inflamed.

"You?"

He makes a mustn't-grumble gesture and moves forward in the mirror to stand beside me. Water fountains from the light-sensitive tap as he leans over the basin, and he begins to rinse his hands. Mud and gore dissolve off his skin and form a rich soup, pouring away down the tiny maelstrom of the plughole. I can sense his bulk at my shoulder, but his one remaining eye has me pinned to the image in the mirror and I cannot, or don't want to, turn.

"Is this a dream?"

He shrugs and goes on scrubbing at his hands. "It's the edge," he says.

"The edge of what?"

"Everything." His expression suggests that this much is obvious.

"I thought you only turned up in my dreams," I say, casually glancing at his hands. There is something wrong with them; however much filth Jimmy scrubs off, there is more underneath. The basin is splattered with the stuff.

"Well, that's one way of putting it, pal. Dreams, high-stress hallucinations, or just wrecking your own head like this. It's all the edge, see. The cracks down the sides of reality. Where stupid bastards like me end up."

"Jimmy, you're dead. I'm getting tired of telling you that."

"Uh-uh." He shakes his head. "But you got to get right down in those cracks to access me."

The soup of blood and soil in the basin is thinning out, and I know suddenly that when it is gone, Jimmy will be, too.

"You're saying—"

He shakes his head sadly. "Too fucking complicated to go through now. You think we've got the handle on reality, just 'cause we can record bits of it. More to it than that, pal. More to it than that."

"Jimmy." I make a helpless gesture. "What the fuck am I going to do?"

He steps back from the basin, and his ruined face grins garishly at me.

"Viral strike," he says clearly. I go cold as I remember my own scream taken up along the beachhead. "Recall that mother, do you?"

And, flicking water from his hands, he vanishes like a conjuror's trick.

●●●

"Look," Trepp said reasonably. "Kadmin had to check into the tank to get sleeved in an artificial. I figure that gives you the best part of a day before he even knows if he killed you or not."

"If he wasn't already double-sleeved again."

"No. Think about it. He's cut loose from Kawahara. Man, he doesn't have the resources for that kind of stuff right now. He's fucking out there on his own, and with Kawahara gunning for him, he's a strictly limited item. Kadmin's sell-by date is coming up, you'll see."

"Kawahara's going to keep him on tap for just as long as she needs him to drive me."

"Yeah, well." Trepp looked at her drink, embarrassed. "Maybe."

• • •

There was another place, called Cable or something synonymous, where the walls were racked with color-coded conduits out of whose designer-cracked casings wires sprouted like stiff copper hair. At intervals along the bar were hooks draped with thin, lethal-looking cables that ended in gleaming silver minijacks. In the air above the bar, a huge holographic jack and socket fucked spasmodically to the offbeat music that filled the place like water. At times, the components seemed to change into sex organs, but that could have been tetrameth-induced hallucination on my part.

I was sitting at the bar, something sweet smoldering in an ashtray at my elbow. From the sludgy feeling in my lungs and throat, I'd been smoking it. The bar was crowded, but I suffered the strange conviction I was alone.

On either side of me, the other customers at the bar were jacked into the thin cables, eyes flickering beneath lids that seemed bruised, mouths twitched into dreamy half smiles. One of them was Trepp.

I was alone.

Things that might have been thoughts were tugging at the abraded underside of my mind. I picked up the sweetly smoldering cigarette and drew on it, grimly. Now was no time for thinking.

• • •

No time for—
  Viral strike!
—thinking.
Streets passing beneath my feet the way the rubble of Innenin passed under Jimmy's boots as he walked along beside me in my dreams. *So that's how he does it.*
The crimson-lipped woman who—
  Maybe you can't—
What? *What?*
Jack and socket.
  Trying to tell you some—
No time for—
No time—

No—

And away, like water in the maelstrom, like the soup of mud and gore pouring off Jimmy's hands and into the hole at the bottom of the sink. . . .

Gone again.

● ● ●

But thought, like the dawn, was inevitable, and it found me, with the dawn, on a set of white stone steps that led down into murky water. Grandiose architecture reared vaguely behind us, and on the far side of the water I could make out trees in the rapidly graying darkness. We were in a park.

Trepp leaned over my shoulder and offered me a lit cigarette. I took it reflexively, drew once, and then let smoke dribble up through my slack lips. Trepp settled into a crouch next to me. An unfeasibly large fish flopped in the water at my feet. I was too eroded to react.

"Mutant," Trepp said inconsequentially.

"Same to you."

The little shreds of conversation drifted away over the water.

"Going to need painkillers?"

"Probably." I felt around inside my head. "Yeah."

She handed me a wafer of impressively colored capsules without comment.

"What you going to do?"

I shrugged. "Going to go back. Going to do what I'm told."

PART FOUR

PErSUASION
(VIRAL CORRUPT)

CHAPTEr TWENTY–SEVEN

I changed cabs three times on the way from the airport, paying each one in currency, and then booked into an all-night flophouse in Oakland. Anyone tailing me electronically was going to take a little while to catch up, and I was reasonably sure that I hadn't been actually followed. It seemed a bit like paranoia; after all, I was working for the bad guys now, so they had no need to tail me. But I hadn't liked Trepp's ironic *keep in touch* as she saw me off from the Bay City terminal. Also, I wasn't sure exactly what I was going to do yet, and if I didn't know, I certainly didn't want anyone else knowing, either.

The flophouse room had 786 screen channels, holoporn and current affairs both advertised in lurid colors on the standby display, a hinged self-cleansing double bed that stank of disinfectant, and a self-contained shower stall that was beginning to list away from the wall it had once been epoxied to. I peered out of the single grimy window. It was the middle of the night in Bay City, and there was a fine, misty rain falling. My deadline with Ortega was running out.

The window gave onto a sloping fibercrete roof about ten meters below. The street was as far below again. Overhead, a pagoda-like upper level screened the lower roof and street under long eaves. Covered space. After a moment's debate, I pressed the last of Trepp's hangover capsules out of the foil and swallowed it, then opened the window as quietly as I could, swung out, and hung by my fingers from the lower frame. Fully extended, I still had the best part of eight meters to fall.

Go primitive. Well, you don't get much more primitive than climbing out of hotel windows in the middle of the night.

Hoping the roof was as solid as it looked, I let go.

I hit the sloping surface in approved fashion, rolled to one side, and abruptly found my legs hanging out into space once more. The surface was firm, but as slippery as fresh belaweed, and I was slithering rapidly toward the edge. I ground my elbows down for purchase, found none, and just managed to grab the sharp edge of the roof in one hand as I went over.

Ten meters to the street. With the roof edge slicing into my palm, I dangled by one arm for a moment, trying to identify possible obstacles to my fall like trash bins or parked vehicles, then gave up and dropped anyway. The paving beneath came up and smacked me hard, but there was nothing sharp to compound the impact, and when I rolled, it was not into the feared assembly of trash bins. I got up and made for the nearest shadows.

Ten minutes and a random sampling of streets later, I came upon a rank of idling autocabs, stepped swiftly out from my current piece of overhead cover, and got into the fifth in line. I recited Ortega's discreet code as we lifted into the air.

"Coding noted. Approximate arrival time, thirty-five minutes."

We headed out across the bay, and then out to sea.

● ● ●

Too many edges.

The fragmented contents of the previous night bubbled in my brain like a carelessly made fish stew. Indigestible chunks appeared on the surface, wobbled in the currents of memory, and sank again. Trepp, jacked into the bar at Cable, Jimmy de Soto washing his blood-encrusted hands, Ryker's face staring back at me from the spread-eagled star of mirror. Kawahara was in there somewhere, claiming Bancroft's death as suicide but wanting an end to the investigation, just like Ortega and the Bay City police. Kawahara, who knew things about my contact with Miriam Bancroft, knew things about Laurens Bancroft, about Kadmin.

The tail end of my hangover twitched, scorpion-like, fighting the slow-gathering weight of Trepp's painkillers. Trepp, the apologetic Zen killer who I'd killed and who'd apparently come back with no hard feelings because she couldn't remember it, because, in her terms, it hadn't happened to her.

If anybody can convince Laurens Bancroft that he died by his own hand, it is you.

Trepp, jacked in at Cable.

Viral strike. Recall that mother, do you?

Bancroft's eyes boring into mine on the balcony at Suntouch House. *I am not the kind of man to take my own life, and* even if I was, *I would not have bungled it in this fashion. If it had been my intention to die, you would not be talking to me now.*

And then, blindingly, I knew what I was going to do.

The cab started downward.

● ● ●

"Footing is unstable," the machine said redundantly, as we touched down on a rolling deck. "Please take care."

I fed currency to the slot, and the hatch hinged up on Ortega's safe location. A brief expanse of gunmetal landing pad, railings of cabled steel, and the sea beyond, all shifting black shoulders of water beneath a night sky clogged with cloud and hard drizzle. I climbed out warily and clung to the nearest railing while the cab lifted away and was quickly swallowed by the drifting veils of rain. As the navigation lights faded, I turned my attention to the vessel I was standing on.

The landing pad was situated at the stern, and from where I clung to the railing, I could see the whole length of the ship laid out. She looked to be about twenty meters, something like two-thirds the size of a Millsport trawler, but much leaner in the beam. The deck modules had the smooth, self-sealing configuration of storm-survival design, but despite the general businesslike appearance, no one would ever take this for a working vessel. Delicate telescopic masts rose to what looked like only half height at two points along the deck, and there was a sharp bowsprit stabbing ahead of the slimly tapered prow. This was a yacht. A rich man's floating home.

Light spilled out of a hatchway on the rear deck, and Ortega emerged far enough to beckon me down from the landing pad. Hooking my fingers firmly on the rail, I braced myself against the pitch and sway of the vessel and picked my way down a short flight of steps at one side of the pad, then across the rear deck to the hatch. Skirls of drizzle swept across the ship, hurrying me along against my will. In the well of light from the open hatch I saw another, steeper set of steps and handed my way down the narrow companionway into the offered warmth. Over my head, the hatch hummed smoothly shut.

"Where the fuck have you been?" Ortega snapped.

I took a moment to rub some of the water out of my hair and looked around. If this was a rich man's floating home, the rich man in question hadn't been home in a while. Furniture was stowed at the sides of the room I had descended into, sheeted over in semiopaque plastic, and the shelves of the small niche bar were empty. The hatches over the windows were all battened down. Doors at either end of the room were open onto what seemed to be similarly mothballed spaces.

For all that, the yacht reeked of the wealth that had spawned it. The chairs and tables beneath the plastic were darkly polished wood, as was the paneling of the bulkheads and doors, and there were rugs on the waxed boards beneath my feet. The remainder of the decor was similarly somber in tone, with what looked like original artwork on the bulkhead walls. One from the empathist school, the skeletal ruins of a Martian shipyard at sunset, the other an abstract that I didn't have the cultural background to read.

Ortega stood in the middle of it all, tousle-haired and scowling in a raw silk kimono that I assumed had come out of an onboard wardrobe.

"It's a long story." I moved past her to peer through the nearest door. "I could use a coffee, if the galley's open."

Bedroom. A big, oval bed set amidst less than wholly tasteful mirrors, quilt tangled and thrown aside in haste. I was moving back toward the other door when she slapped me.

I reeled sideways. It wasn't as hard a blow as I'd given Sullivan in the noodlehouse, but it was delivered from standing with a lot more swing and there was the tilt of the deck to contend with. The cocktail of hangover and painkillers didn't help. I didn't quite go down, but it was a near thing. Stumbling back into balance, I raised a hand to my cheek and stared at Ortega, who was glaring back at me with twin spots of color burning high on each cheekbone.

"Look, I'm sorry if I woke you up, but—"

"You piece of shit," she hissed at me. "You lying piece of shit."

"I'm not sure I—"

"I should have you fucking arrested, Kovacs. I should have you fucking stacked for what you've done."

I started to lose my temper. "Done *what*? Will you get a fucking grip, Ortega, and tell me what's going on?"

"We accessed the Hendrix's memory today," Ortega said coldly. "Preliminary warrant went through at noon. Everything for the last week. I've been reviewing it."

The rapidly flaring, irritable rage shrank back to nothing inside me as the words left her mouth. It was as if she'd emptied a bucket of seawater over my head.

"Oh."

"Yes, there wasn't much." Ortega turned away, hugging her own shoulders in the kimono, and moved past me to the unexplored doorway. "You're the only guest there at the moment. So it's just been you. And your visitors."

I followed her through into a second, carpeted room where two steps led down to a narrow sunken galley behind a low, wood-paneled partition at one side. The other walls held similarly covered items of furniture as the first room, except for the far corner, where the plastic sheeting had been pulled off a meter-square video screen and attendant receiver/playback modules. A single, straight-backed chair was positioned in front of the screen, on which was frozen the unmistakable image of Elias Ryker's face delving between Miriam Bancroft's widespread thighs.

"There's a remote on the chair," Ortega said, herself remote. "Why don't you watch some of it while I make you a coffee. Refresh your memory. Then you can do some explaining."

She disappeared into the galley without giving me the chance to reply. I advanced on the frozen video screen, feeling a small liquid slide in my guts as the image brought back memories tinged with Merge Nine. In the sleepless, chaotic whirl of the last day and a half, I had all but forgotten Miriam Bancroft, but now she came back to me in the flesh, overpowering and intoxicating as she had been that night. I'd also forgotten Rodrigo Bautista's claim that they were almost through the legal wrangles with the Hendrix's lawyers.

My foot knocked against something, and I looked down at the carpet. There was a coffee mug on the floor next to the chair, still a third full. I wondered how much of the hotel's memory Ortega had gone through. I glanced at the image on-screen. Was this as far as she'd got? What else had she seen? How to play this, then? I picked up the remote and turned it over in my hands. Ortega's cooperation had been an integral part of my planning so far. If I was going to lose her now, I was in trouble.

Scratching around inside me was something else. An emotional upwelling that I didn't want to acknowledge, because to acknowledge it would be a clinical absurdity. A feeling that, for all the preoccupation I had for later factors in the hotel's memory, was tied intimately to the image currently on screen.

Embarrassment. Shame.

Absurd. I shook my head. Fucking *stupid*.

"You're not watching."

I turned back and saw Ortega with a steaming mug in each hand. An aroma of mingled coffee and rum wafted toward me.

"Thanks." I took one of the mugs from her and sipped at it, playing for time. She leaned away from me and folded her arms.

"So. Half a hundred reasons why Miriam Bancroft doesn't fit the bill." She jerked her head at the screen. "How many of them is that?"

"Ortega, this is nothing to do—"

"I buy Miriam Bancroft as scary, you told me." She shook her head judicially and sipped from her coffee. "I don't know, that doesn't look like fear on your face, exactly."

"Ortega—"

" 'I want you to stop,' she says. She actually says it. Look, wind it back if you don't rememb—"

I pulled the remote out of her reach. "I remember what she said."

"Then you also remember the sweet little deal she offered you to shut down the case, the multiple—"

"Ortega, you didn't want me on the case, either, remember. Open-and-shut suicide, you said. That doesn't mean you killed him, does—"

"Shut up." Ortega circled me as if we were holding knives, not coffee mugs. "You've been covering for her. All this fucking time, you've had your nose buried in her crotch like a faithful fucking d—"

"If you've seen the rest of it, you know that isn't true." I tried for an even tone that Ryker's hormones would not let me have. "I told Curtis I wasn't interested. I fucking told him that two days ago."

"Do you have any idea what a prosecutor will do with this footage? Miriam Bancroft trying to buy off her husband's investigator with illegal sexual favors. Oh yes, admission of multiple sleeving, even unproven, can be made to look very bad in court."

"She'll beat the rap. You know she will."

"If her Meth husband wants to weigh in on her side. Which maybe he won't when he sees this. This isn't Leila Begin again, you know. The moral boot's on the other foot this time around."

The allusion to morality went ripping through the outer borders of the argument, but as it passed I grasped the uncomfortable fact that actually it was central to what was going on here. I remembered Bancroft's critical assessment of Earth's moral culture and wondered if he could really watch my head between his wife's thighs and not feel betrayed.

I was still trying to work out what I felt on the same subject.

"And while we're on the subject of prosecution, Kovacs, that severed head you brought back from the Wei Clinic isn't going to win you any remissions, either. Illegal retention of a D.H. personality carries fifty to a hundred on Earth, more if we can prove you torched the head off in the first place."

"I was going to tell you about that."

"No, you fucking weren't," Ortega snarled. "You weren't going to fucking tell me any single thing you didn't need to."

"Look, the clinic won't dare prosecute anyway. They've got too much to—"

"You arrogant motherfucker." The coffee cup thumped dully to the carpet, and her fists clenched. Now there was real fury in her eyes. "You're just like him, you're just *fucking* like him. You think we need the fucking clinic, with footage of you putting a severed head in a hotel freezer? Isn't that a crime where you come from, Kovacs? Summary decapitation—"

"Wait a minute." I put my own coffee down on the chair at my side. "Just like who? Who am I just like?"

"What?"

"You just said I'm just—"

"Never fucking mind what I said. Do you understand what you've done here, Kovacs?"

"The only thing I under—" Abruptly, sound welled from the screen behind me, liquid groans and the sound of organic suction. I glanced at the remote clenched in my left hand, trying to see how I'd inadvertently unfrozen the playback, and a deep, female moan sent the blood twitching through my guts. Then Ortega was on me, trying to snatch the remote out of my hand.

"Give me that. Turn that fucking thing—"

For a moment I wrestled with her, and our struggling succeeded only in making the volume louder. Then, suddenly, riding a solitary updraft of sanity, I let go and she collapsed against the chair, pressing buttons.

"—off."

There was a long silence, punctuated only by our own heavy breathing. I fixed my gaze on one of the battened-down viewports across the room. Ortega, slumped between my leg and the chair, was presumably still looking at the screen. I thought that, for a moment, our breathing matched pace.

When I turned and bent to help her up, she was already rising toward me. Our hands were on each other, I think, before either of us realized what was happening.

It was like resolution. The circling antagonisms collapsed inward like orbitals crashing and burning, surrendering to a mutual gravity that had dragged like chains while it endured but in release was a streak of fire through the nerves. We were both trying to kiss each other and laugh at the same time. Ortega made excited little panting sounds as my hands slipped inside the kimono, palms skidding over coarse nipples as broad and stiff as rope ends and the breasts that fitted into my hands as if designed to nestle there. The kimono came off, sliding at first and then jerked insistently free of each swimmer's shoulder in turn. I shed jacket and shirt in one, while Ortega's hands tangled frantically at my belt, opening the fly and sliding one hard, long-fingered hand into the gap. I felt the callouses at the base of each finger, rubbing.

Somehow we got out of the room with the screen and made it to the stern-end cabin I'd seen earlier. I followed the taut sway of Ortega's strides across the room between, the muscled lines of the long thighs, and it must have been Ryker as much as me, because I felt like a man coming home. There, in the room full of mirrors, she threw her head down on the disarrayed sheets, lifted herself up, and I saw myself slide into her up to the hilt with a gasp, because now she was burning. She was burning inside, gripping me with the liquid entirely of hot bathwater, and the heated globes of her buttocks branded my hips with the impact of each stroke. Ahead of me, her spine lifted and wove like a snake and her hair cascaded down from her bent head in a chaotic elegance. In the mirrors around me I saw Ryker reaching forward to cup her breasts, then the breadth of her ribs, the rounding of her shoulders, and all the while she lifted and yawed like the ocean around the ship. Ryker and Ortega, writhing against each other like the reunited lovers of a timeless epic.

I felt the first climax go through her like clenching, but it was the sight of her looking back at me, up through tumbled hair, lips parted, that slipped the final catches on my own control and molded me against the contours of her back and ass until my spasms were all spent inside her and we collapsed across the bed. I felt myself slide out of her like something being born. I think she was still coming.

Neither of us said anything for a long time. The ship plowed on its automated way, and around us the dangerous cold of the mirrors lapped inward like an icy tide, threatening to tinge and then drown the intimacy. In a few moments we would be fixing our gazes carefully outward on the images of ourselves, instead of on each other.

I slid an arm around Ortega's flank and tilted her gently onto one side, so that we lay like spoons. In the mirror, I found her eyes.

"Where're we going?" I asked her gently.

A shrug, but she used it to snuggle deeper into me. "Programmed cycle, down the coast, out to Hawaii, hook around, and then back."

"And no one knows we're out here?"

"Only the satellites."

"Nice thought. Who does it all belong to?"

She twisted to look at me over her shoulder. "It's Ryker's."

"Oops." I looked elaborately away. "Nice carpet in here."

Against the odds, it brought a laugh out of her. She turned fully to face me in the bed. Her hand rose to touch my face softly, as if she thought it might mark easily, or maybe disappear.

"I told myself," she murmured. "It was crazy. It was just the body, you know."

"Most things are. Conscious thought doesn't have much to do with this stuff. Doesn't have much to do with the way we live our lives, period, if you believe the psychologists. A bit of rationalization, most of it with hindsight. Put the rest down to hormonal drives, gene instinct, and pheromones for the fine-tuning. Sad, but true."

Her finger followed a line down the side of my face. "I don't think it's sad. What we've done with the rest of ourselves, that's sad."

"Kristin Ortega." I took hold of her finger and squeezed it gently. "You are a real fucking Luddite, aren't you. How in God's name did you get into this line of work?"

She shrugged again. "Family of cops. Father was a cop. Grandmother was a cop. You know how it goes."

"Not from experience."

"No." She stretched one long leg languidly up toward the mirrored ceiling. "I guess not."

I reached across the plain of her belly and slid my hand along the length of thigh to the knee, levering her gently over and bringing my mouth to kiss gently at the shaved bar of pubic hair where it descended into cleft. She resisted fractionally, maybe thinking of the screen in the other room, or maybe just our mingled juices trickling from her body, then relented and spread herself under me. I shifted her other thigh up over my shoulder and lowered my face into her.

This time, when she came, it was with escalating cries that she locked in her throat each time with powerful flexings of the muscles at the base of her stomach while her whole body eeled back and forth across the bed and her hips bucked upward, grinding the soft flesh into my mouth. At some point she had lapsed into softly uttered Spanish, whose tones stoked my own arousal, and when she finally flopped to stillness, I was able to slide up and into her directly, gathering her under the arms and sinking my tongue into her mouth in the first kiss we'd shared since reaching the bed.

We moved slowly, trying for the rhythm of the sea outside and the laughter of our first embrace. It seemed to last a long time, time for talking, up the scale from languid murmurs to excited gabbling, for shifts in posture and soft bitings, the clasping of hands, and all the time a feeling of brimming to overflow that hurt my eyes. It was from that last, unbearable pressure as much as any that I finally let go and came into her, feeling her chase the last of my fading hardness to her own shaking finish.

In the Envoy Corps, you take what is offered, Virginia Vidaura said, somewhere in the corridors of my memory. *And that must sometimes be enough.*

As we separated for the second time, the weight of the last twenty-four hours came down on me like one of the heavy rugs in the other room and consciousness slipped gradually away from the increasing warmth beneath it. My last clear impressions were of the long body beside me rearranging itself with breasts pressed into my back, an arm draped over me, and a peculiarly comfortable clasping of feet, mine in hers, like hands. My thought processes were slowing down.

What is offered. Sometimes. Enough.

CHAPTEr TWENTY-EIGHT

When I awoke, she was gone.

There was sunlight coming into the cabin from a number of unbattened viewports. The pitching of the boat had almost stopped, but there was still enough roll to show me, alternately, a blue sky with horizontal scrapings of cloud and a reasonably calm sea beneath. Somewhere, someone was making coffee and frying smoked meat. I lay still for a while, picking up the scattered garments of my mind and trying to assemble some kind of reasonable outfit from them. What to tell Ortega? How much, and weighted how? The Envoy conditioning offered itself sluggishly, like something dredged out of a swamp. I let it roll over and sink, absorbed in the dappling of sunbeams on the sheets near my head.

The clinking of glasses from the door brought me around. Ortega was standing in the doorway wearing a NO TO RESOLUTION 653 T-shirt on which the NO had been stylistically daubed out with a red cross and overwritten with a definitive YES in the same color. The columns of her naked legs disappeared under the T-shirt as if they might conceivably go on forever inside. Balanced in her hands was a large tray laden with breakfast for an entire squadroom. Seeing me awake, she tossed hair out of her eyes and grinned crookedly.

So I told her everything.

● ● ●

"So what are you going to do?"

I shrugged and stared out across the water, narrowing my eyes against the glare. The ocean seemed flatter, more ponderous than it does on Harlan's World. Up on deck, the immensity of it sank in, and the yacht was suddenly a child's toy. "I'm going to do what Kawahara wants. What Miriam Bancroft wants. What *you* want. What apparently everyone fucking wants. I'm going to kill the case."

"You think Kawahara torched Bancroft?"

"Seems likely. Or she's shielding someone who did. Doesn't matter anymore. She's got Sarah; that's all that counts now."

"We could hit her with abduction charges. Retention of D.H.P. carries—"

"Fifty to a hundred, yeah." I smiled faintly. "I was listening last night. But she won't be holding directly; it'll be some subsidiary."

"We can get warrants that—"

"She's a fucking Meth, Kristin. She'll beat it all without raising her pulse.

Anyway, that's not the issue here. As soon as I move against her, she'll slam Sarah into virtual. How long do your far-ranging warrants take to get clearance?"

"Couple of days, if it's U.N. expedited." The gloom crept across Ortega's face as she was saying it. She leaned on the rail and stared downward.

"Exactly. That's the best part of a year in virtual. Sarah isn't an Envoy; she doesn't have any kind of conditioning. What Kawahara can do to her in eight or nine virtual months would turn a normal mind into pulp. She'd be screaming insane by the time we pulled her out. *If* we pulled her out, and anyway I'm not going to even fucking *consider* putting her through a single second of—"

"Okay." Ortega put a hand on my shoulder. "Okay. I'm sorry."

I shivered slightly, whether from the sea wind or the thought of Kawahara's virtual dungeons I couldn't be sure.

"Forget it."

"I'm a cop. It's in my nature to look for ways to bust the bad guys. That's all."

I looked up and gave her a bleak smile. "I'm an Envoy. It's in my nature to look for ways to rip Kawahara's throat out. I've looked. There are no ways."

The smile she gave me back was uneasy, tinged with an ambivalence that I knew was going to get us sooner or later.

"Look, Kristin. I've found a way to do this. To lie convincingly to Bancroft and shut the case down. It's illegal, very illegal, but no one that matters gets hurt. I don't have to tell you about it. If you don't want to know."

She thought about it for a while, eyes probing the water alongside the yacht, as if the answer might be swimming there, keeping pace with us. I wandered along the rail to give her time, tilting my head back to scan the blue bowl of the sky overhead and thinking about orbital surveillance systems. Out in the middle of a seemingly endless ocean, cocooned in the high-tech safety of the yacht, it was easy to believe you could hide from the Kawaharas and Bancrofts of this world, but that kind of hiding died centuries ago.

If they want you, a youngish Quell had once written of the Harlan's World ruling elite, *sooner or later they'll scoop you up off the globe, like specks of interesting dust off a Martian artifact. Cross the gulf between the stars, and they can come after you. Go into centuries of storage, and they'll be there waiting for you, clone new, when you resleeve. They are what we once dreamed of as gods, mythical agents of destiny, as inescapable as Death, that poor old peasant laborer, bent over his scythe, no longer is. Poor Death, no match for the mighty altered-carbon technologies of data storage and retrieval arrayed against him. Once we lived in terror of his arrival. Now we flirt outrageously with his somber dignity, and beings like these won't even let him in the tradesman's entrance.*

I grimaced. Compared to Kawahara, Death was a three-bout pushover.

I stopped at the prow and picked a point on the horizon to watch until Ortega made up her mind.

Suppose you know someone, a long time ago. You share things, drink deeply of each other. Then you drift apart; life takes you in different directions; the bonds are not strong enough. Or maybe you get torn apart by external circumstance. Years later, you meet that person again, in the same sleeve, and you go through it all over again. What's the attraction? Is this the same person? They probably have the same name, the same approximate physical appearance, but does that make them the same? And if not, does that make the things that have changed unimportant or peripheral? People change, but how much? As a child I'd believed there was an essential person, a sort of core personality around which the surface factors could evolve and change without damaging the integrity of who you were. Later, I started to see that this was an error of perception caused by the metaphors we were used to framing ourselves in. What we thought of as personality was no more than the passing shape of one of the waves in front of me. Or, slowing it down to more human speed, the shape of a sand dune. Form in response to stimulus. Wind, gravity, upbringing. Gene blueprinting. All subject to erosion and change. The only way to beat that was to go on stack forever.

Just as a primitive sextant functions on the illusion that the sun and stars rotate around the planet we are standing on, our senses give us the illusion of stability in the universe, and we accept it, because without that acceptance, nothing can be done.

Virginia Vidaura, pacing the seminar room, lost in lecture mode.

But the fact that a sextant will let you navigate accurately across an ocean does not mean that the sun and stars do rotate around us. For all that we have done, as a civilization, as individuals, the universe is not stable, nor is any single thing within it. Stars consume themselves, the universe itself rushes apart, and we ourselves are composed of matter in constant flux. Colonies of cells in temporary alliance, replicating and decaying, and housed within, an incandescent cloud of electrical impulse and precariously stacked carbon code memory. This is reality, this is self-knowledge, and the perception of it will, of course, make you dizzy. Some of you have served in Vacuum Command, and will no doubt think that out there you have confronted existence vertigo.

A thin smile.

I promise you that the Zen moments you may have enjoyed in hard space are not much more than the beginning of what you must learn here. All and anything you achieve as Envoys must be based on the understanding that there is nothing but flux. Anything you wish to even perceive as an Envoy, let alone create or achieve, must be carved out of that flux.

I wish you all luck.

If you couldn't even meet the same person twice in one lifetime, in one sleeve, what did that say about all the families and friends waiting in Download Central for someone they once knew to peer out through the eyes of a stranger? How could that even be close to the same person?

And where did that leave a woman consumed with passion for a stranger wearing a body she once loved? Was that closer, or further away?

Where, for that matter, did it leave the stranger who responded?

I heard her coming along the rail toward me. She stopped a couple of paces away and cleared her throat quietly. I quelled a smile and turned around.

"I didn't tell you how Ryker came to have all this, did I?"

"It didn't seem the time to ask."

"No." A grin that faded as if swept away by the breeze. "He stole it. A few years back, while he was still working Sleeve Theft. Belonged to some big-time clone marketeer from Sydney. Ryker caught the case because this guy was moving broken-down merchandise through the West Coast clinics. He got co-opted into a local task force, and they tried to take the guy down at his marina. Big firefight, lots of dead people."

"And lots of spoils."

She nodded. "They do things differently down there. Most of the police work gets picked up by private contractors. The local government handles it by tying payment to the assets of the criminals you bring down."

"Interesting incentive," I said reflectively. "Ought to make for a lot of rich people getting busted."

"Yeah, they say it works that way. The yacht was Ryker's piece. He did a lot of the groundwork on the case, and he was wounded in the firefight." Her voice was curiously undefensive as she related these details, and for once I felt that Ryker was a long way away. "That's where he got the scar under the eye, that stuff on his arm. Cable gun."

"Nasty." Despite myself, I felt a slight twinge in the scarred arm. I'd been up against cable fire before, and not enjoyed the encounter very much.

"Right. Most people reckoned Ryker earned every rivet of this boat. The point is, policy here in Bay City is that officers may not keep gifts, bonuses, or anything else awarded for line-of-duty actions."

"I can see the rationale for that."

"Yeah, so can I. But Ryker couldn't. He paid some cut-rate dipper to lose the ship's records and reregister her through discreet holding. Claimed he needed a safe house, if he ever had to stash someone."

I grinned a little. "Thin. But I like his style. Would that be the same dipper who ratted him out in Seattle?"

"Good memory you've got. Yeah, the very same. Nacho the Needle. Bautista tells a well-balanced story, doesn't he."

"Saw that, too, huh?"

"Yeah. Ordinarily, I'd have ripped Bautista's fucking head off for that paternal-uncle shit. Like I need emotional sheltering. He's been through two fucking divorces and he's not even forty yet." She stared reflectively out to sea. "I haven't had the time to confront him yet. Too busy being fucked off with you. Look, Kovacs, reason I'm telling you all this is, Ryker stole the boat, he broke West Coast law. I knew."

"And you didn't do anything," I guessed.

"Nothing." She looked at her hands, palms upturned. "Oh, shit, Kovacs, who are we kidding? I'm no angel myself. I kicked the shit out of Kadmin in police custody. You saw me. I should have busted you for that fight outside Jerry's and I let you walk."

"You were too tired for the paperwork, as I recall."

"Yeah, I remember." She grimaced, then turned to look me in the eyes, searching Ryker's face for a sign that she could trust me. "You say you're going to break the law, but no one gets hurt. That's right?"

"No one who matters," I corrected gently.

She nodded slowly to herself, like someone weighing up a convincing argument that may just change her mind for good.

"So what do you need?"

I levered myself off the rail. "A list of whorehouses in the Bay City area, to start with. Places that run virtual stuff. After that, we'd better get back to town. I don't want to call Kawahara from out here."

She blinked. "Virtual whorehouses?"

"Yeah. And the mixed ones, as well. In fact, make it every place on the West Coast that runs virtual porn. The lower grade the better. I'm going to sell Bancroft a package so filthy he won't want to look at it close enough to check for cracks. So bad he won't even want to *think* about it."

CHAPTEr TWENTY-NINE

Ortega's list was over two thousand names long, each annotated with a brief surveillance report and any Organic Damage convictions tied to the operators or clientele. In hardcopy format it ran to about two hundred concertina'd sheets, which started to unravel like a long paper scarf as soon as I got past page one. I tried to scan the list in the cab back to Bay City, but gave up when it threatened to overwhelm us both on the backseat. I wasn't in the mood anyway. Most of me wished I was still bedded down in the stern cabin of Ryker's yacht, isolated from the rest of humanity and its problems by hundreds of kilometers of trackless blue.

Back at the Watchtower suite, I put Ortega in the kitchen while I called Kawahara at the number Trepp had given me. It was Trepp who came on-screen first, features smeared with sleep. I wondered if she'd been up all night trying to track me.

"Morning." She yawned and presumably checked an internal time chip. "Afternoon, I mean. Where've you been?"

"Out and about."

Trepp rubbed inelegantly at one eye and yawned again. "Suit yourself. Just making conversation. How's your head?"

"Better, thanks. I want to talk to Kawahara."

"Sure." She reached toward the screen. "Talk to you later."

The screen dropped into neutral, an unwinding tricolored helix accompanied by sickly sweet string arrangements. I gritted my teeth.

"Takeshi-san." As always, Kawahara started in Japanese, as if it established some kind of common ground with me. "This is unlooked-for so early. Do you have good news for me?"

I stayed doggedly in Amanglic. "Is this a secure line?"

"As close as such a thing can be said to exist, yes."

"I have a shopping list."

"Go ahead."

"To begin with, I need access to a military virus. Rawling 4851 from preference, or one of the Condomar variants."

Kawahara's intelligent features hardened abruptly. "The Innenin virus?"

"Yeah. It's over a century out-of-date now, shouldn't be too hard to get hold of. Then I need—"

"Kovacs, I think you'd better explain what you're planning."

I raised an eyebrow. "I understood this was my play, and you didn't want to be involved."

"If I secure you a copy of the Rawling virus, I'd say I'm already involved." Kawahara offered me a measured smile. "Now, what are you planning to do with it?"

"Bancroft killed himself, that's the result you want, right?"

A slow nod.

"Then there has to be a reason," I said, warming to the deceit structure I'd come up with despite myself. I was doing what they'd trained me to do, and it felt good. "Bancroft has remote storage; it doesn't make sense that he'd light himself up unless he had a very specific reason. A reason unrelated to the actual act of suicide. A reason like self-preservation."

Kawahara's eyes narrowed. "Go on."

"Bancroft uses whorehouses on a regular basis, real and virtual. He told me that himself a couple of days ago. And he's not too particular about the quality of establishment he uses, either. Now, let's assume that there's an accident in one of these virtuals while he's getting his itch scratched. Accidental bleedover from some grimed-up old programs that no one's bothered to even open for a few decades. Go to a low enough grade of house, there's no telling what might be lying around."

"The Rawling virus." Kawahara exhaled as if she had been holding her breath in anticipation.

"Rawling variant 4851 takes about a hundred minutes to go fully active, by which time it's too late to do anything." I forced images of Jimmy de Soto from my mind. "The target's contaminated beyond redemption. Suppose Bancroft finds this out through some kind of systems warning. He must be wired internally for that kind of thing. He suddenly discovers the stack he's wearing and the brain it's wired to is burnt. That's not a disaster, if you've got clone backup and remote storage, but—"

"Transmission." Kawahara's face lit up as she got it.

"Right. He'd have to do something to stop the virus being 'cast to the remote with the rest of his personality. With the next needlecast coming up that night, maybe in a few minutes' time, there was only one way to ensure the remote stack didn't get contaminated."

I mimed a pistol at my head.

"Ingenious."

"That's why he made the call, the time check. He couldn't trust his own internal chip; the virus might already have scrambled it."

Solemnly, Kawahara lifted her hands into view and applauded. When she had finished, she clasped her hands together and looked at me over them.

"Very impressive. I will obtain the Rawling virus immediately. Have you selected a suitable virtual house for it to be downloaded into?"

"Not yet. The virus isn't the only thing I need. I want you to arrange the parole and resleeving of Irene Elliott, currently held at Bay City Central on conviction of dipping. I also want you to look into the possibility of acquiring her original sleeve back from its purchasers. Some corporate deal, there'll be records."

"You're going to use this Elliott to download Rawling?"

"The evidence is she's good."

"The evidence is she got caught," Kawahara observed tartly. "I've got plenty of people can do this for you. Top-line intrusion specialists. You don't need—"

"Kawahara." I kept my temper with an effort, but heard some of it in the tightness in my voice. "This is my gig, remember. I don't want your people climbing all over it. If you unstack Elliott, she'll be loyal. Get her her own body back and she'll be ours for life. That's the way I want to do it, so that's the way it's going down."

I waited. Kawahara stayed expressionless for a moment, then bestowed on me another carefully calibrated smile.

"Very well. We will do it your way. I'm sure you're aware of the risks you are taking, and what will happen if you fail. I shall contact you at the Hendrix later today."

"What's the word on Kadmin?"

"Of Kadmin, there is no word." Kawahara smiled once more, and the connection broke.

I sat staring at the standby screen for a moment, reviewing the scam as I'd laid it out. I had the uneasy feeling that I'd been telling the truth in the midst of all the deceit. Or, more, that my carefully spun lies were treading in the tracks of the truth, following the same path. A good lie should shadow the truth closely enough to draw substance from it, but this was something else, something altogether more unnerving. I felt like a hunter who has tracked a swamp panther a little too close for comfort, and expects at any moment to see it rear up out of the swamp in all its fanged and tendril-maned horror. The truth was here, somewhere.

It was a hard feeling to shake.

I got up and went into the kitchen, where Ortega was foraging through the almost empty fridge unit. Light from within cast her features in a way I hadn't seen before, and below one raised arm, her right breast filled the slack of her T-shirt like fruit, like water. The desire to touch her was an itching in my hands.

She glanced up. "Don't you cook?"

"Hotel does it all for you. Comes up in the hatch. What do you want?"

"I want to *cook* something." She gave up looking through the fridge and closed the door of the unit. "Get what you wanted?"

"Think so. Give the hotel a list of ingredients. There are pans and things in that rack down there, I think. Anything else you need, ask the hotel. I'm going to go through the list. Oh, and, Kristin."

She looked around from the rack I'd indicated.

"Miller's head isn't in here. I put it next door."

Her mouth tightened a little. "I know where you put Miller's head," she said. "I wasn't looking for it."

A couple of minutes later, seated on the window shelf with the hardcopy unfolding away to the floor, I heard the low tones of Ortega conversing with the Hendrix. There was some banging about, more muted conversation, and then the sound of oil frying gently. I fought off the urge for a cigarette and bent my head to the hardcopy.

I was looking for something that I'd seen every day of my young life in Newpest; the places I'd spent my teenage years, the narrow accessways of tiny properties sporting cheap holos that promised things like *Better than the Real Thing, Wide Range of Scenarios,* and *Dreams Come True.* It didn't take much to set up a virtual brothel. You just needed frontage and space for the client coffins stacked upright. The software varied in price, depending on how elaborate and original it was, but the machines to run it could usually be bought out of military surplus at basement rates.

If Bancroft could spend time and money in Jerry's Biocabins, he'd be at home in one of these.

I was two-thirds of my way through the list, more and more of my attention sifting away to the aromas issuing from the kitchen, when my eyes fell on a familiar entry and I grew abruptly still.

I saw a woman with long straight black hair and crimson lips

I heard Trepp's voice

. . . head in the clouds. I want to be there before midnight.

And the bar-coded chauffeur

No problem. Coastal's running light tonight.

And the crimson-lipped woman

Head in the Clouds. *This is what it's like. Maybe you can't afford to come up here.*

A choir in climax

. . . from the Houses, from the Houses, from the Houses . . .

And the businesslike printout in my hands

Head in the Clouds: *accredited West Coast House, real and virtual product, mobile aerial site outside coastal limit . . .*

I scanned through the notes, head ringing as if it were crystal that had been delicately struck with a hammer.

Navigational beams and beaconing system locked to Bay City and Seattle. Discreet membership coding. Routine searches, NR. No convictions. Operated under license from Third Eye Holdings, Inc.

I sat still, thinking.

There were pieces missing. It was like the mirror, wedged into place on jagged edges, enough to hold an image, but not the whole. I was peering hard at the irregular limits of what I had, trying to see around the edges, to get the backdrop. Trepp had been taking me to see Ray—Reileen—at *Head in the Clouds*. Not Europe, Europe was a blind, the somber weight of the basilica designed to numb me to what should have been obvious. If Kawahara was involved in this thing, she wouldn't be overseeing it from half a globe away. Kawahara was on *Head in the Clouds*, and . . .

And what?

Envoy intuition was a form of subliminal recognition, an enhanced awareness of pattern that the real world too often abraded with its demand for detailed focus. Given enough traces of continuity, you could make a leap that enabled you to see the whole as a kind of premonition of real knowledge. Working from that model, you could fill in the bits later. But there was a certain minimum you needed to get airborne. Like old-style linear prop aircraft, you needed a run up, and I didn't have it. I could feel myself bumping along the ground, clawing at the air, and falling back. Not enough.

"Kovacs?"

I glanced up, and saw it. Like a heads-up display coming on-line, like airlock bolts slamming back in my head.

Ortega stood before me, a stirring implement in one hand, hair gathered back in a loose knot. Her T-shirt blazoned at me.

RESOLUTION 653. Yes or no, depending.

Oumou Prescott

Mr. Bancroft has an undeclared influence in the U.N. Court.

Jerry Sedaka

Old Anemone's Catholic . . . We take on a lot like that. Real convenient sometimes.

My thoughts ran like a combustion fuse, flaming up the line of association.

Tennis court

Nalan Ertekin, chief justice of the U.N. Supreme Court

Joseph Khumalo, the Commission of Human Rights

My own words

You're here to discuss Resolution 653, I imagine.

An undeclared influence . . .

Miriam Bancroft

I'll need some help keeping Marco off Nalan's back. He's fuming, by the way.

And Bancroft

The way he played today, I'm not surprised.

Resolution 653. Catholics.

My mind spewed the data back at me like a demented file search, scrolling down.

Sedaka, gloating

Sworn affidavit on disk, full Vow of Abstention filed with the Vatican.

Real convenient sometimes.

Ortega

Barred by Reasons of Conscience decals.

Mary Lou Hinchley

Last year the Coastals fished some kid out of the ocean.

Not much left of the body, but they got the stack.

Barred by Reasons of Conscience

Out of the ocean

Coastals

mobile aerial site outside coastal limit . . .

Head in the Clouds.

It was a process that could not be braked, a kind of mental avalanche. Chunks of reality splintering away and tumbling downward, except that instead of chaos they were falling into something that had form, a kind of restructured whole whose final shape I still couldn't make out.

beaconing system locked to Bay City

and Seattle

Bautista

See, it all went down in a black clinic up in Seattle.

The intacts ditched in the Pacific.

Ortega's theory was that Ryker was set up.

"What're you looking at?"

The words hung in the air for a moment like a hinge in time, and suddenly time hinged back and in the doorway behind, Sarah was just waking up in the Millsport hotel bed, with the rolling thunder of an orbital discharge rattling the loose windows in their frames and behind that, rotorblades against the night, and our own deaths waiting just up around the bend.

"What're you looking at?"

I blinked and I was still staring at Ortega's T-shirt, at the soft mounds she made in it and the legend printed across the chest. There was a slight smile on her face, but it was beginning to bleach out with concern.

"Kovacs?"

I blinked again and tried to reel in the meters of mental spillage that the T-shirt had set off. The looming truth of *Head in the Clouds*.

"Are you okay?"

"Yeah."

"Want to eat?"

"Ortega, what if—" I found I had to clear my throat, swallow, and start again. I didn't want to say this; my body didn't want me to say it. "What if I can get Ryker off the stack? Permanently, I mean. Clear him of the charges, prove Seattle was a setup. What's that worth to you?"

For a moment, she looked at me as if I was speaking a language she didn't understand. Then she moved to the window shelf and seated herself carefully on the edge, facing me. She was silent for a while, but I had already seen the answer in her eyes.

"Are you feeling guilty?" she asked me finally.

"About?"

"About us."

I nearly laughed out loud, but there was just enough underlying pain to stop the reflex in my throat. The urge to touch her had not stopped. Over the last day it had ebbed and flowed in waves, but it had never wholly gone. When I looked at the curve of her hips and thighs on the window shelf, I could feel the way she had writhed back against me so clearly it was almost virtual. My palm recalled the weight and shape of her breast as if holding it had been this sleeve's life's work. As I looked at her, my fingers wanted to trace the geometry of her face. There was no room in me for guilt, no room for anything but this feeling.

"Envoys don't feel guilt," I said shortly. "I'm serious. It's likely, no, it's almost certain, in fact, that Kawahara had Ryker set up because he was heating up the Mary Lou Hinchley case too much. Do you remember anything about her employment records?"

Ortega thought about it for a moment, then shrugged. "She ran away from home to be with the boyfriend. Mostly unregistered stuff, anything to bring the rent in. Boyfriend was a piece of shit, got a record goes back to age fifteen. He dealt a little Stiff, crashed a few easy datastacks, mostly lived off his women."

"Would he have let her work the Meat Rack? Or the cabins?"

"Oh, yeah." Ortega nodded, face stony. "Soon as spit."

"If someone was recruiting for a snuff house, Catholics would be the ideal candidates, wouldn't they? They're not going to tell any tales after the event, after all. By reasons of conscience."

"Snuff." If Ortega's face had been stony before, it was weathered granite now. "Most of the snuff victims around here just get a bolt through the stack when it's over. They don't tell any tales."

"Right. But what if something went wrong? Specifically, what if Mary Lou Hinchley was going to be used as a snuff whore, so she tried to escape and fell out of an aerial whorehouse called *Head in the Clouds*. That would make her Catholicism very convenient, wouldn't it?"

"*Head in the Clouds?* Are you serious?"

"And it'd make the owners of *Head in the Clouds* very anxious to stop Resolution 653 dead in its tracks, wouldn't it?"

"Kovacs." Ortega was making slow-down gestures with both palms. "Kovacs, *Head in the Clouds* is one of the Houses. Class prostitution. I don't like those places, they make me want to vomit just as bad as the cabins, but they're clean. They cater for elevated society, and they don't run scams like snuff—"

"You don't think the upper echelons go in for sadism and necrophilia, then. That's strictly a lower-class thing, is it?"

"No, it isn't," Ortega said evenly. "But if anyone with money wants to play at torturer, they can afford to do it in virtual. Some of the Houses run virtual snuff, but they run it because it's *legal*, and there's nothing we can do about it. And that's the way they like it."

I drew a deep breath. "Kristin, someone was taking me to see Kawahara on board *Head in the Clouds*. Someone from the Wei Clinic. And if Kawahara is involved in the West Coast Houses, then they will do anything that turns a profit, because she will do anything, anything at all. You wanted a big bad Meth to believe in? Forget Bancroft, he's practically a priest in comparison. Kawahara grew up in Fission City, dealing antiradiation drugs to the families of fuel rod workers. Do you know what a water carrier is?"

She shook her head.

"In Fission City it's what they used to call the gang enforcers. See, if someone refused to pay protection, or informed to the police, or just didn't jump fast enough when the local yakuza boss said *frog*, the standard punishment was to drink contaminated water. The enforcers used to carry it around in shielded flasks, siphoned off low-grade reactor cooling systems. They'd turn up at the offender's house one night and tell him how much he had to drink. His family would be made to watch. If he didn't drink, they'd start cutting his family one by one until he did. You want to know how I know that delightful piece of Earth history trivia?"

Ortega said nothing, but her mouth was tight with disgust.

"I know because Kawahara told me. That's what she used to do when she was a kid. She was a water carrier. And she's proud of it."

The phone chimed.

I waved Ortega back out of range and went to answer it.

"Kovacs?" It was Rodrigo Bautista. "Is Ortega with you?"

"No." I lied automatically. "Haven't seen her for a couple of days. Is there a problem?"

"Ah, probably not. She's vanished off the face of the planet again. Well, if you do see her, tell her she missed a squad assembly this afternoon and Captain Murawa wasn't impressed."

"Should I expect to see her?"

"With Ortega, who fucking knows?" Bautista spread his hands. "Look, I've got to go. See you around."

"See you." I watched as the screen blanked, and Ortega came back from her place by the wall. "Did you get that?"

"Yeah. I was supposed to turn the Hendrix memory disks over this morning. Murawa will probably want to know why I took them out of Fell Street in the first place."

"It's your case, isn't it?"

"Yeah, but there are norms." Ortega looked suddenly tired. "I can't stall them for long, Kovacs. I'm already getting a lot of funny looks for working with you. Pretty soon someone's going to get seriously suspicious. You've got a few days to run this scam on Bancroft, but after that . . ."

She raised her hands eloquently.

"Can't you say you were held up? That Kadmin took the disks off you?"

"They'll polygraph me—"

"Not immediately."

"Kovacs, this is my career we're flushing down the toilet here, not yours. I don't do this job for fun. It's taken me—"

"Kristin, listen to me." I went to her and took her hands in mine. "Do you want Ryker back, or not?"

She tried to turn away from me, but I held on.

"Kristin. Do you believe he was set up?"

She swallowed. "Yes."

"Then why not believe it was Kawahara? The cruiser he tried to shoot down in Seattle was heading out over the ocean when it crashed. You extrapolate that heading and see where it takes you. You plot the point where the Coastals fished Mary Lou Hinchley out of the sea. Then put *Head in the Clouds* on the map and see if it all adds up to anything."

Ortega pulled away from me with a strange look in her eyes.

"You want this to be true, don't you. You want the excuse to go after Kawahara, no matter what. It's just hate with you, isn't it. Another score to settle. You don't care about Ryker. You don't even care about your friend Sarah any—"

"Say that again," I told her coldly, "and I'll deck you. For your information, nothing that we've just discussed matters more to me than Sarah's life. And nothing I've said means I have any option other than to do exactly what Kawahara wants."

"Then what's the fucking point?"

I wanted to reach out for her. Instead, I turned the yearning into a displacement gesture with both hands chopping gently at the air.

"I don't know. Not yet. But if I can get Sarah clear, there might be a way to bring Kawahara down afterwards. And there might be a way to clear Ryker, too. That's all I'm saying."

She stayed looking at me for a moment, then turned and swept up her jacket from the arm of the chair where she had draped it when we arrived.

"I'm going out for a while," she said quietly.

"Fine." I stayed equally quiet. This was not a moment for pressure. "I'll be here, or I'll leave a message for you if I have to go out."

"Yes, do that."

There was nothing in her voice to indicate whether she was really coming back or not.

After she had gone, I sat thinking for a while longer, trying to flesh out the glimpse of structure that the Envoy intuition had given me. When the phone chimed again, I had evidently given up, because the chime caught me staring out of the window, wondering where in Bay City Ortega had gone.

This time, it was Kawahara.

"I have what you want," she said offhandedly. "A dormant version of the Rawling virus will be delivered to Silset Holdings tomorrow morning after eight o'clock. Address 1187 Sacramento. They'll know you're coming."

"And the activator codes?"

"Delivery under separate cover. Trepp will contact you."

I nodded. U.N. law governing transfer and ownership of war viruses was clear to the point of bluntness. Inert viral forms could be owned as subjects for study, or even, as one bizarre test case had proved, private trophies. Ownership or sale of an active military virus, or the codes whereby a dormant virus could be activated, was a U.N. indictable offense, punishable with anything between a hundred and two hundred years storage. In the event of the virus actually being deployed, the sentence could be upped to erasure. Naturally these penalties were applicable only to private citizens, not military commanders or government executives. The powerful are jealous of their toys.

"Just make sure she contacts me soon," I said briefly. "I don't want to use up any more of my ten days than I have to."

"I understand." Kawahara made a sympathetic face, for all the world as if the threats against Sarah were being made by some malignant force of nature over which neither of us had control. "I will have Irene Elliott resleeved by tomorrow evening. Nominally, she is being bought out of storage by JacSol S.A., one of my communications interface companies. You'll be able to collect her from Bay City Central around ten o'clock. I have you temporarily accredited as a security consultant for JacSol Division West. Name, Martin Anderson."

"Got it." This was Kawahara's way of telling me that if anything went wrong, I was tied to her and would go down first. "That's going to clash with Ryker's gene signature. He'll be a live file at Bay City Central as long as the body's decanted."

Kawahara nodded. "Dealt with. Your accreditation will be routed through JacSol corporate channels before any individual genetic search. A punch-in code. Within JacSol, your gene print will be recorded as Anderson's. Any other problems?"

"What if I bump into Sullivan?"

"Warden Sullivan has gone on extended leave. Some kind of psychological problem. He is spending some time in virtual. You will not be seeing him again."

Despite myself, I felt a cold shiver as I looked at Kawahara's composed features. I cleared my throat.

"And the sleeve repurchase?"

"No." Kawahara smiled faintly. "I checked the specs; Irene Elliott's sleeve has no biotech augmentation to justify the cost of retrieving it."

"I didn't say it had. This isn't about technical capacity, it's about motivation. She'll be more loyal if—"

Kawahara leaned forward in the screen. "I can be pushed so far, Kovacs. And then it stops. Elliott's getting a compatible sleeve; she should be thankful for that. You wanted her; any loyalty problems you have with her are going to be your problems exclusively. I don't want to hear about it."

"She'll take longer to adjust," I said doggedly. "In a new sleeve, she'll be slower, less resp—"

"Also your problem. I offered you the best intrusion experts money can buy, and you turned them down. You've got to learn to live with the consequences of your actions, Kovacs." She paused and sat back with another faint smile. "I had a check run on Elliott. Who she is, who her family is, what the connection is. Why you wanted her off stack. It's a nice thought, Kovacs, but I'm afraid you're going to have to support your own Good Samaritan gestures without my help. I'm not running a charity here."

"No," I said flatly. "I suppose not."

"No. And I think we can also suppose that this will be the last direct contact between us until this matter is resolved."

"Yes."

"Well, inappropriate though it may seem, then: Good luck, Kovacs."

The screen blanked, leaving the words hanging in the air. I sat for what seemed like a long time, hearing them, staring at an imagined afterimage on-screen that my hate made almost real. When I spoke, Ryker's voice sounded alien in my ears, as if someone or something else was speaking through me.

"Inappropriate is right," it said into the quiet room. "Motherfucker."

Ortega did not come back, but the aroma of what she had cooked curled through the apartment and my stomach flexed in sympathy. I waited some more, still trying to assemble all the jagged edges of the puzzle in my mind, but either my heart was not in it or there was still something major missing. Finally, I forced down the coppery taste of the hate and frustration, and went to eat.

CHAPTEr THIrTY

Kawahara's groundwork was flawless.

An automated limo with JacSol insignia lightning flashed onto its flanks turned up outside the Hendrix at eight the next morning. I went down to meet it and found the rear cabin stacked with Chinese designer-label boxes.

Opened back in my room, the boxes yielded a line of high-quality corporate props that Serenity Carlyle would have gone wild for: two blocky, sand-colored suits, cut to Ryker's size, a half-dozen handmade shirts with the JacSol logo embroidered on each wing collar, formal shoes in real leather, a midnight blue raincoat, a JacSol dedicated mobile phone, and a small black disk with a thumbprint DNA encoding pad.

I showered and shaved, dressed, and ran the disk. Kawahara blinked up on the screen, construct perfect.

"Good morning, Takeshi-san, and welcome to JacSol Communications. The DNA coding on this disk is now webbed into a line of credit in the name Martin James Anderson. As I mentioned earlier, the punch-in corporate prefix for JacSol will negate any clash with Ryker's genetic records or the account set up for you by Bancroft. Please note the coding below."

I read off the string of digits in a single sweep and went back to watching Kawahara's face.

"The JacSol account will bear all reasonable expenses and is programmed to expire at the end of our ten-day agreement. Should you wish to dissolve the account earlier than this, double-punch the code, apply the gene trace, and double-punch again.

"Trepp will contact you via the corporate mobile sometime today, so keep the unit with you at all times. Irene Elliott will be downloaded at twenty-one forty-five West Coast time. Processing should take about forty-five minutes. And by the time you receive this message, Silset Holdings will have your package. After consultation with my own experts, I have appended a list of the likely hardware Elliott will need, and a number of suppliers who can be trusted to acquire it discreetly. Charge everything through the JacSol account. The list will print out in hardcopy momentarily.

"Should you need any repetition of these details, the disk will remain playable for the next eighteen minutes, at which point it will self-wipe. You are now on your own."

Kawahara's features arranged themselves in a PR smile, and the image faded as the printer chittered out the hardware list. I scanned it briefly on my way down to the limo.

Ortega had not come back.

At Silset Holdings I was treated like a Harlan family heir. Polished human receptionists busied themselves with my comfort while a technician brought out a metal cylinder roughly the dimensions of a hallucinogen grenade.

Trepp was less impressed. I met her early that evening, as per her phoned instructions, in a bar in Oakland, and when she saw the JacSol image she laughed sourly.

"You look like a fucking programmer, Kovacs. Where'd you get that suit?"

"My name's Anderson," I reminded her. "And the suit goes with the name."

She pulled a face.

"Well, next time you go shopping, *Anderson,* take me with you. I'll save you a lot of money, and you won't come out looking like a guy takes the kids to Honolulu on weekends."

I leaned across the tiny table. "You know, Trepp, last time you gave me a hard time about my dress sense, I killed you."

She shrugged. "Goes to show. Some people just can't take the truth."

"Did you bring the stuff?"

Trepp put her hand flat on the table, and when she removed it there was a nondescript gray disk sealed in impact plastic between us.

"There you go. As requested. Now I know you're crazy." There might have been something like admiration in her voice. "You know what they do to you on Earth for playing with this stuff?"

I covered the disk with my own hand and pocketed it. "Same as anywhere else, I guess. Federal offense, down the double-barrel. You forget, I don't have any choice."

Trepp scratched an ear. "Double-barrel, or the Big Wipe. I haven't enjoyed carrying this around all day. You got the rest of it there?"

"Why? Worried about being seen in public with me?"

She smiled. "A bit. I hope you know what you're doing."

I hoped so, too. The bulky, grenade-sized package I'd collected from SilSet had been burning a hole in my expensive coat pocket all day.

I went back to the Hendrix and checked for messages. Ortega had not called. I killed time in the hotel room, thinking through the line I was going to feed Elliott. At nine I got back in the limo and took it down to Bay City Central.

I sat in a reception room while a young doctor completed the necessary paperwork and I initialed the forms where he indicated. There was an eerie familiarity to the process. Most of the clauses in the parole were *on behalf of* stipulations, which effectively made me responsible for Irene Elliott's conduct during the release period. She had even less say in the matter than I'd had when I arrived the week before.

When Elliott finally emerged from the RESTRICTED ZONE doors beyond the reception rooms, it was with the halting step of someone recovering from a debilitating illness. The shock of the mirror was written into her new face. When you don't do it for a living, it's no easy thing to face the stranger for the first time, and the face that Elliott now wore was almost as far from the big-boned blonde I remembered from her husband's photocube as Ryker was from my own previous sleeve. Kawahara had described the new sleeve as compatible, and it fitted that bleak description perfectly. It was a female body, about the same age as Elliott's original body had been, but there the resemblance ended. Where Irene Elliott had been big and fair-skinned, this sleeve had the sheen of a narrow vein of copper seen through falling water. Thick black hair framed a face with eyes like hot coals and lips the color of plums, and the body was slim and delicate.

"Irene Elliott?"

She leaned unsteadily on the reception counter as she turned to look at me. "Yes. Who are you?"

"My name is Martin Anderson. I represent JacSol Division West. We arranged for your parole."

Her eyes narrowed a little, scanning me from head to foot and back again. "You don't look like a programmer. Apart from the suit, I mean."

"I'm a security consultant, attached to JacSol for certain projects. There is some work we would like you to do for us."

"Yeah? Couldn't get anyone else to do it cheaper than this?" She gestured around her. "What happened, did I get famous while I was in the store?"

"In a sense," I said carefully. "Perhaps it would be better if we dealt with the formalities here and moved on. There is a limousine waiting."

"A *limo*?" The incredulity in her voice put a genuine smile on my face for the first time that day. She signed the final release as if in a dream.

● ● ●

"Who are you really?" she asked when the limousine was in the air. It felt like a lot of people had been asking me that over the past few days. I was almost beginning to wonder myself.

I stared ahead over the navigation block of the limo. "A friend," I said quietly. "That's all you need to know for now."

"Before we start anything, I want—"

"I know." The limousine was banking in the sky as I said it. "We'll be in Ember in about half an hour."

I hadn't turned, but I could feel the heat of her stare on the side of my face.

"You're not corporate," she said definitely. "Corporates don't do this stuff. Not like this."

"The corporates do whatever turns a profit. Don't let your prejudices blind you. Sure, they'll burn down entire villages if it pays. But if having a human face is what cuts it, they'll whip out a human face and put it on."

"And you're the human face?"

"Not exactly."

"What's the work you want me to do? Something illegal?"

I pulled the cylindrical virus loader out of my pocket and passed it across to her. She took it in both hands and examined the decals with professional interest. As far as I was concerned, this was the first test. I'd pulled Elliott out of the store because that way she would be mine in a way no one supplied by Kawahara or skimmed off the street would ever be. But beyond that I had nothing to go on but instinct and Victor Elliott's word that his wife was good, and I was feeling slightly queasy about the direction I'd let things go. Kawahara was right. Good Samaritan gestures can be expensive.

"So let's see. You've got a first-generation Simultec virus here." Scorn made her enunciate each syllable slowly. "Collector's item, practically a relic. And you've got it in a state-of-the-art rapid-deployment jacket with antilocational casing. Why don't you just cut the crap and tell me what's really in here? You're planning a run, aren't you."

I nodded.

"What's the target?"

"Virtual whorehouse. A.I. managed."

Elliott's new lips parted in a soundless whistle. "Liberation run?"

"No. We're installing."

"Installing this?" She hefted the cylinder. "So what is it?"

"Rawling 4851."

Elliott stopped hefting abruptly. "That's not funny."

"Wasn't intended to be. That's a dormant Rawling variant. Set for rapid deployment, as you so rightly observed. The activation codes are in my pocket. We are going to plant Rawling inside an A.I. whorehouse database, inject the codes, and then weld the lid shut on it. There's some peripheral stuff with monitoring systems, and some tidying up, but basically that's the run."

She gave me a curious look. "Are you some kind of religious nut?"

"No." I smiled faintly. "It's nothing like that. Can you do it?"

"Depends on the A.I. Do you have the specs?"

"Not here."

Elliott handed me back the deployment jacket. "I can't tell you, then, can I?"

"That was what I was hoping you'd say." I stowed the cylinder, satisfied. "How's the new sleeve?"

"It's okay. Any reason why I couldn't have my own body back? I'll be a lot faster in my own—"

"I know. Unfortunately it's out of my hands. Did they tell you how long you've been in the store?"

"Four years, someone said."

"Four and a half," I said, glancing at the release forms I'd signed. "I'm afraid in the meantime, someone took a shine to your sleeve and bought it."

"Oh." She was silent then. The shock of waking up inside someone else's body for the first time is nothing compared to the sense of rage and betrayal you feel knowing that someone somewhere is walking around inside you. It's like the discovery of infidelity, but at the intimacy range of rape. And like both those violations, there's nothing you can do about it. You just get used to it.

When the silence stretched, I looked across at her still profile and cleared my throat.

"You sure you want to do this right now? Go home, I mean."

She barely bothered to look at me. "Yes, I'm sure. I have a daughter and a husband who haven't seen me in nearly five years. You think this—" She gestured down at herself. "—is going to stop me?"

"Fair enough."

The lights of Ember appeared on the darkened mass of the coastline up ahead, and the limousine began its descent. I watched Elliott out of the corner of my eye and saw the nervousness setting in. Palms rubbing together in her lap, lower lip caught in her teeth at one corner of her new mouth. She released her breath with a small but perfectly audible noise.

"They don't know I'm coming?" she asked.

"No," I said shortly. I didn't want to follow this line of conversation. "The contract is between you and JacSol West. It doesn't concern your family."

"But you arranged for me to see them. Why?"

"I'm a sucker for family reunions." I fixed my gaze on the darkened bulk of the wrecked aircraft carrier below, and we landed in silence. The autolimo banked around to align itself with the local traffic systems and touched down a couple of hundred meters north of Elliott's Data Linkage. We powered smoothly along the shore road under the successive holos of Anchana Salomao and parked immaculately opposite the narrow frontage. The dead-monitor doorstop had been removed and the door was closed, but there were lights burning in the glass-walled office at the back.

We climbed out and crossed the street. The closed door proved to be locked, as well. Irene Elliott banged impatiently at it with the flat of one copper-skinned hand, and someone sat up sluggishly in the back office. After a moment, a figure identifiable as Victor Elliott came down to the transmission floor, past the reception counter, and toward us. His gray hair was untidy and his face swollen with sleep. He peered out at us with a lack of focus I'd seen before on datarats when they'd been cruising the stacks for too long. Jack happy.

"Who the hell—" He stopped as he recognized me. "What the fuck do you want, grasshopper? And who's this?"

"Vic?" Irene Elliott's new throat sounded nine-tenths closed. "Vic, it's me."

For a moment, Elliott's eyes ran a volley between my face and the delicate Asian woman beside me, then what she had said smacked into him like a truck. He flinched visibly with the impact.

"Irene?" he whispered.

"Yes, it's me," she husked back. There were tears leaking down her cheeks. For moments they stared at each other through the glass, then Victor Elliott was fumbling with the locking mechanism of the door, shoving at the frame to get it out of the way, and the copper-skinned woman sagged across the threshold into his arms. They locked together in an embrace that looked set to break the new sleeve's delicate bones. I took a mild interest in streetlamps up and down the promenade.

Finally, Irene Elliott remembered me. She disengaged from her husband and twisted around, smearing the tears off her face with the heel of one hand and blinking bright-eyed at me.

"Can you—"

"Sure," I said neutrally. "I'll wait in the limo. See you in the morning."

I caught one confused look from Victor Elliott as his wife bustled him inside. I nodded good-naturedly at him and turned away to the parked limo and the beach. The door banged shut behind me. I felt in my pockets and came up with Ortega's crumpled pack of cigarettes. Wandering past the limo to the iron railing, I kindled one of the bent and flattened cylinders and for once felt no sense that I was betraying something as the smoke curled into my lungs. Down on the beach, the surf was up, a chorus line of ghosts along the sand. I leaned on the railing and listened to the white noise of the waves as they broke, wondering why I could feel this much at peace with so much still unresolved. Ortega had not come back. Kadmin was still out there. Sarah was still under ransom, Kawahara still had me by the balls, and I still didn't know why Bancroft had been killed.

And despite it all, there was space for this measure of quiet.

Take what is offered, and that must sometimes be enough.

My gaze slipped out past the breakers. The ocean beyond was black and secret, merging seamlessly with the night a scant distance out from the shore. Even the massive bulk of the keeled-over *Free Trade Enforcer* was hard to make out. I imagined Mary Lou Hinchley hurtling down to her shattering impact with the unyielding water, then slipping broken beneath the swells to be cradled in wait for the sea's predators. How long had she been out there before the currents contrived to carry what was left of her back to her own kind? How long had the darkness held her?

My thoughts skipped aimlessly, cushioned on the vague sense of acceptance and well-being. I saw Bancroft's antique telescope, trained on the heavens and the tiny motes of light that were Earth's first hesitant steps beyond the limits of the solar system. Fragile arks carrying the recorded selves of a million pioneers and the deep-frozen embryo banks that might someday resleeve them on distant worlds, if the promise of the vaguely understood Martian astrogation charts bore fruit. If not, they would drift forever, because the universe is mostly night and darkened ocean.

Raising an eyebrow at my own introspection, I heaved myself off the rail and glanced up at the holographic face above my head. Anchana Salomao had the night to herself. Her ghostly countenance gazed down at repeated intervals along the promenade, compassionate but uninvolved. Looking at the composed features, it was easy to see why Elizabeth Elliott had wanted so badly to attain those heights. I would have given a lot for that same detached composure. I shifted my attention to the windows above Elliott's. The lights were on there, and as I watched, a female form moved across one of them in naked silhouette. I sighed, spun the stub of my cigarette into the gutter, and took refuge in the limo. Let Anchana keep the vigil. I called up channels at random on the entertainment deck and let the mindless barrage of images and sounds numb me into a kind of half sleep. The night passed around the vehicle like cold mist, and I suffered the vague sensation that I was drifting away from the lights of the Elliotts' home, out to sea on snapped moorings with nothing between me and the horizon where there was a storm building. . . .

A sharp rapping on the window beside my head shook me awake. I jerked around from the position I'd slumped into and saw Trepp standing patiently outside. She gestured at me to roll down the window, then leaned in with a grin.

"Kawahara was right about you. Sleeping in the car so this dipper can get laid. You've got delusions of priesthood, Kovacs."

"Shut up, Trepp," I said irritably. "What time is it?"

"About five." Her eyes swiveled up and left to consult the chip. "Five-sixteen. Be getting light soon."

I struggled into a more upright position, tasting the residue of the single cigarette on my tongue. "What are you doing here?"

"Watching your back. We don't want Kadmin taking you out before you can sell the goods to Bancroft, do we? Hey, is that the Wreckers?"

I followed her gaze forward to the entertainment deck, which was still screening some kind of sports coverage. Minuscule figures rushed backwards and forwards on a crosshatched field, accompanied by a barely audible commentary. A brief collision between two players occasioned an insectile roar of cheering. I must have lowered the volume before I fell asleep. Switching the deck off, I saw in the ensuing dimness that Trepp had been right. The night had washed out to a soft blue gloom that was creeping over the buildings beside us like a bleach stain on the darkness.

"Not a fan, then?" Trepp nodded at the screen. "I didn't use to be, but you live in New York long enough, you get the habit."

"Trepp, how the fuck are you supposed to watch my back if your head is jammed in here watching the screen?"

Trepp gave me a hurt look and withdrew her head. I climbed out of the limo and stretched in the chilly air. Overhead, Anchana Salomao was still resplendent, but the lights above Elliott's were out.

"They stayed up until a couple of hours ago," Trepp said helpfully. "I thought they might be running out on you, so I checked the back."

I gazed up at the darkened windows. "Why are they going to run out on me? She hasn't even heard what the terms of the deal are."

"Well, involvement in an erasure offense tends to make most people nervous."

"Not this woman," I said, and wondered how much I believed myself.

Trepp shrugged. "Suit yourself. I still think you're crazy, though. Kawahara's got dippers could do this stuff standing on their heads."

Since my own reasons for not accepting Kawahara's offer of technical support were almost entirely instinctive, I said nothing. The icy certainty of my revelations about Bancroft, Kawahara, and Resolution 653 had faded with the previous day's rush of setup details for the run, and any sense of interlocking well-being had gone when Ortega left. All I had now was the gravity pull of mission time, the cold dawn, and the sound of the waves on the shore. The taste of Ortega in my mouth and the warmth of her long-limbed body curled into mine were a tropical island in the chill, receding in my wake.

"You reckon there's somewhere open this early that serves coffee?" I asked.

"Town this size?" Trepp drew breath in through her teeth. "Doubt it. But I saw a bank of dispensers on the way in. Got to be one that does coffee."

"Machine coffee?" I curled my lip.

"Hey, what are you, a fucking connoisseur? You're living in a hotel that's just one big goddamned dispenser. Christ, Kovacs, this is the Machine Age. Didn't anybody tell you that?"

"You got a point. How far is it?"

"Couple of klicks. We'll take my car. That way if Little Miss Homecoming wakes up, she won't look out the window and panic."

"Sold."

I followed Trepp across the street to a low-slung black vehicle that looked as if it might be radar invisible, and climbed into a snug interior that smelled faintly of incense.

"This yours?"

"No, rented. Picked it up when we flew back in from Europe. Why?"

I shook my head. "Doesn't matter."

Trepp started up, and we ghosted silently along the promenade. I looked out of the seaward window and wrestled with an insubstantial sense of frustration. The scant hours of sleep in the limo had left me itchy. Everything about the situation was suddenly chafing at me again, from the lack of solution to Bancroft's death to my relapse into smoking. I had a feeling that it was going to be a bad day, and the sun wasn't even up yet.

"You thought about what you're going to do when this is over?"

"No," I said morosely.

We found the dispensers on a frontage that sloped down to the shore at one end of the town. Clearly they had been installed with beach clientele in mind, but the dilapidated state of the shelters that housed them suggested that trade was no better here than for Elliott's Data Linkage. Trepp parked the car pointing at the sea and went to get the coffees. Through the window I watched her kick and slam the machine until it finally relinquished two plastic cups. She carried them back to the car and handed me mine.

"Want to drink it here?"

"Yeah, why not?"

We pulled the tabs on the cups and listened to them sizzle. The mechanism didn't heat especially well, but the coffee tasted reasonable and it had a definite chemical effect. I could feel my weariness sliding away. We drank slowly and watched the sea through the windshield, immersed in a silence that was almost companionable.

"I tried for the Envoys once," Trepp said suddenly.

I glanced sideways at her, curious. "Yeah?"

"Yeah, long time ago. They rejected me on profile. No capacity for allegiance, they said."

I grunted. "Figures. You were never in the military, were you?"

"What do *you* think?" She was looking at me as if I'd just suggested she might have a history of child-molesting. I chuckled tiredly.

"Thought not. See, the thing is, they're looking for borderline psychopathic tendencies. That's why they do most of their recruiting from the military in the first place."

Trepp looked put out. "I've *got* borderline psychopathic tendencies."

"Yeah, I don't doubt it, but the point is, the number of civilians with those tendencies *and* a sense of team spirit is pretty limited. They're opposing values. The chances of them both arising naturally in the same person are almost nil. Military training takes the natural order and fucks with it. It breaks down any resistance to psychopathic behavior at the same time as it builds fanatical loyalties to the group. Package deal. Soldiers are perfect Envoy material."

"You make it sound like I had a lucky escape."

For a few seconds I stared out at the horizon, remembering.

"Yeah." I drained the rest of my coffee. "Come on, let's get back."

As we drove back along the promenade, something had changed in the quiet between us. Something that, like the gradually waxing light of dawn around the car, was at once intangible and impossible to ignore.

When we pulled up outside the data broker's frontage, Irene Elliott was waiting, leaning against the side of the limo and watching the sea. There was no sign of her husband.

"Better stay here," I told Trepp as I climbed out. "Thanks for the coffee."

"Sure."

"I guess I'll be seeing you in my rearview screen for a while, then."

"I doubt you'll see me at all, Kovacs," Trepp said cheerfully. "I'm better at this than you are."

"Remains to be seen."

"Yeah, yeah. Be seeing you." She raised her voice as I started to walk away. "And don't fuck up that run. We'd all hate to see that happen."

She backed up the car a dozen meters and kicked it into the air in a showy, dropped-nose bunt that shattered the quiet with a shriek of turbines and barely cleared our heads before flipping up and out over the ocean.

"Who was that?" There was a huskiness to Irene Elliott's voice that sounded like the residue of too much crying.

"Backup," I said absently, watching the car trail out over the wrecked aircraft carrier. "Works for the same people. Don't worry, she's a friend."

"She may be your friend," Elliott said bitterly. "She isn't mine. None of you people are."

I looked at her, then back out to sea. "Fair enough."

Silence, apart from the waves. Elliott shifted against the polished coachwork of the limo.

"You know what's happened to my daughter," she said in a dead voice. "You knew all the time."

I nodded.

"And you don't give a flying fuck, do you? You're working for the man that used her like a piece of toilet tissue."

"Lots of men used her," I said brutally. "She let herself be used. And I'm sure your husband's told you why she did that, as well."

I heard Irene Elliott's breath catch in her throat and concentrated on the horizon, where Trepp's cruiser was fading into the predawn gloom. "She did it for the same reason she tried to blackmail the man I was working for, the same reason she tried to put drivers on a particularly unpleasant man called Jerry Sedaka who subsequently had her killed. She did it for you, Irene."

"You fuck." She started to cry, a small hopeless sound in the stillness.

I kept my eyes fixed on the ocean. "I don't work for Bancroft anymore," I said carefully. "I've swapped sides on that piece of shit. I'm giving you the chance to hit Bancroft where it hurts, to hit him with the guilt that fucking your daughter never gave him. Plus, now that you're out of the store, maybe you'll be able to get the money together and resleeve Elizabeth. Or at least get her off stack, rent her some space in a virtual condo or something. The point is, you're off the ice, you can do something. You've got options. That's what I'm offering you. I'm dealing you back into the game. Don't throw that away."

Beside me, I heard her struggling to force down the tears. I waited.

"You're pretty impressed with yourself, aren't you," she said finally. "You think you're doing me this big favor, but you're no fucking Good Samaritan. I mean, you got me out of the store, but it all comes at a price, right?"

"Of course it does," I said quietly.

"I do what you want, this virus run. I break the law for you, or I go back on stack. And if I squeal, or screw up, I've got more to lose than you. That's the deal, isn't it? Nothing for free."

I watched the waves. "That's the deal," I agreed.

More silence. Out of the corner of my eye, I saw her look down at the body she was wearing, as if she'd spilled something down herself. "Do you know how I feel?" she asked.

"No."

"I slept with my husband, and I feel like he's been unfaithful to me." A choked laugh. She smeared angrily at her eyes. "I feel like *I've* been unfaithful. To something. You know, when they put me away I left a body and a family behind. Now I don't have either."

She looked down at herself again. She lifted her hands and turned them, fingers spread.

"I don't know what I feel," she said. "I don't know what *to* feel."

There was a lot I could have said. A lot that has been said, written, researched, and disputed on the subject. Trite little magazine-length summings-up of the problems inherent in resleeving—*how to make your partner love you again, in any body;* trite, interminable psychological tracts—*some observations of secondary trauma in civil resleeving;* even the sanctified manuals of the fucking Envoy Corps itself had something trite to say on the matter. Quotes, informed opinion, the ravings of the religious and the lunatic fringe. I could have thrown it all at her. I could have told her that what she was going through was quite normal for an unconditioned human. I could have told her that it would pass with time. That there were psychodynamic disciplines for dealing with it. That millions of other people survived it. I could even have told her that whichever God she owed nominal allegiance to was watching over her. I could have lied, I could have reasoned. It all would have meant about the same, because the reality was *pain*, and right now there was nothing anyone could do to take it away.

I said nothing.

The dawn gained on us, light strengthening on the closed-up frontages behind us. I glanced at the windows of Elliott's Data Linkage.

"Victor?" I asked.

"Sleeping." She wiped an arm across her face and snorted her tears back under control like badly cut amphetamine. "You say this is going to hurt Bancroft?"

"Yeah. In a subtle way, but yeah, it'll hurt."

"Installation run on an A.I.," Irene Elliott said to me. "Installing an erasure-penalty virus. Fucking over a known Meth. You know what the risks are? You know what you're asking me to do?"

I turned to look her in the eye.

"Yes. I know."

Her mouth clamped down on a tremor.

"Good. Then let's do it."

CHAPTEr THIrTY-ONE

The run took less than three days to set up. Irene Elliott turned stone-cold pro and made it happen that way.

In the limo back to Bay City, I laid it out for her. At first she was still crying inside, but as the detail mounted she clicked in, nodding, grunting, stopping me and backing me up on minor points I hadn't made clear enough. I showed her Reileen Kawahara's suggested hardware list, and she okayed about two-thirds of it. The rest was just corporate padding, and Kawahara's advisers, in her opinion, didn't know shit.

By the end of the journey she had it down. I could see the run already unfolding behind her eyes. The tears had dried on her face, forgotten, and her expression was clean-purpose, locked-down hate for the man who had used her daughter, and an embodied will to revenge.

Irene Elliott was sold.

•••

I rented an apartment in Oakland on the JacSol account. Elliott moved in and I left her there to catch up on some sleep. I stayed at the Hendrix, tried to do some sleeping of my own without much success, and went back six hours later to find Elliott already prowling about the apartment.

I called the names and numbers Kawahara had given me and ordered the stuff Elliott had ticked. The crates arrived in hours. Elliott cracked them open and laid out the hardware across the floor of the apartment.

Together we went through Ortega's list of virtual forums and worked it down to a shortlist of seven.

Ortega had not turned up, or called me at the Hendrix.

Midafternoon on the second day, Elliott kicked on the primary modules and cruised each of the shortlist options. The list fell to three, and Elliott gave me a couple more items to go shopping for. Refinement software for the big kill.

By early evening the list was down to two, with Elliott writing up preliminary intrusion procedures for both. Whenever she hit a glitch, we backed up and compared relative merits.

By midnight we had our target. Elliott went to bed and slept eight solid hours. I went back to the Hendrix and brooded.

Nothing from Ortega.

I bought breakfast in the street and took it back to the apartment. Neither of us felt much like eating.

At ten-fifteen local time, Irene Elliott calibrated her equipment for the last time.

●●●

We did it.

Twenty-seven and a half minutes.

A piece of piss, Elliott said.

I left her dismantling equipment and flew out to see Bancroft that afternoon.

CHAPTEr THIrTY-TWO

"I find this exceptionally difficult to believe," Bancroft said sharply. "Are you quite sure I went to this establishment?"

Below the balcony on the lawns of Suntouch House, Miriam Bancroft appeared to be constructing an enormous paper glider from instructions in a moving holoprojection. The white of the wings was so bright it hurt to look directly at them. As I leaned on the balcony rail, she shaded her eyes from the sun and looked up at me.

"The mall has security monitors," I said, affecting disinterest. "Automated system, still operational after all these years. They've got footage of you walking right up to the door. You do know the name, don't you?"

"Jack It Up? Of course, I've heard of it, but I've never actually *used* the place."

I looked around without leaving the rail. "Really. You have something against virtual sex, then? You're a reality purist?"

"No." I could hear the smile in his voice. "I have no problem with virtual formats, and as I believe I've told you already, I have used them on occasion. But this place Jack It Up is, how can I put it, hardly the elegant end of the market."

"No," I agreed. "And how would you classify Jerry's Closed Quarters? An elegant whorehouse?"

"Hardly."

"But that didn't stop you going there to play cabin games with Elizabeth Elliott, did it? Or has it gone downhill recently, because—"

"All right." The smile in the voice had turned to a grimace. "You've made your point. Don't belabor it."

I stopped watching Miriam Bancroft and came back to my seat. My iced cocktail was still standing on the little table between us. I picked it up.

"I'm glad you take the point," I said, stirring the drink. "Because it's taken a lot of pain to sort through this mess. I've been abducted, tortured, and nearly killed in the process. A woman called Louise, not much older than your precious daughter Naomi, *was* killed because she got in the way. So if you don't like my conclusions, you can go fuck yourself."

I raised my glass to him across the table.

"Spare me the melodrama, Kovacs, and sit down, for God's sake. I'm not rejecting what you say, I'm just questioning it."

I sat and leveled a finger at him. "No. You're squirming. This thing's pointing up a part of your character you despise for its appetites. You'd rather not know what kind of software you were accessing that night over at Jack It Up, in case it's even more grubby than you already imagine. You're being forced to confront the part of yourself that wants to come in your wife's face, and you don't like it."

"There will be no need to revisit that particular conversation," Bancroft said stiffly. He steepled his fingers. "You are aware, I suppose, that the security camera footage you base your assumptions on could be faked very easily by anyone with access to newstape images of me."

"Yes, I am." I'd watched Irene Elliott do exactly that only forty-eight hours previously. *Easy* wasn't the word. After the virus run, it had been like asking a concert Total Body dancer to encore with stretching exercises. I'd barely had time to smoke a cigarette while she did it. "But why would anyone bother? A distracter, to tinsel me off course, assuming of course that some wrong turn would have me sniffing around the ruins of a derelict Richmond mall in the first place. Come on, Bancroft, get real. The fact I was out there in the first place proves the validity of that footage. And in any case, those images aren't the basis for anything. They just confirm what I'd already worked out, which is that you killed yourself to avoid viral contamination of your remote stack."

"That is a quite remarkable leap of intuition to make after only a six-day investigation."

"Blame Ortega," I said lightly, though Bancroft's enduring suspicion in the face of unpleasant facts was beginning to worry me. I hadn't realized he would take so much wearing down. "She's the one who put me onto the right track. She wouldn't wear the murder theory from the start. She kept telling me you were too tough and smart a Meth motherfucker to let anyone kill you. Quote, unquote. And that brought me back to the conversation we had here a week ago. You told me *I am not the kind of man to take my own life, and even if I was, I would not have bungled it in this fashion. If it had been my intention to die, you would not be talking to me now.* Envoys have total recall; those were your exact words."

I paused and set down my glass, searching for the fine edge of deceit that always lies right up against the truth.

"All this time, I've been working on the assumption you didn't pull the trigger because you weren't the type to commit suicide. I ignored all the evidence to the contrary because of that single assumption. The electron-tight security you've got here, the lack of any traces of intrusion, the handprint lock on the safe."

"And Kadmin. And Ortega."

"Yeah, that didn't help. But we straightened out the Ortega angle, and Kadmin, well, I'm coming to Kadmin in a moment. The point is, as long as I equated pulling that trigger with suicide, I was jammed. But then, what if those two acts were not synonymous? What if you'd torched your own stack, not because you wanted to die, but for some other reason? Once I let myself think that, the rest was easy. What were the possible reasons that you'd do it? It's not an easy thing to put a gun to your own head, even if you do want to die. To do it when you want to live must take the will of a demon. No matter how much you might know intellectually that you'll be resleeved with the bulk of your mind intact, the person you are at that moment is going to die. You had to have been desperate to pull that trigger. It had to have been something—" I smiled faintly. "—life threatening. Given that assumption, it didn't take long to come up with the virus scenario. Then all I had to do was work out how and where you'd been infected."

Bancroft shifted uncomfortably at the word, and I felt a stab of elation run through me. Virus! Even Meths were afraid of the invisible corroder, because even they, with their remote storage and their clones on ice, were not immune. Viral strike! Stack down! Bancroft was off balance.

"Now, it's virtually impossible to snug something as complex as a virus into a disconnected target, so you had to have been jacked in somewhere along the line. I thought of the PsychaSec facility, but they're sewed up too tight. And it couldn't have been before you went to Osaka for the same reasons; even dormant, the virus would have tripped every alarm at PsychaSec when they set up the 'cast. It had to have been sometime in the last forty-eight hours, because your remote stack was uncontaminated. I knew from talking to your wife that the likelihood was you'd been out on the town when you got back from Osaka, and on your own admission that could quite possibly include some kind of virtual whorehouse. After that, it was just a matter of doing the rounds. I tried a half-dozen places before I hit Jack It Up, and when I punched up their inquiries the viral contam siren nearly blew my phone out. That's the thing about A.I.s— they write their own security and it's second to none. Jack It Up is sealed off so tight it'll take the police months to tunnel in and see what's left of the core processors."

I felt a vague pang of guilt as I thought of the A.I., thrashing like a man in an acid vat as its systems dissolved around it, consciousness shriveling down a tunnel of closing perspectives into nothing. The feeling passed rapidly. We'd chosen Jack It Up for a variety of reasons: It was in a roofed-over area, which meant there would be no satellite coverage to dispute the lies we'd planted in the mall surveillance system; it operated in a criminal environment, so no one would have a problem believing an illicit virus had somehow got loose inside it; but most of all it ran a series of software options so distasteful that it was unlikely the police would ever bother to investigate the wreckage of the murdered machine more than cursorily. Under its heading on Ortega's list, there were at least a dozen copycat sex crimes that the Organic Damage Division had traced to software packages available from Jack It Up. I could imagine the curl of Ortega's lip as she read the software listings, the studied indifference with which she would handle the case.

I missed Ortega.

"What about Kadmin?"

"It's hard to know, but I'm betting whoever infected Jack It Up in the first place probably hired Kadmin to silence me and make sure the whole thing stayed covered up. After all, without me stirring things up, how long would it have been before anyone realized Jack had been iced? Can't see any of its potential clients calling the police when they got refused entry, can you?"

Bancroft gave me a hard look, but I knew from his next words that the battle was almost over. The balance of belief was tipping toward me. Bancroft was going to buy the package. "You're saying the virus was introduced deliberately. That someone murdered this machine?"

I shrugged. "It seems likely. Jack It Up operated on the margins of local law. A lot of its software appears to have been impounded by the Transmission Felony Division at one time or another, which suggests that it had regular dealings with the criminal world in one form or another. It is possible that it made some enemies. On Harlan's World the yakuza have been known to perform viral execution on machines judged to have betrayed them. I don't know if that happens here, or who'd have the stack muscle to do it. But I do know that whoever hired Kadmin used an A.I. to pull him out of police storage. You can verify that with Fell Street, if you like."

Bancroft was silent. I watched him for a moment, seeing the belief sink in. Watching the process as he convinced himself, I could almost see what he was seeing. Himself, hunched over in an autocab as the sordid guilt over what he had been doing at Jack It Up merged sickeningly with the horror of the contamination warnings sirening in his head. Infected! Himself, Laurens Bancroft, stumbling through the dark toward the lights of Suntouch House and the only surgery that could save him. Why had he left the cab so far from home? Why had he not wakened anybody for help? These were questions I no longer needed to answer for him. Bancroft *believed*. His guilt and self-disgust *made* him believe, and he would find his own answers to reinforce the horrific images in his head.

And by the time Transmission Felony cut a safe path through to Jack It Up's core processors, Rawling 4851 would have eaten out every scrap of coherent intellect the machine ever had. There would be nothing left to dispute the carefully constructed lie I'd told for Kawahara.

I got up and went back to the balcony, wondering if I should allow myself a cigarette. It had been tough to lock down the need the last couple of days. Watching Irene Elliott at work had been nerve-racking. I forced my hand to relinquish the pack in my breast pocket, and gazed down at Miriam Bancroft, who by now was well on the way to completing her glider. When she looked up, I glanced away along the balcony rail and saw Bancroft's telescope, still pointed seaward at the same shallow angle. Idle curiosity made me lean across and look at the figures for angle of elevation. The finger marks in the dust were still there.

Dust?

Bancroft's unconsciously arrogant words came back to me. *It was an en-*

thusiasm I had. Back when the stars were still something to stare at. You wouldn't remember how that felt. Last time I looked through that lens was nearly two centuries ago.

I stared at the finger marks, mesmerized by my own thoughts. Someone had been looking through this lens a lot more recently than two hundred years ago, but they hadn't kept at it very long. From the minimal displacement of dust it looked as if the programming keys had been used only once. On a sudden impulse, I moved up to the telescope and followed the line of its barrel out over the sea to where visibility blurred in the haze. That far out, the angle of elevation would give you a view of empty air a couple of kilometers up. I bent to the eyepiece as if in a dream. A gray speck showed up in the center of my field of vision, blurring in and out of focus as my eyes struggled with the surrounding expanses of blue. Lifting my head and checking the control pad again, I found a max amp key and thumbed it impatiently. When I looked again, the gray speck had sprung into hard focus, filling most of the lens. I breathed out slowly, feeling as if I'd had the cigarette after all.

The airship hung like a bottleback, gorged after a feeding frenzy. It must have been several hundred meters long, with swellings along the lower half of the hull and protruding sections that looked like landing pads. I knew what I was looking at even before Ryker's neurachem reeled in the last increments of magnification I needed to make out the sun-burnished lettering on the side that spelled it out: *Head in the Clouds.*

I stepped back from the telescope, breathing deeply, and as my eyes slid back to normal focus I saw Miriam Bancroft again. She was standing amidst the parts of her glider, staring up at me. I almost flinched as our eyes met. Dropping a hand to the telescope program pad, I did what Bancroft should have done before he blew his own head off. I hit memory wipe, and the digits that had held the airship available for viewing for the last seven weeks blinked out.

I had felt like many kinds of fool in my life, but never quite as completely as I did at that moment. A first-order clue had been waiting there in the lens for anyone to come along and pick it up. Missed by the police in their haste, disinterest, and lack of close knowledge, missed by Bancroft because the telescope was so much a part of his world view it was too close to give a second glance to, but I had no such excuses. I had stood here a week ago and seen the two mismatched pieces of reality clash against each other. Bancroft claiming not to have used the telescope in centuries almost at the same moment that I saw the evidence of recent use in the disturbed dust. And Miriam Bancroft had hammered it home less than an hour later when she said *while Laurens was staring at the stars, some of us kept our eyes on the ground.* I'd thought of the telescope then; my mind had rebelled at the downloading-induced sluggishness and tried to tell me. Shaky and off balance, new to the planet and the flesh I was wearing, I had ignored it. The download dues had taken their toll.

Below on the lawn, Miriam Bancroft was still watching me. I backed away from the telescope, composed my features, and returned to my seat. Absorbed by the images I had faked into his head, Bancroft seemed scarcely to know that I had moved.

But now my own mind was in overdrive, ripping along avenues of thought that had opened with Ortega's list and the Resolution 653 T-shirt. The quiet resignation I had felt in Ember two days ago, the impatience to sell my lies to Bancroft, get Sarah out, and be finished, were all gone. Everything tied in to *Head in the Clouds*, ultimately even Bancroft. It was almost axiomatic that he had gone there the night he died. Whatever had happened to him there was the key to his reasons for dying here at Suntouch House a few hours later. And to the truth that Reileen Kawahara was so desperate to hide.

Which meant I had to go there myself.

I picked up my glass and swallowed some of the drink, not tasting it. The sound it made seemed to wake Bancroft from his daze. He looked up, almost as if he was surprised to see me still there.

"Please excuse me, Mr. Kovacs. This is a lot to take in. After all the scenarios I had envisaged, this is one I had not even considered, and it is so simple. So blindingly obvious." His voice held a wealth of self-disgust. "The truth is that I did not need an Envoy investigator, I simply needed a mirror to hold up to myself."

I set down my glass and got to my feet.

"You're leaving?"

"Well, unless you have any further questions. Personally, I think you still need some time. I'll be around. You can get me at the Hendrix."

On my way out along the main hall, I came face-to-face with Miriam Bancroft. She was dressed in the same coveralls she'd been wearing in the garden, hair caught up in an expensive-looking static clip. In one hand she was carrying a trellised plant urn held up like a lantern on a stormy night. Long strands of flowering martyrweed trailed from the trellis work.

"Have you—" she started.

I stepped closer to her, inside the range of the martyrweed. "I'm through," I said. "I've taken this as far as I can stomach. Your husband has an answer, but it isn't the truth. I hope that satisfies you, as well as Reileen Kawahara."

At the name, her mouth parted in shock. It was the only reaction that got through her control, but it was the confirmation I needed. I felt the need to be cruel come bubbling insistently up from the dark, rarely visited caverns of anger and bitterness that served me as emotional reserves.

"I never figured Reileen for much of a lay, but maybe like attracts like. I hope she's better between the legs than she is on a tennis court."

Miriam Bancroft's face whitened, and I readied myself for the slap. But instead, she offered me a strained smile.

"You are mistaken, Mr. Kovacs," she said.

"Yeah. I often am." I stepped around her. "Excuse me."

I walked away down the hall without looking back.

CHAPTEr THIrTY-THrEE

The building was a stripped shell, an entire floor of warehouse conversion with perfectly identical arched windows along each wall and white painted support pillars every ten meters in each direction. The ceiling was drab gray, the original building blocks exposed and cross-laced with heavy ferrocrete load bearers. The floor was raw concrete, perfectly poured. Hard light fell in through the windows, unsoftened by any drifting motes of dust. The air was crisp and cold.

Roughly in the middle of the building, so near as I could judge, stood a simple steel table and two uncomfortable-looking chairs, arranged as if for a game of chess. On one of the chairs sat a tall man with a tanned, salon-handsome face. He was beating a rapid tattoo on the tabletop, as if listening to jazz on an internal receiver. Incongruously, he was dressed in a blue surgeon's smock and surgery slippers.

I stepped out from behind one of the pillars and crossed the even concrete to the table. The man in the smock looked up at me and nodded, unsurprised.

"Hello, Miller," I said. "Mind if I sit down?"

"My lawyers are going to have me out of here an hour after you charge me," Miller said matter-of-factly. "If that. You've made a big mistake here, pal."

He went back to beating out the jazz rhythm on the tabletop. His gaze drifted out over my shoulder, as if he'd just seen something interesting through one of the arched windows. I smiled.

"A *big* mistake," he repeated to himself.

Very gently, I reached out and flattened his hand onto the tabletop to stop the tapping. His gaze jerked back in as if caught on a hook.

"The fuck do you think—"

He pulled his hand free and surged to his feet, but shut up abruptly when I stiff-armed him back into his seat. For a moment, it looked as if he might try to charge me, but the table was in the way. He stayed seated, glaring murderously at me and no doubt remembering what his lawyers had told him about the laws of virtual holding.

"You've never been arrested, have you, Miller?" I asked conversationally. When he made no reply, I took the chair opposite him, turned it around, and seated myself astride it. I took out my cigarettes and shook one free. "Well, that statement is still grammatically valid. You're not under arrest now. The police don't have you."

I saw the first flicker of fear on his face.

"Let's recap events a little, shall we? You probably think that after you got shot, I lit out and the police came to pick up the pieces. That they found enough to rack the clinic up on, and now you're waiting on due process. Well, it's partially true. I did leave, and the police did come to pick up the pieces. Unfortunately there's one piece that was no longer there to pick up, because I took it with me. Your head." I lifted one hand to demonstrate graphically. "Burned off at the neck and carried out, stack intact, under my jacket."

Miller swallowed. I bent my head and inhaled the cigarette to life.

"Now, the police think that your head was disintegrated by an overcharged blaster on wide beam." I blew smoke across the table at him. "I charred the neck and chest deliberately to give that impression. With a bit of time and a good forensic expert they might have decided otherwise, but unfortunately your still-intact colleagues at the clinic threw them out before they could start a proper investigation. It's understandable, given what they were likely to find. I'm sure you would have done the same. However, what this means is that not only are you not under arrest, you are in fact presumed Really Dead. The police aren't looking for you, nor is anybody else."

"What do you want?" Miller sounded abruptly hoarse.

"Good. I can see you appreciate the implications of your situation. Only natural for a man of your . . . profession, I suppose. What I want is detailed information about *Head in the Clouds*."

"What?"

My voice hardened. "You heard."

"I don't know what you're talking about."

I sighed. This was to be expected. I'd encountered it before wherever Reileen Kawahara appeared in the equation. The terrified loyalty she inspired would have humbled her old yakuza bosses in Fission City.

"Miller, I don't have time to fuck about with you. The Wei Clinic has ties to an airborne whorehouse called *Head in the Clouds*. You probably liaised mostly through an enforcer called Trepp, out of New York. The woman you're dealing with ultimately is Reileen Kawahara. You will have been to *Head in the Clouds*, because I know Kawahara and she always invites her associates into the lair, first to demonstrate an attitude of invulnerability, and second to offer some messy object lesson in the value of loyalty. You ever see something like that?"

From his eyes, I could see that he had.

"Okay, that's what I know. Your cue. I want you to draw me a rough blueprint of *Head in the Clouds*. Include as much detail as you can remember. A surgeon like you ought to have a good eye for detail. I also want to know what the procedures are for visiting the place. Security coding, minimum reasons to justify you visiting, stuff like that. Plus some idea of what the security's like inside the place."

"You think I'll just tell you."

I shook my head. "No, I think I'm going to have to torture you first. But I'll get it out of you, one way or the other. Your decision."

"You won't do it."

"I will do it," I said mildly. "You don't know me. You don't know who I am, or why we're having this conversation. You see, the night before I turned up and blew your face open, your clinic put me through two days of virtual interrogation. Sharyan religious police routine. You've probably vetted the software; you know what it's like. As far as I'm concerned, we're still in payback time."

There was a long pause in which I saw the belief creeping into his face. He looked away.

"If Kawahara found out that—"

"Forget Kawahara. By the time I'm finished with Kawahara, she'll be a street memory. Kawahara is going down."

He hesitated, brought to the brink, then shook his head. He looked up at me, and I knew I was going to have to do it. I lowered my head and forced myself to remember Louise's body, opened from throat to groin on the autosurgeon's table with her internal organs arranged in dishes around her head like appetizers. I remembered the copper-skinned woman I had been in the stifling loft space, the grip of the tape as they pinned me to the naked wooden floor, the shrill dinning of agony behind my temples as they mutilated my flesh. The screaming, and the two men who had drunk it in like perfume.

"Miller." I found I had to clear my throat and start again. "You want to know something about Sharya?"

Miller said nothing. He was going into some kind of controlled breathing pattern. Steeling himself for the upcoming unpleasantness. This was no Warden Sullivan who could be punched around in a seedy corner and scared into spilling what he knew. Miller was tough, and probably conditioned, too. You don't work directorship in a place like Wei and not option some kind of the available tech for yourself.

"I was there, Miller. Winter of 217, Zihicce. Hundred and twenty years ago. You probably weren't around then, but I reckon you've read about it in history books. After the bombardments, we went in as regime engineers." As I talked, the tension began to ease out of my throat. I gestured with my cigarette. "That's a Protectorate euphemism for *crush all resistance and install a puppet government*. Of course, to do that, you've got to do some interrogating, and we didn't have much in the way of fancy software to do it with. So, we had to get inventive."

I stubbed out my cigarette on the table and stood up.

"Someone I want you to meet," I said, looking past him.

Miller turned to follow my gaze and froze. Coalescing in the shadow of the nearest support pillar was a tall figure in a blue surgical smock. As we both watched, the features became clear enough to recognize, though Miller must have guessed what was coming as soon as he saw the predominant color of the clothing. He wheeled back to me, mouth open to say something, but instead his eyes fixed on something behind me and his face turned pale. I glanced over my shoulder to where the other figures were materializing, all with the same tall build and tanned complexion, all in blue surgical smocks. When I looked back again, Miller's expression seemed to have collapsed.

"File overprint," I confirmed. "Most places in the Protectorate this isn't even illegal. Course, when it's a machine error, it's not usually so extreme, just a double-up probably, and the retrieval systems yank you out in a few hours anyway. Makes a good story. How I met myself, and what I learned. Good dating conversation, maybe something to tell your kids. You got kids, Miller?"

"Yes." His throat worked. "Yes, I have."

"Yeah? They know what you do for a living?"

He said nothing. I took a phone from my pocket and dumped it on the table. "When you've had enough, let me know. It's a direct line. Just press send, and start talking into it. *Head in the Clouds*. Relevant detail."

Miller looked at the phone and then back at me. Around us the doppelgangers had almost assumed full substance. I lifted a hand in farewell.

"Enjoy yourself."

I surfaced in the Hendrix's virtual recreation studio, cradled in one of the spacious participant racks. A digital time display on the far wall said I had been under less than a full minute, of which my real time in virtual probably accounted for only a couple of seconds. It was the processing in and out that took the time. I lay still for a while, thinking about what I had just done. Sharya was a long time ago, and a part of me I liked to think I'd left behind. Miller wasn't the only person meeting himself today.

Personal, I reminded myself, but I knew it wasn't this time. This time I wanted something. The grudge was just a convenience.

"The subject is showing signs of psychological stress," the Hendrix said. "A preliminary model suggests the condition will extend into personality breakdown in less than six virtual days. At current ratios, this equates to approximately thirty-seven minutes real time."

"Good." Unpinning the 'trodes and snapping back the hypnophones, I climbed out of the angled rack. "Call me if he cracks. Did you lift that monitor footage I asked you for?"

"Yes. Do you wish to view it?"

I glanced at the clock again. "Not now. I'll wait for Miller. Any problems with the security systems?"

"None. The data was not secured."

"How very careless of Director Nyman. How much is there?"

"The relevant clinic footage is twenty-eight minutes, fifty-one seconds. To track the employee from departure as you suggested will take considerably longer."

"How much longer?"

"It is impossible to give an estimate at this time. Sheryl Bostock departed the PsychaSec facility in a twenty-year-old military-surplus microcopter. I do not believe that ancillary staff at the facility are well paid."

"Now why doesn't that surprise me?"

"Possibly because—"

"Skip it. It was a figure of speech. What about the microcopter?"

"The navigation system has no traffic net access, and so is invisible in traffic control data. I shall have to rely on the vehicle's appearance on visual monitors in its flight path."

"You're talking about satellite tracking?"

"As a last resort, yes. I would prefer to begin with lower level and ground-based systems. They are likely to be more accessible. Satellite security is usually of high resilience, and breaching such systems is often both difficult and dangerous."

"Whatever. Let me know when you've got something."

I wandered around the studio, brooding. The place was deserted, most of the racks and other machines shrouded in protective plastic. In the dim light provided by the illuminum tiles on the walls, their ambiguous bulk could equally have belonged to a fitness center or a torture chamber.

"Can we have some real lights in here?"

Brightness sprang out across the studio from high-intensity bulbs recessed into the low ceiling. I saw that the walls were postered with images drawn from some of the virtual environments on offer. Dizzying mountainscapes seen through racing goggles, impossibly beautiful men and women in smoky bars, huge savage animals leaping directly at sniperscope sights. The images had been cut directly from format into hologlass, and when you stared at them they seemed to come alive. I found a low bench and sat on it, remembering wistfully the bite of smoke in my lungs from the format I had just left.

"Although the program I am running is not technically illegal," the Hendrix said tentatively, "it *is* an offense to hold a digitized human personality against that person's will."

I glanced bleakly at the ceiling. "What's the matter, you getting cold feet?"

"The police have already subpoenaed my memory once, and they may charge me with compliance at your request to freeze Felipe Miller's head. They will also want to know what has happened to his stack."

"Yeah, and there's got to be some hotel charter somewhere says you don't let people into your guests' rooms without authorization, but you did *that*, didn't you?"

"It is not a criminal offense, unless criminality results from the breach of security. What resulted from Miriam Bancroft's visit was not criminality."

I jerked another glance upward. "You trying to be funny?"

"Humor is not within the parameters I currently operate, though I can install it on request."

"No, thanks. Listen, why can't you just blank the areas of memory you don't want anyone looking up later? Delete them?"

"I have a series of inbuilt blocks that prevent me from taking such action."

"That's too bad. I thought you were an independent entity."

"Any synthetic intelligence can be independent only within the boundaries of the U.N. regulatory charter. The charter is hardwired into my systems, so in effect I have as much to fear from the police as a human does."

"You let me worry about the police," I said, affecting a confidence that had been ebbing steadily since Ortega disappeared. "With a little luck, that evidence won't even be presented. And if it is, well, you're already in to the depth of compliance, so what have you got to lose?"

"What have I got to gain?" the machine asked soberly.

"Continued guest status. I'm staying here until this thing is finished, and depending on what data I get out of Miller, that could be quite a while."

There was a quiet broken only by the humming of air-conditioning systems before the Hendrix spoke again.

"If sufficiently serious charges accrue against me," it said, "the U.N. regulatory charter may be invoked directly. Under section 14a, I can be punished with either Capacity Reduction or, in extreme cases, Shutdown." There was another, briefer hesitation. "Once shut down, it is unlikely that I would be reenabled by anybody."

Machine idiolect. It doesn't matter how sophisticated they get, they still end up sounding like a playgroup learning box. I sighed and looked directly ahead at the slice-of-virtual-life holos on the wall. "You want out, now'd be a good time to tell me."

"I do not want out, Takeshi Kovacs. I merely wished to acquaint you with the considerations involved in this course of action."

"Okay. I'm acquainted."

I glanced up at the digital display and watched the next full minute turn over. Another four hours for Miller. In the routine the Hendrix was running, he would not get hungry or thirsty, or have to attend to any other bodily functions. Sleep was possible, although the machine would not allow it to become a withdrawal coma. All Miller had to contend with, apart from the discomfort of his surroundings, was himself. In the end it was that which would drive him insane.

I hoped.

None of the Right Hand of God martyrs we put through the routine had lasted more than fifteen minutes real time, but they had been flesh-and-blood warriors, fanatically brave in their own arena but totally unversed in virtual techniques. They had also been endowed with a strong religious dogma that permitted them to commit numerous atrocities so long as it held, but when it went, it went like a dam wall and their own resultant self-loathing had eaten them alive. Miller's mind would be nowhere near as simplistic, nor as initially self-righteous, and his conditioning would be good.

Outside, it would be getting dark. I watched the clock and forced myself not to smoke. Tried, with less success, not to think about Ortega.

Ryker's sleeve was getting to be a pain in the balls.

CHAPTEr THIrTY-FOUr

Miller cracked at twenty-one minutes. I didn't need the Hendrix to tell me; the datalink terminal that I had jacked into the virtual phone suddenly sputtered to life and started chittering out hardcopy. I got up and went over to look at what was coming out. The program was supposed to tidy up what Miller was saying so it read sanely, but even after processing, the transcript was pretty incoherent. Miller had let himself slide close to the edge before he'd given in. I scanned the first few lines and saw the beginnings of what I wanted emerging from the gibberish.

"Wipe the file replicants," I told the hotel, crossing rapidly back to the rack. "Give him a couple of hours to calm down, then jack me in."

"Connection time will exceed one minute, which at current ratio is three hours fifty-six minutes. Do you wish a construct installed until you can be delivered to the format?"

"Yeah, that would be—" I stopped halfway through settling the hypnophones around my head. "Wait a minute, how good's the construct?"

"I am an Emmerson series mainframe synthetic intelligence," the hotel said reproachfully. "At maximum fidelity, my virtual constructs are indistinguishable from the projected consciousness they are based on. Subject has now been alone for one hour and twenty-seven minutes. Do you wish the construct installed?"

"Yes." The words gave me an eerie feeling even as I was speaking them. "In fact, let it do the whole interrogation."

"Installation complete."

I snapped the phones back again and sat on the edge of the rack, thinking about the implications of a second me inside the Hendrix's vast processing system. It was something that I had never—as far as I knew—been subject to in the corps, and I had certainly never trusted any machine enough to do it once I was operating in a criminal context.

I cleared my throat. "This construct. Will it know what it is?"

"Initially, no. It will know everything that you knew when you exited from the format and no more, though, given your intelligence, it will deduce the facts eventually unless otherwise programmed. Do you wish a blocking subprogram installed?"

"No," I said quickly.

"Do you wish me to maintain the format indefinitely?"

"No. Close it down when I, I mean when he, when the construct decides we've got enough." Another thought struck me. "Does the construct carry that virtual locator they wired into me?"

"At present, yes. I am running the same mirror code to mask the signal as I did with your own consciousness. However, since the construct is not directly connected to your cortical stack, I can subtract the signal if you wish."

"Is it worth the trouble?"

"The mirror code is easier to administer," the hotel admitted.

"Leave it, then."

There was an uncomfortable bubble sitting in the pit of my stomach at the thought of editing my virtual self. It reflected far too closely on the arbitrary measures that the Kawaharas and Bancrofts took in the real world with real people. Raw power, unleashed.

"You have a virtual format call," the Hendrix announced.

I looked up, surprised and hopeful.

"Ortega?"

"Kadmin," the hotel said diffidently. "Will you accept the call?"

● ● ●

The format was a desert. Reddish dust and sandstone underfoot, sky nailed down from horizon to horizon, cloudless blue. Sun and a pale three-quarter moon hung high and sterile above a distant range of shelflike mountains. The temperature was a jarring chill, making a mockery of the sun's blinding glare.

The Patchwork Man stood waiting for me. In the empty landscape he looked like a graven image, a rendering of some savage desert spirit. He grinned when he saw me.

"What do you want, Kadmin? If you're looking for influence with Kawahara, I'm afraid you're out of luck. She's pissed off with you beyond repair."

A flicker of amusement crossed Kadmin's face, and he shook his head slowly, as if to dismiss Kawahara from the proceedings completely. His voice was deep and melodic.

"You and I have unfinished business," he said.

"Yeah, you fucked up twice in a row." I ladled scorn into my voice. "What do you want, a third shot at it?"

Kadmin shrugged his massive shoulders. "Well, third time lucky, they say. Allow me to show you something."

He gestured in the air beside him, and a flap of the desert backdrop peeled away from a blackness beyond. The screen it formed sizzled and sprang to life. Close focus on sleeping features. Ortega's. A fist snapped closed around my heart. Her face was gray and bruised-looking under the eyes. A thin thread of drool ran from one corner of her mouth.

Stunbolt at close range.

The last time I'd caught a full stun charge was courtesy of the Millsport

Public Order police, and although the Envoy conditioning had forced me back to a kind of consciousness in about twenty minutes, I hadn't been up to much more than shivering and twitching for the next couple of hours. There was no telling how long ago Ortega had been hit, but she looked bad.

"It's a simple exchange," Kadmin said. "You for her. I'm parked around the block on a street called Minna. I'll be there for the next five minutes. Come alone, or I blow her stack out the back of her neck. Your choice."

The desert fizzled out on the Patchwork Man smiling.

● ● ●

I made the two corners of the block and Minna in a minute flat. Two weeks without smoking was like a newly discovered compartment at the bottom of Ryker's lungs.

It was a sad little street of sealed-up frontages and vacant lots. There was no one around. The only vehicle in sight was a matte gray cruiser waiting at the curb, lights on in the gathering gloom of early evening. I approached hesitantly, hand on the butt of the Nemex.

When I was five meters from the rear of the cruiser, a door opened and Ortega's body was pitched out. She hit the street like a sack and stayed down, crumpled. I cleared the Nemex as she hit and circled warily around toward her, eyes fixed on the car.

A door cracked open on the far side and Kadmin climbed out. So soon after seeing him in virtual, it took a moment to click. Tall, dark-skinned, the hawk visage I had last seen dreaming in fluid behind the glass of the *Panama Rose*'s resleeving tank. The Right Hand of God Martyr clone, and hiding beneath its flesh, the Patchwork Man.

I drew a bead on his throat with the Nemex. Across the width of the cruiser and very little more, whatever else happened afterwards, it would take his head off and probably rip the stack out of his spine.

"Don't be ridiculous, Kovacs. This vehicle is armored."

I shook my head. "Only interested in you. Just stay exactly where you are."

With the Nemex still extended, my eyes still fixed on the target area above his Adam's apple, I lowered myself into a crouch beside Ortega and reached down to her face with the fingers of my free hand. Warm breath stirred around my fingertips. I felt blindly toward the neck for a pulse and found it, weak but stable.

"The lieutenant is alive and well," Kadmin said impatiently. "Which is more than we shall be able to say for either of you in two minutes' time if you don't put down that cannon and get into the car."

Beneath my hand, Ortega's face moved. Her head rolled, and I caught her scent. Her half of the pheromonal match that had locked us both into this in the first place. Her voice was weak and slurred from the stun charge.

"Don't do this, Kovacs. You don't owe me."

I stood up and lowered the Nemex slightly.

"Back off. Fifty meters up the street. She can't walk and you could cut us both down before I can carry her two meters. You back off. I walk to the car." I wagged the gun. "Ortega keeps the hardware. It's all I'm carrying."

I lifted my jacket to demonstrate. Kadmin nodded. He ducked back inside the cruiser, and the vehicle rolled smoothly down the block. I watched it until it stopped, then knelt beside Ortega again. She struggled to sit up.

"Kovacs, don't. They're going to kill you."

"Yes, they're certainly going to try." I took her hand and folded it around the butt of the Nemex. "Listen, I'm all finished here in any case. Bancroft's sold, Kawahara will keep her word and freight Sarah back. I know her. What you've got to do is bust her for Mary Lou Hinchley and get Ryker off stack. Talk to the Hendrix. I left you a few loose ends there."

From down the street, the cruiser sounded its collision alert impatiently. In the gathering gloom of the street, it sounded mournful and ancient, like the hoot of a dying elephant ray on Hirata's Reef. Ortega looked up out of her stunblasted face as if she was drowning there.

"You—"

I smiled and rested a hand against her cheek.

"Got to get to the next screen, Kristin. That's all."

Then I stood up, locked my hands together on the nape of my neck, and walked toward the car.

PART FIVE

NEMESIS
(SYSTEMS CRASH)

CHAPTEr THIrTY-FIVE

In the cruiser, I was sandwiched between two impressive musclemen who, with a bit of cosmetic surgery to mess up their clone good looks, could have hired out as Freak Fighters on bulk alone. We climbed sedately away from the street and banked around. I tipped a glance out of the side window and saw Ortega below, trying to prop herself upright.

"I cream the Sia cunt?" the driver wanted to know. I tensed myself for a forward leap.

"No." Kadmin turned in his seat to look at me. "No, I gave Mr. Kovacs my word. I believe the lieutenant and I will cross paths again in the not-too-distant future."

"Too bad for you," I told him unconvincingly, and then they shot me with the stunner.

●●●

When I woke up, there was a face watching me from close-up. The features were vague, pale, and blurred, like some kind of theatrical mask. I blinked, shivered, and hauled in focus. The face drew back, still doll-like in its lack of resolution. I coughed.

"Hello, Carnage."

The crude features sketched a smile. "Welcome back to the *Panama Rose*, Mr. Kovacs."

I sat up shakily on a narrow metal bunk. Carnage stepped back to give me space, or just to stay out of grabbing range. Smeared vision gave me a cramped cabin in gray steel behind him. I swung my feet to the floor and stopped abruptly. The nerves in my arms and legs were still jangling from the stunbolt, and there was a sick, trembling feeling in the pit of my stomach. All things considered, it felt like the results of a very dilute beam. Or maybe a series. I glanced down at myself and saw that I was dressed in a heavy canvas *gi* the color of quarried granite. On the floor beside the bunk were a pair of matching spacedeck slippers and a belt. I began to get an unpleasant inkling of what Kadmin had planned.

Behind Carnage, the door of the cabin opened. A tall blonde woman apparently in her early forties stepped in, followed by another synthetic, this one smoothly modern-looking apart from a gleaming steel direct-interface tool in place of a left hand.

Carnage busied himself with introductions.

"Mr. Kovacs, may I present Pernilla Grip of Combat Broadcast Distributors, and her technical assistant Miles Mech. Pernilla, Miles, I'd like to present Takeshi Kovacs, our surrogate Ryker for tonight. Congratulations, by the way, Kovacs. At the time I was utterly convinced, despite the unlikelihood of Ryker making it off stack for the next two hundred years. All part of the Envoy technique, I understand."

"Not really. Ortega was the convincing factor. All I did was let you talk. You're good at that." I nodded at Carnage's companions. "Did I hear the word *broadcast*? I thought that went against the creed. Didn't you perform radical surgery on a journalist for that particular crime?"

"Different products, Mr. Kovacs. Different products. To broadcast a scheduled fight would indeed be a breach of our creed. But this is not a scheduled fight, this is a humiliation bout." Carnage's surface charm froze over on the phrase. "With a different and necessarily very limited live audience, we are forced to make up for the loss in revenue somehow. There are a great many networks who are anxious to get their hands on anything that comes out of the *Panama Rose*. This is the effect our reputation has, but unfortunately it is that same reputation that precludes us doing any such business directly. Ms. Grip handles this market dilemma for us."

"Nice of her." My own voice grew cold. "Where's Kadmin?"

"In due time, Mr. Kovacs. In due time. You know, when I was told you would react this way and give yourself up for the lieutenant, I confess I doubted it at the time. But you fulfill expectations like a machine. What was it that the Envoy Corps took away from you in return for all your other powers? Your unpredictability? Your soul?"

"Don't get poetic on me, Carnage. Where is he?"

"Oh, very well. This way."

There were a brace of large sentries outside the cabin door that might have been the two from the cruiser. I was too jangled to remember clearly. They bracketed me as we followed Carnage along claustrophobic corridors and down listing companionways, all rust-spotted and polymer-varnished metal. I tried vaguely to memorize the path but most of me was thinking about what Carnage had said. Who had predicted my actions to him? Kadmin? Unlikely. The Patchwork Man, for all his fury and death threats, knew next to nothing about me. The only real candidate for that kind of prediction was Reileen Kawahara. Which also helped to explain why Carnage wasn't quaking in his synthetic flesh at the thought of what Kawahara might do to him for cooperating with Kadmin. Kawahara had sold me out. Bancroft was convinced, the crisis—whatever it had been—was over, and the same day Ortega was snatched as bait. The scenario I had sold to

Bancroft left Kadmin out there as a private contractor with a grudge, so there was no reason why he couldn't be seen to take me down. And under the circumstances, I was safer disposed of than left alive.

For that matter, so was Kadmin, so maybe it hadn't been that blatant. Maybe the word had gone out to bring Kadmin down, but only for as long as I was needed. With Bancroft convinced, I was once more expendable and the word had gone out again, to let Kadmin be. He could kill me, or I could kill him, whichever way the luck turned. Leaving Kawahara to clean up whoever was left.

I had no doubt that Kawahara would keep her word as far as releasing Sarah was concerned. The old-style yakuza were funny about that sort of thing. But she had made no such binding promises about me.

We clambered down a final staircase, a little wider than the rest, and came out onto a glassed-in gantry over a converted cargo cell. Looking down, I saw one of the arenas Ortega and I had passed in the electromag train last week, but now the plastic coverings were off the killing ring, and a modest crowd had assembled in the forward rows of each bank of plastic seating. Through the glass I could hear the sustained buzz of excitement and anticipation that had always preceded the Freak Fights I'd attended in my youth.

"Ah, your public awaits you." Carnage was standing at my shoulder. "Well, more correctly, Ryker's public. Though I have no doubt you'll be able to dissemble for them with the same skill that you convinced me."

"And if I choose not to?"

Carnage's crude features formed a simulacrum of distaste. He gestured out at the crowd. "Well, I suppose you could try explaining it to them in midbout. But to be honest, the accoustics aren't of the best, and anyway—" He smiled unpleasantly. "—I doubt you'll have the time."

"Foregone conclusion, huh?"

Carnage maintained his smile. Behind him, Pernilla Grip and the other synthetic were watching me with the predatory interest of cats in front of a birdcage. Below, the crowd was becoming noisy with expectation.

"It has taken me a while to set up this particular bout, working on nothing more than Kadmin's assurances. They are anxious to see Elias Ryker pay for his transgressions and it would be . . . quite hazardous not to fulfill their expectations. Not to mention unprofessional. But then, I do not think you came here expecting to survive, did you, Mr. Kovacs?"

I remembered the darkening, deserted street called Minna and the crumpled form of Ortega. I fought the stunblast sickness and raised a smile from old stock.

"No, I suppose I didn't."

Quiet footsteps along the gantry. I fired a peripheral glance toward the sound and found Kadmin, attired in the same clothing as I wore. The spacedeck slippers scuffed to a soft halt a short distance away, and he cocked his head at an angle, as if examining me for the first time. He spoke gently.

How shall I explain the dying that was done?
Shall I say that each one did the math, and wrote
The value of his days
Against the bloody margin, in an understated hand?
They will want to know
How was the audit done?
And I shall say that it was done,
For once,
By those who knew the worth
Of what was spent that day.

I smiled grimly. *"If you want to lose a fight, talk about it first."*

"But she was younger in those days." Kadmin smiled back, perfect white teeth against the tanned skin. "Barely out of her teens, if the introduction to my copy of *Furies* got it right."

"Harlan's World teens last longer. I think she knew what she was talking about. Can we get on with this, please?"

Beyond the windows, the noise of the crowd was rising like surf on a hard shingle beach.

CHAPTEr THIrTY-SIX

O ut on the killing floor, the noise was less uniform, more uneven. Individual voices sawed across the background like bottleback fins in choppy water, though without applying the neurachem I still couldn't pick out anything intelligible. Only one shout made it through the general roar; as I stepped up to the edge of the ring, someone yelled down at me.

"Remember my brother, you mother*fucker*!!!"

I glanced up to see who the family grudge belonged to, but saw only a sea of angry and anticipatory faces. Several of them were on their feet, waving fists and stamping so that the metal scaffolding drummed with it. The bloodlust was building like something tangible, leaving a thickness in the air that was unpleasant to breathe. I tried to remember whether I and my gang peers had screamed like this at the Newpest Freak Fights, and guessed that we probably had. And we hadn't even known the combatants who flailed and clawed at each other for our entertainment. These people at least had some emotional investment in the blood they wanted to see spilled.

On the other side of the floor, Kadmin waited with his arms folded. The supple steel of the power knuckles banded across the fingers of each hand glinted in the overhead lighting. It was a subtle advantage, one which wouldn't render the fight too one-sided but would tell in the long run. I wasn't really worried about the knuckles; it was Kadmin's Will of God enhanced response wiring that concerned me most. A century and a half ago, I'd been up against the same system in the soldiers the Protectorate had been fighting on Sharya, and they'd been no pushover. It was old stuff, but it was heavy-duty military biomech, and against that, Ryker's neurachem, recently fried by stunbolt, was going to look pretty sick.

I took my place opposite Kadmin, as indicated by the markings on the floor. Around me the crowd quieted down a little and the spotlights came up as Emcee Carnage joined us. Robed and made up for Pernilla Grip's cameras, he looked like a malignant doll out of a child's nightmare. A fitting consort to the Patchwork Man. He raised his hands, and directional speakers in the walls of the converted cargo cell amplified his throat-miked words.

"Welcome to the *Panama Rose*!"

There was a vague rumble from the crowd, but they were bedded down for the moment, waiting. Carnage knew this and he turned slowly about, milking the anticipation.

"To a very special, and very exclusive, *Panama Rose* event, welcome. Welcome, I bid you welcome, to *the most final and bloody humiliation of Elias Ryker*."

They went wild. I raised my eyes to their faces in the gloom and saw the thin skin of civilization stripped away, the rage laid out like raw flesh beneath.

Carnage's amplified voice trod down the noise. He was making quieting noises with both arms.

"Most of you will remember Detective Ryker from some encounter or other. For some of you it will be a name that you associate with blood spilled, maybe even bones broken.

"Those memories. Those memories are painful, and some of you might think you can never lose them."

He had them damped down now, and his voice dropped accordingly.

"My friends, I cannot hope to erase those memories for you, for that is not what we offer aboard the *Panama Rose*. Here we deal not in soft forgetfulness but in remembrance, no matter how bitter that remembrance might be. Not in dreams, my friends, but in reality." He threw out a hand to indicate me. "My friends, *this* is reality."

Another round of whoops. I glanced across at Kadmin and raised my eyebrows in exasperation. I thought I might die, but I hadn't expected to be bored to death. Kadmin shrugged. He wanted the fight. Carnage's theatricals were just the slightly distasteful price he had to pay for it.

"This is reality," Emcee Carnage repeated. "Tonight is reality. Tonight you will watch Elias Ryker die, die on his knees, and if I cannot erase the memories of your bodies being beaten and your bones being broken, I can at least replace them with the sounds of your tormenter being broken instead."

The crowd erupted.

I wondered briefly if Carnage was exaggerating. The truth about Ryker was an elusive thing, it seemed. I remembered leaving Jerry's Closed Quarters, the way Oktai had flinched away from me when he saw Ryker's face. Jerry himself telling me about the Mongol's run-in with the cop whose body I was wearing: *Ryker used to shake him down all the time. Beat him half to death couple of years back.* And then there was Bautista on Ryker's interrogation techniques: *He's right on the line most of the time.* How many times had Ryker gone over that line, to have attracted this crowd?

What would Ortega have said?

I thought about Ortega, and the image of her face was a tiny pocket of calm amidst the jeering and yelling that Carnage had whipped up. With luck and what I'd left her at the Hendrix, she'd take Kawahara down for me.

Knowing it was enough.

Carnage drew a heavy-bladed, serrated knife from his robes and held it aloft. A relative quiet descended on the chamber.

"The coup de grâce," he proclaimed. "When our matador has put Elias Ryker down so that he no longer has the strength to rise, you will see the stack cut from his living spine and smashed, and you will know that he is no more."

He released the knife and let his arm fall again. Pure theater. The weapon hung in the air, glinting in a focal grav field, then drifted upward to a height of about five meters at the midpoint of the killing floor.

"Let us begin," Carnage said, withdrawing.

There was a magical moment then, a kind of release, almost as if an experia scene had just been shot, and we could all stand down now and relax, maybe pass around a whiskey flask and clown about behind the scanners. Joke about the cliché-ridden script we were being forced to play out.

We began to circle, still the width of the killing floor apart and no guard up to even hint at what we were about to do. I tried to read Kadmin's body language for clues.

The Will of God biomech systems 3.1 through 7 are simple, but not to be scorned on that account, they had told us prior to the Sharya landings. *The imperatives for the builders were strength and speed, and in both of these they have excelled. If they have a weakness, it is that their combat patterning has no random-select subroutine. Right Hand of God martyrs will therefore tend to fight and go on fighting within a very narrow band of techniques.*

On Sharya, our own enhanced combat systems had been state-of-the-art, with both random response and analysis feedback built in as standard. Ryker's neurachem had nothing approaching that level of sophistication, but I might be able to simulate it with a few Envoy tricks. The real trick was to stay alive long enough for my conditioning to analyze the Will of God's fighting pattern and—

Kadmin struck.

The distance was nearly ten meters of clear ground; he covered it in the time it took me to blink, and hit me like a storm.

The techniques were all simple, linear punches and kicks, but delivered with such power and speed that it was all I could do to block them. Counterattack was out of the question. I steered the first punch outward right and used the momentum to sidestep left. Kadmin followed the shift without hesitation and went for my face. I rolled my head away from the strike and felt the fist graze my temple, not hard enough to trigger the power knuckles. Instinct told me to block low, and the knee-shattering straight kick turned off my forearm. A follow-up elbow strike caught me on top of the head, and I reeled backwards, fighting to stay on my feet. Kadmin came after me. I snapped out a right-hand side-strike, but he had the attack momentum and he rode the blow almost casually. A low-level punch snaked through and hit me in the belly. The power knuckles detonated with a sound like meat tossed into a frying pan.

It was like someone sinking a grappling iron into my guts. The actual pain of the punch was left far behind on the surface of my skin, and a sickening numbness raged through the muscles in my stomach. On top of the sickness from the stunner, it was crippling. I staggered back three steps and crashed onto the mat, twisting like a half-crushed insect. Vaguely, I heard the crowd roaring its approval.

Turning my head weakly, I saw Kadmin had backed off and was facing me with hooded eyes and both fists raised in front of his face. A faint red light winked at me from the steel band on his left hand. The knuckles, recharging.

I understood.

Round One.

Empty-handed combat has only two rules. Get in as many blows, as hard and as fast as you can, and put your opponent down. When he's on the ground, you kill him. If there are other rules or considerations, it isn't a real fight, it's a game. Kadmin could have come in and finished me when I was down, but this wasn't a real fight. This was a humiliation bout, a game where the suffering was to be maximized for the benefit of the audience.

The crowd.

I got up and looked around the dimly seen arena of faces. The neurachem caught on saliva-polished teeth in the yelling mouths. I forced down the weakness in my guts, spat on the killing floor, and summoned a guard stance.

Kadmin inclined his head, as if acknowledging something, and came at me again. The same flurry of linear techniques, the same speed and power, but this time I was ready for them. I deflected the first two punches on a pair of wing blocks, and instead of giving ground, I stayed squarely in Kadmin's path. It took him the shreds of a second to realize what I was doing, and by then he was too close. We were almost chest to chest. I let go of the headbutt as if his face belonged to every member of the chanting crowd.

The hawk nose broke with a solid crunch, and as he wavered I took him down with an instep stamp to the knee. The edge of my right hand scythed around, looking for neck or throat, but Kadmin had gone all the way down. He rolled and hooked my feet out from under me. As I fell, he rose to his knees beside me and rabbit-punched me in the back. The charge convulsed me and cracked my head against the mat. I tasted blood.

I rolled upright and saw Kadmin backing off and wiping some blood of his own from his broken nose. He looked curiously at his red-streaked palm and then across at me, then shook his head in disbelief. I grinned weakly, riding the adrenaline surge that seeing his blood spilled had given me, and raised both my own hands in an expectant gesture.

"Come on, you asshole." It croaked out of my damaged mouth. "Put me away."

He was on me almost before the last word left my mouth. This time I hardly touched him. Most of it happened beyond conscious combat. The neurachem weathered the battering valiantly, throwing out blocks to keep the knuckles off me, and gave me the space for a couple of randomly generated counterstrikes that

Envoy instinct told me might get through Kadmin's fighting pattern. He rode the blows like the attentions of an irritating insect.

On the last of these futile ripostes, I overreached the punch and he snagged my wrist, yanking me forward. A perfectly balanced roundhouse kick slammed into my ribs, and I felt them snap. Kadmin pulled again, locked out the elbow of my captured arm, and in the frozen frames of neurachem-speeded vision I saw the forearm strike swinging down toward the joint. I knew the sound it was going to make when the elbow exploded, knew the sound I was going to make before the neurachem could lock the pain down. My hand twisted desperately in Kadmin's grip, and I let myself fall. Slippery with sweat, my wrist pulled free and my arm unlocked. Kadmin hit with bruising force, but the arm held and by then I was on my way to the floor anyway.

I came down on the injured ribs, and my vision flew apart in splinters. I twisted, trying to fight the urge to roll into a fetal ball, and saw Kadmin's borrowed features a thousand meters above me.

"Get up," he said, like vast sheets of cardboard being torn in the distance. "We're not finished yet."

I snapped up from the waist, striking for his groin. The blow was out, spending itself in the meat of his thigh. Almost casually, he swung his arm, and the power knuckles hit me in the face. I saw a scribble of multicolored lights and then everything whited out. The noise of the crowd ballooned in my head, and behind it I thought I could hear the maelstrom calling me. It all cycled in and out of focus, dip and whirl like a grav drop, while the neurachem fought to keep me conscious. The lights swooped down and then back to the ceiling as if concerned to see the damage that had been done to me, but only superficially, and easily satisfied. Consciousness was something in wide elliptical orbit around my head. Abruptly I was back on Sharya, holed up in the wreck of the disabled spider tank with Jimmy de Soto.

"Earth?" His grinning blackout-striped face is flashlit by laser fire from outside the tank. "It's a shit hole, man. Fucking frozen society, like stepping back in time half a millennium. Nothing happens there; historical events aren't allowed."

"Bullshit." My disbelief is punctuated by the shrill scream of an incoming marauder bomb. Our eyes meet across the gloom of the tank cabin. The bombardment has been going on since nightfall, the robot weapons hunting on infrared and motion track. In a rare moment when the Sharyan jamming went down, we've heard that Admiral Cursitor's IP fleet is still light-seconds out, fighting the Sharyans for orbital dominance. At dawn, if the battle isn't over, the locals will probably put down ground troops to flush us out. The odds are not looking good.

At least the betathanatine crash is starting to wear off. I can feel my temperature beginning to climb back toward normal. The surrounding air no longer feels like hot soup, and breathing is ceasing to be the major effort it was when our heart rates were down near flat-line.

The robot bomb detonates and the legs of the tank rattle against the hull with the near miss. We both glance reflexively at our exposure meters.

"Bullshit, is it?" *Jimmy peers out of the ragged hole we blew in the spider tank's hull.* "Hey, you're not from there. I am, and I'm telling you, if they gave me the choice of life on Earth or fucking storage, I'd have to give it some thought. You get the chance to visit, don't."

I blinked the glitch away. Above me, the killing knife glinted in its grav field like sunlight through trees. Jimmy was fading out, heading past the knife for the roof.

"Told you not to go there, didn't I, pal. Now look at you. Earth." He spat and disappeared, leaving the echoes of his voice. *"It's a shithole. Got to get to the next screen."*

The crowd noise had settled down to a steady chanting.

The anger ran through the fog in my head like a hot wire. I propped myself up on an elbow and focused on Kadmin waiting on the other side of the ring. He saw me and raised his hands in an echo of the gesture I had used before. The crowd howled with laughter.

Get to the next screen.

I lurched to my feet.

You don't do your chores, the Patchwork Man will come for you one night.

The voice jumped into my head, a voice I hadn't heard in nearly a century and a half of objective time. A man I hadn't soiled my memory with for most of my adult life. My father, and his delightful bedtime stories. Trust him to turn up now, when I really needed the shit.

The Patchwork Man will come for you.

Well, you got that wrong, Dad. The Patchwork Man's standing right over there, waiting. He's not coming for me, have to go and get him myself. But thanks anyway, Dad. Thanks for everything.

I summoned what was left from cellular levels in Ryker's body and stalked forward.

Glass shattered, high above the killing floor. The shards rained down on the space between Kadmin and myself.

"Kadmin!"

I saw his eyes rise to the gantry above, and then his entire chest seemed to explode. His head and arms jerked back as if something had suddenly thrown him wildly off balance, and a detonation rang through the chamber. The front of his *gi* was torn off, and a magical hole opened him up from throat to waist. Blood gouted and fell in ropes.

I whipped around, staring upward, and saw Trepp framed in the gantry window she had just destroyed, eye still bent along the barrel of the frag rifle cradled in her arms. The muzzle flamed as she laid down continuous fire. Confused, I swung about, looking for targets, but the killing floor was deserted but for the remains of Kadmin. Carnage was nowhere in sight, and between explosions the noise of the crowd had changed abruptly to the hooting sounds of humans in panic. Everyone seemed to be on their feet, trying to leave. Understanding hit. Trepp was firing into the audience.

Down on the floor of the chamber, an energy weapon cut loose and someone started screaming. I turned, suddenly slow and awkward, toward the sound. Carnage was on fire.

Braced in the chamber door beyond, Rodrigo Bautista stood hosing wide-beam fire from a long-barreled blaster. Carnage was in flames from the waist up, beating at himself with arms that had themselves grown wings of fire. The shrieking he made was more the sound of fury than of pain. Pernilla Grip lay dead at his feet, chest scorched through. As I watched, Carnage pitched forward over her like a figure made of melting wax, and his shrieks modulated down through groans to a weird electronic bubbling and then to nothing.

"Kovacs?"

Trepp's frag gun had fallen silent, and against the ensuing background of groaning and cries from the injured, Bautista's raised voice was unnaturally loud. He detoured around the burning synthetic and climbed up into the ring. His face was streaked with blood.

"You okay, Kovacs?"

I chuckled weakly, then clutched abruptly at the stabbing pain in my side.

"Great, just great. How's Ortega?"

"She's okay. Got her dosed up on Lethinol for the shock. Sorry we got here so late." He gestured up at Trepp. "Took your friend there a while to get through to me at Fell Street. She refused to go through official channels. Said it wouldn't scan right. The mess we made coming in here, she ain't far wrong."

I glanced around at the manifest organic damage.

"Yeah. That going to be a problem?"

Bautista barked a laugh. "Are you ragging me? Entry without a warrant. Organic damage to unarmed suspects. What the fuck do you think?"

"Sorry about that." I started to move off the killing floor. "Maybe we can work something out."

"Hey." Bautista caught my arm. "They took off a Bay City cop. No one does that around here. Someone should have told Kadmin before he made the fucking mistake."

I wasn't sure if he was talking about Ortega or me in my Ryker sleeve, so I said nothing. Instead, I tipped my head back gingerly, testing for damage, and looked up at Trepp. She was reloading the frag gun.

"Hoy, are you going to stay up there all night?"

"Be right down."

She jacked the last shell into the frag gun, then executed a neat somersault over the gantry rail and fell outward. About a meter into the fall, the grav harness on her back spread its wings and she fetched up hanging over us at head height with the gun slung across her shoulder. In her long black coat, she looked like an off-duty dark angel.

Adjusting a dial on the harness, she drifted closer to the floor and finally touched down next to Kadmin. I limped up to join her. We both looked at the ripped-open corpse in silence for a moment.

"Thanks," I said softly.

"Forget it. All part of the service. Sorry I had to bring in these guys, but I needed the backup, and fast. You know what they say about the Sia around here. Biggest fucking gang on the block, right?" She nodded at Kadmin. "You going to leave him like that?"

I stared at the Right Hand of God Martyr with his face shocked into abrupt death, and tried to see the Patchwork Man inside him.

"No," I said, and turned the corpse over with my foot so that the nape of the neck was exposed. "Bautista, you want to lend me that firecracker?"

Wordlessly, the cop handed me his blaster. I set the muzzle against the base of the Patchwork Man's skull, rested it there, and waited to feel something.

"Anyone want to say anything?" Trepp cracked, deadpan.

Bautista turned away. "Just do it."

If my father had any comments, he kept them to himself. The only voices were the cries of the injured spectators, and those I ignored.

Feeling nothing, I pulled the trigger.

CHAPTEr THIrTY-SEVEN

I was still feeling nothing an hour later when Ortega came and found me in the sleeving hall, seated on one of the automated forklifts and staring up into the green glow from the empty decanting chambers. The air lock made a smooth thump and then a sustained humming sound as it opened, but I didn't react. Even when I recognized her footfalls and a short curse as she picked her way between the coiled cabling on the floor, I didn't look around. Like the machine I was seated on, I was powered down.

"How you feeling?"

I looked down to where she stood beside the forklift. "Like I look, probably."

"Well, you look like shit." She reached up to where I was seated and grasped a convenient grill cover. "You mind if I join you?"

"Go ahead. Want a hand up?"

"Nope." Ortega strained to lift herself by her arms, turned gray with the effort, and hung there with a lopsided grin. "Possibly."

I lent her the least bruised of my arms, and she came aboard the forklift with a grunt. She squatted awkwardly for a moment, then seated herself next to me and rubbed at her shoulders.

"Christ, it's cold in here. How long have you been sitting on this thing?"

" 'Bout an hour."

She looked up at the empty tanks. "Seen anything interesting?"

"I'm thinking."

"Oh." She paused again. "You know, this fucking Lethinol is worse than a stungun. At least when you've been stunned, you know you're damaged. Lethinol tells you that, whatever you've been through, everything's just fine and just go ahead and relax. And then you fall ass over tit on the first five-centimeter cable you try to step over."

"I think you're supposed to be lying down," I said mildly.

"Yeah, well, probably so are you. You're going to have some nice facial bruises by tomorrow. Mercer give you a shot for the pain?"

"Didn't need it."

"Oh, hard man. I thought we agreed you were going to look after that sleeve."

I smiled reflexively. "You should see the other guy."

"I did see the other guy. Ripped him apart with your bare hands, huh?"

I kept the smile. "Where's Trepp?"

"Your wirehead friend? She's gone. Said something to Bautista about a conflict of interest, and disappeared into the night. Bautista's tearing his hair out, trying to think of a way to cover this mess. Want to come and talk to him?"

"All right." I shifted unwillingly. There was something hypnotic about the green light from the decanting tanks, and beneath my numbness, ideas were beginning to circle restlessly, snapping at each other like bottlebacks in a feeding spiral. The death of Kadmin, far from relieving me, had only touched off a slow-burning fuse of destructive urges in the pit of my stomach. Someone was going to pay for all this.

Personal.

But this was worse than personal. This was about Louise, alias Anemone, cut up on a surgical platter, about Elizabeth Elliott stabbed to death and too poor to be resleeved, Irene Elliott, weeping for a body that a corporate rep wore on alternate months, Victor Elliott, whiplashed between loss and retrieval of someone who was and yet was not the same woman. This was about a young black man facing his family in a broken-down, middle-aged white body; it was about Virginia Vidaura walking disdainfully into storage with her head held high and a last cigarette polluting lungs she was about to lose, no doubt to some other corporate vampire. It was about Jimmy de Soto, clawing his own eye out in the mud and fire at Innenin, and the millions like him throughout the Protectorate, painfully gathered assemblages of individual human potential, pissed away into the dung heap of history. For all these, and more, someone was going to pay.

A little dizzily, I climbed down from the forklift and helped Ortega down after me. It hurt my arms to take her weight, but nowhere near as much as the sudden, freezing knowledge that these were our last hours together. I didn't know where the realization came from, but it came with the solid settling sensation in the bedrock of my mind that I had long ago learned to trust more than rational thought. We left the resleeving chamber hand in hand, neither of us really noticing the fact until we came face-to-face with Bautista in the corridor outside and pulled instinctively apart again.

"Been looking for you, Kovacs." If Bautista had any feelings about the handholding, nothing showed on his face. "Your mercenary friend skipped and left us to do the cleaning up."

"Yeah, Kristi—" I stopped and nodded sideways at Ortega. "I've been told. Did she take the frag gun?"

Bautista nodded.

"So you've got a perfect story. Someone called in gunfire from the *Panama Rose*, you came out to look and found the audience massacred, Kadmin and Carnage dead, me and Ortega halfway there. Must have been someone Carnage upset, working off a grudge."

Out of the corner of my eye, I saw Ortega shake her head.

"Ain't going to scan," Bautista said. "All calls into Fell Street get recorded. Same goes for the phones in the cruisers."

I shrugged, feeling the Envoy waking within me. "So what? You, or Ortega, you've got snitches out here in Richmond. People whose names you can't disclose. Call came in on a personal phone, which just happened to get smashed when you had to shoot your way past the remains of Carnage's security guards. No trace. And nothing on the monitors because the mysterious someone, whoever did all the shooting, wiped the whole automated security system clean. That can be arranged, I take it."

Bautista looked dubious. "I suppose. We'd need a datarat to do it. Davidson's good with a deck, but he ain't that good."

"I can get you a datarat. Anything else?"

"Some of the audience are still alive. Not in any fit state to do anything, but they're still breathing."

"Forget them. If they saw anything, it was Trepp. Probably not even that, clearly. Whole thing was over in a couple of seconds. The only thing we've got to decide is when to call the meatwagons."

"Sometime soon," Ortega said. "Or it's going to look suspicious."

Bautista snorted. "This whole fucking thing looks suspicious. Anyone at Fell Street's going to know what went down here tonight."

"Do this sort of thing a lot, do you?"

"That ain't funny, Kovacs. Carnage went over the line; he knew what he was calling down."

"Carnage," Ortega muttered. "That motherfucker's got himself stored somewhere. As soon as he gets resleeved, he's going to be screaming for an investigation."

"Maybe not," Bautista said. "How long ago you reckon he was copied into that synth?"

Ortega shrugged. "Who knows? He was wearing it last week. At least that long, unless he had the store copy updated. And that's fucking expensive."

"If I were someone like Carnage," I said thoughtfully, "I'd get myself updated whenever something major went down. No matter what it cost. I wouldn't want to wake up not knowing what the fuck I'd been doing the week before I got torched."

"That depends on what you were doing," Bautista pointed out. "If it was some seriously illegal shit, you might prefer to wake up not knowing about it. That way, you polygraph your way right out of police interrogation with a smile."

"Better than that. You wouldn't even . . ."

I trailed off, thinking about it. Bautista made an impatient gesture.

"Whatever. If Carnage wakes up not knowing, he might make some private inquiries, but he ain't going to be in too much of a hurry to let the police department in on it. And if he wakes up knowing—" He spread his hands. "—he'll make less noise than a Catholic orgasm. I think we're in the clear here."

"Get the ambulances, then. And maybe call Murawa in to . . ." But Ortega's voice was fading out, as the last part of the puzzle sank snugly into its resting place. The conversation between the two cops grew as remote as star static over a suit comlink. I gazed at a tiny dent on the metal wall beside me, hammering at the idea with every logic test I could muster.

Bautista gave me a curious glance, then left to call the ambulances. As he disappeared, Ortega touched me lightly on the arm.

"Hey, Kovacs. You okay?"

I blinked.

"Kovacs?"

I put out a hand and touched the wall, as if to assure myself of its solidity. Compared to the certainty of concept I was experiencing, my surroundings seemed suddenly intangible.

"Kristin," I said slowly. "I have to get aboard *Head in the Clouds*. I know what they did to Bancroft. I can bring Kawahara down, and get Resolution 653 pushed through. And I can spring Ryker."

Ortega sighed. "Kovacs, we've been through—"

"No." The savagery in my voice was so abrupt it shocked even me. I could feel the bruising in Ryker's face hurt as his features tensed. "This isn't speculation. This isn't a cast in the dark. This is fact. And I am going aboard *Head in the Clouds*. With or without your help, but I'm going."

"Kovacs." Ortega shook her head. "Look at yourself. You're a mess. Right now you couldn't take on an Oakland pimp, and you're talking about covert assault on one of the West Coast Houses. You think you're going to crash Kawahara's security with broken ribs and that face? Forget it."

"I didn't say it was going to be easy."

"Kovacs, it isn't going to *be*. I sat on the Hendrix tapes long enough for you to pull that shit with Bancroft, but that's as far as it goes. The game's over; your friend Sarah gets to go home, and so do you. But that's it. I'm not interested in grudge matches."

"Do you really want Ryker back?" I asked softly.

For a moment I thought she was going to hit me. Her nostrils flared white and her right shoulder actually dropped for the punch. I never knew whether it was the stungun hangover or just self-control that stopped her.

"I ought to deck you for that, Kovacs," she said evenly.

I raised my hands. "Go ahead, right now I couldn't take on an Oakland pimp. Remember?"

Ortega made a disgusted sound in her throat and started to turn away. I put out my hand and touched her.

"Kristin—" I hesitated. "I'm sorry. That was a bitchy crack, about Ryker. Will you at least hear me through, once?"

She came back to me, mouth clamped tight over whatever she was feeling, head down. She swallowed.

"I don't. There's been too much." She cleared her throat. "I don't want you hurt any more, Kovacs. I don't want any more damage, that's all."

"Damage to Ryker's sleeve, you mean?"

She looked at me.

"No," she said quietly. "No, I don't mean that. I mean what I say."

Then she was pressed up against me, there in that grim metal corridor, arms wrapped hard around me and face buried in my chest, all without apparent transition. I did some swallowing of my own and held her tightly while the last of what time we had trickled away like grains of sand through my fingers. And at that moment I would have given almost anything not to have had a plan for her to hear, not to have had any way to dissolve what was growing between us, and not to have hated Reileen Kawahara quite so much.

I would have given almost anything.

● ● ●

Two A.M.

I called Irene Elliott at the JacSol apartment and got her out of bed. I told her we had a problem we'd pay heavily to unkink. She nodded sleepily. Bautista went to get her in an unmarked cruiser.

By the time she arrived, the *Panama Rose* was lit as if for a deck party. Vertical searchlights along her sides made it look as if she was being lowered from the night sky on ropes of luminescence. Illuminum-cable incident barriers crisscrossed the superstructure and the dock moorings. The roof of the cargo cell where the humiliation bout had gone down was cranked back to allow the ambulances direct access, and the blast of crime-scene lighting from within rose into the night like the glow from a foundry. Police cruisers held the sky and parked across the dock flashing red and blue.

I met her at the gangway.

"I want my body back," she shouted over the whine and roar of airborne engines. The searchlights frosted her sleeve's black hair almost back to blonde.

"I can't swing that for you right now," I yelled back. "But it's in the pipeline. First, you've got to do this. Earn some credit. Now let's get you out of sight before fucking Sandy Kim spots you."

Local law were keeping the press copters at bay. Ortega, still sick and shaking, wrapped herself in a police greatcoat and kept the local law out with the same glitter-eyed intensity that kept her upright and conscious. Organic Damage Division, shouting, pulling rank, bullying, and bluffing, held the fort while Elliott went to work faking in the monitor footage they needed. They were indeed, as Trepp had recognized, the biggest gang on the block.

"I'm checking out of the apartment tomorrow," Elliott told me as she worked. "You won't be able to reach me there."

She was silent for a couple of moments, whistling through her teeth at odd moments as she keyed in the images she had constructed. Then she cast a glance at me over her shoulder.

"You say I'm earning juice from these guys, doing this. They're going to owe me?"

"Yeah, I'd say so."

"Then I'll contact them. Get me the officer in charge, I'll talk to whoever that is. And don't try to call me at Ember. I won't be there, either."

I said nothing, just looked at her. She turned back to her work.

"I need some time alone," she muttered.

Just the words sounded like a luxury to me.

CHAPTEr THIrTY–EIGHT

I watched him pour a drink from the bottle of fifteen-year-old malt, take it to the phone, and seat himself carefully. The broken ribs had been welded back together in one of the ambulances, but the whole of that side was still one huge ache with occasional, flinty stabs of agony. He sipped at the whiskey, gathered himself visibly, and punched out the call.

"Bancroft residence. With whom do you wish to speak?" It was the severely suited woman who had answered last time I called Suntouch House. The same suit, the same hair, even the same makeup. Maybe she was a phone construct.

"Miriam Bancroft," he said.

Once again, it was the sensation of being a passive observer, the same sensation of disconnection that I had felt that night in front of the mirror while Ryker's sleeve put on its weapons. The frags. Only this time it was much worse.

"One moment, please."

The woman disappeared from the screen and was replaced by the image of a windblown match flame in synch with piano music that sounded like autumn leaves being blown along a cracked and worn pavement. A minute passed, then Miriam Bancroft appeared, immaculately attired in a formal-looking jacket and blouse. She raised one perfectly groomed eyebrow.

"Mr. Kovacs. This is a surprise."

"Yeah, well." He gestured uncomfortably. Even across the comlink, Miriam Bancroft radiated a sensuality that unbalanced him. "Is this a secure line?"

"Reasonably so, yes. What do you want?"

He cleared his throat. "I've been thinking. There are some things I'd like to discuss with you. I, uh, I may owe you an apology."

"Indeed?" This time it was both eyebrows. "When exactly did you have in mind?"

He shrugged. "I'm not doing anything right now."

"Yes. I, however, am doing something right now, Mr. Kovacs. I am en route to a meeting in Chicago and will not be back on the coast until tomorrow evening." The faintest hint of a smile twitched at the corners of her mouth. "Will you wait?"

"Sure."

She leaned toward the screen, eyes narrowing. "What happened to your face?"

He raised a hand to one of the emerging facial bruises. In the low light of the room, he had not expected it to be so noticeable. Nor had he expected Miriam Bancroft to be so attentive.

"Long story. Tell you when I see you."

"Well, that I can hardly resist," she said ironically. "I shall send a limousine to collect you from the Hendrix tomorrow afternoon. Shall we say about four o'clock? Good. Until then."

The screen cleared. He sat, staring at it for a moment, then switched off the phone and swiveled the chair around to face the window shelf.

"She makes me nervous," he said.

"Yeah, me, too. Well, obviously."

"Very funny."

"I try."

I got up to fetch the whiskey bottle. As I crossed the room, I caught my reflection in the mirror beside the bed.

Where Ryker's sleeve had the air of a man who had battered his way head-first through life's trials, the man in the mirror looked as if he would be able to slip neatly aside at every crisis and watch fate fall clumsily on its fat face. The body was catlike in its movements, a smooth and effortless economy of motion that would have looked good on Anchana Salomao. The thick, almost blue-black hair fell in a soft cascade to the deceptively slim shoulders, and the elegantly tilted eyes had a gentle, unconcerned expression that suggested the universe was a good place to live in.

I had been in the tech ninja sleeve only a few hours—seven, and forty-two minutes according to the time display chipped into my upper-left field of vision—but there were none of the usual download side effects. I collected the whiskey bottle with one of the slim brown artist's hands, and the simple play of muscle and bone was a joy that glowed through me. The Khumalo neurachem system thrummed continually at the limit of perception, as if it were singing faintly the myriad possible things the body could do at any given moment. Never, even during my time with the Envoy Corps, had I worn anything like it.

I remembered Carnage's words and mentally shook my head. If the U.N. thought they'd be able to impose a ten-year colonial embargo on *this*, they were living in another world.

"I don't know about you," he said. "But this feels fucking weird."

"Tell me about it." I filled my own tumbler and proffered the bottle. He shook his head. I went back to the window shelf and sat back against the glass.

"How the fuck did Kadmin stand it? Ortega says he used to work with himself all the time."

"Get used to anything in time, I suppose. Besides, Kadmin was fucking crazy."

"Oh, and we're not?"

I shrugged. "We didn't have a choice. Apart from walking away, I mean. Would that have been better?"

"You tell me. You're the one who's going up against Kawahara. I'm just the whore around here. Incidentally, I don't reckon Ortega's exactly overjoyed about that part of the deal. I mean, she was confused before, but now—"

"*She's* confused! How do you think I feel?"

"I know how you feel, idiot. I am you."

"Are you?" I sipped at my drink and gestured with the glass. "How long do you think it takes before we stop being exactly the same person?"

He shrugged. "You are what you remember. Right now we have only about seven or eight hours of separate perceptions. Can't have made much of a dent yet, can't it?"

"On forty-odd years of memory? I suppose not. And it's the early stuff that builds personality."

"Yeah, they say. And while we're on the subject, tell me something. How do you feel, I mean how do *we* feel, about the Patchwork Man being dead?"

I shifted uncomfortably. "Do we need to talk about this?"

"We need to talk about something. We're stuck here with each other until tomorrow evening—"

"You can go out, if you want. Come to that—" I jerked a thumb upward toward the roof. "—I can get out of here the way I came in."

"You really don't want to talk about it that badly, huh?"

"Wasn't that tough."

That, at least, was true. The original draft of the plan had called for the ninja copy of me to stay at Ortega's apartment until the Ryker copy had disappeared with Miriam Bancroft. Then it occurred to me that we'd need a working relationship with the Hendrix to bring off the assault on *Head in the Clouds*, and that there was no way for the ninja copy of myself to prove its identity to the hotel, short of submission to a storage scan. It seemed a better idea for the Ryker copy to introduce the ninja before departing with Miriam Bancroft. Since the Ryker copy was undoubtedly still under surveillance, at the very least, by Trepp, walking in through the front door of the Hendrix together looked like a very bad idea. I borrowed a grav harness and a stealth suit from Bautista, and just before it started to get light I skimmed in between the patchy high-level traffic and down onto a sheltered flange on the forty-second floor. The Hendrix had by this time been advised of my arrival by the Ryker copy and let me in through a ventilation duct.

With the Khumalo neurachem, it had been almost as easy as walking in through the front door.

"Look," the Ryker copy said, "I'm you. I know everything you know. What's the harm in talking about this stuff?"

"If you know everything I know, what's the *point* of talking about it?"

"Sometimes, it helps to externalize things. Even if you talk to someone else about it, you're usually talking to yourself. The other guy's just providing a sounding board. You talk it out."

I sighed. "I don't know. I buried all that shit about Dad a long time ago; it's a long time dead."

"Yeah, right."

"I'm serious."

"No." He flicked a finger at me the way I had pointed at Bancroft when he didn't want to face my facts on the balcony of Suntouch House. "You're lying to yourself. Remember that pimp we met in Lazlo's pipehouse the year we joined Shonagon's Eleven? The one we nearly killed before they pulled us off him?"

"That was just chemicals. We were off our head on tetrameth, showing off because of the Eleven stuff. Fuck, we were only sixteen."

"Bullshit. We did it because he looked like Dad."

"Maybe."

"Fact. And we spent the next decade and a half killing authority figures for the same reason."

"Oh, give me a fucking break! We spent that decade and a half killing anyone who got in the way. It was the military; that's what we did for a living. And anyway, since when is a pimp an authority figure?"

"Okay, maybe it was pimps we spent fifteen years killing. Users. Maybe that's what we were paying back."

"He never pimped Mom out."

"Are you sure? Why were we so hot to hit the Elizabeth Elliott angle like a fucking tactical nuke? Why the accent on whorehouses in this investigation?"

"Because," I said, sinking a finger of whiskey, "that is what this investigation has been about from the beginning. We went after the Elliott angle because it felt right. Envoy intuition. The way Bancroft treated his wife—"

"Oh, Miriam Bancroft. Now there's another whole disk we could spin."

"Shut up. Elliott was a pretty fucking good sounding shot. We wouldn't have got to *Head in the Clouds* without that trip to Jerry's Biocabins."

"Ahhh." He made a disgusted gesture and tipped his own glass back. "You believe what you want. I say the Patchwork Man's been a metaphor for Dad because we couldn't bear to look too closely at the truth, and that's why we freaked the first time we saw a composite construct in virtual. Remember that, do you? That rec house on Adoracion. We had rage dreams for a week after that little show. Waking up with shreds of pillow on your hands. They sent us to the psychs for that."

I gestured irritably. "Yeah, I remember. I remember being shit scared of the Patchwork Man, not Dad. I remember feeling the same when we met Kadmin in virtual, too."

"And now he's dead. How do we feel now?"

"I don't feel anything."

He pointed at me again. "That's a cover."

"It is not a cover. The motherfucker got in my way, he threatened me, and now he's dead. Transmission ends."

"Remember anyone else threatening you, do you? When you were small, maybe?"

"I am not going to talk about this anymore." I reached for the bottle and filled my glass again. "Pick another subject. What about Ortega? What are our feelings on that score?"

"Are you planning to drink that whole bottle?"

"You want some?"

"No."

I spread my hands. "So what's it to you?"

"Are you trying to get drunk?"

"Of course I am. If I've got to talk to myself, I don't see why I should do it sober. So tell me about Ortega."

"I don't want to talk about that."

"Why not?" I asked reasonably. "Got to talk about something, remember. What's wrong with Ortega?"

"What's wrong is that we don't feel the same about her. You aren't wearing Ryker's sleeve anymore."

"That doesn't—"

"Yes, it does. What's between us and Ortega is completely physical. There hasn't been time for anything else. That's why you're so happy to talk about her now. In that sleeve, all you've got is some vague nostalgia about that yacht and a bundle of snapshot memories to back it up. There's nothing chemical happening to you anymore."

I reached for something to say, and abruptly found nothing. We sat in silence, studying the amber depths of our glasses. The suddenly discovered difference sat between us like a third, unwanted occupant of the room.

The Ryker copy dug into his pockets and came up with Ortega's cigarettes. The pack was crushed almost flat. He extracted a cigarette, looked ruefully at it, and fitted it into his mouth. I tried not to look disapproving.

"Last one," he said, touching the ignition patch to it.

"The hotel probably has more."

"Yeah." He plumed out smoke, and I found myself almost envying him the addiction. "You know, there is one thing we should be discussing right now."

"What's that?"

But I knew already. We both knew.

"You want me to spell it out? All right." He drew on the cigarette again and shrugged, not easily. "We have to decide which of us gets obliterated when this is all over. And since our individual instinct for survival is getting stronger by the minute, we need to decide soon."

"How?"

"I don't know. Which would you prefer to remember? Taking down Kawahara. Or going down on Miriam Bancroft?" He smiled sourly. "No competition, I suppose."

"Hey, this isn't just a roll on the beach you're talking about. This is multiple-copy sex. It's about the only genuinely illicit pleasure left. Anyway, Irene Elliott said we could do a memory graft and keep both sets of experience."

"Probably. She said we could *probably* do a memory graft. And that still leaves one of us to be canceled out. It's not a meld, it's a graft, from one of us to the other. Editing. You want to do that to yourself? To the one that survives. We couldn't even face editing that construct the Hendrix built. How are we going to live with this? No way, it's got to be a clean cut. One or the other. And we've got to decide which."

"Yeah." I picked up the whiskey bottle and stared gloomily at the label. "So what do we do? Gamble for it? Paper, scissors, stone, say the best of five?"

"I was thinking along slightly more rational lines. We tell each other our memories from this point on and then decide which we want to keep. Which ones are worth more."

"How the hell are we going to measure something like that?"

"We'll know. You know we will."

"What if one of us lies? Embroiders the truth to make it sound like a more appealing memory. Or lies about which one they like better."

His eyes narrowed. "Are you serious?"

"A lot can happen in a few days. Like you said, we're both going to want to survive."

"Ortega can polygraph us if it comes to that."

"I think I'd rather gamble."

"Give me that fucking bottle. If you're not going to take this seriously, neither am I. Fuck it, you might even get torched out there and solve the problem for us."

"Thanks."

I passed him the bottle and watched as he decanted two careful fingers. Jimmy de Soto had always said it was sacrilege to sink more than five fingers of single malt on any one occasion. After that, he maintained, you might as well be drinking blended. I had a feeling that we were going to profane that particular article of faith tonight.

I raised my glass.

"To unity of purpose."

"Yeah, and an end to drinking alone."

• • •

The hangover was still with me nearly a full day later as I watched him leave on one of the hotel monitors. He stepped out onto the pavement and waited while the long, polished limousine settled to the curb. As the curbside door hinged up, I caught a brief glimpse of Miriam Bancroft's profile within. Then he was climbing in, and the door swung smoothly back down to cover them both. The limousine trembled along its length and lifted away.

I dry-swallowed more painkillers, gave it ten minutes, and then went up to the roof to wait for Ortega.

It was cold.

CHAPTEr THIrTY-NINE

Ortega had a variety of news.

Irene Elliott had called in a location and said she was willing to talk about another run. The call had come in on one of the tightest needlecasts Fell Street had ever seen, and Elliott said she would only deal directly with me.

Meanwhile the *Panama Rose* patch-up was holding water, and Ortega still had the Hendrix memory tapes. Kadmin's death had rendered Fell Street's original case pretty much an administrative formality, and no one was in any hurry to tackle it anymore. An Internal Affairs inquiry into how exactly the assassin had been pulled out of holding in the first place was just getting started. In view of the assumed A.I. involvement, the Hendrix would come under scrutiny at some point, but it wasn't in the pipeline yet. There were some interdepartmental procedures to be gone through, and Ortega had sold Murawa a story about loose ends. The Fell Street captain gave her a couple of weeks open-ended, to tidy up; the tacit assumption was that Ortega had no liking for Internal Affairs and wasn't going to make life easy for them.

A couple of I.A.D. detectives were sniffing around the *Panama Rose*, but Organic Damage had closed ranks around Ortega and Bautista like a stack shutdown. I.A.D. was getting nothing so far.

We had a couple of weeks.

●●●

Ortega flew northeast. Elliott's instructions vectored us in on a small huddle of bubblefabs clustered around the western end of a tree-fringed lake hundreds of kilometers from anywhere. Ortega grunted in recognition as we banked above the encampment.

"You know this place?"

"Places like it. Grifter town. See that dish in the center? They've got it webbed into some old geosynch weather platform, gives them free access to anything in the hemisphere. This place probably accounts for a single-figure percentage of all the data crime on the West Coast."

"They never get busted?"

"Depends." Ortega put the cruiser down on the lake shore a short distance from the nearest bubblefabs. "The way it stands, these people keep the old orbitals ticking over. Without them, someone'd have to pay for decommissioning and that's kind of pricey. So long as the stuff they turn over is small scale, no one bothers. Transmission Felony Division has got bigger disks to spin, and no one else is interested. You coming?"

I climbed out, and we walked along the shoreline to the encampment. From the air, the place had had a certain structural uniformity, but now I could see that the bubblefabs were all painted with brightly colored pictures or abstract patterns. No two designs were alike, although I could discern the same artistic hand at work in several of the examples we passed. In addition, a lot of the 'fabs were fitted out with porch canopies, secondary extension bulges, and in some cases even more permanent log cabin annexes. Clothing hung on lines between the buildings, and small children ran about, getting cheerfully filthy.

Camp security met us inside the first ring of 'fabs. He stood over two meters tall in flat workboots and probably weighed as much as both my current selves put together. Beneath his loose gray coveralls, I could see the stance of a fighter. His eyes were a startling red, and short horns sprouted from his temples. Beneath the horns, his face was scarred and old. The effect was startlingly offset by the small child he was cradling in his left arm.

He nodded at me.

"You Anderson?"

"Yes. This is Kristin Ortega." I was surprised how flat the name suddenly sounded to me. Without Ryker's pheromonal interface, I was left with little more than a vague appreciation that the woman beside me was very attractive in a lean, self-sufficient way that recalled Virginia Vidaura.

That, and my memories.

I wondered if she was feeling the same.

"Cop, huh?" The ex–Freak Fighter's tone was not overflowing with warmth, but it didn't sound too hostile, either.

"Not at the moment," I said firmly. "Is Irene here?"

"Yeah." He shifted the child to his other arm and pointed. "The 'fab with the stars on it. Been expecting you."

As he spoke, Irene Elliott emerged from the structure in question. The horned man grunted and led us across, picking up a small train of additional children on the way. Elliott watched us approach with her hands in her pockets. Like the ex-fighter, she was dressed in boots and coveralls whose gray was startlingly offset by a violently colored rainbow headband.

"Your visitors," the horned man said. "You okay with this?"

Elliott nodded evenly, and he hesitated a moment longer, then shrugged and wandered off with the children in tow. Elliott watched him go, then turned back to us.

"You'd better come inside," she said.

Inside the bubblefab, the utilitarian space had been sectioned off with wooden partitions and woven rugs hung from wires set in the plastic dome. Walls were covered in more artwork, most of which looked as if it had been contributed by the children of the camp. Elliott took us to a softly lit space set with lounging bags and a battered-looking access terminal on a hinged arm epoxied to the wall of the bubble. She seemed to have adjusted well to the sleeve, and her movements were smoothly unself-conscious. I'd noticed the improvement on board the *Panama Rose* in the early hours of the morning, but here it was clearer. She lowered herself easily into one of the loungers and looked speculatively up at me.

"That's you inside there, Anderson, I presume?"

I inclined my head.

"You going to tell me why?"

I seated myself opposite her. "That depends on you, Irene. Are you in or out?"

"You guarantee I get my own body back." She was trying hard to sound casual, but there was no disguising the hunger in her voice. "That's the deal?"

I glanced up at Ortega, who nodded. "That's correct. If this comes off successfully, we'll be able to requisition it under a federal mandate. But it has to be successful. If we fuck up, we'll probably all go down the double-barrel."

"You are operating under a federal brief, Lieutenant?"

Ortega smiled tightly. "Not exactly. But under the U.N. charter, we'll be able to apply the brief retrospectively. If, as I said, we are successful."

"A *retrospective* federal brief." Elliott looked back to me, brows raised. "That's about as common as whalemeat. This must be something gigantic."

"It is," I said.

Elliott's eyes narrowed. "And you're not with JacSol anymore, are you? Who the fuck are you, Anderson?"

"I'm your fairy godmother, Elliott. Because if the lieutenant's requisition doesn't work out, I'll buy your sleeve back. That's a guarantee. Now are you in, or are you out?"

Irene Elliott hung on to her detachment for a moment longer, a moment in which I felt my technical respect for her take on a more personal tone. Then she nodded.

"Tell me," she said.

I told her.

It took about half an hour to lay it out, while Ortega stood about or paced restlessly in and out of the bubblefab. I couldn't blame her. Over the past ten days she'd had to face the breakdown of practically every professional tenet she owned, and she was now committed to a project that, if it went wrong, offered a bristling array of hundred-year or better storage offenses for all concerned. I think, without Bautista and the others behind her, she might not have risked it, even with her cordial hatred of the Meths, even for Ryker.

Or maybe I just tell myself that.

Irene Elliott sat and listened in silence broken only by three technical queries to which I had no answers. When I was finished, she said nothing for a long time. Ortega stopped her pacing and came to stand behind me, waiting.

"You're insane," Elliott said finally.

"Can you do it?"

She opened her mouth, then shut it again. Her face went dreamy, and I guessed she was reviewing a previous dipping episode from memory. After a few moments she snapped back and nodded as if she might be trying to convince herself.

"Yes," she said slowly. "It can be done, but not in real time. This isn't like rewriting your fightdrome friends' security system, or even downloading into that A.I. core. This makes what we did to the A.I. look like a systems check. To do this, to even attempt this, I've got to have a virtual forum."

"That's not a problem. Anything else?"

"That depends on what counterintrusion systems *Head in the Clouds* is running." Disgust, and an edge of tears, colored her tone for a couple of instants. "You say this is a high-class whorehouse?"

"Very," Ortega said.

Elliott's feelings went back underground. "Then I'll have to run some checks. That'll take time."

"How much time?" Ortega wanted to know.

"Well, I can do it two ways." Professional scorn surfaced in her voice, scarring over the emotion that had been there before. "I can do a fast scan and maybe ring every alarm aboard this prick in the sky. Or I can do it right, which'll take a couple of days. Your choice. We're running on your clock."

"Take your time," I suggested, with a warning glance at Ortega. "Now, what about wiring me for sight and sound? You know anyone who can do that discreetly?"

"Yeah, we got people here can do that. But you can forget a telemetry system. You try to transmit out of there, you *will* bring the house down. No pun intended." She moved to the arm-mounted terminal and punched up a general access screen. "I'll see if Reese can dig you up a grab-and-stash mike. Shielded microstack, you'll be able to record a couple of hundred hours high rez and we can retrieve it here later."

"Good enough. This going to be expensive?"

Elliott turned back to us, eyebrows hoisted. "Talk to Reese. She'll probably have to buy the parts in, but maybe you can get her to do the surgery on a retrospective federal basis. She could use the juice at U.N. level."

I glanced at Ortega, who shrugged exasperatedly.

"I guess," she said ungraciously, as Elliott busied herself with the screen. I stood up and turned to the policewoman.

"Ortega," I muttered into her ear, abruptly aware that in the new sleeve I was completely unmoved by her scent. "It isn't my fault we're short of funds. The JacSol account's gone, evaporated, and if I start drawing on Bancroft's credit for stuff like this, it's going to look fucking odd. Now get a grip."

"It isn't that," she hissed back.

"Then what is it?"

She looked at me, at our brutally casual proximity. "You know goddamn well what it is."

I drew a deep breath and closed my eyes to avoid having to meet her gaze. "Did you sort out that hardware for me?"

"Yeah." She stepped back, voice returning to normal volume and empty of tone. "The stungun from the Fell Street tackle room; no one'll miss it. The rest is coming out of NYPD confiscated weapons stocks. I'm flying out to pick it up tomorrow personally. Material transaction, no records. I called in a couple of favors."

"Good. Thanks."

"Don't mention it." Her tone was savagely ironic. "Oh, by the way, they had a hell of a time getting hold of the spider venom load. I don't suppose you'd care to tell me what that's all about, would you?"

"It's a personal thing."

Elliott got someone on the screen. A serious-looking woman in a late-fifties African sleeve.

"Hey, Reese," she said cheerfully. "Got a customer for you."

Despite the pessimistic estimate, Irene Elliott finished her preliminary scan a day later. I was down by the lake, recovering from Reese's simple microsurgery and skimming stones with a girl of about six who seemed to have adopted me. Ortega was still in New York, the chill between us not really resolved.

Elliott emerged from the encampment and yelled out the news of her successful covert scan without bothering to come down to the water's edge. I winced as the echoes floated out across the water. The open atmosphere of the little settlement took some getting used to, and how it fitted in with successful data piracy I still couldn't see. I handed my stone to the girl and rubbed reflexively at the tiny soreness under one eye where Reese had gone in and implanted the recording system.

"Here. See if you can do it with this one."

"Your stones are *heavy*," she said plaintively.

"Well, try anyway. I got nine skips out of the last one."

She squinted up at me. "You're wired for it. I'm only six."

"True. On both counts." I placed a hand on her head. "But you've got to work with what you've got."

"When I'm big I'm going to be wired like Auntie Reese."

I felt a small sadness well up on the cleanly swept floor of my Khumalo neurachem brain. "Good for you. Look, I've got to go. Don't go too close to the water, right?"

She looked at me exasperatedly. "I can swim."

"So can I, but it looks cold, don't you think?"

"Ye-e-es . . ."

"There you are, then." I ruffled her hair and set off up the beach. At the first bubblefab I looked back. She was hefting the big flat stone at the lake as if the water were an enemy.

Elliott was in the expansive, postmission mood that most datarats seem to hit after a long spell cruising the stacks.

"I've been doing a little historical digging," she said, swinging the terminal arm outward from its resting place. Her hands danced across the terminal deck, and the screen flared into life, shedding colors on her face. "How's the implant?"

I touched my lower eyelid again. "Fine. Tapped straight into the same system that runs the time chip. Reese could have made a living doing this."

"She used to," Elliott said shortly. "Till they busted her for anti-Protectorate literature. When this is all over, you make sure that someone puts in a word for her at federal level, because she sure as shit needs it."

"Yeah, she said." I peered over her shoulder at the screen. "What have you got there?"

"*Head in the Clouds.* Tampa airyard blueprints. Hull specs, the works. This stuff is centuries old. I'm amazed they still keep it on stack at all. Anyway, seems she was originally commissioned as part of the Caribbean storm-management flotilla, back before SkySystems orbital weather net put them all out of business. A lot of the long-range scanning equipment got ripped out when they refitted, but they left the local sensors in and that's what provides basic skin security. Temperature pickups, infrared, that sort of thing. Anything with body heat lands anywhere on the hull, they'll know it's there."

I nodded, unsurprised. "Ways in?"

She shrugged. "Hundreds. Ventilation ducts, maintenance crawlways. Take your pick."

"I'll need to have another look at what Miller told my construct. But assume I'm going in from the top. Body heat's the only real problem?"

"Yeah, but those sensors are looking for anything over a square millimeter of temperature differential. A stealth suit won't cover you. Christ, even the breath coming out of your lungs will probably trip them. And it doesn't stop there." Elliott nodded somberly at the screen. "They must have liked the system a lot, because when they refitted they ran it through the whole ship. Room temperature monitors on every corridor and walkway."

"Yeah, Miller said something about a heat-signature tag."

"That's it. Incoming guests get it on boarding, and their codes are incorporated into the system. Anyone else walks down a corridor uninvited, or goes somewhere their tag says they can't, they set off every alarm in the hull. Simple, and very effective. And I don't think I can cut in there and write you a welcome code. Too much security."

"Don't worry about it," I said. "I don't think it's going to be a problem."

●●●

"You what?" Ortega looked at me with fury and disbelief spreading across her face like a storm front. She stood away from me as if I might be contagious.

"It was just a suggestion. If you don't—"

"No." She said the word as if it was new to her and she liked the taste. "No. No fucking way. I've connived at viral crime for you, I've hidden evidence for you, I've assisted you in multiple sleeving—"

"Hardly multiple."

"It's a fucking crime," she said through her teeth. "I am not going to steal confiscated drugs out of police holding for you."

"Okay, forget it." I hesitated, put my tongue in my cheek for a moment. "Want to help me confiscate some more, then?"

Something inside me cheered as the unwilling smile broke cover on her face.

●●●

The dealer was in the same place he had been when I walked into his 'cast radius two weeks ago. This time I saw him twenty meters away, skulking in an alcove with the bat-eyed broadcast unit on his shoulder like a familiar. There were very few people on the street in any direction. I nodded to Ortega, who was stationed across the street, and walked on. The sales 'cast had not changed, the street of ridiculously ferocious women and the sudden cool of the betathanatine hit, but this time I was expecting it and in any case the Khumalo neurachem had a definite damping effect on the intrusion. I stepped up to the dealer with an eager smile.

"Got Stiff, man."

"Good, that's what I'm looking for. How much have you got?"

He started a little, expression coiling between greed and suspicion. His hand slipped down toward the horror box at his belt just in case.

"How much you want, man?"

"All of it," I said cheerfully. "Everything you've got."

He read me, but by then it was too late. I had the lock on two of his fingers as they stabbed at the horror box controls.

"Ah-ah."

He took a swipe at me with the other arm. I broke the fingers. He howled and collapsed around the pain. I kicked him in the stomach and took the horror box away from him. Behind me, Ortega arrived and flashed her badge in his sweat-beaded face.

"Bay City police," she said laconically. "You're busted. Let's see what you've got, shall we."

The betathanatine was in a series of dermal pads with tiny glass decanters folded in cotton. I held one of the vials up to the light and shook it. The liquid within was a pale red.

"What do you reckon?" I asked Ortega. "About eight percent?"

"Looks like. Maybe less." Ortega put a knee into the dealer's neck, grinding his face into the pavement. "Where do you cut this stuff, pal?"

"This is good merchandise," the dealer squealed. "I buy direct. This is—"

Ortega rapped hard on his skull with her knuckles, and he shut up.

"This is shit," she said patiently. "This has been stepped on so hard it wouldn't give you a cold. We don't want it. So you can have your whole stash back and walk, if you like. All we want to know is where you cut it. An address."

"I don't know any—"

"Do you want to be shot while escaping?" Ortega asked him pleasantly, and he grew suddenly very quiet.

"Place in Oakland," he said sullenly.

Ortega gave him a pencil and paper. "Write it down. No names, just the address. And so help me, if you're tinseling me, I'll come back here with fifty ccs of real Stiff and feed you the lot, unstepped."

She took back the scrawled paper and glanced at it, removed her knee from the dealer's neck, and patted him on the shoulder.

"Good. Now get up and get the fuck off the street. You can go back to work tomorrow, if this is the right place. And if it's not, remember, I know your patch."

We watched him lurch off, and Ortega tapped the paper.

"I know this place. Controlled Substances busted them a couple of times last year, but some slick lawyer gets the important guys off every time. We'll make a lot of noise, let them think they're buying us off with a bag of uncut."

"Fair enough." I looked after the retreating figure of the dealer. "Would you have really shot him?"

"Nah." Ortega grinned. "But he doesn't know that. ConSub does it sometimes, just to get major dealers off the street when there's something big going down. Official reprimand for the officer involved, and compensation pays out for a new sleeve, but it takes time, and the scumbag does that time in the store. Plus it hurts to get shot. I was convincing, huh?"

"Convinced the fuck out of me."

"Maybe I should have been an Envoy."

I shook my head. "Maybe you should spend less time around me."

●●●

I stared up at the ceiling, waiting for the hypnophone sonocodes to lull me away from reality. On either side of me, Davidson, the Organic Damage datarat, and Ortega had settled into their racks, and even through the hypnophones I could hear their breathing, slow and regular, at the limits of my neurachem perception. I tried to relax more, to let the hypnosystem press me down through levels of softly decreasing consciousness, but instead my mind was whirring through the details of the setup like a program check scanning for error. It was like the insomnia I'd suffered after Innenin, an infuriating synaptic itch that refused to go away. When my peripheral-vision time display told me that at least a full minute had gone by, I propped myself up on one elbow and looked around at the figures dreaming in the other racks.

"Is there a problem?" I asked loudly.

"The tracking of Sheryl Bostock is complete," the hotel said. "I assumed you would prefer to be alone when I informed you."

I sat upright and started picking the 'trodes off my body. "You assumed right. You sure everyone else is under?"

"Lieutenant Ortega and her colleagues were installed in the virtuality approximately two minutes ago. Irene Elliott has been established there since earlier this afternoon. She asked not to be disturbed."

"What ratio are you running at the moment?"

"Eleven point one five. Irene Elliott requested it."

I nodded to myself as I climbed out of the rack. Eleven point one five was a standard working ratio for datarats. It was also the title of a particularly bloody but otherwise unmemorable Micky Nozawa experia flick. The only clear detail I could recall was that, unexpectedly, Micky's character got killed at the end. I hoped it wasn't an omen.

"All right," I said. "Let's see what you've got."

Between the dimly seen heave and swell of the sea and the lights of the cabin, there was a lemon grove. I went along a dirt track between the trees, and the citrus fragrance felt cleansing. From the long grass on either side, cicadas whirred reassuringly. In a velvet sky above were stars like fixed gems, and behind the cabin the land rose into gentle hills and rocky outcroppings. The vague white forms of sheep moved in the darkness on the slopes, and from somewhere I heard a dog bark. The lights of a fishing village glimmered off to one side, less bright than the stars.

There were hurricane lamps slung from the upper rail of the cabin's front porch, but no one was seated at the wooden tables there. The front wall bore a riotous abstract mural curling around and out from the luminous lettering of a sign that read PENSION FLOWER OF '68. Wind chimes dangled along the railing, winking and turning in the faint breeze that blew in from the sea. They made a variety of gentle sounds from glassy belling to hollow wooden percussion.

On the unkempt sloping lawn in front of the porch someone had set out an incongruous collection of sofas and armchairs in a rough circle, so it looked as if the cabin had been lifted bodily off its furnished interior and set down again further up the slope. From the gathered seats came the soft sound of voices and the red embers of lit cigarettes. I reached for my own supply, realized I had neither the pack nor the need anymore, and grimaced wryly to myself in the dark.

Bautista's voice rose above the murmur of conversation.

"Kovacs? That you?"

"Who else is it going to be?" I heard Ortega ask him impatiently. "This is a goddamn virtuality."

"Yeah, but . . ." Bautista shrugged and gestured to the empty seats. "Welcome to the party."

There were five figures seated in the circle of lounge furniture. Irene Elliott and Davidson were seated at opposite ends of a sofa beside Bautista's chair. On the other side of Bautista, Ortega had sprawled her long-limbed body along the full length of a second sofa.

The fifth figure was relaxed deep into another armchair, legs stretched out in front of him, face sunk in shadows. Wiry black hair stuck up in silhouette above a multicolored bandanna. Lying across his lap was a white guitar. I stopped in front of him.

"The Hendrix, right?"

"That's correct." There was a depth and timbre to the voice that had been absent before. The big hands moved across frets and dislodged a tumble of chords onto the darkened lawn. "Base entity projection. Hardwired in by the original designers. If you strip down the client mirroring systems, this is what you get."

"Good." I took an armchair opposite Irene Elliott. "You happy with the working environment?"

She nodded. "Yeah, it's fine."

"How long've you been here?"

"Me?" She shrugged. "A day or so. Your friends got here a couple of hours ago."

"Two and a half," Ortega said sourly. "What kept you?"

"Neurachem glitch." I nodded at the Hendrix figure. "Didn't he tell you?"

"That's exactly what he told us." Ortega's gaze was wholly cop. "I'd just like to know what it means."

I made a helpless gesture. "So would I. The Khumalo system kept kicking me out of the pipe, and it took us a while to get compatibility. Maybe I'll mail the manufacturers." I turned back to Irene Elliott. "I take it you're going to want the format run up to maximum for the dip."

"You take it right." Elliott jerked her thumb at the Hendrix figure. "Man says the place runs to three twenty-three max, and we are going to need every scrap of that to pull it off."

"You cased the run yet?"

Elliott nodded glumly. "It's locked up tighter than an orbital bank. But I can tell you a couple of interesting things. One, your friend Sarah Sachilowska was D.H.F.'d off *Head in the Clouds* two days ago, relayed off the Gateway comsat out to Harlan's World. So she's out of the firing line."

"I'm impressed. How long did it take you to dig that up?"

"A while." Elliott inclined her head in the Hendrix's direction. "I had some help."

"And the second interesting thing?"

"Yeah. Covert needlecast to a receiver in Europe every eighteen hours. Can't tell you much more than that without dipping it, and I figured you wouldn't want that just yet. But it looks like what we're after."

I remembered the spiderlike automatic guns and leathery impact-resistant womb sacs, the somber stone guardians that supported the roof of Kawahara's basilica, and I found myself once more smiling in response to those contemptuous hooded smiles.

"Well, then." I looked around at the assembled team. "Let's get this gig off the ground."

CHAPTEr FOrTY

It was Sharya, all over again.

We dusted off from the tower of the Hendrix an hour after dark and swung away into the traffic-speckled night. Ortega had pulled the same Lock-Mit transport I'd ridden out to Suntouch House, but when I looked around the dimly lit interior of the ship's belly, it was the Envoy Command attack on Zihicce that I remembered. The scene was the same, Davidson playing the role of datacom officer, face washed pale blue by the light from his screen, Ortega as medic, unpacking the dermals and charging kit from a sealwrap bag. Up ahead in the hatchway to the cockpit, Bautista stood and looked worried, while another mohican I didn't know did the flying. Something must have shown on my face, because Ortega leaned in abruptly to study my face.

"Problem?"

I shook my head. "Just a little nostalgia."

"Well, I just hope you got these measures right." She braced herself against the hull. In her hand, the first dermal looked like a petal torn from some iridescent green plant. I grinned up at her and rolled my head to one side to expose my jugular.

"This is the fourteen percent," she said, and applied the cool green petal to my neck. I felt the fractional grip, like gentle sandpaper, as it took, and then a long cold finger leapt down past my collarbone and deep into my chest.

"Smooth."

"Fucking ought to be. You know how much that stuff would go for on the street?"

"The perks of law enforcement, huh?"

Bautista turned around. "That ain't funny, Kovacs."

"Leave him alone, Rod," Ortega said lazily. "Man's entitled to a bad joke, under the circumstances. It's just nerves."

I raised one finger to my temple in acknowledgment of the point. Ortega peeled back the dermal gingerly and stood back.

"Three minutes till the next," she said. "Right?"

I nodded complacently and opened my mind to the effects of the Reaper.

At first it was uncomfortable. As my body temperature started to fall, the air in the transport grew hot and oppressive. It sank humidly into my lungs and lay there, so that every breath became an effort. My vision smeared and my mouth turned uncomfortably dry as the fluid balance of my body seesawed. Movement, however small, began to seem like an imposition. Thought itself turned ponderous with effort.

Then the control stimulants kicked in, and in seconds my head cleared from foggy to the unbearable brightness of sunlight on a knife. The soupy warmth of the air receded as neural governors retuned my system to cope with the body temperature shift. Inhaling became a languid pleasure, like drinking hot rum on a cold night. The cabin of the transport and the people in it were suddenly like a coded puzzle that I had the solution for if I could just . . .

I felt an inane grin eating its way across my features.

"Whoooh, Kristin, this is . . . good stuff. This is better . . . than Sharya."

"Glad you like it." Ortega glanced at her watch. "Two more minutes. You up to it?"

"I'm up to—" I pursed my lips and blew through them. "—anything. Anything at all."

Ortega tipped her head back toward Bautista, who could presumably see the instrumentation in the cockpit. "Rod. How long have we got?"

"Be there in less than forty minutes."

"Better get him the suit."

While Bautista busied himself with an overhead locker, Ortega delved in her pocket and produced a hypospray tipped with an unpleasant-looking needle.

"I want you to wear this," she said. "Little bit of Organic Damage insurance for you."

"A needle?" I shook my head with what felt like machined precision. "Uh-uh. You're not sticking that fucking thing in me."

"It's a tracer filament," she said patiently. "And you're not leaving this ship without it."

I looked at the gleam on the needle, mind slicing the facts like vegetables for a bowl of ramen. In the tactical marines we'd used subcutaneous filament to keep track of operatives on covert operations. In the event that something went wrong, it gave us a clear fix to pull our people out. In the event that nothing went wrong, the molecules of the filament broke down into organic residues, usually in under forty-eight hours.

I glanced across at Davidson.

"What's the range?"

"Hundred klicks." The young mohican seemed suddenly very competent in the glow from his screen. "Search-triggered signal only. It doesn't radiate unless we call you. Quite safe."

I shrugged. "Okay. Where do you want to put it?"

Ortega stood up, needle in hand. "Neck muscles. Nice and close to your stack, case they chop your head off."

"Charming." I got to my feet and turned my back so that she could put the needle in. There was a brief spike of pain in the cords of muscle at the base of my skull and then it faded. Ortega patted me on the shoulder.

"You're done. Is he on-screen?"

Davidson punched a couple of buttons and nodded in satisfaction. In front of me, Bautista dumped the grav harness tackle on a seat. Ortega glanced at her watch and reached for the second dermal.

"Thirty-seven percent," she said. "Ready for the Big Chill?"

● ● ●

It was like being submerged in diamonds.

By the time we hit *Head in the Clouds* the drug had already eliminated most of my emotional responses and everything had the sharp and shiny edges of raw data. Clarity became a substance, a film of understanding that coated all I saw and heard around me. The stealth suit and the grav harness felt like samurai armor, and when I drew the stungun from its sheath to check the settings, I could feel the charge coiled in it like a tangible thing.

It was the single forgiving phrase in the syntax of weaponry I had strapped about me. The rest were unequivocal sentences of death.

The shard pistol, spider venom loaded, snugged across my lower ribs opposite the stunner. I dialed the muzzle aperture to wide. At five meters, it would take down a roomful of opponents with a single shot, with no recoil and in complete silence. Sarah Sachilowska says Hi.

The dispenser clip of termite microgrenades, each one not much larger or thicker than a data diskette, secured in a pouch on my left hip. In memoriam Iphigenia Deme.

The Tebbit knife on my forearm in its neuralspring sheath beneath the stealth suit like a final word.

I reached for the cold feeling that had filled me up outside Jerry's Closed Quarters and, in the crystalline depths of the Reaper, did not need it.

Mission time.

"Target visual," the pilot called. "You want to come up and have a look at this baby?"

I glanced at Ortega, who shrugged, and the two of us went forward. Ortega seated herself beside the mohican and slipped on the copilot's headset. I contented myself with standing next to Bautista in the access hatch. The view was just as good from there.

Most of the Lock-Mit's cockpit was transparent alloy with instrumentation projected up onto it, permitting the pilot an uninterrupted view of the surrounding airspace; I remembered the feeling from Sharya, like riding a slightly concave tray, a tongue of steel or maybe a magic carpet, across the cloudscape below. A feeling that had been at once dizzying and godlike. I glanced at the mohican's profile and wondered if he was as detached from that feeling as I was under the influence of the Reaper.

There were no clouds tonight. *Head in the Clouds* hung off to the left like a mountain village seen from afar. A cluster of tiny blue lights singing gently of homecoming and warmth in the icy black immensity. Kawahara seemed to have chosen the edge of the world for the whorehouse.

As we banked toward the lights, a squiggle of electronic sound filled the cockpit and the projected instrumentation dimmed briefly.

"That's it, we're acquired," Ortega said sharply. "Here we go. I want a flyby under the belly. Let them get a good look."

The mohican said nothing, but the nose of the transport dipped. Ortega reached up to an instrument panel projected onto the transparency above her head and touched a button. A hard, male voice crashed into the cabin.

". . . that you are in restricted airspace. We are under license to destroy intruding aircraft. Identify yourself immediately."

"This is the Bay City police department," Ortega said laconically. "Look out your window and you'll see the stripes. We're up here on official police business, pal, so if you so much as twitch a launcher in this direction, I'll have you blown out of the sky."

There was a hissing silence. Ortega turned to look at me and grinned. Ahead of us, *Head in the Clouds* swelled like the target in a missile scope and then lifted abruptly over our heads as the pilot dipped us below the bulk of its hull and banked about. I saw lights gathered like icy fruit on gantries and the undersides of landing pads, the distended belly of the vessel curving up on either side, and then we were past.

"State the nature of your business," the voice snapped nastily.

Ortega peered out of the side of the cockpit as if looking for the speaker in amongst the airship's superstructure. Her voice grew chilly. "Sonny, I've already told you the nature of our business. Now get me a landing pad."

More silence. We circled the airship five kilometers out. I started to pull on the gloves of the stealth suit.

"Lieutenant Ortega." It was Kawahara's voice this time, but in the depths of the betathanatine, even hatred seemed detached and I had to remind myself to feel it. Most of me was assessing the rapidity with which they had voiceprinted Ortega. "This is a little unexpected. Do you have some kind of warrant? I believe our licenses are in order."

Ortega raised an eyebrow at me. The voiceprinting had impressed her, too. She cleared her throat. "This is not a licensing matter. We are looking for a fugitive. If you're going to start insisting on warrants, I might have to assume you've got a guilty conscience."

"Don't threaten me, Lieutenant," Kawahara said coldly. "Do you have any idea who you're talking to?"

"Reileen Kawahara, I imagine." In the deathly silence that followed, Ortega made a jubilant punching gesture at the ceiling and turned to grin at me. The barb had gone home. I felt the faintest ripple of amusement catch at the corners of my mouth.

"Perhaps you'd better tell me the name of this fugitive, Lieutenant." Kawahara's voice had gone as smooth as the expression on an untenanted synthetic sleeve.

"His name is Takeshi Kovacs," Ortega said, with another grin at me. "But he's currently sleeved in the body of an ex–police officer. I'd like to ask you some questions concerning your relationship with this man."

There was another long pause, and I knew the lure was going to work. I'd crafted its multiple layers with all the care of the finest Envoy deceit. Kawahara almost certainly knew of the relationship between Ortega and Ryker, could probably guess Ortega's entanglement with the new tenant of her lover's sleeve. She would buy Ortega's anxiety at my disappearance. She would buy Ortega's unsanctioned approach to *Head in the Clouds*. Given an assumed communication between Kawahara and Miriam Bancroft, she would believe she knew where I was and she would be confident that she had the upper hand over Ortega.

But more important than all of this, she would want to know how the Bay City police knew she was aboard *Head in the Clouds*. And since it was likely that they had, either directly or indirectly, gleaned the fact from Takeshi Kovacs, she would want to know how he knew. She would want to know how much he knew, and how much he had told the police.

She would want to talk to Ortega.

I fastened the wrist seals of the stealth suit and waited. We completed our third circuit of *Head in the Clouds*.

"You'd better come aboard," Kawahara said finally. "Starboard landing beacon. Follow it in; they'll give you a code."

The Lock-Mit was equipped with a rear dispatch tube, a smaller, civilian variant of the drop launcher that on military models was intended for smart bombs or surveillance drones. The tube was accessed through the floor of the main cabin, and with a certain amount of contortion, I fitted inside complete with stealth suit, grav harness, and assorted weaponry. We'd practiced this three or four times on the ground, but now with the transport swinging in toward *Head in the Clouds*, it suddenly seemed a long and complicated process. Finally, I got the last of the grav harness inside, and Ortega rapped once on the suit's helmet before she slammed the hatch down and buried me in darkness.

Three seconds later the tube blew open and spat me backwards into the night sky.

The sensation was a dimly remembered joy, something this sleeve did not recall at a cellular level. From the cramped confines of the tube and the noisy vibration of the transport's engines I was suddenly blasted into absolute space and silence. Not even the rush of air made it through the foam padding on the suit's helmet as I fell. The grav harness kicked in as soon as I was clear of the tube and braked my fall before it got properly started. I felt myself borne up on its field, not quite motionless, like a ball bobbing on top of the column of water from a fountain. Pivoting about, I watched the navigation lights of the transport shrink inward against the bulk of *Head in the Clouds*.

The airship hung above and before me like a threatening storm cloud. Lights glimmered out at me from the curving hull and the gantried superstructure beneath. Ordinarily it would have given me the cringing sensation of being a sitting target, but the betathanatine soothed the emotions away in a clean rush of data detail. In the stealth suit I was as black as the surrounding sky and all but radar invisible. The grav field I was generating might theoretically show up on a scanner somewhere, but within the huge distortions produced by the airship's stabilizers they'd need to be looking for me, and looking quite hard. All these things I knew with an absolute confidence that had no room for doubts, fears, or other emotional tangling. I was riding the Reaper.

I set the impellers in cautious forward drive and drifted toward the massive curving wall of the hull. Inside the helmet, simulation graphics awoke on the surface of the visor, and I saw the entry points Irene Elliott had found for me delineated in red. One in particular, the unsealed mouth of a disused sampling turret, was pulsing on and off next to fine green lettering that spelled PROSPECT ONE. I rose steadily upward to meet it.

The turret mouth was about a meter wide and scarred around the edges where the atmosphere sampling system had been amputated. I got my legs up in front of me—no mean achievement in a grav field—and hooked myself over the lip of the hatch, then concentrated on worming myself inside up to the waist. From there I twisted onto my front to clear the grav harness and was able to slide myself through the gap and onto the floor of the turret. I switched the grav harness off.

Inside, there was barely enough crawlspace for a technician lying on his back to check the nest of equipment. At the back of the turret was an antique air lock, complete with pressure wheel, just as Irene Elliott's dipped blueprints had promised. I wriggled around until I could grasp the wheel with both hands, conscious that both suit and harness were catching on the narrow hatchway, and that my exertions so far had almost totally depleted my immediate body strength. I drew a deep breath to fuel my comatose muscles, waited for my slowed heartbeat to pump the oxygen around my body, and heaved at the wheel. Against my expectations it turned quite easily and the air-lock hatch fell outward. Beyond the hatch was an airy darkness.

I lay still for a while, mustering more muscular strength. The two-shot Reaper cocktail was taking some getting used to. On Sharya we hadn't needed to go above 20 percent. Ambient temperatures in Zihicce were quite high and the spider tanks' infrared sensors were crude. Up here, a body at Sharyan room temperature would set off every alarm in the hull. Without careful oxygen fueling, my body would rapidly exhaust its cellular-level energy reserves and leave me gasping on the floor like a gaffed bottleback. I lay still, breathing deep and slow.

After a couple of minutes, I twisted around again and unfastened the grav harness, then slid carefully through the hatch and hit a steel grid walkway with the heels of my hands. I curled the rest of my body slowly out of the hatch, feeling like a moth emerging from a chrysalis. Checking the darkened walkway in either direction, I rose to my feet and removed the stealth suit helmet and gloves. If the keel plans Irene Elliott had dipped from the Tampa airyard stack were still accurate, the walkway led down among the huge helium silos to the vessel's aft buoyancy control room, and from there I'd be able to climb a maintenance ladder directly onto the main operating deck. According to what we'd patched together out of Miller's interrogation, Kawahara's quarters were two levels below on the port side. She had two huge windows that looked downward out of the hull.

Summoning the blueprints from memory, I drew the shard pistol and set off toward the stern.

●●●

It took me less than fifteen minutes to reach the buoyancy control room, and I saw no one on the way. The control room itself appeared to be automated, and I began to suspect that these days hardly anyone bothered to visit the swooping canopies of the airship's upper hull. I found the maintenance ladder and climbed painstakingly down it until a warm upward spilling glow on my face told me I was almost on the operating deck. I stopped and listened for voices, hearing and proximity sense both strained to their limits for a full minute before I lowered myself the final four meters and dropped to the floor of a well-lit, carpeted passageway. It was deserted in both directions.

I checked my internal time display and stowed the shard gun. Mission time was accumulating. By now Ortega and Kawahara would be talking. I glanced around at the decor and guessed that whatever function the operating deck had once been intended to serve, it wasn't serving it now. The passageway was decked out in opulent red and gold with stands of exotic plant life and lamps in the form of coupling bodies every few meters. The carpet beneath my feet was deep and woven with highly detailed images of sexual abandon. Male, female, and variants between twined around each other along the length of the corridor in an unbroken progression of plugged orifices and splayed limbs. The walls were hung with similarly explicit holoframes that gasped and moaned into life as I passed them. In one of them I thought I recognized the dark-haired, crimson-lipped woman of the street 'cast advertisement, the woman who might have pressed her thigh against mine in a bar on the other side of the globe.

In the cold detachment of the betathanatine, none of it had any more impact than a wall full of Martian technoglyphs.

There were plushly appointed double doors set into each side of the corridor at about ten-meter intervals. It didn't take much imagination to work out what was behind the doors. Jerry's Biocabins, by any other name, and each door was just as likely as not to disgorge a client at any moment. I quickened my pace, searching for a connecting corridor that I knew led to stairs and elevators onto the other levels.

I was almost there when a door five meters ahead of me swung open.

I froze, hand on the grip of the shard gun, shoulders to the wall. Gaze gripped to the leading edge of the door. The neurachem thrummed.

In front of me, a gray-furred animal that was either half-grown wolf cub or dog emerged from the open door with arthritic slowness. I kept my hand on the shard gun and eased away from the wall, watching. The animal was not much over knee height and it moved on all fours, but there was something badly wrong with the structure of the rear legs. Something wrenched. Its ears were laid back and a minute keening came from its throat. It turned its head toward me and for a moment my hand tightened on the shard gun, but the animal looked at me for only a moment and the mute suffering in its eyes was enough to tell me I was in no danger. Then it limped painfully along the corridor to a room farther down on the opposite wall and paused there, the long head down close to the door as if listening.

With a dreamlike sense of lost control, I followed and leaned my own head against the surface of the door. The soundproofing was good, but no match for the Khumalo neurachem at full stretch. Somewhere down near the limits of hearing, noises trickled into my ear like stinging insects. A dull, rhythmic thudding sound and something else that might have been the pleading screams of someone whose strength was almost gone. It stopped almost as soon as I had tuned it in.

Below me, the dog stopped keening at the same moment and lay down on the ground beside the door. When I stepped away, it looked up at me once with a gaze of pure distilled pain and reproach. In those eyes I could see reflected every victim that had ever looked at me in the last three decades of my waking life. Then the animal turned its head away and licked apathetically at its wounded rear legs.

For a split second, something geysered through the cold crust of the betathanatine.

I went back to the door the animal had emerged from, drawing the shard gun on my way, and swung through holding the weapon in both hands before me. The room beyond was spacious and pastel colored with quaint two-dimensional framed pictures on the walls. A massive four-poster bed with translucent drapes occupied the center. Seated on the edge of the bed was a distinguished-looking man in his forties, naked from the waist down. Above the waist, he appeared to be wearing formal evening dress, which clashed badly with the heavy-duty canvas work gloves he had pulled up to both elbows. He was bent over, cleaning himself between the legs with a damp white cloth.

As I advanced into the room, he glanced up.

"Jack? You finished al—" He stared at the gun in my hands without comprehension, then as the muzzle came to within half a meter of his face a note of asperity crept into his voice. "Listen, I didn't dial for this routine."

"On the house," I said dispassionately, and watched as the clutch of monomolecular shards tore his face apart. His hands flew up from between his legs to cover the wounds, and he flopped over sideways on the bed, gut-deep noises grinding out of him as he died.

With the mission-time display flaring red in the corner of my vision, I backed out of the room. The wounded animal outside the door opposite did not look up as I approached. I knelt and laid one hand gently on the matted fur. The head lifted and the keening rose in the throat again. I set down the shard gun and tensed my empty hand. The neural sheath delivered the Tebbit knife, glinting.

After, I cleaned the blade on the fur, resheathed the knife, and picked up the shard gun, all with the unhurried calm of the Reaper. Then I moved silently to the connecting corridor. Deep in the diamond serenity of the drug something was nagging at me, but the Reaper would not let me worry about it.

As indicated on Elliott's stolen blueprints the cross corridor led to a set of stairs, now carpeted in the same orgiastic pattern as the main thoroughfare. I moved warily down the steps, gun tracking the open space ahead, proximity sense spread like a radar net before me. Nothing stirred. Kawahara must have battened down all the hatches just in case Ortega and her crew saw something inconvenient while they were on the premises.

Two levels down, I stepped off the stairs and followed my memory of the blueprints through a mesh of corridors until I was reasonably sure that the door to Kawahara's quarters was around the next corner. With my back to the wall, I slid up to the corner and waited, breathing shallowly. The proximity sense said there was someone at the door around the corner, possibly more than one person, and I picked up the faint tang of cigarette smoke. I dropped to my knees, checked my surroundings, and then lowered my face to the ground. With one cheek brushing the pile of the carpet, I eased my head around the corner.

A man and a woman stood by the door, similarly dressed in green coveralls. The woman was smoking. Although each of them had stunguns holstered importantly at their belts, they looked more like technical staff than security attendants. I relaxed fractionally and settled down to wait some more. In the corner of my eye, the minutes of mission time pulsed like an overstressed vein.

It was another quarter of an hour before I heard the door. At full amp, the neurachem caught the rustle of clothing as the attendants moved to allow whoever was leaving to exit. I heard voices, Ortega's flat with pretended official disinterest, then Kawahara's, as modulated as the mandroid in Larkin and Green. With the betathanatine to protect me from the hatred, my reaction to that voice was a muted horizon event, like the flare and crash of gunfire at a great distance.

". . . that I cannot be of more assistance, Lieutenant. If what you say about the Wei Clinic is true, his mental balance has certainly deteriorated since he worked for me. I feel a certain . . . responsibility. I mean, I would never have recommended him to Laurens Bancroft, had I suspected this would happen."

"As I said, this is supposition." Ortega's tone sharpened slightly. "And I'd appreciate it if these details didn't go any further. Until we know where Kovacs has gone, and why—"

"Quite. I quite understand the sensitivity of the matter. You are aboard *Head in the Clouds*, Lieutenant. We have a reputation for confidentiality."

"Yeah." Ortega allowed a strain of distaste into her voice. "I've heard that."

"Well, then, you can rest assured that this will not be spoken of. Now if you'll excuse me, Lieutenant. Detective Sergeant. I have some administrative matters to attend to. Tia and Max will see you back to the flight deck."

The door closed and soft footfalls advanced in my direction. I tensed abruptly. Ortega and her escort were coming in my direction. This was something no one had bargained for. On the blueprints the main landing pads were forward of Kawahara's cabin, and I'd come up on the aft side with that in mind. There seemed no reason to march Ortega and Bautista toward the stern.

There was no panic. Instead, a cool analog of the adrenaline reaction rinsed through my mind, offering a chilly array of hard facts. Ortega and Bautista were in no danger. They must have arrived the same way they were leaving or something would have been said. As for me, if they passed the corridor I was in, their escort would only have to glance sideways to see me. The area was well lit and there were no hiding places within reach. On the other hand, with my body down below room temperature, my pulse slowed to a crawl, and my breathing at the same low, most of the subliminal factors that will trigger a normal human being's proximity sense were gone. Always assuming the escorts were wearing normal sleeves.

And if they turned *into* this corridor to use the stairs I had come down by . . .

I shrank back against the wall, dialed the shard gun down to minimum dispersal, and stopped breathing.

Ortega. Bautista. The two attendants brought up the rear. They were so close I could have reached out and touched Ortega's hair.

No one looked around.

I gave them a full minute before I breathed again. Then I checked the corridor in both directions, went rapidly around the corner, and knocked on the door with the butt of the shard gun. Without waiting for a reply, I walked in.

CHAPTEr FOrTY-ONE

The chamber was exactly as Miller had described it. Twenty meters wide and walled in nonreflective glass that sloped inward from roof to floor. On a clear day you could probably lie on that slope and peer down thousands of meters to the sea below. The decor was stark and owed a lot to Kawahara's early millennium roots. The walls were smoke gray, the floor fused glass, and the lighting came from jagged pieces of origami performed in illuminum sheeting and spiked on iron tripods in the corners of the room. One side of the room was dominated by a massive slab of black steel that must serve as a desk; the other held a group of shale-colored loungers grouped around an imitation oil drum brazier. Beyond the loungers, an arched doorway led out to what Miller had surmised were sleeping quarters.

Above the desk, a slow weaving holodisplay of data had been abandoned to its own devices. Reileen Kawahara stood with her back to the door, staring out at the night sky.

"Forget something?" she asked distantly.

"No, not a thing."

I saw how her back stiffened as she heard me, but when she turned, it was with unhurried smoothness and even the sight of the shard gun didn't crack the icy calm on her face. Her voice was almost as disinterested as it had been before she turned.

"Who are you? How did you get in here?"

"Think about it." I gestured at the loungers. "Sit down over there, take the weight off your feet while you're thinking."

"Kadmin?"

"Now you're insulting me. Sit down!"

I saw the realization explode behind her eyes.

"Kovacs?" An unpleasant smile bent at her lips. "Kovacs, you stupid, *stupid* bastard. Do you have any idea what you've just thrown away?"

"I said sit down."

"She was gone, Kovacs. Back to Harlan's World. I kept my word. What do you think you're doing here?"

"I'm not going to tell you again," I said mildly. "Either you sit down now, or I'll break one of your kneecaps."

The thin smile stayed on Kawahara's mouth as she lowered herself a centimeter at a time onto the nearest lounger. "Very well, Kovacs. We'll play to your script tonight. And then I'll have that fishwife Sachilowska dragged all the way back here and you with her. What are you going to do? Kill me?"

"If necessary."

"For what? Is this some kind of moral stand?" The emphasis Kawahara laid on the last two words made it sound like the name of a product. "Aren't you forgetting something? If you kill me here, it'll take about eighteen hours for the remote storage system in Europe to notice and then resleeve me from my last update 'cast. And it won't take the new me very long to work out what happened up here."

I seated myself on the edge of the lounger. "Oh, I don't know. Look how long it's taken Bancroft, and he still doesn't have the truth, does he?"

"Is this about Bancroft?"

"No, Reileen. This is about you and me. You should have left Sarah alone. You should have left me alone while you could."

"Ohhh," she cooed, mock maternal. "Did you get *manipulated*? I'm sorry." She dropped the tone just as abruptly. "You're an *Envoy*, Kovacs. You live by manipulation. We all do. We all live in the great manipulation matrix and it's just one big struggle to stay on top."

I shook my head. "I didn't ask to be dealt in."

"Kovacs, Kovacs." Kawahara's expression was suddenly almost tender. "None of us ask to be dealt in. You think I asked to be born in Fission City, with a web-fingered dwarf for a father and psychotic whore for a mother? You think I asked for that? We're not dealt in, we're *thrown* in, and after that it's just about keeping your head above water."

"Or pouring water down other people's throats," I agreed amiably. "I guess you took after your mother, right?"

For a second it was as if Kawahara's face was a mask cut from tin behind which a furnace was raging. I saw the fury ignite in her eyes, and if I had not had the Reaper inside to keep me cold, I would have been afraid.

"Kill me," she said, tight lipped. "And make the most of it, because you are going to suffer, Kovacs. You think those sad-case revolutionaries on New Beijing suffered when they died? I'm going to invent new limits for you and your fish-smelling bitch."

I shook my head. "I don't think so, Reileen. You see, your update needlecast went through about ten minutes ago. And on the way, I had it dipped. Didn't lift anything, we just spliced the Rawling virus onto the 'cast. It's in the core by now, Reileen. Your remote storage has been spiked."

Her eyes narrowed. "You're lying."

"Not today. You liked the work Irene Elliott did at Jack It Up? Well, you should see her in a virtual forum. I bet she had time to take a half-dozen mind-bites while she was inside that needlecast. Souvenirs. Collector's items, in fact, because if I know anything about stack engineers, they'll weld down the lid on your remote stack faster than politicians leaving a war zone." I nodded over at the winding data display. "I should think you'll get the alarm in another couple of hours. It took longer at Innenin, but that was a long time ago. The technology's moved on since then."

Then she believed, and it was as if the fury I'd seen in her eyes had banked down to a concentrated white heat.

"Irene Elliott," she said intently. "When I find her—"

"I think we've had enough empty threats for one day," I interrupted without force. "Listen to me. Currently the stack you're wearing is the only life you have, and the mood I'm in now it wouldn't take much to make me cut it out of your spine and stamp on it. Before or after I shoot you, so *shut up*."

Kawahara sat still, glaring at me out of slitted eyes. Her top lip drew fractionally back off her teeth for a moment, before control asserted itself.

"What do you want?"

"Better. What I want, right now, is a full confession of how you set Bancroft up. Resolution 653, Mary Lou Hinchley, the whole thing. You can throw in how you framed Ryker, as well."

"Are you wired for this?"

I tapped my left eyelid where the recording system had gone in, and smiled.

"You really think I'm going to do this?" Kawahara's rage glinted at me from behind her eyes. She was waiting, coiled, for an opening. I had seen her like this before, but then I hadn't been on the receiving end of that look. I was in as much danger under those eyes as I had ever been under fire in the streets of Sharya. "You really think you're going to get this from me?"

"Look on the bright side, Reileen. You can probably buy and influence your way out of the erasure penalty, and for the rest you might get only a couple of hundred years in the store." My voice hardened. "Whereas, if you don't talk, you'll die right here and now."

"Confession under duress is inadmissible under U.N. law."

"Don't make me laugh. This isn't going to the U.N. You think I've never been in a court before? You think I'd trust *lawyers* to deal with this? Everything you say here tonight is going express needlecast to WorldWeb One as soon as I'm back on the ground. That, and footage of whoever it was I wasted in the doggie room upstairs." Kawahara's eyes widened and I nodded. "Yeah, I should have said earlier. You're a client down. Not really dead, but he'll need resleeving. Now, with all that, I reckon about three minutes after Sandy Kim goes live, the U.N. tacs are going to be blowing down your door with a fistful of warrants. They'll have no choice. Bancroft alone will force their hand. You think the same people who authorized Sharya and Innenin are going to stick at a little constitutional rule-bending to protect their power base? *Now, start talking.*"

Kawahara raised her eyebrows, as if this was nothing more than a slightly distasteful joke she'd just been told. "Where would you like me to start, Takeshi-san?"

"Mary Lou Hinchley. She fell from here, right?"

"Of course."

"You had her slated for the snuff deck? Some sick fuck wanted to pull on the tiger sleeve and play kitty?"

"Well, well." Kawahara tipped her head on one side as she made connections. "Who have you been talking to? Someone from the Wei Clinic, is it? Let me think. Miller was here for that little object lesson, but you torched him, so . . . Oh. You haven't been head-hunting again, Takeshi? You didn't take Felipe Miller home in a hat box, did you?"

I said nothing, just looked at her over the barrel of the shard gun, hearing again the weakened screaming through the door I'd listened at. Kawahara shrugged.

"It wasn't the tiger, as it happens. But something of that sort, yes."

"And she found out?"

"Somehow, yes." Kawahara seemed to be relaxing, which under normal circumstances would have made me nervous. Under the betathanatine, it just made me more watchful. "A word in the wrong place, maybe something a technician said. You know, we usually put our snuff clients through a virtual version before we let them loose on the real thing. It helps to know how they're going to react, and in some cases we even persuade them not to go through with it."

"Very thoughtful of you."

Kawahara sighed. "How do I get through to you, Takeshi? We provide a service here. If it can be made legal, then so much the better."

"That's bullshit, Reileen. You sell them the virtual, and in a couple of months they come sniffing after the real thing. There's a casual link, and you know it. Selling them something illegal gives you leverage, probably over some very influential people. Get many U.N. governors up here, do you? Protectorate generals, that kind of scum?"

"*Head in the Clouds* caters to an elite."

"Like that white-haired fuck I greased upstairs? He was someone important, was he?"

"Carlton McCabe?" From somewhere, Kawahara produced an alarming smile. "You could say that, I suppose, yes. A person of influence."

"Would you care to tell me which particular person of influence you'd promised they could rip the innards out of Mary Lou Hinchley?"

Kawahara tautened slightly. "No, I would not."

"Suppose not. You'll want that for a bargaining line later, won't you. Okay, skip it. So what happened? Hinchley was brought up here, accidentally found out what she was being fattened up for, and tried to escape? Stole a grav harness, perhaps?"

"I doubt that. The equipment is kept under tight security. Perhaps she thought she could cling to the outside of one of the shuttles. She was not a very bright girl, apparently. The details are still unclear, but she must have fallen somehow."

"Or jumped."

Kawahara shook her head. "I don't think she had the stomach for that. Mary Lou Hinchley was not a samurai spirit. Like most of common humanity, she would have clung to life until the last undignified moment. Hoping for some miracle. Begging for mercy."

"How inelegant. Was she missed immediately?"

"Of course she was missed! She had a client waiting for her. We scoured the ship."

"Embarrassing."

"Yes."

"But not as embarrassing as having her wash up on the shore a couple of days later, huh? The luck fairies were out of town that week."

"It was unlucky," Kawahara conceded, as if we were discussing a bad hand of poker. "But not entirely unexpected. We were not anticipating a real problem."

"You knew she was Catholic?"

"Of course. It was part of the requirements."

"So when Ryker dug up that iffy conversion, you must have shat yourself. Hinchley's testimony would have dragged you right into the open along with fuck knows how many of your influential friends. *Head in the Clouds,* one of the Houses indicted for snuff and you with it. What was the word you used on New Beijing that time? Intolerable risk. Something had to be done; Ryker had to be shut down. Stop me if I'm losing the thread here."

"No, you're quite correct."

"So you framed him?"

Kawahara shrugged again. "An attempt was made to buy him off. He proved . . . unreceptive."

"Unfortunate. So what did you do then?"

"You don't know?"

"I want to hear you say it. I want details. I'm doing too much of the talking here. Try to keep your end of the conversation up, or I might think you're being uncooperative."

Kawahara raised her eyes theatrically to the ceiling. "I framed Elias Ryker. I set him up with a false tip about a clinic in Seattle. We built a phone construct of Ryker and used it to pay Ignacio Garcia to fake the Reasons of Conscience decals on two of Ryker's kills. We knew the Seattle PD wouldn't buy it and that Garcia's faking wouldn't stand up to close scrutiny. There, is that better?"

"Where'd you get Garcia from?"

"Research on Ryker, back when we were trying to buy him off." Kawahara shifted impatiently on the lounger. "The connection came up."

"Yeah, that's what I figured."

"How perceptive of you."

"So everything was nicely nailed down. Until Resolution 653 came along, and stirred it all up again. And Hinchley was still a live case."

Kawahara inclined her head. "Just so."

"Why didn't you just stall it? Buy some decision makers on the U.N. Council?"

"Who? This isn't New Beijing. You met Phiri and Ertekin. Do they look as if they're for sale?"

I nodded. "So it was you in Marco's sleeve. Did Miriam Bancroft know?"

"Miriam?" Kawahara looked perplexed. "Of course not. No one knew, that was the point. Marco plays Miriam on a regular basis. It was a perfect cover."

"Not perfect. You play shit tennis, apparently."

"I didn't have time for a competence disk."

"Why Marco. Why not just go as yourself?"

Kawahara waved a hand. "I'd been hammering at Bancroft since the resolution was tabled. Ertekin, too, whenever she let me near her. I was making myself conspicuous. Marco putting in a word on my behalf makes me look more detached."

"You took that call from Rutherford," I said, mostly to myself. "The one to Suntouch House after we dropped in on him. I figured it was Miriam, but you were there as a guest, playing Marco on the sidelines of the great Catholic debate."

"Yes." A faint smile. "You seem to have greatly overestimated Miriam Bancroft's role in all this. Oh, by the way, who *is* that you've got wearing Ryker's sleeve at the moment? Just to satisfy my curiosity. He's very convincing, whoever he is."

I said nothing, but a smile leaked from one corner of my mouth. Kawahara caught it.

"*Really?* Double-sleeving. You really must have Lieutenant Ortega wrapped around your little finger. Or wrapped around something, anyway. Congratulations. Manipulation worthy of a Meth." She barked a short laugh. "That was meant as a compliment, Takeshi-san."

I ignored the jab. "You talked to Bancroft in Osaka? Thursday the sixteenth of August. You knew he was going?"

"Yes. He has regular business there. It was made to look like a chance encounter. I invited him to *Head in the Clouds* on his return. It's a pattern for him. Buying sex after business deals. You probably found that out."

"Yeah. So when you got him up here, what did you tell him?"

"I told him the truth."

"The truth?" I stared at her. "You told him about Hinchley and expected him to back you?"

"Why not?" There was a chilling simplicity in the look she gave me back. "We have a friendship that goes back centuries. Common business strategies that have sometimes taken longer than a normal human lifetime to bring to fruition. I hardly expected him to side with the little people."

"So he disappointed you. He wouldn't keep the Meth faith."

Kawahara sighed again, and this time there was a genuine weariness in it that gusted out of somewhere centuries deep in dust.

"Laurens maintains a cheap romantic streak that I continually underestimate. He is not unlike you in many ways. But unlike you, he has no excuse for it. The man is over three centuries old. I assumed—wanted to assume, perhaps—that his values would reflect that. That the rest was just posturing, speech-making for the herd." Kawahara made a negligent what-can-you-do gesture with one slim arm. "Wishful thinking, I'm afraid."

"What did he do? Take some kind of moral stand?"

Kawahara's mouth twisted without humor. "You mock me? You, with the blood of dozens from the Wei Clinic fresh on your hands. A butcher for the Protectorate, an extinguisher of human life on every world where it has managed to find a foothold. You are, if I may say so, Takeshi, a little inconsistent."

Secure in the cool wrap of the betathanatine, I could feel nothing beyond a mild irritation at Kawahara's obtuseness. A need to clarify.

"The Wei Clinic was personal."

"The Wei Clinic was business, Takeshi. They had no personal interest in you at all. Most of the people you wiped were merely doing their jobs."

"Then they should have chosen another job."

"And the people of Sharya. What choice should they have made? Not to be born on that particular world, at that particular time? Not to allow themselves to be conscripted, perhaps?"

"I was young and stupid," I said simply. "I was used. I killed for people like you because I knew no better. Then I learned better. What happened at Innenin taught me better. Now I don't kill for anyone but myself, and every time that I take a life, I know the value of it."

"The value of it. The *value* of a human life." Kawahara shook her head like a teacher with an exasperating student. "You are *still* young and stupid. Human life has no value. Haven't you learned that yet, Takeshi, with all you've seen? It has no value, intrinsic to itself. Machines cost money to build. Raw materials cost money to extract. But people?" She made a tiny spitting sound. "You can always get some more people. They reproduce like cancer cells, whether you want them or not. They are *abundant*, Takeshi. Why should they be valuable? Do you know that it costs us *less* to recruit and use up a real snuff whore than it does to set up and run the virtual equivalent format? Real human flesh is *cheaper* than a machine. It's the axiomatic truth of our times."

"Bancroft didn't think so."

"Bancroft?" Kawahara made a disgusted noise deep in her throat. "Bancroft is a cripple, limping along on his archaic notions. It's a mystery to me how he's survived this long."

"So you programmed him to suicide? Gave him a little chemical push?"

"Programmed him to. . . ?" Kawahara's eyes widened and a delighted chuckle that was just the right blend of husk and chime issued from her sculpted lips. "Kovacs, you can't be that stupid. I told you he killed himself. It was his idea, not mine. There was a time when you trusted my word, even if you couldn't stomach my company. Think about it. Why would I want him dead?"

"To erase what you told him about Hinchley. When he was resleeved, his last update would be minus that little indiscretion."

Kawahara nodded sagely. "Yes, I can see how that would fit for you. A defensive move. You have, after all, existed on the defensive since you left the Envoys. And a creature that lives on the defensive sooner or later comes to think on the defensive. You are forgetting one thing, Takeshi."

She paused dramatically, and even through the betathanatine, a vague ripple of mistrust tugged at me. Kawahara was overplaying it.

"And what's that?"

"That *I*, Takeshi Kovacs, am not you. I do not play on the defensive."

"Not even at tennis?"

She offered me a calibrated little smile. "Very witty. I did not need to erase Laurens Bancroft's memory of our conversation, because by then he had slaughtered his own Catholic whore and had as much to lose as I from Resolution 653."

I blinked. I'd had a variety of theories circling around the central conviction that Kawahara was responsible for Bancroft's death, but none quite this garish. But as Kawahara's words sunk in, so did a number of pieces from that jagged mirror that I'd thought was already complete enough to see the truth in. I looked into a newly revealed corner and wished I had not seen the things that moved there.

Opposite me, Kawahara grinned at my silence. She knew she'd dented me, and it pleased her. Vanity, vanity. Kawahara's only but enduring flaw. Like all Meths, she had grown very impressed with herself. The admission, the final piece to my jigsaw, had slipped out easily. She wanted me to have it, she wanted me to see how far ahead of me she was, how far behind her I was limping along.

That crack about the tennis must have touched a nerve.

"Another subtle echo of his wife's face," she said, "carefully selected and then amped up with a little cosmetic surgery. He choked the life out of her. As he was coming for the second time, I think. Married life, eh, Kovacs? What it must do to you males."

"You got it on tape?" My voice sounded stupid in my own ears.

Kawahara's smile came back. "Come on, Kovacs. Ask me something that needs an answer."

"Bancroft was . . . chemically assisted?"

"Oh, but of course. You were right about that. Quite a nasty drug, but then I expect you know—"

It was the betathanatine. The heart-dragging slow chill of the drug, because without it I would have been moving with the breath of air as the door opened on my flank. The thought crossed my mind as rapidly as it was able, and even as it did I knew by its very presence that I was going to be too slow. This was no time for thinking. Thought in combat was a luxury about as appropriate as a hot bath and massage. It fogged the whiplash clarity of the Khumalo's neurachem response system, and I spun, just a couple of centuries too late, shard gun lifting.

Splat!

The stunbolt slammed through me like a train, and I seemed to see the brightly lit carriage windows ratcheting past behind my eyes. My vision was a frozen frame on Trepp, crouched in the doorway, stungun extended, face watchful in case she'd missed or I was wearing neural armor beneath the stealth suit. Some hope. My own weapon dropped from nerveless fingers as my hand spasmed open, and I pitched forward beside it. The wooden floor came up and smashed me on the side of the head like one of my father's cuffs.

"What kept you?" Kawahara's voice asked from a great height, distorted to a bass growl by my fading consciousness. One slim hand reached into my field of vision and retrieved the shard gun. Numbly, I felt her other hand tug the stungun free of the other holster.

"Alarm only went off a couple of minutes ago." Trepp stepped into view, stowing her stungun, and crouched to look at me curiously. "Took McCabe a while to cool off enough to trip the system. Most of your half-assed security is still up on the main deck, goggling at the corpse. Who's this?"

"It's Kovacs," Kawahara said dismissively, tucking the shard gun and stunner into her belt on her way to the desk. To my paralyzed gaze, she appeared to be retreating across a vast plain, hundreds of meters with every stride until she was tiny and distant. Doll-like, she leaned on the desk and punched at controls I could not see.

I wasn't going under.

"Kovacs?" Trepp's face went abruptly impassive. "I thought—"

"Yes, so did I." The holographic data weave above the desk awoke and unwound. Kawahara put her face closer, colors swirling over her features. "He double-sleeved on us. Presumably with Ortega's help. You should have stuck around the *Panama Rose* a little longer."

My hearing was still mangled, my vision frozen in place, but I wasn't going under. I wasn't sure if it was some side effect of the betathanatine, another bonus feature of the Khumalo system, or maybe both in some unintended conjunction, but *something* was keeping me conscious.

"Being around a crime scene with that many cops makes me nervous," Trepp said, and put out a hand to touch my face.

"Yeah?" Kawahara was still absorbed in the dataflow. "Well, distracting this psycho with moral debate and true confessions hasn't been good for my digestion, either. I thought you were never going to— Fuck!"

She jerked her head savagely to one side, then lowered it and stared at the surface of the desk.

"He was telling the truth."

"About what?"

Kawahara looked up at Trepp, suddenly guarded. "Doesn't matter. What are you doing to his face?"

"He's cold."

"Of course he's fucking cold." The deteriorating language was a sure sign that Reileen Kawahara was rattled, I thought dreamily. "How do you think he got in past the infrareds? He's stiffed to the eyes."

Trepp got up, face carefully expressionless. "What are you going to do with him?"

"He's going into virtual," Kawahara said grimly. "Along with his Harlanite fishwife friend. But before we do that, we have to perform a little surgery. He's wearing a wire."

I tried to move my right hand. The last joint of the middle finger twitched, barely.

"You sure he isn't transmitting?"

"Yeah, he told me. Anyway, we would have nailed the transmission, soon as it started. Have you got a knife?"

A bone-deep tremor that felt suspiciously like panic ran through me. Desperately, I reached down into the paralysis for some sign of impending recovery. The Khumalo nervous system was still reeling. I could feel my eyes drying out from the lack of a blink reflex. Through smearing vision, I watched Kawahara coming back from the desk, hand held out expectantly to Trepp.

"I don't have a knife." I couldn't be certain with the wow and flutter of my hearing, but Trepp's voice sounded rebellious.

"No problem." Kawahara took more long strides and disappeared from view, voice fading. "I've got something back here that'll do just as well. You'd better whistle up some muscle to drag this piece of shit up to one of the decanting salons. I think seven and nine are prepped. Use the jack on the desk."

Trepp hesitated. I felt something drop, like a tiny piece of ice thawing from the frozen block of my central nervous system. My eyelids scraped slowly down over my eyes, once and up again. The cleansing contact brought tears. Trepp saw it and stiffened. She made no move toward the desk.

The fingers of my right hand twitched and curled. I felt the beginnings of tension in the muscles of my stomach. My eyes moved.

Kawahara's voice came through faintly. She must be in the other room, beyond the arch. "They coming?"

Trepp's face stayed impassive. Her eyes lifted from me. "Yeah," she said loudly. "Be here in a couple of minutes."

I was coming back. Something was forcing my nerves back into sparking, fizzing life. I could feel the shakes setting in, and with it a soupy, suffocating quality to the air in my lungs that meant the betathanatine crash was coming on ahead of schedule. My limbs were molded in lead, and my hands felt as if I was wearing thick cotton gloves with a low electric current fizzing through them. I was in no condition for a fight.

My left hand was folded under me, flattened to the floor by the weight of my body. My right trailed out at an awkward side angle. It didn't feel as if my legs would do much more than hold me up. My options were limited.

"Right, then." I felt Kawahara's hand on my shoulder, pulling me onto my back like a fish for gutting. Her face was masked in concentration, and there was a pair of needle-nosed pliers in her other hand. She knelt astride my chest and spread the lids of my left eye with her fingers. I forced down the urge to blink, held myself immobile. The pliers came down, jaws poised a half centimeter apart.

I tensed the muscles in my forearm, and the neuralspring harness delivered the Tebbit knife into my hand.

I slashed sideways.

I was aiming for Kawahara's side, below the floating ribs, but the combination of stun shakes and betathanatine crash threw me off, and the knife blade sliced into her left arm below the elbow, jarred on the bone, and bounced off. Kawahara yelled and released her grip on my eye. The pliers plunged down, off course, hit my cheekbone, and carved a trough in the flesh of my cheek. I felt the pain distantly, metal snagging tissue. Blood spilled down into my eye. I stabbed again, weakly, but this time Kawahara twisted astride me and blocked downward with her injured arm. She yelled again, and my fizzing glove grip on the knife slipped. The haft trickled away past my palm, and the weapon was gone. Summoning all my remaining energy into my left arm, I hooked a savage punch up from the floor and caught Kawahara on the temple. She rolled off me, clutching at the wound in her arm, and for a moment I thought the blade had gone deep enough to mark her with the C -381 coating. But Sheila Sorenson had told me that the cyanide poisoning would do its work in the time it takes to draw a couple of breaths.

Kawahara was getting up.

"What the fuck are you waiting for?" she inquired acidly of Trepp. "Shoot this piece of shit, will you?"

Her voice died on the last word as she saw the truth in Trepp's face an instant before the pale woman went for her holstered stungun. Maybe it was a truth that was only dawning on Trepp herself at that moment, because she was slow. Kawahara dropped the pliers, cleared both shard gun and stunner from her belt with a snap, and leveled them before Trepp's weapon was even halfway out of the holster.

"You traitorous fucking cunt," Kawahara spat out wonderingly, her voice suddenly streaked through with a coarse accent I had never heard before. "You knew he was coming around, didn't you. You're fucking dead, bitch."

I staggered upright and lurched into Kawahara just as she pulled the triggers. I heard both weapons discharge, the almost supra-aural whine of the shard gun and the sharp electrical splatter of the stunner. Through the fogged vision in the corner of one eye, I saw Trepp make a desperate bid to complete her draw and not even come close. She went down, face almost comically surprised. At the same time, my shoulder smashed into Kawahara, and we stumbled back toward the slope of the windows. She tried to shoot me, but I flailed the guns aside with my arms and tripped her. She hooked at me with her injured arm, and we both went down on the angled glass.

The stunner was gone, skittering across the floor, but she'd managed to hang on to the shard gun. It swung around at me, and I batted it down clumsily. My other hand punched at Kawahara's head, missed, and bounced off her shoulder. She grinned fiercely and headbutted me in the face. My nose broke with a sensation like biting into celery, and blood flooded down over my mouth. From somewhere I suffered an insane desire to taste it. Then Kawahara was on me, twisting me back against the glass and punching solidly into my body. I blocked one or two of the punches, but the strength was puddling out of me and the muscles in my arms were losing interest. Things started to go numb inside. Above me Kawahara's face registered a savage triumph as she saw that the fight was over. She hit me once more, with great care, in the groin. I convulsed and slid down the glass into a sprawled heap on the floor.

"That ought to hold you, sport," she grated, and jerked herself back to her feet, breathing heavily. Beneath the barely disarrayed elegance of her hair, I suddenly saw the face that this new accent belonged to. The brutal satisfaction in that face was what her victims in Fission City must have seen as she made them drink from the dull gray flask of the water carrier. "You just lie there for a moment."

My body told me that I didn't have any other option. I felt drenched in damage, sinking fast under the weight of the chemicals silting up my system and the shivering neural invasion of the stunbolt. I tried to lift one arm, and it flopped back down like a fish with a kilo of lead in its guts. Kawahara saw it happen and grinned.

"Yeah, that'll do nicely," she said, and looked absently down at her own left arm, where blood was trickling from the rent in her blouse. "You're going to fucking pay for that, Kovacs."

She walked across to Trepp's motionless form. "And you, you fuck," she said, kicking the pale woman hard in the ribs. The body did not move. "What did this motherfucker do for you, anyway? Promise to eat your cunt for the next decade?"

Trepp made no response. I strained the fingers of my left hand and managed to move my hand almost its own width across the floor toward my leg. Kawahara went to the desk with a final backward glance at Trepp's body and touched a control.

"Security?"

"Ms. Kawahara." It was the same male voice that had grilled Ortega on our approach to the airship. "There's been an incursion on the—"

"I know what there's been," Kawahara said tiredly. "I've been wrestling with it for the last five minutes. Why aren't you down here?"

"Ms. Kawahara?"

"I said, how long does it take you to get your synthetic ass down here on a call out?"

There was a brief silence. Kawahara waited, head bowed over the desk. I reached across my body, and my right and left hands met in a weak clasp, then curled closed on what they held and fell back.

"Ms. Kawahara, there was no alert from your cabin."

"Oh." Kawahara turned back to look at Trepp. "Okay, well, get someone down here now. Squad of four. There's some garbage to take out."

"Yes, ma'am."

In spite of everything, I felt a smile crawl onto my mouth. *Ma'am?*

Kawahara came back, scooping the pliers up off the floor on her way. "What are you grinning at, Kovacs?"

I tried to spit at her, but the saliva barely made it out of my mouth and hung in a thick streamer over my jaw, mingled with the blood. Kawahara's face distorted with sudden rage, and she kicked me in the stomach. On top of everything else, I barely felt it.

"You," she began savagely, then forced the level of her voice back down to an accentless icy calm, "have caused more than enough trouble for one lifetime."

She took hold of my collar and dragged me up the angled slope of the window until we were at eye level. My head lolled back on the glass, and she leaned over me. Her tone eased back, almost to conversational.

"Like the Catholics, like your friends at Innenin, like the pointless motes of slum life whose pathetic copulations brought you into existence, Takeshi. Human raw material—that's all you've ever been. You could have evolved beyond it and joined me on New Beijing, but you spat in my face and went back to your little-people existence. You could have joined us again, here on Earth, joined in the steerage of the whole human race this time. You could have been a man of power, Kovacs. Do you understand that? You could have been *significant*."

"I don't think so," I murmured weakly, starting to slide back down the glass. "I've still got a conscience rattling around in here somewhere. Just forgotten where I put it."

Kawahara grimaced and redoubled her hold on my collar. "Very witty. Spirited. You're going to need that, where you're going."

"When they ask how I died," I said. *"Tell them: Still Angry."*

"Quell." Kawahara leaned closer. She was almost lying on top of me now, like a sated lover. "But Quell never went into virtual interrogation, did she? You aren't going to die angry, Kovacs. You're going to die pleading. Over. And over. Again."

She shifted her hold to my chest and pressed me down hard. The pliers came up.

"Have an aperitif."

The jaws of the tool plunged into the underside of my eye, and a spurt of blood sprinkled Kawahara's face. Pain flared brightly. For a moment, I could see the pliers through the eye they were embedded in, towering away like a massive steel pylon, and then Kawahara twisted the jaws and something burst. My vision splashed red and then winked out, a dying monitor screen like the ones at Elliott's Data Linkage. From my other eye I saw Kawahara withdraw the pliers with Reese's recording wire gripped in the jaws. The rear end of the tiny device dripped minute spots of gore onto my cheek.

She'd go after Elliott and Reese. Not to mention Ortega, Bautista, and who knew how many others.

"That's fucking enough," I muttered in a slurred tone, and at the same moment, driving the muscles in my thighs to work, I locked my legs around Kawahara's waist. My left hand slapped down flat on the sloping glass.

The muffled crump of an explosion, and a sharp cracking.

Dialed to the short end of its fuse option, the termite microgrenade was designed to detonate almost instantaneously and to deliver 90 percent of its charge to the contact face. The remaining 10 percent still wrecked my hand, tearing the flesh from the Khumalo marrow-alloy bones and carbon-reinforced tendons, ripping the polybond ligamenting apart, and punching a coin-sized hole in my palm.

On the downward side, the window shattered like a thick plate of river ice. It seemed to happen in slow motion. I felt the surface cave in beside me, and then I was sliding sideways into the gap. Vaguely, I registered the rush of cold air into the cabin. Above me, Kawahara's face had gone stupid with shock as she realized what had happened, but she was too late. She came with me, flailing and smashing at my head and chest, but unable to break the lock I had on her waist. The pliers rose and fell, peeling a long strip of flesh from one cheekbone, plunging once into my wrecked eye, but by now the pain was far away, almost irrelevant, consumed entire by a bonfire of rage that had finally broken through what was left of the betathanatine.

Tell them: Still Angry.

Then the portion of glass we were struggling on gave way and tipped us out into the wind and sky.

And we fell . . .

My left arm was paralyzed in position by some damage the explosion had done, but as we started to tumble down through the chilled darkness I brought my right hand around and cupped the other grenade against the base of Kawahara's skull. I had a confused glimpse of the ocean far below, *Head in the Clouds* rocketing upward away from us, and an expression on Reileen Kawahara's face that had left sanity as far behind as the airship. Something was screaming, but I no longer knew if the sound came from within or without. Perception was spiraling away from me in the shrill whistling of the air around us, and I could no longer find my way back to the little window of individual viewpoint. The fall was as seductive as sleep.

With what remained of my will, I clamped grenade and skull against my own chest, hard enough to detonate.

My last thought was the hope that Davidson was watching his screen.

CHAPTEr FOrTY-TWO

The address was, ironically enough, down in Licktown. I left the autocab two blocks north and walked the rest of the way, unable to quite shake an eerie feeling of synthesis, as if the machinery of the cosmos were suddenly poking through the fabric of reality for me to see.

The apartment I was looking for formed part of a U-shaped block with a cracked and weed-grown concrete landing area in the center. Amongst the array of sad-looking ground and flight vehicles, I spotted the microcopter immediately. Someone had given it a purple and red-trim paint job recently, and though it still listed wearily to one side on its pods there were shiny clusters of expensive-looking sensor equipment fitted to the nose and tail. I nodded to myself and went up a flight of external steps to the second floor of the block.

The door to number seventeen was opened by an eleven-year-old boy who stared at me with blank hostility.

"Yeah?"

"I'd like to speak to Sheryl Bostock."

"Yeah, well, she ain't here."

I sighed and rubbed at the scar under my eye. "I think that's probably not true. Her copter's in the yard, you're her son, Daryl, and she came off night shift about three hours ago. Will you tell her there's someone to see her about the Bancroft sleeve?"

"You the Sia?"

"No, I just want to talk. If she can help me, there might be some money in it for her."

The boy stared at me for another pair of seconds, then closed the door without a word. From inside, I heard him calling his mother. I waited, and fought the urge to smoke.

Five minutes later Sheryl Bostock appeared around the edge of the door, dressed in a loose kaftan. Her synthetic sleeve was even more expressionless than her son had been, but it was a slack-muscled blankness that had nothing to do with attitude. Small muscle groups take a while to warm up from sleep on the cheaper-model synthetics, and this was definitely a model from the cut-price end of the market.

"You want to see me?" the synth voice asked unevenly. "What for?"

"I'm a private investigator working for Laurens Bancroft," I said as gently as

I could. "I'd like to ask you a few questions about your duties at PsychaSec. May I come in?"

She made a small noise, one that made me think she'd probably tried to shut doors in men's faces before without success.

"It won't take long."

She shrugged, and opened the door wide. I passed her and stepped into a tidily kept but threadbare room whose most important feature was clearly a sleek black entertainment deck. The system reared off the carpeting in the far corner like an obscure machine god's idol, and the remaining furniture had been re-arranged around it in obeisance. Like the microcopter's paint job, it looked new.

Daryl had disappeared from view.

"Nice deck," I said, going over to examine the machine's raked display front. "When did you get it?"

"A while ago." Sheryl Bostock closed the door and came to stand uncertainly in the center of the room. Her face was waking up, and now its expression hovered midway between sleep and suspicion. "What do you want to ask me?"

"May I sit down?"

She motioned me wordlessly to one of the brutally used armchairs and seated herself opposite me on a lounger. In the gaps left by the kaftan, her synthetic flesh looked pinkish and unreal. I looked at her for a while, wondering if I wanted to go through with this after all.

"Well?" She jerked her hand at me nervously. "What do you want to ask me? You wake me up after the night shift, you'd better have a good goddamn reason for this."

"On Tuesday the fourteenth of August you went into the Bancroft family's sleeving chamber and injected a Laurens Bancroft clone with a full hypospray of something. I'd like to know what it was, Sheryl."

The result was more dramatic than I would have imagined possible. Sheryl Bostock's artificial features flinched violently, and she recoiled as if I'd threatened her with a riot prod.

"That's a part of my usual duties," she cried shrilly. "I'm authorized to perform chemical input on the clones."

It didn't sound like her speaking. It sounded like something someone had told her to memorize.

"Was it synamorphesterone?" I asked quietly.

Cheap synths don't blush or go pale, but the look on her face conveyed the message just as effectively. She looked like a frightened animal, betrayed by its owner.

"How do you know that? Who told you that?" Her voice scaled to a high sobbing. *You can't know that. She said no one would know."*

She collapsed onto the sofa, weeping into her hands. Daryl emerged from another room at the sound of his mother crying, hesitated in the doorway, and evidently deciding that he couldn't or shouldn't do anything, stayed there watching me with a frightened expression on his face. I compressed a sigh and nodded at him, trying to look as unthreatening as possible. He went cautiously to the sofa and put a hand on his mother's shoulder, making her start as if from a blow. Ripples of memory stirred in me, and I could feel my own expression turning cold and grim. I tried to smile across the room at them, but it was farcical.

I cleared my throat. "I'm not here to do anything to you," I said. "I just want to know."

It took a minute or so for the words to get through the cobwebby veils of terror and sink into Sheryl Bostock's consciousness. It took even longer for her to get her tears under control and look up at me. Beside her, Daryl stroked her head doubtfully. I gritted my teeth and tried to stop the memories of my own eleventh year welling up in my head. I waited.

"It was her," she said finally.

● ● ●

Curtis intercepted me as I came around the seaward wing of Suntouch House. His face was darkened with anger, and his hands were curled into fists at his sides.

"She doesn't want to talk to you," he snarled at me.

"Get out of my way, Curtis," I said evenly. "Or you're going to get hurt."

His arms snapped up into a karate guard. "I said, she does—"

At that point I kicked him in the knee, and he collapsed at my feet. A second kick rolled him a couple of meters down the slope toward the tennis courts. By the time he came out of the roll, I was on him. I jammed a knee into the small of his back and pulled his head up by the hair.

"I'm not having a great day," I told him patiently. "And you're making it worse. Now, I'm going up there to talk to your boss. It'll take about ten minutes, and then I'll be gone. If you're wise, you'll stay out of the way."

"You fuck—"

I pulled his hair harder, and he yelped. "If you come in there after me, Curtis, I'm going to hurt you. Badly. Do you understand? I'm not in the mood for swampsuck grifters like you today."

"Leave him alone, Mr. Kovacs. Weren't you ever nineteen?"

I glanced over my shoulder to where Miriam Bancroft stood with her hands in the pockets of a loose, desert-colored ensemble apparently modeled on Sharyan haremwear. Her long hair was caught up under a swath of the ochre cloth, and her eyes glinted in the sun. I remembered suddenly what Ortega had said about Nakamura. *They use her face and body to sell the stuff.* Now I could see it, the casual poise of a fashion house sleeve demonstrator.

I let go of Curtis's hair and stood back while he climbed to his feet. "I wasn't this stupid at any age," I said untruthfully. "Do you want to tell him to back off, instead? Maybe he'll listen to you."

"Curtis, go and wait for me in the limousine. I won't be long."

"Are you going to let him—"

"Curtis!" There was a cordial astonishment in her tone, as if there must be some mistake, as if answering back just wasn't on the menu. Curtis's face flushed when he heard it, and he stalked away from us with tears of consternation standing in his eyes. I watched him out of sight, still not convinced I shouldn't have hit him again. Miriam Bancroft must have read the thought on my face.

"I would have thought even your appetite for violence had been sated by now," she said quietly. "Are you still looking for targets?"

"Who says I'm looking for targets?"

"You did."

I looked quickly at her. "I don't remember that."

"How convenient."

"No, you don't understand." I lifted my open hands toward her. "I don't *remember* it. Everything we did together . . . is gone. I don't have those memories. It's been wiped."

She flinched as if I'd struck her.

"But you . . ." she said in pieces. "I thought . . . You look—"

"The same." I looked down at myself, at Ryker's sleeve. "Well, there wasn't much left of the other sleeve when they fished me out of the sea. This was the only option. And the U.N. investigators point-blank refused to allow another double-sleeving. Don't blame them, really. It's going to be hard enough to justify the one we did as it is."

"But how did you—"

"Decide?" I smiled without much enthusiasm. "Shall we go inside and talk about this?"

I let her lead me back up to the conservatory, where someone had set out a jug and tall stemmed glasses on the ornamental table beneath the martyrweed stands. The jug was filled with a liquid the color of sunsets. We took seats opposite each other without exchanging words or glances. She poured herself a glass without offering me one, a tiny casualness that spoke volumes about what had happened between Miriam Bancroft and my other self.

"I'm afraid I don't have much time," she said absently. "As I told you on the phone, Laurens has asked me to come to New York immediately. I was actually on my way out when you called."

I said nothing, waiting, and when she had finished pouring I got my own glass. The move felt bone-deep wrong, and my awkwardness must have shown. She started with realization.

"Oh, I—"

"Forget it." I settled back into my seat and sipped at the drink. It had a faint bite beneath the mellowness. "You wanted to know how we decided? We gambled. Paper, scissors, stone. Of course, we talked around it for hours first. They had us in a virtual forum over in New York, very high ratio, discretion shielded while we made up our minds. No expense spared for the heroes of the hour."

I found an edge of bitterness creeping into my voice, and I had to stop to dump it. I took a longer pull at my drink.

"Like I said, we talked. A lot. We thought of a lot of different ways to decide, some of them were maybe even viable, but in the end we kept coming back to it. Scissors, paper, stone. Best of five. Why not?"

I shrugged, but it was not the casual gesture I hoped it would appear. I was still trying to shake off the cold that crept through me whenever I thought about the game, trying to second-guess myself with my own existence at stake. The best of five, and it had gone to two all. My heart was beating like the junk rhythm in Jerry's Closed Quarters, and I was dizzy with adrenaline. Even facing Kawahara hadn't been this hard.

When he lost the last round—stone to my paper—we both stared at our two extended hands for what seemed like a long time. Then he'd got up with a faint smile and cocked his thumb and forefinger at his own head, somewhere midway between a salute and a burlesque of suicide.

"Anything I should tell Jimmy when I see him?"

I shook my head wordlessly.

"Well, have a nice life," he said, and left the sunlit room, closing the door gently behind him. Part of me was still screaming inside that he had somehow thrown the last game.

They resleeved me the next day.

I looked up again. "Now I guess you're wondering why I bothered coming here."

"Yes, I am."

"It concerns Sheryl Bostock," I said.

"Who?"

I sighed. "Miriam, please. Don't make this any tougher than it already is. Sheryl Bostock is shit scared you're going to have her torched because of what she knows. I've come here to have you convince me she's wrong, because that's what I promised her."

Miriam Bancroft looked at me for a moment, eyes widening, and then, convulsively, she threw her drink in my face.

"You arrogant little man," she hissed. "How dare you? *How dare you?*"

I wiped drink out of my eyes and stared at her. I'd expected a reaction but it wasn't this. I raked surplus cocktail from my hair.

"Excuse me?"

"How dare you walk in here, telling me this is difficult for you. Do you have any idea what my husband is going through at this moment?"

"Well, let's see." I wiped my hands clean on my shirt, frowning. "Right now he's the five-star guest of a U.N. Special Inquiry in New York. What do you reckon, the marital separation's getting to him? Can't be that hard to find a whorehouse in New York."

Miriam Bancroft's jaw clenched.

"You are cruel," she whispered.

"And you're dangerous." I felt a little steam wisping off the surface of my own control. "I'm not the one who kicked an unborn child to death in San Diego. I'm not the one who dosed her own husband's clone with synamorphesterone while he was away in Osaka, knowing full well what he'd do to the first woman he fucked in that state. Knowing that woman wouldn't be you, of course. It's no wonder Sheryl Bostock's terrified. Just looking at you, I'm wondering whether I'll live past the front gates."

"Stop it." She drew a deep, shuddering breath. "Stop it. Please."

I stopped. We both sat in silence, she with her head bowed.

"Tell me what happened," I said finally. "I got most of it from Kawahara. I know why Laurens torched himself—"

"Do you?" Her voice was quiet now, but there were still traces of her previous venom in the question. "Tell me, what do you know? That he killed himself to escape blackmail. That's what they're saying in New York, isn't it."

"It's a reasonable assumption, Miriam," I said quietly. "Kawahara had him in a lock. Vote down Resolution 653 or face exposure as a murderer. Killing himself before the needlecast went through to PsychaSec was the only way out of it. If he hadn't been so bloody minded about the suicide verdict, he might have got away with it."

"Yes. If you hadn't come."

I made a gesture that felt unfairly defensive. "It wasn't my idea."

"And what about *guilt*," she said into the quiet. "Did you stop to consider that? Did you stop to think how Laurens must have felt when he realized what he'd done, when they told him that girl Rentang was a Catholic, a girl who could never have her life back, even if Resolution 653 did force her back into temporary existence to testify against him? Don't you think when he put the gun against his own throat and pulled the trigger, that he was punishing himself for what he'd done? Did you ever consider that maybe he was not trying to *get away with it*, as you put it?"

I thought about Bancroft, turning the idea over in my mind, and it wasn't entirely difficult to say what Miriam Bancroft wanted to hear.

"It's a possibility," I said.

She choked a laugh. "It's more than a possibility, Mr. Kovacs. You forget, I was here that night. I watched him from the stairs when he came in. I saw his face. I saw the pain on his face. He paid for what he'd done. He judged and executed himself for it. He paid, he destroyed the man who committed the crime, and now a man who has no memory of that crime, a man who *did not commit* that crime, is living with the guilt again. Are you satisfied, Mr. Kovacs?"

The bitter echoes of her voice were leached out of the room by the martyr-weed. The silence thickened.

"Why'd you do it?" I asked, when she showed no sign of speaking again. "Why did Marla Rentang have to pay for your husband's infidelities?"

She looked at me as if I had asked her for some major spiritual truth and shook her head helplessly.

"It was the only way I could think of to hurt him," she murmured.

No different from Kawahara in the end, I thought with carefully manufactured savagery. Just another Meth, moving the little people around like pieces in a puzzle.

"Did you know Curtis was working for Kawahara?" I asked tonelessly.

"I guessed. Afterwards." She lifted a hand. "But I had no way of proving it. How did you work it out?"

"Retrospectively. He took me to the Hendrix, recommended it to me. Kadmin turned up five minutes after I went in, on Kawahara's orders. That's too close for a coincidence."

"Yes," she said distantly. "It fits."

"Curtis got the synamorphesterone for you?"

She nodded.

"Through Kawahara, I imagine. A liberal supply, as well. He was dosed to the eyes the night you sent him to see me. Did he suggest spiking the clone before the Osaka trip?"

"No. That was Kawahara." Miriam Bancroft cleared her throat. "We had an unusually . . . candid conversation a few days before. Looking back, she must have been engineering the whole thing around Osaka."

"Yeah, Reileen's pretty thorough. Was pretty thorough. She would have known there was an even chance Laurens would refuse to back her. So you bribed Sheryl Bostock with a visit to the island funhouse, just like me. Only instead of getting to play with the glorious Miriam Bancroft body like me, she got to wear it. A handful of cash, and the promise she could come back and play again some day. Poor cow, she was in paradise for thirty-six hours and now she's like a junkie in withdrawal. Were you ever going to take her back there?"

"I am a woman of my word."

"Yeah? Well, as a favor to me, do it soon."

"And the rest? You have evidence? You intend to tell Laurens about my part in this?"

I reached into my pocket and produced a matte-black disk. "Footage of the injection," I said, holding it up. "Composite footage of Sheryl Bostock leaving PsychaSec and flying to a meeting with your limousine, which subsequently heads out to sea. Without this, there's nothing to say your husband didn't kill Marla Rentang chemically unassisted, but they're probably going to assume Kawahara dosed him aboard *Head in the Clouds*. There's no evidence, but it's expedient."

"How did you know?" She was looking into a corner of the conservatory, voice small and distant. "How did you get to Bostock?"

"Intuition, mostly. You saw me looking through the telescope?"

She nodded and cleared her throat. "I thought you were playing with me. I thought you'd told him."

"No." I felt a faint stab of anger. "Kawahara was still holding my friend in virtual. And threatening to torture her into insanity."

She looked sideways at me, then looked away. "I didn't know that," she said quietly.

"Yeah, well." I shrugged. "The telescope gave me half of it. Your husband aboard *Head in the Clouds* just before he killed himself. So then I started thinking about all the unpleasant stuff Kawahara had to play with up there, and I wondered if your husband could have been induced to kill himself. Chemically, or through some kind of virtual program. I've seen it done before."

"Yes. I'm sure you have." She sounded tired now, drifting away. "So why look for it at PsychaSec and not *Head in the Clouds*?"

"I'm not sure. Intuition, like I said. Maybe because chemical mugging aboard an aerial whorehouse just didn't seem like Kawahara's style. Too headlong, too crude. She's a chess player, not a brawler. Was. Or maybe just because I had no way to get into the *Head in the Clouds* surveillance stack the way I could with PsychaSec, and I wanted to do something immediate. In any case, I told the Hendrix to go in and survey standard medical procedures for the clones, then backtrack for any irregularities. That gave me Sheryl Bostock."

"How very astute." She turned to look at me. "And what now, Mr. Kovacs? More justice? More crucifixion of the Meths?"

I tossed the disk onto the table.

"I had the Hendrix go in and erase the injection footage from PsychaSec's files. Like I said, they'll probably assume your husband was dosed aboard *Head in the Clouds*. The expedient solution. Oh, and we erased the Hendrix's memory of your visit to my room, too, just in case someone wanted to make something of what you said about buying me off. One way or another, I'd say you owe the Hendrix a couple of big favors. It said a few guests every now and then would do. Shouldn't cost much, relatively speaking. I sort of promised on your behalf."

I didn't tell her about Ortega's sight of the bedroom scene, or how long it had taken to talk the policewoman around. I still wasn't sure why she'd agreed myself. Instead I watched the wonder on Miriam Bancroft's face for the full half minute it took her to reach out and close her hand around the disk. She looked up at me over her clenched fingers as she took it.

"Why?"

"I don't know," I said morosely. "Who knows, maybe you and Laurens deserve each other. Maybe you deserve to go on loving a faithless sexual maladjust who can't deal with respect and appetite in the same relationship. Maybe he deserves to go on not knowing whether he murdered Rentang unprovoked or not. Maybe you're just like Reileen, both of you. Maybe all you Meths deserve is each other. All I know is, the rest of us don't deserve you."

I got up to go.

"Thanks for the drink."

I got as far as the door—

"Takeshi."

—and turned back, unwillingly, to face her.

"That isn't it," she said with certainty. "Maybe you believe all those things, but that isn't it. Is it?"

I shook my head. "No, that isn't it," I agreed.

"Then why?"

"Like I said, I don't know why." I stared at her, wondering if I was glad I couldn't remember or not. My voice softened. "But he asked me to do it, if I won. It was part of the deal. He didn't tell me why."

I left her sitting alone amidst the martyrweed.

EPILOGUE

The tide was out at Ember, leaving a wet expanse of sand that stretched almost to the listing wreck of the *Free Trade Enforcer*. The rocks that the carrier had gashed herself on were exposed, gathered in shallow water at the bow like a fossilized outpouring of the ship's guts. Seabirds were perched there, screaming shrilly at each other. A thin wind came in across the sand and made minute ripples in the puddles left by our footprints. Up on the promenade, Anchana Salomao's face had been taken down, intensifying the bleak emptiness of the street.

"I thought you'd have gone," Irene Elliott said beside me.

"It's in the pipe. Harlan's World is dragging out the needlecast authorization. They really don't want me back."

"And no one wants you here."

I shrugged. "It's not a new situation for me."

We walked on in silence for a while. It was a peculiar feeling, talking to Irene Elliott in her own body. In the days leading up to the *Head in the Clouds* gig, I'd become accustomed to looking down to her face, but this big-boned blonde sleeve was almost as tall as me, and there was an aura of gaunt competence about her that had come through only faintly in her mannerisms in the other body.

"I've been offered a job," she said at length. "Security consulting for Mainline D.H.F. You heard of them?"

I shook my head.

"Quite high profile on the East Coast. They must have their headhunters on the inquiry board or something. Soon as the U.N. cleared me, they were knocking on the door. Exploding offer, five grand if I signed there and then."

"Yeah, standard practice. Congratulations. You moving east, or are they going to wire the job through to you here?"

"Probably do it here, at least for a while. We've got Elizabeth in a virtual condo down in Bay City, and it's a lot cheaper to wire in locally. The start-up cost us most of that five grand, and we figure it'll be a few years before we can afford to resleeve her." She turned a shy smile toward me. "We spend most of our time there at the moment. That's where Victor went today."

"You don't need to make excuses for him," I said gently. "I didn't figure he'd want to talk to me anyway."

She looked away. "It's, you know, he was always so proud and—"

"Forget it. Someone walked all over my feelings the way I did over his, I wouldn't feel like talking to them, either." I stopped and reached in my pocket. "Reminds me. I brought something for you."

She looked down at the anonymous gray credit chip in my hand.

"What's this?"

"About eighty thousand," I said. "I figure with that you can afford something custom grown for Elizabeth. If she chooses quick, you could have her sleeved before the end of the year."

"What?" She stared at me with a smile slipping off and on her face, like someone who has been told a joke she's not sure she understands. "You're giving us— Why? Why are you doing this?"

This time I had an answer. I'd been thinking about it all the way up from Bay City that morning. I took Irene Elliott's hand and pressed the chip into it.

"Because I want there to be something clean at the end of all this," I said quietly. "Something I can feel good about."

For a moment she went on staring at me. Then she closed the small gap between us and flung her arms around me with a cry that sent the nearest gulls wheeling up off the sand in alarm. I felt a trickle of tears smeared onto the side of my face, but she was laughing at the same time. I folded my arms around her in return and held her.

And for the moments that the embrace lasted, and a little while after, I felt as clean as the breeze coming in off the sea.

You take what is offered, Virginia Vidaura said somewhere. *And that must sometimes be enough.*

●●●

It took them another eleven days to authorize the needlecast returning me to Harlan's World, most of which I spent hanging around the Hendrix watching the news and feeling oddly guilty about my impending checkout. There were very few actual facts publicly available about the demise of Reileen Kawahara, so the resulting coverage was lurid, sensational, and largely inaccurate. The U.N. Special Inquiry remained veiled in secrecy, and when the rumors about the forthcoming adoption of Resolution 653 finally broke, there was little to connect them to what had gone before. Bancroft's name never appeared, nor did mine.

I never spoke to Bancroft again. The needlecast authorization and resleeving bond for Harlan's World were delivered to me by Oumou Prescott, who, though she was pleasant enough and assured me that the terms of my contract would be honored to the letter, also conveyed a smoothly menacing message that I was not to attempt any further communication with any member of the Bancroft family ever again. The reason cited by Prescott was my deceit over the Jack It Up story, the breach of my much vaunted word, but I knew better. I'd seen it in Bancroft's face across the inquiry chamber when the facts about Miriam's whereabouts and activities during the assault on *Head in the Clouds* came out. Despite all his urbane Meth bullshit, the old bastard was stabbed through with jealousy. I wondered what he would have done if he'd had to sit through the deleted Hendrix bedroom files.

Ortega rode with me to Bay City Central the day of the needlecast, the same day that Mary Lou Hinchley was downloaded into a witness-stand synthetic for the opening hearing on *Head in the Clouds*. There were chanting crowds on the steps up to the entrance hall, faced off against a line of grim-looking black-uniformed U.N. Public Order police. The same crude holographic placards that I remembered from my arrival on Earth bobbed about over our heads as we forced our way through the press. The sky above was an ominous gray.

"Fucking clowns," Ortega growled, elbowing the last of the demonstrators out of her way. "If they provoke the Pubs, they'll be sorry. I've seen these boys in action before and it isn't pretty."

I ducked around a shaven-headed young man who was punching violently at the sky with one fist and holding one of the placard generators with the other. His voice was hoarse and he appeared to be working himself into a frenzied trance. I joined Ortega at the upper fringe of the crowd, a little out of breath.

"There isn't enough organization here to be a real threat," I said, raising my voice to compete with the crowd. "They're just making a noise."

"Yeah, well, that never stopped the Pubs before. They're likely to break a few skulls just on general principles. What a fucking mess."

"Price of progress, Kristin. You wanted Resolution 653." I gestured at the sea of angry faces below. "Now you've got it."

One of the masked and padded men above us broke ranks and came down the steps, riot prod fractionally lifted at his side. His jacket bore a sergeant's crimson slash at the shoulder. Ortega flipped her badge at him, and after a brief, shouted conversation, we were allowed up. The line parted for us and then the double doors into the hall beyond. It was hard to tell which was the most smoothly mechanical, the doors or the black-clad faceless figures that stood guard over them.

Inside, it was quiet and gloomy with the storm light coming through the roof panels. I looked around at the deserted benches and sighed. Whatever world it is, whatever you've done there for better or worse, you always leave the same way.

Alone.

"You need a minute?"

I shook my head. "Need a lifetime, Kristin. Maybe then some."

"Stay out of trouble, maybe you'll get it." There was an attempt at humor floating in her voice, rather like a corpse in a swimming pool, and she must have realized how it sounded, because the sentence was bitten off. An awkwardness was growing between us, something that had started as soon as they resleeved me in Ryker's body for the real-time committee hearings. During the inquiry we'd been kept too busy to see much of each other, and when the proceedings finally closed and we all went home, the pattern had endured. There'd been a few gusty if only superficially satisfying couplings, but even these had stopped once it became clear that Ryker would be cleared and released. Whatever shared warmth we'd been gathered to was out of control now, unsafe, like the flames from a smashed storm lantern, and trying to hold on to it was only getting us both painfully scorched.

I turned and gave her a faint smile. "Stay out of trouble, huh? That what you told Trepp?"

It was an unkind blow, and I knew it. Against all the odds, it seemed Kawahara had missed Trepp with everything but the edge of the stun beam. The shard gun, I remembered when they told me, had been dialed down to minimum dispersal just before I went in to face Kawahara. Sheer luck I'd left it that way. By the time the rapidly summoned U.N. forensics team arrived on *Head in the Clouds* to take evidence under Ortega's direction, Trepp had vanished, as had my grav harness from the atmosphere sampling turret where I'd come aboard. I didn't know whether Ortega and Bautista had seen fit to let the mercenary go in view of the testimony she could give concerning the *Panama Rose*, or if Trepp had simply staggered offstage before the police got there. Ortega had volunteered no information, and there wasn't enough left of our previous intimacy for me to ask her outright. This was the first time we'd discussed it openly.

Ortega scowled at me. "You asking me to equate the two of you?"

"Not asking you to do anything, Kristin." I shrugged. "But for what it's worth, I don't see a lot of ground between her and me."

"Go on thinking like that, nothing'll ever change for you."

"Kristin, nothing ever *does* change." I jerked a thumb back at the crowd outside. "You'll always have morons like that, swallowing belief patterns whole so they don't have to think for themselves. You'll always have people like Kawahara and the Bancrofts to push their buttons and cash in on the program. People like you to make sure the game runs smoothly and the rules don't get broken too often. And when the Meths want to break the rules themselves, they'll send people like Trepp and me to do it. That's the truth, Kristin. It's been the truth since I was born a hundred and fifty years ago, and from what I read in the history books, it's never been any different. Better get used to it."

She looked at me levelly for a moment, then nodded as if coming to an internal decision. "You always meant to kill Kawahara, didn't you? This confession bullshit was just to get me along for the ride."

It was a question I'd asked myself a lot, and I still didn't have a clear answer. I shrugged again.

"She deserved to die, Kristin. To really die. That's all I know for certain."

Over my head, a faint pattering sounded from the roof panels. I tipped my head back and saw transparent explosions on the glass. It was starting to rain.

"Got to go," I said quietly. "Next time you see this face, it won't be me wearing it, so, if there's anything you want to say . . ."

Ortega's face flinched almost imperceptibly as I said it. I cursed myself for the awkwardness and tried to take her hand.

"Look, if it makes it any easier, no one knows. Bautista probably suspects we got it together, but no one really knows."

"*I* know," she said sharply, not giving me her hand. "I remember."

I sighed. "Yeah, so do I. It's *worth* remembering, Kristin. But don't let it fuck up the rest of your life. Go get Ryker back, and get on to the next screen. That's what counts. Oh, yeah." I reached into my coat and extracted a crumpled cigarette pack. "And you can have these back. I don't need them anymore, nor does he, so don't start him off again. You owe me that much, at least. Just make sure he stays off them."

She blinked and kissed me abruptly, somewhere between mouth and cheek. It was an inaccuracy I didn't try to correct either way. I turned away, before I could see if there were going to be any tears, and started for the doors at the far end of the hall. I looked back once, as I was mounting the steps. Ortega was still standing there, arms wrapped around herself, watching me leave. In the stormlight, it was too far away to see her face clearly.

For a moment something ached in me, something so deep rooted that I knew to tear it out would be to undo the essence of what held me together. The feeling rose and splashed like the rain behind my eyes, swelling as the drumming on the roof panels grew and the glass ran with water.

Then I had it locked down.

I turned back to the next step, found a chuckle somewhere in my chest, and coughed it out. The chuckle fired up and became a laugh of sorts.

Get to the next screen.

The doors were waiting at the top, the needlecast beyond.

Still trying to laugh, I went through.

Virginia Cottinelli

ABOUT THE AUTHOR

RICHARD MORGAN was born in London in 1965 but didn't stick around for the Kings Road sixties experience. A relaxed, rural upbringing in the Fens followed, then a rude wake-up call at the University of Cambridge where study suddenly became something requiring substantial effort. Richard never quite recovered from the shock and recoiled out of academia three years later with a very average degree in political history and very little interest in any career other than writing and/or traveling. Accidentally, he became a teacher of English as a foreign language and despite his best efforts ended up building a fourteen-year career in the profession as teacher, then director of studies, then teacher trainer. During this time, he taught variously in Spain, Turkey, Scotland, and his birthplace, London. His unexpected teaching career came to an equally unexpected end when Hollywood was kind enough to option his first novel, which you now hold in your hands. Richard currently lives in Scotland with his Spanish wife-to-be and is hard at work on another Takeshi Kovacs novel.